Kentucky State Geologist, Henry Nettelroth

Kentucky Fossil Shells

a monograph of the fossil shells of the Silurian and Devonian rocks of Kentucky

Kentucky State Geologist, Henry Nettelroth

Kentucky Fossil Shells
a monograph of the fossil shells of the Silurian and Devonian rocks of Kentucky

ISBN/EAN: 9783337387488

Printed in Europe, USA, Canada, Australia, Japan

Cover: Foto ©Andreas Hilbeck / pixelio.de

More available books at **www.hansebooks.com**

KENTUCKY GEOLOGICAL SURVEY, J. R. PROCTER, Director.

Kentucky Fossil Shells

A MONOGRAPH OF THE FOSSIL SHELLS

f Kentucky

By Henry Nettelroth, C. E.

1889.

FRANKFORT, KENTUCKY
ELECTROTYPED AND PRINTED BY E. POLK JOHNSON, PUBLIC PRINTER AND BINDER
1889.

KENTUCKY GEOLOGICAL SURVEY, J. R. PROCTER, Director.

Kentucky Fossil Shells

A MONOGRAPH OF THE FOSSIL SHELLS

Silurian and Devonian Rocks of Kentucky

By Henry Nettelroth, C. E.

1889.

FRANKFORT, KENTUCKY
ELECTROTYPED AND PRINTED BY E. POLK JOHNSON, PUBLIC PRINTER AND BINDER
1889.

TABLE OF CONTENTS.

	PAGE.
Letter from the Author	3–4
A Short Sketch of Geology	5–27
Description of Genera and Species	28–230
Index to Genera and Species described	231-239
Index to Species described	240–245
Plates and Explanatory Text	I–XXXVI

LETTER FROM THE AUTHOR.

Mr. John R. Procter,

Director Kentucky Geological Survey:

Dear Sir: The work of describing the fossil shells, or Mollusca, from the Falls of the Ohio, which you kindly assigned to me some years ago, has, unfortunately, been delayed by severe illness of several years' duration. It was only during the past winter that I regained sufficient strength to complete it. This monograph contains about two hundred and twenty species, forty-three of which are new, and originally described by me. The descriptions and illustrations of the balance are scattered over many different State Reports, Monographs and Periodicals, accessible to only a few persons in Kentucky, and, for this reason, it was necessary either to copy those figures and descriptions, or to reproduce them from our own material. All of our illustrations are original, with the exception of three or four, which are copied from Prof. Hall's 27th Regents' Report. The drawing and engraving was done by Mr. Chas. Starck, of the Louisville Lithographing Co., who deserves great credit for the pains taken and the skill shown in the execution of this work. Of the original descriptions of known species, I copied some entirely. Coming, as they were, from the skillful pen of Prof. Hall, it was impossible to improve them. Others I have remodeled, and some set aside and replaced by new ones. In many cases, the descriptions were made from single, not well preserved, specimens, which rarely showed the true characters of the shells in their original condition, and, therefore, led to errors in the descriptions. The large and excellent material now found in about a dozen collections here in the Falls Cities, while enabling me to correct those mistakes, has also compelled me to change descriptions coming from far superior palæontologists. The larger number of our fossil shells were, heretofore, described and figured by Prof. James Hall, of Albany, New York, in his numerous reports and pamphlets, most all of which he presented to me, with the kind permission to make the broadest use of his illustrations and descriptions. For such exceptional generosity I can thank him only by this public acknowledgment. The material used in the preparation of this monograph belongs partly to my own cabinet, and partly to the collections of the following gentlemen:

Major Wm. J. Davis, Profs. Wm. J. McConathy and J. T. Gaines and Dr. James Knapp, of Louisville, Ky., Prof. A. C. Goodwin, of Charlestown, Messrs. Orlando Hobbs, Henry Peters and Mr. Fogg, of Jeffersonville, Indiana. These gentlemen have rendered me all the assistance I desired or needed, for which I here express my thanks. To Major Wm. J. Davis, the author of "Kentucky Fossil Corals," I am especially indebted for much valuable information given me, while on our numerous collecting trips, and during the preparation of this work. It has pained me to see the valuable collection of the late Dr. James Knapp, from which Prof. Hall received most of his Ohio Falls specimens, leave our State. Though in corals it was greatly inferior to the cabinet of Major Wm. J. Davis, and in shells not equal to my own, it contained some very rare specimens which it may be impossible to replace.

Our shells have generally retained their original form, not having suffered from compression or distortion, as is the case with so many fossils from other localities, and their silicification has prevented all wear and rubbing after separation from their matrix, while, on the other hand, their changing into hornstone has, in many instances, obliterated the original fine surface-markings, for the study and description of which we have to acquire material from other localities.

The descriptions of fossils I have prefaced by a short article on geology and palæontology in general, containing information indispensable to any one who wishes to gain an understanding of the fossil remains of the fauna and flora of former ages. In preparing said article, I have made extensive use of the works of Dana, Lyell and others.

Hoping that this monograph will meet with your approval, and that it may be of service to the students of geology, in spite of its many shortcomings, which, knowing your kind disposition, I feel assured you will overlook or excuse, I express here to you, dear sir, my many thanks for your kind consideration and indulgence, and remain

Very respectfully, your obedient servant,

HENRY NETTELROTH.

LOUISVILLE, 1887.

FOSSIL SHELLS

SILURIAN AND DEVONIAN ROCKS.

BY

HENRY NETTELROTH.

PART I,

A SHORT SKETCH OF GEOLOGY.

A SKETCH OF GEOLOGY.

The name "Geology" is derived from the Greek words "ge," the earth, and "logos," a discourse, thus indicating a science of the earth, a science investigating the different materials of which the earth is composed, and also the manner in which these materials are arranged. Geology gives us, also, the history of our planet from its beginning to the present time—examining all the processes through which the earth has passed, from its original gaseous condition until it acquired its present form and structure. It furthermore enables us to obtain extensive and valuable information about the animal and vegetable life which covered our globe during bygone ages.

Geology is a science of comparatively recent date, though we find some geological knowledge among the ancient Romans and Greeks, and in the writings of the middle age. All that knowledge, however, amounted only to a few isolated speculations, nearly always based upon erroneous suppositions, and never resulting in the establishment of a regular system. Geology as a science was originated during the last century, but received its main development during the present one. In spite of its short existence, it has outgrown many of its sister sciences, and ranks to-day among the most important ones at the head of the scale. Its founders and chief promoters are mainly found among the English, German and French savants, and during the present century our own country has contributed its full share to its advancement. The names of Lyell and Murchison, of Leopold von Buch and Goldfuss, of Cuvier and Verneuil, and of our own eminent geologist, Professor James Hall, of New York, and many others, will be known to the students of this noble science throughout the coming ages.

Geology has for its territory the whole earth, as far as the same is accessible to its investigations. These are not confined to the surface, but penetrate as deep into the interior as artificial excavations for mines and artesian wells allow. Still greater and better opportunities than these artificial openings, which are limited in numbers and dimensions, are offered the geologist, for his researches, by the peculiar figuration of our planet's surface, where deep valleys alternate with high mountains, and where the strata are bent to such a degree that we find them at one place deep below the surface, whilst at a distance of a few miles the very same layers may be outcropping at the slope of a hill, or may even form the surface rocks of extensive districts.

Vast as the geological field appears, and in reality is, it, nevertheless, forms only a small portion of the whole contents of our globe. The deepest excavations rarely extend to a depth of 2,000 feet below the level of the sea, though their absolute depth may be greatly in excess of this, inasmuch as most of them are in mountainous regions. The bending of the strata very often gives us an insight into greater depths, but even this amounts only to a few miles, and forms only a small portion of the earth's radius. Beyond these depths geology is barred, as far as actual observations are concerned, but its inquiries may penetrate deeper; it may speculate about the nature and condition of the earth's interior. About this matter different theories have been advanced, but as all of them are based on mere speculation, none have met with a general acceptance by the scientific world. Whether the center of our globe is solid or fluid, whether it is a vacuum or filled with compressed air, we are unable to decide with certainty. Some facts speak for a solid and others for a fluid center, and still others can not be accounted for by either condition.

Some European scientists, like Leslie and Halley, consider the earth a hollow sphere, which, according to Leslie, was filled with imponderable material, possessing an enormous repulsive force. These philosophic speculations of savants were taken up by Captain Symmes, of Kentucky, who, by adding his own fantastic dreams, enlarged them to the so-called "Symmes' Theory." Symmes insists that the interior of our globe is not only hollow, but that it is also inhabited by animals and plants; that it possesses a very mild climate, and is illuminated by two planets, which he calls Pluto and Proserpina. He felt so convinced of the existence of his subterranean country, that he repeatedly extended private and public invitations to Alexander von Humboldt, Sir Humphrey Davy, and other celebrated scientists of this country, and of the old world, to accompany him on his intended subterranean expedition.

ROCKS.

The solid portion of the earth is composed of different materials or rocks. The term "rock," as commonly understood, signifies a hard and stony mass, such as granite, quartz or limestone, but in its geological meaning, it embraces all solid constituents of our globe, the hard and stony, as well as the soft and incoherent matter; thus, loose sand and soft clay are just as well included in that term as basalt and quarrystone. Before geology enlightened the people, it was the general belief that all the rocks, with their present form and arrangement, were thus created. This belief, though still adhered to by the ignorant masses, and by bigots, has disappeared from the minds of all who ever came under the influence of geological reasoning. Geology informs us, that all the rocks in their present structure, composition and arrangement, are the products and results of many different conditions under which our earth existed, and of many different processes through which it has passed during the many ages of its existence. By whatever influences the rocks may have received their present characters, they received their original form and structure by the agency of fire. All the rocks, without exception, passed, in the beginning, through a molten condition, out of which, by subsequent cooling, they received their first form as solids. But in the course of time another agent appeared and changed many of the existing forms. Water, the powerful opponent of fire, went into action, and by its chemical, as well as mechanical influence, dissolved a large portion of the fire-produced formations, and carried them to distant localities, where, under favorable conditions, they were deposited as sediments, forming those rocks which are mainly characterized by their arrangement into strata or layers. Again, we find many of these sediment-formations have been subjected to the influence of heat, by which they lost some of their former characteristics. Their crystallization, and the total absence of organic remains, prove the action of heat, while, on the other hand, their stratification, which is generally retained, testifies to their sedimentary origin. Thus we will notice a natural division of all the rocks into the following three classes:

1. Rocks originally formed by fire and not afterwards changed, the igneous rocks.

2. Rocks formed in water by sediments, the stratified or sedimentary rocks.

3. Rocks originally formed as sedimentary deposits, but afterwards changed by heat, without losing their stratification, called metamorphic rocks.

The igneous rocks are generally subdivided into volcanic and plutonic rocks. Their difference is caused by the condition under which the cooling of the molten masses took place. In the volcanic rocks, the molten matter appeared either on the surface of the earth, or at least very near to the same, where the cooling was rapid, and where the forming rocks were not subjected to the heavy pressure of the superimposed strata.

The plutonic rocks resulted from greatly different conditions. Here the molten masses did not penetrate the surface strata, but remained deep in the interior of the earth, or at least at the bottom of deep oceans, where the cooling process was retarded, and where the new formations were compressed by the weight of the overlying layers.

In the column of strata we generally find the plutonic rock at the bottom. Next above come the metamorphic formations, which are superimposed by the sedimentary and volcanic rocks. This arrangement led the earlier geologists to the belief that the plutonic and metamorphic rocks were older than the others, consequently, they called the lower primary formations, and the upper the secondary formations. The older school of geologists adhered to the so-called neptunian theory, according to which all the rocks, with the only exception of the volcanic lava formations, were considered as produced by water, or to be of aqueous origin. If this theory had proved correct, the views of the old school about the comparative age of the different rocks would be sustained. But progress in geological science has upset the neptunian theory, and established in its place the plutonic theory, which makes fire or subterranean heat the main agency in the production of the plutonic and metamorphic rocks.

This new theory does not admit the classification of primary and secondary rocks. The first rocks ever produced, which formed the first thin crust of our globe, were dissolved by water and removed to other localities, where they furnished the constituents of the sedimentary formations. Even a large portion of these have been ground up by weather and water, to provide the material for later deposits. Rocks of all the different classes have been formed, during the past, simultaneously, and may be in process of formation at the present time. The terms primary and secondary are, therefore, obsolete, inasmuch as they indicate the comparative age of the different rocks.

SEDIMENTARY OR STRATIFIED ROCKS.

Though all the different classes of rocks are of great interest to the geologist, still the most important of all is that including the sedimentary formations. The rocks of this class are always arranged in layers or strata, and they are, therefore, generally referred to as stratified rocks. They are of greater importance to the geologist than the other formations, because they furnish him the main material for his investigations. Most, if not all, of them have been formed since the beginning of organic life on our planet, as proved by the remains or traces of animal and vegetable organism preserved in their strata.

The most important among the different points which the geologist has to consider in regard to the sedimentary rocks, are: their mineral composition, their arrangement in strata, their relative age, and, most of all, their organic remains.

In regard to their mineral composition, we may divide them into three groups, the siliceous, or arenaceous rocks; the clayey, or argillaceous rocks; and the calcareous rocks, or limestone. The main constituent of the first group is silica, in the form of quartz-grains or sand; that of the second group is clay, a mixture of siliceous matter, with a large amount of alumina and oxide of iron, and that of the third group is carbonate of lime. It is impossible to separate these three groups by a well defined division line. Some rocks form a kind of connecting link between the first and second, and others between the second and third group, while again, others may combine the siliceous and calcareous rocks. The first group is represented by sandstone, the second by shale, and the third by limestone. Argillaceous rocks are easily identified by the peculiar earthy odor which they emit when breathed upon, while the limestones may be detected by the aid of muriatic acid, which causes effervescing when applied to them. Upon sandstone acids have no effect whatever.

STRATIFICATION.—Stratification is the arrangement of rocks into different layers or beds. It is a characteristic feature of all the sedimentary formations. Stratification can only be produced by sedimentation, and the latter can, as far as geological strata are concerned, only take place in water charged with solid or earthy matter, which is kept in suspense in the shape of mud. Solid material has generally a greater density, or specific gravity, than water, and, therefore, can be kept in suspense by the latter only so long as the lateral motion of the water overcomes the action of gravitation. As soon as the water ceases to move, the mud falls to the bottom, where it forms the sediment which afterwards, under the enormous pressure of superimposed masses, transforms into solid rock. If such sediment formation had gone on continuously, and always under exactly the same conditions, throughout a whole geological period, all the rocks of that formation would form a solid, unbroken mass. But the sediment formation suffered frequent interruptions, extending over shorter or longer periods, and was subjected to many changes in its material. These circumstances caused a differentiation in the deposits. Any interruption of the formation, or any change in the material, were indicated by lines or planes of separation, while the different layers, thus produced, were distinguished by color and texture.

The solid or earthy materials with which the waters are charged, are derived partly from the dry land by the influence of heat, frost and rain, and partly by the never-resting waves of the oceans grinding up the cliffs and beaches of the seashores. These agencies are employed to reduce the elevations of the dry lands to the level of the oceans, and, if they were not counteracted by other forces, would accomplish their task in less than six millions of years. It is estimated that the average elevation of all the continents and islands does not amount to fully one thousand feet; and, on the other hand, the work accomplished by denudation is computed to be one foot in six thousand years, extending over the whole area elevated above the ocean. Such calculations are only mere approximations, based upon conditions which may change considerably in the course of time, and should never be used for framing deductions, without making great allowances. That the work of denudation must have been different during the different ages of the past, can not be doubted. There were periods when a very high temperature prevailed all over the earth, from the poles to the equator, causing a heavy rainfall, and lending the water a greater dissolving power, circumstances which must have produced greater denudation. Then, again, other periods set in, when the temperature of our globe was very low, when the excessive heat of former ages was replaced by excessive cold. Frost is a very powerful agent in the destruction of rocks. The hardest material which admits water into its pores will be crumbled to dust by this destructive force. Here, again, denudation must have been very large. Between these extremes in temperature, our planet experienced some moderate climate which had not such a destructive influence upon the solid material of our earth's crust.

STRATA AND LAYERS.—These two terms are generally used as synonymous, but some geologists make a distinction between them. They use the term layer for each single member of stratified rock, and apply the term strata to beds of the same material. Thus, if a section shows in its lower half limestone, and in its upper half sandstone, it contains only two strata, though it may show a great many layers.

Layers and strata vary in thickness from an inch, and less, to many feet. Very thin layers are called laminæ, and for thin strata, the term seams is used. If all the strata had remained undisturbed in their original position, all would be nearly horizontal, and parallel to each other; but the many upheavals and depressions to which our earth's crust has been subjected, have disturbed their original horizontal and parallel arrangement, and we now find them occupying every imaginable position in relation to each other. Wherever two sets of strata or layers are nearly parallel to each other, it proves that the older set was not disturbed in its original position before the younger or later one was deposited upon it; but whenever the upper strata rests on the edges of those below, these latter have been disturbed before the formation of the upper ones took place. In the first case, where the parallelism of the strata is maintained, they are said to be conformable; but whenever the planes of the upper layers rest on the edges of the lower ones, they are called unconformable. Conformability of strata indicates a period of rest, whilst unconformability is a certain proof of disturbance. Any movement in the earth's crust must produce some changes in its layers or strata, resulting either in a bending or breaking of the same, whereby fissures, folds and faults are originated. Fissures are rents caused by breakage, without any displacement of the rock on either side of the fracture, below or above their former level; but, whenever the masses on one side or the other have changed their positions, either by elevation or depression, the rent becomes a fault. According to the great difference in the magnitude of the forces producing the faults, the size of the latter must also differ greatly. We find them measuring from an inch and less, to many hundred feet. Faults are of great inconvenience to miners, especially where they appear of considerable size. Folds of strata are the result of their bending without breaking; they differ in size from a few feet to many miles, and form, very often, extensive valleys and mountains. Strata are very seldom found perfectly horizontal; they may be so for a short distance, but, extending over a larger area, they will always show a certain amount of curvature. These curves bending inward—that is, with their convexity toward the center of earth—are forming troughs; bending outward, they form arches. A line running, in a series of strata, through the highest point of their arches, is called their anticlinal axis, and the line running through the lowest point of their troughs is known as their synclinal axis. If no denudation had inter-fered, we would always find the anticlinal axis to correspond with elevations, and the synclinal with valleys; but, since, by the influence of weather and water the figuration of our earth's surface has greatly changed, we often meet with anticlinal valleys and synclinal hills. The correct location of these lines is often of great importance to the geologist in surveying a certain district or country, which he can easily accomplish if he bears in mind that his proceed-ing from older upon younger strata leads him towards the synclinal; and *vice versa*, if he proceeds from younger upon older formation he approaches an anticlinal.

Two other important features of the stratified rocks are their dip and strike. Upon these, to a great extent, depends the peculiar topography of the earth's surface.

Dip is the amount of the deflection of strata from the horizontal or level line; it is measured by, or expressed in, degrees. If a layer has a dip of forty-five degrees, it is bent downward, and forms with the horizontal surface an angle of forty-five degrees. Wherever the dip increases to an angle of ninety degrees, the strata stand on their edges in a vertical position. Strike is the horizontal line drawn at right-angles to the direction of the dip. Rocks with a southern or northern dip, will have an eastern or western strike. As long as the dip of certain strata runs in the same direction, their strike is indicated by a straight line; but as soon as the dip changes its direction, the strike will assume the shape of either a broken or curved line. Rocks with great dip produce a broken undulating country, and in accordance with the curved or straight lines of the strike, we find the hills and valleys respectively winding or rectilineal.

PALÆONTOLOGY.

Palæontology treats of the animals and plants which inhabited our planet during former periods, and may, therefore, be properly styled the natural history of by-gone ages. From zoölogy and botany, it differs only in so far as its objects belong mostly to an extinct fauna and flora, the remains or traces of which are imbedded in the rocks and soils of the earth's crust. Palæ-ontology forms a science of itself; but on account of its intimate connection with geology, it is generally considered as only a branch of the latter. The objects with which palæontology deals are known under the name of "fossils," a term designating bodies "dug out of the ground," and which was formerly applied to metals and rocks, as well as to organic remains. At present the word fossil is used in a more restricted sense, applying only to such geological objects from which science may deduce information about the organic life of the past. These objects mainly consist in remains of animals and plants, such as shells, teeth and bones; or stems, leaves and fruits; but they also include the burrows and tracks of annelids, the footprints of saurians and other animals, and even the droppings of fishes and reptiles, which are known under the name of coprolites. Some geologists class among the fossils even objects produced by man, such as arrow-heads, spear-heads and canoes found in the gravel and clay beds of our fields and river shores; but, inasmuch as they properly belong to archæology, they can not be counted among the fossils.

The real nature of fossils was known more than five hundred years before the Christian era, by Xenophanes. He observed the fossil remains in the quarries of Syracuse, consisting of marine shells and fish-bones. He recognized them as the remains of real animals, that had lived there at the bottom of the sea, where they were imbedded in mud, which afterwards hardened into the rocks then inclosing them. He also laid down the general proposition, that the geographical features of our earth are not constant, but that, where land now is, sea has been, and where sea now is, land has been. Afterwards this clear conception of the real nature of fossils appears to have been lost, until the end of the seventeenth century, when Nicholas Steno, Professor of anatomy in Florence, though a Dane by birth, gave them again a correct explanation, and revived the theory of Xenophanes.

Before Steno, during the fourteenth, fifteenth, sixteenth and seventeenth centuries, fossils were regarded as mere figured stones, portions of mineral matter which have assumed the forms of leaves and shells and bones, just as those portions of mineral matter which we call crystals, take on the form of regular geometrical bodies. Others considered them the products of the germs of animals and of the seeds of plants, which have, as it were, lost their way, in the bowels of the earth, and achieved only an imperfect and abortive development. These opinions appear to us ridiculous, and we are inclined to sneer at our ancestors for entertaining such ideas about a matter which is now so clear and simple. People who believed in spontaneous generation, could have no difficulty in taking fossils for sports of nature, and we know that spontaneous generation was generally believed in up to the present century; and, even to-day, thousands of people, laying claim to a fair education, still adhere to that belief These erroneous ideas about the nature of fossils were, long after Steno's correct interpretation, maintained among common people, but men of science became more and more convinced of the correctness of

Xenophanes' theory. To-day, every person who has gained an insight into palæontology, knows that the fossils found in most of the sedimentary rocks are originated by animal or vegetable remains, which became imbedded in the mud at the bottom of the sea, during former ages. In speaking of fossils, we generally describe them as remains of animals and of plants, which is not in accordance with the facts, at least not for the majority of them, inasmuch as, in the larger number, not a particle of organic matter is preserved, and only the form of the imbedded body retained. The original animal or vegetable substances dissolved and became replaced by calcareous, siliceous and other minerals. The remains, therefore, underwent an active transformation into stone, or became, as we call it, petrified. Fossils thus transformed or changed, are classed together under the name of petrifactions.

This term is very often used as a synonym for fossils, but erroneously; because not every fossil has passed through a petrifying process, while there are many belonging to younger formations, that have, outside of form and structure, retained also the color and organic matter of the original remains. Every petrifaction is a fossil, but not every fossil is a petrifaction. The process by which the transformation of organic remains into mineral bodies is produced, is of a chemical nature, and depends upon conditions not yet fully understood.

We must distinguish between petrifactions and incrustations, although the latter are often classed among the former. Incrustations are generally produced in springs, whose waters are charged with a considerable amount of calcareous matter, which settles upon immersed bodies, like flowers and branches, or shells and bones, inclosing them with a mineral coat or crust, but never permeating them, as is done in the case of petrifaction. By breaking such incrustations we find, either the inclosed bodies unchanged, or, if they have disappeared, the place formerly occupied by them a hollow mould.

Another transformation of animal matter is by many erroneously classed among petrifactions. We sometimes notice in public papers reports of cases where human bodies, resurrected after some years of interment, have been found, not only well preserved in form, but so hard and stiff, and so much increased in weight, as to appear completely changed into stone. Such cases are looked upon by a great many people as a kind of miracle, while, really, they are nothing more than the result of a chemical process by which the animal fat has been converted into a sort of wax. Transformations of this kind occur only in bodies buried in wet places, where they are completely submerged by underground water charged with antiseptic ingredients. As soon as these bodies are removed from their original resting place, they commence to decompose, a fact clearly showing that they never underwent the process of petrifaction. The wax-like material into which the fat is converted is called adipocere. It was first discovered by the French scientist Fourcroy, in the year 1787, during the removal of the cemetery of the Innocents, in Paris.

USE OF FOSSILS.

Collectors of geological and palæontological specimens are often objects of wonder and curiosity to people who notice them closely examining rock-piles and clay-banks. What are those fellows doing there ? What are they hunting for ? These questions are asked, without exception, by almost every person passing by, and if the men of science show the things they are looking for, and explain their origin and meaning, they may consider themselves very fortunate if, in ninety-nine out of a hundred cases, they are not looked upon as fit recruits for a lunatic asylum. The ignorance prevailing among the mass of the people, about objects of natural, science, and especially of geology and palæontology, is appalling. Such ignorance might be excused among the lower classes, who had neither time nor opportunity to acquire knowledge, but to find it, even at the end of the nineteenth century, among the majority of persons who lay claim to a fair and liberal education, is very humiliating, and proves the inefficiency of our schools, at least in that direction.

Fossils are picked up, by people in general and by curiosity hunters in particular, because they look so "pretty" or so "strange," as the expression may be; but that these pretty and strange-looking things are of the greatest importance to science, and of immense service to industry, is, so far, known only to very few, outside of the scientific world. Fossils are the letters with which Nature has written the earth's history, in a language intelligible to every student of natural science, whatever nationality he may claim. They faithfully report to us the different processes and changes through which our globe has passed, from its beginning as a solid body to the present day. In them, the animal and vegetable kingdoms of by-gone ages arise from their tombs, and present themselves to the investigation of science. They furnish the indisputable proof that the organized world commenced with its lowest forms, and developed gradually into its higher types. Mantell, an English geologist, says of them : "Fossils have been eloquently and appropriately termed medals of creation, for, as an accomplished numismatist, even when the inscription of an ancient and unknown coin is illegible, can, from the half obliterated effigy and from the style of art, determine with precision, the people by whom, and the period when it was struck ; so, in like manner, the geologist can decipher these natural memorials, interpret the hieroglyphics with which they are inscribed, and, from apparently most insignificant relics, trace the history of beings, of whom no other records are extant, and ascertain the forms and habits of unknown types of organization, whose races were swept from the face of the earth long before the appearance of man and his contemporaries." The fact that fossils show the gradual development of organic life from its lowest to its highest types, affords to science the means of determining the relative age of the different strata in which they are imbedded ; rocks, for instance, embracing remains and traces of fishes, must be younger than others in which only fossils of shells and corals are contained ; or, again, strata only imbedding seaweeds and other low forms of the vegetable kingdom, must be older than those in which leaves and fruits of the trees of our present forests are found. Fossils tell us by their character, and by their mode of preservation, whether they have lived at the bottom of the ocean, in fresh water lakes or rivers, or on the dry land. If they lived in the seas, they also inform us whether these were quiet or stormy, deep or shallow. By the data deduced from fossils, geologists are able, to-day, to write the geographies of former geological epochs, and to mark out on maps the exact distribution of land and water prevailing on our globe during those periods. What the compass is to the navigator, guiding him across the pathless ocean into the intended port, are the fossils to the geologist in his scientific investigations, and in his explorations for economical and industrial purposes. They not only tell him the history of the earth, and of its former .inhabitants, they also show him the fields where the gold and diamond hunter may find those brilliant treasures with which our daughters like to heighten and brighten their natural charms. They indicate the places where to dig successfully for the briny water which furnishes our table with the most indispensable spice, or for the valuable oil illuminating our. houses and parlors. They also locate the mines from which we extract that invaluable mineral which not only affords us comfort at home, but also speeds our travels across the oceans and the plains.

Fossils are the letters in the geological alphabet. To read the latter you must know the former. Without their thorough understanding, no successful study of geology is possible.

GEOLOGICAL PERIODS.

During the infancy of the geological science, it was generally believed that different periods had existed in former ages, which were separated by sharply defined division lines, and that each period possessed its own creation ; which meant that all the different species of animals and plants of a certain period were created and destroyed during that period, and that, for the succeeding epoch, an entirely new creation had to take place. This belief in the total destruction of all existing life at the end of the different geological periods, called cataclysm, originated from the fact that different groups of strata contain different groups of fossils, and was upheld by the belief in a priori creation of each species. Corresponding with those periods, the stratified rocks were divided into different formations.

The rapid progress of the geological science has expunged the division lines between the periods, and has upset the theory of cataclysm. The existence of different groups of fossils in different strata can not be denied; but a more careful examination of the fossils has already shown, and hereafter will show more conclusively, that the existing differences are not the result of new creations, but are produced by the gradual modifications occurring in species exposed to changes in their surroundings during the course of many centuries. The theory of evolution, now generally accepted by all men of science, has destroyed the theory of cataclysm, as well as the belief in an a priori creation of each single species. The division of the geological time into periods, and of the stratified rocks into formations, though based upon erroneous suppositions, has proved to be of great convenience to geologists, and is, therefore, maintained. The dividing lines, however, are not fixed by nature, but may be shifted by arbitration. The whole geological time, from its beginning to the present day, is divided into four great divisions called ages. These are as follows:

1. Azoic Age, embracing the time from the beginning of the earth as a solid body to the appearance of life in the shape of either animals or plants.

2. Palæozic Age, beginning with the appearance of organic forms, and terminating with the close of the coal formation.

3. Mesozoic Age, beginning at the end of the coal formation, and closing at the appearance of mammals.

4. Cenozoic Age, embracing the balance of time up to the present day.

Corresponding with this division of time, we divide all the rocks into the four groups of azoic, palæozoic, mesozoic and cenozoic rocks, according to the age in which their respective formation took place. The first group of rocks is of little or no interest to the palæontologist, inasmuch as it does not contain any traces of life; still, what we to-day consider azoic, or bare of life, may, to-morrow, disclose forms of undoubted organic character. Not many years ago all the metamorphic rocks were considered azoic; but since Canadian geologists have discovered the Eozoan canadense, and have also established the fact that numerous traces of coal and graphite are to be found in these rocks, the existence of some kind of life during the formation of that group can not be doubted any longer. As soon as the presence of life during the formation of those rocks, which heretofore were classed among the azoic, is definitely settled, those rocks have either to be removed to the palæozoic group, or, as Professor Dawson, of Canada, has proposed, a new group, to be called the Eozoic, has to be established for their reception.

All the different metamorphic rocks constitute together the Archaean formation, which is subdivided into the Laurentian and Huronian groups. The Laurentian group forms the base of the whole geological column of sedimentary rocks. It derives its name either from the St. Lawrence river or from the Laurentian mountains in Canada, where it is exposed over an extensive area. In the United States we find it cropping out in New York, where it forms the Adirondack mountains; also in Michigan and Tennessee, and in a few other States. Its thickness in Canada is estimated to be about six miles, or more than 30,000 feet. About the middle of its column are the strata containing the Eozoan canadense, the real nature of which is still involved in some doubt. However, it appears that a majority of geologists have accepted it as the fossil remains of a Rhizopod, and consider it as the commencing point of animal life.

The Huronian group has received its name from Lake Huron, in the vicinity of which it is largely developed and exposed. It overlies the rocks of the previous group in a manner proving its later origin. The dividing line between these two Archaean groups is not sharply drawn. The absence of fossils in these rocks compels us to base their distinction altogether upon their lithological characters, which, alone, seldom affords a safe criterion for the determination of groups. The thickness of the Huronian group in Canada is estimated to exceed 10,000 feet. None of these Archaean rocks are exposed in the State of Kentucky, though their presence at great depth can not be doubted.

The rocks formed during the Palæozic age are divided into three formations : the Silurian, the Devonian and the Carboniferous.

SILURIAN FORMATION.—This formation was first established by Sir R. T. Murchison, the celebrated English geologist. He named it after the ancient Silures, the former inhabitants of that portion of Britain where he first studied this class of rocks. Murchison divided this formation into the Upper and Lower Silurian, a subdivision generally accepted by the geologists of Europe and America, and which answers fully for most purposes. The Lower Silurian formation is the most important on account of its large extent in thickness, as well as in area. It is subdivided into the following groups, which are given in ascending order.

1. St. John's Group; 2. Potsdam Group; 3. Calciferous Group; 4. Quebec Group; 5. Chazy Group; 6. Birdseye Limestone; 7. Black River Group 8. Trenton Group; 9. Utica Slate; 10. Hudson River Group. Some of these groups, as will be seen, are named after localities where they are prominently exposed, while others have received their name from the peculiar character of the rocks which they embrace. Of all these different groups, the Trenton

GEOL. SUR.—3

and the Hudson River groups are of main importance to Kentucky geologists. These two cover extensive areas of our State, and show in some places considerable thickness. The balance are either wanting in Kentucky altogether, or exposed in only very few and very limited spots.

The Hudson River Group is generally known as the Cincinnati Group, on account of its excellent exposure at and around Cincinnati. In Kentucky, the blue limestone of the Trenton forms the surface-rock of that rich and world-renowned district known as the "Blue-grass Country," and is, there, the source of the most productive soil of the United States. In consequence of the rapid decomposition of this rock, when exposed to the influence of sunshine and rain, it keeps the soil in an everlasting virginity, a soil which, a thousand years from to-day, will produce as well as it does at present, provided all other conditions remain the same. The Upper Silurian is divided into the following groups:

1. The Oneida Conglomerate; 2. The Medina Sandstone; 3. The Clinton Group; 4. The Niagara Group; 5. The Onondaga Salt Group; 6. The Lower Helderberg Group. Of these subdivisions of the Upper Silurian, only the Clinton and the Niagara groups deserve especial notice as Kentucky formations. The Clinton Group is only found in few and isolated places, and never attains a thickness of any consideration. The Niagara Group embraces the same kind of rocks which form the bed of the Niagara river at its world-renowned falls, whence it derives its name. In Kentucky it neither covers extensive areas nor attains great thickness; but it furnishes, in some places, excellent building stone. Near Louisville, we find it well exposed in the quarries east of the city, providing Louisville with most of the limestone required for building purposes. Here the Niagara rocks are very rich in fossils, which are mostly well preserved, and have furnished a great deal of the material now in the valuable collections of several Louisville geologists, and which enables science to acquire an extensive knowledge of the fauna of the Niagara period.

DEVONIAN FORMATION.—This formation is named by Murchison after Devonshire, in England, where it is prominently represented in the surface-rocks. Here in America we have subdivided it in the following groups:

1. Oriskany Sandstone; 2. Upper Helderberg Group; 3. Hamilton Group; 4. Portage Group; 5. Chemung Group; and 6. Catskill Group.

The Oriskany sandstone is placed here at the base of the Devonian column, whilst others consider it as the youngest member of the Silurian groups. It is extremely difficult to decide which of the two places assigned by different geologists to the Oriskany sandstone, is the proper and correct one. If, in accordance with the opinion of the older geologists, the Silurian period had been closed by a cataclysm, extinguishing all life of the Silurian time, Nature itself would have drawn a dividing line between Silurian and Devonian formations which could not be misunderstood by anybody; but no cataclysm ever took place; on the contrary, the transformation of the Silurian fauna and flora into their Devonian forms was accomplished by slow and gradual modifications, a process which did not produce partition lines, the establishment of which is thus left to arbitration. The proper way to find out the correct position of the Oriskany sandstone, is to carefully examine its fossils; if these show a nearer relationship to those of the Devonian than to the Silurian, the questionable group belongs to the younger formation; but if the relationship is closer to the Silurian forms, said group should be transferred to the Silurian column. In our own State, we find the Devonian formation represented only by the upper Helderberg and Hamilton groups, which are so blended together that it is entirely impossible to separate them from each other. Fossils characteristic of either of these groups are found from bottom to top of the whole Devonian columns in Kentucky. The Devonian formation does not cover a very extensive field in our State, still it is of great importance for economic, as well as for scientific purposes. It furnishes to the builder rock, cement and lime; to the farmer, a healthy and productive soil; and to the geologist, those precious specimens of fossil corals, crinoids and shells, which nowhere on the whole globe can be found in such abundance of specimens and species, and in such excellent state of preservation, as at Louisville and its vicinity. The widely known Falls of the Ohio River are not only known here in this country as an obstruction to navigation, but they are known to geologists of the whole civilized world as the great store-house where the Devonian world has collected the choicest specimens of its animal kingdom.

The Upper Helderberg group is often called the Corniferous limestone, or the Corniferous group, on account of the great mass of hornstone which it contains. This hornstone is found in great abundance in all of our Devonian strata, and it would, therefore, be advisable to designate the whole Devonian column in Kentucky as the Corniferous group.

CARBONIFEROUS FORMATION.—This formation is divided into Subcarboniferous and Coal Measures; both are still covering a large territory in Kentucky, though it appears that their former original extent has been greatly reduced by denudation. At present we have two large coal fields in our State; the eastern, which forms a part of the Appalachian coal region, and the western, belonging to the Illinois coal fields. Both these districts, it appears, were formerly united, though they are at present separated from each other by a broad strip of land whose surface-rocks belong either to the Devonian or to the Silurian. That the Carboniferous strata originally covered this dividing strip can scarcely be doubted, when we find the many knobs by which it is covered capped with the Carboniferous formation. Those knobs can not be the products of volcanic action. The undisturbed horizontality of their layers proves them to be the result of denudation. The denuding influence of heat, frost and rain appears to be too insignificant to have produced such an amount of excavation as would have been necessary to cut down many square miles of land from their former to their present level—a difference in some places amounting to several hundred feet. However, we must always bear in mind that geological agencies are enabled to do their enormous work, not so much by their magnitude, but mainly by their perseverance throughout the endless spaces of geological times.

Of the Subcarboniferous we distinguish the following five subdivisions: Kinderhook, Burlington, Keokuk, St. Louis and Chester groups. It is doubtful whether the Kinderhook group is really different from the Chemung group, and, even if a difference exists, it remains questionable where to place it properly, whether with the Devonian or the Subcarboniferous; its fossils show a nearer relationship to the Devonian fauna than to that of the superimposed strata of the Subcarboniferous. In Kentucky we find only the three younger formations, viz.: the Keokuk, the St. Louis and the Chester, which form a kind of border around the coal fields. The St. Louis limestone gives a peculiar feature to the country of which it forms the surface-rock. In its strata we find the many, often very extensive caverns, and the surface covered over with numerous funnel-shaped sink-holes. All the formations and groups so far enumerated, originated during the Palæozoic Period; they alone are of interest to Kentucky, inasmuch as they embrace all the surface-rocks of our State.

MESOZOIC AGE. —This produced the following three groups: Triassic, Jurassic and Cretaceous. None of these are represented in our State, though they cover vast areas of our continent, especially the Triassic and Cretaceous, whilst the Jurassic is only recognized in the Rocky Mountains and on its western slope.

CENOZOIC AGE.—During this age, which reaches to the present time, the Tertiary formation was called into existence. In it we find the earliest representatives of the different genera and species of animals and plants which to-day inhabit our planet. The subdivisions of the Tertiary are Eocene, Miocene and Pliocene.

Of living or recent species, the Eocene contains 3 to 4 per cent.; the Miocene from 18 to 20 per cent., and the Pliocene from 35 to 95 per cent., according to Lyell's definition of these different groups.

In the localities where Lyell studied these different rocks, there was a clear line of demarkation between the groups as he organized them, and in each group he found the above stated percentage of recent species ; but other localities of Tertiary rocks showed more than 4 and less than 18 per cent., and others again more than 20 and less than 35 per cent. of living species among their fossils. The question there and then arose, to which of the groups such strata should be attached? This question is solved by placing them in those groups with which their fossils show the nearest relationship.

MOLLUSCA.

Mollusca form one of the great animal sub-kingdoms ; their name is derived from the Latin word "Mollis," meaning soft, on account of the soft consistency of their body. This name was given to them by the French savant, Cuvier. This sub-kingdom embraces the Mollusca proper and the Molluscoids. The latter include the Polyzoa or Bryozoa and the Ascidians. The Ascidians having no shell, but instead only a kind of leathery sack, are not, so far, found in a fossil condition. The Bryozoa were formerly classed with the Corals on account of the resemblance of their calcareous support with those forms, but a closer study of the animals themselves proves their nearer relationship with the Mollusca. Inasmuch as the following monograph only treats of the fossil remains of the Mollusca proper, I deem it sufficient to limit my description to the latter.

The soft condition of the animals of this class makes it necessary to provide them with a protection in some shape or form. This is given them either by a calcareous envelope called their shell, or by a leathery sack or mantle surrounding the body. This mantle is possessed by every Mollusca, whether it is provided with a shell or not; but the mantle of those without shell is more leathery and better adapted for protection than the mantle of the shell-bearers. The shells are either of one, two or several pieces, and are accordingly called univalves, bivalves and multivalves. The common garden snail belongs to the first, the river mussel to the second, and the Chitons to the last group. Some of the Mollusca have a regular head furnished with eyes, tentacles, and a mouth with jaws and teeth. This class is called Encephala. The balance, having no head, are known as Acephala. The first group is divided into Cephalopoda, Gasteropoda and Pteropoda; the second into Brachiopoda and Lamellibranchiata.

CEPHALOPODA, meaning head-footed, so named because their arms or feet are arranged around their mouth. To this class belong the Nautilus, the Argonaut and the cuttle-fish of the present fauna, and the Ammonites, Cereatites and Belemnites of former ages. The bodies of most of them are symmetrical, that is, both halves of their bodies are identical in parts and size; their loco-

motion is produced either by the muscular feet surrounding their mouths, or
by two fins attached to the sides of their body, or, again, by the forcible ex-
pulsion of water through a tube, called the siphon. There are two orders of
Cephalopods: Dibranchiata and Tetrabranchiata, the first possessing two and
the second four branchiae.

The first order includes the cuttle-fishes ; they are all naked, with the exception of the Argonaut. Their soft body is supported by an internal shell.
Plate I, figure 12, shows the complete animal of the Sepia officinalis; and Plate
I, figure 16, is a Belemnite, or the internal shell of one of the dibranchiate
Cephalopods. Most all the species of this order are provided with an ink-bag,
the contents of which they discharge when pursued by their enemies. Of the
second order, the Tetrabranchiata, only very few species are living at the present time. Plate I, figure 24, shows the Nautilus pompilius, the main representative of the tetrabranchiate Cephalopods of the present seas. The oceans
of former ages were swarming with species of this order, fossil forms of which
are figured on Plate I, figures 1, 2, 18 and 19. Their shells are internally
divided into cells or chambers (see Plate I, figures 1 and 24), by a series of
partitions called the septa (see Plate I, figure 24b), connected by a tube called
the siphon or siphuncle, shown by c, Plate I, figure 24. Only the last chamber,
called the body-chamber, is occupied by the animal, while the others are empty
and serve as air-chambers. In fossil specimens very often the outer shell is
removed, and the edges of the septa are seen (Plate I, figures 18 and 19),
which are called sutures. Their form serves to distinguish different genera ;
they are curved in Nautilus and Orthoceras, zigzag in Goniotites, or foliaceous
in Ammonite.

The siphuncle is also of great importance in determining genera; its shape
and location have to be noticed by the student of Palæontology. Its shape is
so variable that it is impossible to give here a sufficient explanation of the
same, whilst its siphuncle may be located either in the center of the shell or
in its dorsal or ventral lines, or even on either of its sides. The opening of
the body-chamber is called its aperture, which, in different species and genera,
assume different shapes, and is generally closed by a calcareous plate, called
the operculum.

GASTEROPODA.—This class includes land and water-snails, which are either
naked or provided with a shell. They received their name because their locomotion is accomplished by the lower part of their body, which is provided
with strong muscles, and, by its contractions and expansions, serves them as a
foot. (See Plate I, figure 13.) Their shells are generally univalve, either
spiral or tubular, but a few are multivalve, the Chitons (see Plate I, figure 11).
In the spiral shells we have to notice the following parts: see Plate I, figure

2, a, the apex; C, c and d, sutures; a to f, the spire; g, the aperture. In figure 14 of the same plate, "a" is the posterior canal, "C" the anterior canal, and "d" the outer lip of the aperture. Each full turn of the spiral is called a whorl. The axis (see Plate I, figure 23), ("a"), around which the whorls are coiled, is either solid or it is hollow, as may be seen in Plate I, figure 10. In this case the shell is called perforated or umbellicated. Nearly all the shells are dextral, or right-handed; others are sinistral, or left-handed; see Plate I, figures 14 and 15. The first is dextral, the second sinistral. In a few species the shell is regularly sinistral; for instance, in Clausilia, while among those with dextral spires, sometimes sinistral aberrations are found. The last turn of the shell is called the body-whorl, and the aperture is generally closed by an operculum.

The aperture is either entire, as in Plate I, figures 10 and 21, or drawn out or produced into a canal, see Plate I, figures 14 and 15. Species having shells with an entire aperture, are generally vegetable feeders, whilst, on the other hand, the siphonated shells belong to carnivorous families. The Gasteropoda are found all over the world on land, in rivers and fresh-water lakes, and in the different oceans. Their fossil representatives run through all the different geological strata, from the lowest Silurian up to recent formation of the Pliocene.

PTEROPODA.—(Wing-footed.) Their locomotion is accomplished by means of a pair of large fins attached to the sides of their head (see Plate I, figure 4). Their shells are univalve, but of very different forms. Plate I, figure 5, shows the fossil shell of one genera of Pteropoda, a Conularia. Animals of this class are very abundant in all our oceans, and furnish food for a good many inhabitants of the sea. In former ages they lived in all the oceans from the Silurian age to those just preceding the now existing ones.

BRACHIOPODA.—The Brachiopoda are bivalve shell-fish, which differ from the ordinary mussels, cockles, etc., in being always equal-sided, but never quite equal-valve. Their forms are symmetrical, and so commonly resemble antique lamps that they were called lampades, or lamp shells, by the old naturalists. The hole which, in a lamp, admits the wick, serves, in the shell, for the passage of the pedicle by which it is attached to submarine objects. The valves of the Brachiopoda are respectively dorsal and ventral. The ventral valve is usually the larger, and has a prominent beak, by which it is attached or through which the organ of adhesion, the pedicle, passes. The valves are articulated by two curved teeth in the ventral valve, which are received by sockets of the dorsal valve; some genera and species are not provided with such hinges. In both the articulated and unarticulated Brachiopods, the valves are opened and closed by strong muscles, whose places of attachment are seen in

Plate I, figure 25. Among the fossil shells of even the older Palæozoic strata, we find sometimes Brachiopod shells so well preserved that even the valves may be opened as far as the teeth and sockets of the hinge will allow. Most of the shells of Brachiopods have a peculiar structure, consisting of flattened prisms of considerable length, arranged parallel to each other with great regularity, and obliquely to the surfaces of the shell, which is also perforated by canals (see Plate I, figure 22). This great class of Mollusca has derived its name from the two long ciliated arms developed from the sides of the mouth, with which each animal is provided as means to create currents which bring to it its food. These arms (Plate I, figure 9) were considered by former naturalists as instruments of locomotion; but it is now ascertained that they, outside of their first mentioned purpose, serve mainly as breathing organs; the erroneous name Brachiopoda (arm-footed), should, therefore, be corrected into Brachionabranchia (arm-breathers). Most of the Brachiopoda are provided with an internal skeleton, consisting of two spiral processes in the Spiriferidæ (see Plate I, figures 7 and 8), whilst in others, the Terebratula and Thecidia, this skeleton takes the form of a loop, as seen in Plate I, figures 6 and 26. This skeleton serves as a support for the brachial membrane. The prominent parts of the Brachiopod shell are the following: Dorsal valve, the upper one, which is usually the smaller, ventral valve, the lower one, which is generally the larger. The beak is that portion of the valve which terminates above the hinge-line in a sharp point or in a perforation (as seen in Plate I, figure 25 "a"). This perforation is called the foramen. The most convex portion of the valve near the beak is known as the umbo. Most of the shells have below the beak a triangular opening, which, in valves without hinge line, is closed by a separate body, consisting of either one or two pieces, the deltidium. In shells with a hinge area, as the Spirifera and Cyrtina, said area is divided in two by the triangular opening, which is partly or entirely closed by the growth of the shell. This is known as the pseudo-deltidium. In some shells the outline of the valve forms on both sides of the hinge a straight line, the hinge line, which may be as long as the greatest breadth of the shell, or may be so short as scarcely to be noticeable. The area which sometimes exists between hinge-line and beak is the hinge-area, best developed in the shells of Cyrtina. The hinge-area may be straight or curved, and is always divided by the pseudo-deltidium.

The valves of a shell are either both convex, or one convex and the other plane, or one convex and the other concave. In some shells, as in Spirifera, the ventral valve has a strong depression extending and enlarging from the beak to the front, dividing the valve into two equal halves. This depression is known as the mesial sinus. Corresponding with this mesial sinus is an elevation in the dorsal valve, extending and enlarging also from beak to front, and called the mesial fold. Cardinal area is a synonym for hinge-area, and cardinal extremities are the extreme points of the hinge-line. Of all the Mollusca, the Brachiopoda enjoy the greatest range both of climate and depth and time; they are found in tropical and polar seas. The living species prefer the deep waters to shallow lakes, though some of them are found even here. Of the population of the seas of former ages, they formed a very large part. Their fossil remains are found in almost every strata of the whole geological column. They are not only very abundant, but also well preserved, and form the principal treasures of many palæontological collections.

LAMELLIBRANCHIATA.—The Mollusca of this class are familiar to every one; they are represented by the oysters, mussels and cockles. The animal is without head, and the shell is bivalve. The valves are attached to the sides of the animal. We have, therefore, in this class, a right and left valve. Plate I, figures 3 and 20, show the left valves. In figure 17, the upper valve is a right one, and the lower a left one. The mouth of the animal is generally directed towards the shorter slope of the shell. The hinge is on the back of the animal and formed by teeth and sockets, together with an elastic ligament. The shells are closed by powerful adductor muscles, but open when the animal relaxes the muscles, or when it is dead. We distinguish in the shells of this class the dorsal, ventral, anterior, and posterior margins. The dorsal margin contains the hinge, whilst the ventral margin is opposite to this. The anterior margin forms the end of the shell on the shorter slope, and the posterior margin the end of the longer slope.

Plate I, figure 3, is the left valve of Cytherea dione, separate from Cytherea, with the following prominent parts: h, the hinge ligament; d, the umbo; f, the lunule; c, cardinal tooth; tt, lateral teeth; a, anterior adductor muscle; a, posterior adductor muscle; p, pallial impression; s, sinus, occupied by retractor of the siphons. The line designated as pallial impression, which in many shells is prominently marked, indicates the place where the mantle is attached to the shell. The presence of a bay or sinus (s), in the line of the pallial impression, proves the animal to have possessed retractile siphons. All the Mollusca belonging to this class live in the water, in rivers, lakes and oceans. They are abundant at the present time, and have been so in all the seas of former ages. Their fossil remains are often extremely well preserved, and add greatly to the beauty of many Palæozoic collections.

Within the here described five classes, the different Mollusca are divided into families, genera and species. The naturalists of former centuries were able to give a more precise definition of these terms. They believed that each species was a priori created, and thus by sharply defined lines of distinction, separated from all the other forms, and only related to some of these by accidental similarity in certain features. Inasmuch as relation between organic beings depends upon their origin from common ancestors, no real relation could exist outside of a species among the animals and plants, if the former belief in the stability of species had remained. The erroneous views of the old school were based upon observations among the more highly developed animals and plants, where the division lines between the species are more pronounced.

Had the scientists of olden times directed their investigation to the lower organisms, they would soon have met with difficulties, and in many cases even with impossibilities, to accomplish a specific differentiation. The evolution theory has upset the views of the old school. It does not believe in a separate original creation for every species, but, according to it, new ones are produced by gradual modifications of old forms. Changes in organisms may be either temporary, that is, dying out with the same specimen in which they first occur, or they may be constant, when they reappear in all the succeeding generations. Only these constant alterations will lead towards new species, and in order to do this, they must intensify in every succeeding specimen, until they become so characteristic as to afford an easy and sure distinction between the original and the new species. It is obvious that this procedure in the creation of species will leave some specimens in a doubtful position ; their modifications may separate them from the old forms and still be insufficient to place them among the new ones. These forms are connecting links, and serve to establish a general relationship in larger groups of organism ; but they cause considerable trouble as far as classification is concerned.

It is impossible to state the exact amount of similarity required between two animals or two plants, which will place them both either in the same family, the same genus, or the same species. In recent years a real mania has sprung up among some naturalists to manufacture as many genera and species as possible. By such proceedings science is not benefited, but only becomes incumbered with synonyms, of which, sooner or later, it has to be purged. Such a cleaning process will be necessary in Palæontology. This science, which has lately passed its childhood, and which handled material, the character of which was little known, has certainly established species and genera which will require revision. We find, for instance, of some fossil shells specimens showing the outside shell with all the markings well preserved, and again, others in the condition of internal casts, with all the shell exfoliated between such specimens exist differences rendering it impossible to recognize their intimate relation without closer investigation. That the first geologists, noticing these two different forms, described them as different species, is quite natural ; but as soon as material of this kind increased, some forms were found, showing partly the internal cast and partly the exterior shell, combining the two fossils which were so far considered as different species. Again, we have certain species in which the extreme forms are so different from each other that any one finding only these two extremes, would be fully justified in describing them as different species, but increased material furnishes intermediate forms connecting those extremes into one species.

Before closing these introductory remarks, I will copy from an English writer some observations which show the beneficial influence of the cultivation of natural sciences upon the minds and morals of the people, words which should be well remembered by every parent looking to the welfare of his child ; by every teacher aiming by his labors to ennoble the mind and character of his students ; and by every trustee of schools endeavoring to elevate those institutions to real nurseries of the highest type of civilization. He remarks : "It is fearfully true, that nine-tenths of the immorality which pervades the better classes of society, originate from the want of an interesting occupation to fill up their vacant time ; and as the study of natural sciences is as attractive as it is beneficial, it must necessarily exert a moral and even religious influence upon the young and inquiring mind. The youth who is fond of scientific pursuits will not enter into revelry, for frivolous or vicious excitement will have no fascinations for him. The overflowing cup, the unmeaning or dishonest game, will not entice him. If any one doubts the beneficial influence of these studies on the morals and character, I would ask him to point out the immoral young man who is devotedly attached to any branch of natural science. I never knew such an one, and if there are any, they are rare exceptions ; and the loud clamors which are always raised against the man of science who errs, prove how rarely the study of the works of nature fails to exert an ennobling effect upon a well regulated mind. Fortunate, indeed, are the youth of either sex, who early imbibe a taste for natural knowledge, and whose predilections are not thwarted by injudicious friends."

These remarks, based upon indisputable facts, show that the value of the natural sciences ought not to be estimated only by their financial result, which is, unfortunately, the only scale with which most people nowadays measure, but also, and more deservedly so, by their ennobling influence upon the hearts and brains of the human race.

FOSSIL SHELLS

OF THE

SILURIAN AND DEVONIAN ROCKS.

BY

HENRY NETTELROTH.

———

PART II.

———

DESCRIPTION OF SPECIES.

FOSSILS

OF THE

SILURIAN AND DEVONIAN ROCKS.

COELENTERATA.

SPONGIA.

Genus Brachiospongia. Marsh.

Described by Marsh in Am. Journal of Scie. and Arts., 2d series, Vol. 44, 1867—Etymology: brachium, an arm; spongia a sponge.

Brachiospongia digitata. Owen

Plate XXXV., figure 3, and Plate XXXVI., figures 1 and 3.
Scyphia digitata, Owen. First Ky. Geol. Rep., Vol. II., p. 111—1857.

This fossil is very peculiar and very interesting; Prof. D. D. Owen, who described it in his Kentucky Report, placed it in the genus Scyphia of Schweigg, but its proper place is in the later established genus Brachiospongia of Marsh. It consists of a circular or elliptical central body, which is hollow, and has on its lower side an elliptical aperture occupying about one-third of the lower surface. This aperture is surrounded by an elevated thick brim, which rises in the specimen before me more than an inch and a quarter above the general surface; its greater diameter measures four and its smaller two inches and a quarter. From the circumference of the central body radiate in my shell twelve large, cylindrical, geniculated tubes, while in fossils seen by Prof. Owen he counted only from eight to eleven. These tubes start from the periphery with a downward direction for about a little more than an inch, where they make an abrupt turn of about ninety degrees upwards, to the extent of more than three inches. If the interspaces between the tubes were closed, the fossil would form a medium sized basin or bowl, with an elevated center. The tubes are all of about the same size and shape; all have an aperture on top, which is different in shape; in some the opening is elliptical, while in others, it extends to the knee; but there is no doubt that, in original specimens, the aperture was limited to the top, and the lateral enlargement of the opening is due to wear and rubbing in its fossil condition. The internal structure is destroyed, and only the outline or general form preserved. The central body measures six inches in diameter, while the circle, formed by the tops of the tubes, has a diameter of nine inches.

Formation and Locality.—This interesting fossil is limited to one locality; it is found in the lower strata of the Cincinnati or Hudson River group, at Bright's Mill, on Benson Creek, a few miles west of Frankfort, Ky., where, altogether, not more than about a dozen fair specimens have been found, while ractional specimens are more numerous.

MOLLUSCA.

BRYOZOA.

Genus Ptilodictya. Lonsdale.

Ptilodictya, Lonsdale. Murch. Sil. Syst.—1830.
Etymology: *ptilon*, a wing; *dictyon*, a net.
The correct orthography would be Ptilodictyon.

Fronds simple or branched, springing from a pointed or wedge-shaped, sub-solid, and finely striated base or articulating process, which fitted loosely in the socket of the expanded and firmly attached base. The free portion of the zoarium is two-edged, with the transverse or cross section acutely elliptical, with the surface either smooth, montiferous, or marked by transverse ridges, and composed of two equal but distinct sides; each side is provided with a delicate epithacal membrane, from which the cells rise to open on the two opposite faces of the frond. Cells quadrate, rhomboidal, or hexagonal, and arranged in longitudinal series, or in a quincuncial manner; pseudo-septa are frequently present; the walls are pierced in many species by connecting foramina. The interstitial cells are usually absent; but in the nodose species the summits of the monticules are often occupied by smaller cells than the average. In the robust species the tubes are crossed by diaphragms placed upon the same level in contiguous tubes.

Ptilodictya hilli. James.

Plate XXXV., figures 1, 2, 4 and 5.
Ptilodictya hilli, James.   Cin. Journ. of Nat. Hist., Vol. V., pt. 3, plate 7, figure 7, no descpt.—1882.

Zoarium digitate, the number of prongs not known; the specimen before me shows one complete branch, which deflects from the original stem, just above the wedge-shaped articulating process, out of the sharp edge, and extending in the same plane with the main stem. On one of the broad sides of the main stem, and in its center line, are two protuberances, the one opposite the center line of the deflecting branch, and the other about one-fourth of an inch above it, which appear to be the buds of two new branches, but whose positions make it somewhat doubtful, inasmuch as those new stems would leave the plane of the two existing prongs. In similar species, as P. ramosa and P. briareus, the branches start always from the sharp edge, and I do not doubt that the same is the case with P. hilli. We may, therefore, assume, that very few branches are formed. This species is generally found in more or less straight, thin strips, of different width, the cross sections of which are either acutely elliptical or elliptic-lanceolate. Both sides are entirely equal; they are most convex in their central line, from where they slope in a regular but gentle curve to the lateral margins, where the surfaces of both sides meet at a very acute angle. The surfaces of both sides are covered by transverse, sharply angular ridges, with interspaces of about twice their own width. Some of these plications cross the branches from one edge to the other in a straight line, rectangular with the margin, the course of others is somewhat oblique, and others again cross the surface only partly. These shorter ribs are always intercalated, and never produced by bifurcation. The whole zoarium is covered by closely arranged rhomboidal cells of about equal size, the walls of which form nearly straight lines, crossing each other obliquely. The largest specimen in my possession measures nearly four inches in length, by more than an inch in width ; in its whole extent it does not show any branch ; it has thirteen transverse ribs in the space of an inch. A smaller specimen measures one inch and three-eighths in length, by one-fourth of an inch in width, with nineteen cross ribs in the space of an inch.

Formation and Locality.—This species is named after Dr. O. O. Hill, formerly of Cincinnati, Ohio, who first discovered it. It was afterwards found rather abundantly in the upper strata of the Hudson River group at Danville, Ky., by Prof. Linney, of the Kentucky Geological Survey.

MOLLUSCA.

BRACHIOPODA.

Genus Crania. Retzius.

Crania. Retzius. Schrift der Berliner Gesellschaft Nat. Freunde. 1781. Etymology: Kranion the upper part of the skull.

Shell smooth or striated by radiating striae ; umbo of the dorsal valve sub-central ; umbo of the ventral valve sub-central, marginal or prominent and cap-like, with an obscure triangular area traversed by a central line. Shell usually attached to other shells or marine bodies. The large muscular impressions of the attached valve are sometimes convex, in other species, deeply excavated; those of the upper valve are usually convex. In C. tripartita of Münster, the nasal process divides the fixed valve into three cells. Some of the species are either entirely free or but slightly attached. Crania craniolaris is the type of the genus, which extends from the Lower Silurian to the present day.

Crania bordeni. HALL AND WHITFIELD.

Plate II., Fig. 14.

Crania bordeni, H. & W.   24th Regent's Report, p. 187—1872.
Crania bordeni, H. & W.   27th Regent's Report, pl. 9—1875.

Shell depressed conical, about half as high as wide; beak sub-central, slightly nearer the anterior end. Surface marked by fine radiating striae, and somewhat strong lines of growth, giving a rugose character to surface, especially toward the margin. This species resembles Crania crenistria, from the Hamilton group of New York, but that species is more coarsely striated than our shell.

Formation and Locality. Found in the rotten hornstone and in the cherty layers on top of the hydraulic limestone of the Devonian formation in Jefferson county, Kentucky, and in Clark county, Indiana. The quarries for hydraulic cement rock at Watson's Station, on the Ohio and Mississippi Railroad, furnished the fine specimen of Modiomorpha concentrica, to which two fine individuals of Crania bordeni are attached.

Genus Discina. Lamarck.

Discina. Lamarck. Hist. Nat. des Animaux sans vertebres. 1819. Etymology: *discus*, a flat round plate; the termination *ina* implying resemblance.

The following are some of the exterior characters of the shells of this genus, as given by Mr. Davidson: "Circular, longitudinally and transversely oval. Upper or dorsal valve conical, patelliform, with apex inclining towards the anterior margin. Lower or ventral valve opercular, flat or partly convex, and perforated by a narrow oval longitudinal slit, reaching to near the posterior margin, and placed in the middle of an oval depressed disk. Surface smooth, ornamented by numerous striae, radiating from the apex to the margin, or by concentric lines of growth produced in foliaceous expansions. Shell structure horny, and perforated by minute tubuli."

Discina doria. HALL.

Discina doria, Hall. Pal. N. Y., Vol. IV., page 19—1867.

Shell very small, sub-circular or oblate, the transverse diameter usually the greater, but in some specimens it is reverse. Dorsal valve moderately convex, apex elevated sub-terminal. Ventral valve flat or concave, the apex excentric; foramen comparatively large, oval, with margins depressed. The shell itself is very thin.

The surface is marked by fine, closely arranged concentric striae, which are plainly visible on our specimens, though they are internal casts, and entirely silicified.

This species closely resembles the D. newberry, from Cuyahoga Falls, Ohio; but that shell is somewhat thicker and stronger, with the apex of the dorsal valve more elevated, and the shell is altogether larger than our specimens. One of the specimens before me measures three lines and a half in length, by three lines in width, and its elevation about one line.

Formation and Locality.—The specimens of this species are adhering to other fossils, a fact which would make their identity with Discina doubtful, if not both valves were found so attached. The specimens before me, three in number, occupy the valve of a Spir. oweni, and were found in the Devonian rocks of Clark county, Indiana.

Discina grandis. VANUXEM.

Plate III., Figure 3.

Orbicula grandis, Vanuxem. Geol. Rep. 3d dist—1842.
Discina grandis, Hall. Pal. N. Y., Vol. IV., p. 7—1867.
Discina grandis, H. & W. 24th Reg. Report, p. 187—1872.
Discina grandis, H. & W. 27th Reg. Rep., pl. 9—1875.

General form broadly and transversely elliptical; either plano-convex or concavo-convex. Dorsal valve sometimes extremely elevated; apex sub-central, a little on one side of the transverse axis. Ventral valve usually moderately concave; foramen reaching from the center or near the center towards one side, but varying somewhat in different individuals. Surface is marked by fine concentric striae, crowded near the center, and more distant and sharply elevated towards the margin. This species is easily recognized by its larger size, and in the ventral valve by the direction of the foramen being in the shorter diameter of the shell. This valve is somewhat unequally concave, and, on the side of the foramen, often a little convex. The specimen here described and figured, has diameters of fourteen and twelve lines, and a height of six lines and one-half, it may be considered as of average size among the shells found here.

Formation and Locality. This species is often met with in our rocks, but only the dorsal valve is preserved, it is always entirely silicified, and occurs in the cherty layers, superimposed upon the hydraulic limestone of the Devonian formation, in Jefferson county, Kentucky, and in Clark county, Indiana. All my specimens of this species I found in the cement quarries at Watson's Station, on the Ohio and Mississippi Railroad, where the chert beds come near the surface.

Genus Lingula. Bruguiere.

Lingula. Bruguiere. Encycl. Meth.—1792. *Etymology : lingula,* a little tongue.

Shell oblong, compressed, sub-equivalve, attached by a pedicle passing out between the valves. Shell structure minutely tubular, texture horny. Shell slightly gaping at each end, truncated in front, rather pointed at the umbones ; dorsal valve rather shorter, with a thickened hinge-margin and a raised central ridge inside. (Woodward.)

Lingula triangulata. n. sp.

Plate XXVI., Figure 1.

Shell of medium size ; sub-triangular or broadly sub-ovate. The lateral margins form, at the apex, an angle of about sixty degrees ; the sides slope from apex to two-thirds of the length of shell in a straight line ; from there they curve gently to basal margin, which is broadly rounded. Shell is moderately convex from beak down to front, but depressed almost flat at margins. The greatest width is about one-third of length of shell from the front ; width is smaller than length. The specimen before me measures twelve lines in length by ten lines in width. Shell itself is thick. The surface is marked by fine concentric lines of growth, and also by fine radiating striae, both of which are somewhat obscure on account of exfoliated condition of fossils, which are mostly internal casts. It appears to have some resemblance with Lingula paliformis of the Hamilton group, but differs from it by its shape and surface-markings.

Formation and Locality. Found in the Hydraulic limestone of the Devonian formation at the Falls of the Ohio, in Kentucky.

Genus Orthis. Dalman.

Orthis, Dalman. Kongl. Vet. Acad. Handl.—1817.

Etymology: Orthis, straight, in allusion to the straight hinge line.

Shell variable in shape, sub-circular or quadrate ; valves equally or unequally convex, socket valve sometimes slightly concave, with or without a mesial fold or sinus ; hinge line straight, generally shorter than width of shell. Both valves furnished with an area, divided by an open, triangular fissure for passage of the pedicle. Beaks more or less incurved, that of larger valve generally more produced. Surface smooth, striated, or ornamented by single, bifurcated, or intercalated ribs. Structure minutely or largely punctate. Valves articulating by means of teeth and sockets.

In interior of ventral valve the vertical dental plates form the walls of the fissure, and extend from beak to bottom of shell; between these a small rounded mesial ridge divides the 'muscular scars, which extend over two elongated depressions, margined on their outer side by the prolonged bases of the dental plates. The cardinal muscles appear to have occupied greater portion of anterior division of these two depressions; the pedicle muscles occupying the external and posterior part of same space.

The adductor was probably attached to each side and close to mesial ridge. In the socket valve the fissure is partly or entirely occupied by a more or less produced simple shelly process, to which were affixed the cardinal muscular fibres, the inner socket walls are considerably prolonged into cavity of the shell, under shape of projecting laminæ, to the extremity of which free, fleshy, spiral arms may, perhaps, have been affixed. Under this shelly process a longitudinal ridge separates the quadruple impressions of the adductor, which on each side forms two deep oval depressions, placed obliquely one above the other, and separated by lateral ridges, branching from the center one. The genus Orthis is very nearly related to Strophomena, from which the more typical forms may in general be easily separated by their usually greater convexity, and the rounder and shorter hinge-line.

Orthis biforata. Schlotheim.

Plate XXIX., figures 18 to 22.

Terebratulites biforatus, Schlotheim, Petrefact. P. 265—1820
Orthis biforata, Meek. Pal. of Ohio, Vol. I., p. 112—1873.
See the list of synonyms in last cited Report.

Shell small, transversely oval-subquadrate, moderately convex, wider than long; hinge-line a little less than the greatest width of the shell; cardinal angles obtuse, seldom rounded. Surface plicate.

Ventral valve depressed convex; mesial sinus well defined from beak to front, deep, with flattened bottom, containing four plications, the central ones starting from the beak, while the lateral start about the middle of valve from marginal slopes of the sinus.

In one of my specimens one of the lateral plications within the sinus is wanting; beak a little more elevated, and somewhat stronger than that of the opposite valve, only faintly curved, almost straight; cardinal area narrow, but increasing in height towards beak; foramen almost an equilateral triangle.

Dorsal valve generally a little more convex than other, greatest convexity at the umbo, from where it curves gently and regularly to lateral and front margins.

Mesial fold prominent and well-defined from beak to front, somewhat flat-tened on top, bearing five plications in its lower half. In younger specimens the fold has only three plications, of which in older individuals the lateral ones dichostomize at about the middle of shell, and thus form the five costae of the lower part. The umbo is more, and the beak less prominent than that of the other valve; hinge-area also somewhat smaller than the ventral. Size of shell variable, the largest specimen in my collection, figured on plate XXIX., sub-figures 18, 19 and 20, has a width of seven-eighths of an inch, a length of five-eighths of an inch, by a depth of three-eighths of an inch.

Surface marked by from five to seven strong angular plications, counted at the margins, some of which are formed by bifurcation. No other surface-mark-ings are visible.

Formation and Locality.—Found in the lower strata of the Niagara formation in the quarries east of Louisville, Ky. This species is very common and of larger forms in the Lower Silurian, but to find its representatives in the Niagara rocks is somewhat of a surprise. They are rather belated stragglers.

Orthis borealis. BILLINGS.

Plate XXXIV., figures 14 to 20.

Orthis borealis, Billings. Can. Nat., Vol. IV., p. 436—1859.
Orthis frankfortensis, James. Cat. Low. Sill. Foss., Cin. gr., p. 10—1871.
Orthis borealis, Meek. Pal. of Ohio, Vol. I, p. 101., pl. 8—1873

Shell of rather less than medium size, transversely oval-sub-quadrate, or truncato-sub-oval, the length and breadth varying with relation to each other from 9 to 11, to 11 to 12; both valves convex; hinge-line generally less than the greatest width of the shell, and meeting the lateral margins under a more or less obtuse angle; lateral margins, from cardinal extremities to base, form-ing a compound, reversed curve of regular form, concave at the cardinal angles and thence convex to base, which is broadly rounded, but sometimes showing also a faint sinuosity. Ventral valve most convex near umbo, sloping from there somewhat abruptly, but in a gentle curve to posteriolateral margins, while the anterior central region is depressed so as to form a broad, very shallow mesial sinus which extends backwards to middle of shell; beak more prominent than that of the other valve, sharply pointed, inclined backward and slightly arched; cardinal area broad-triangular, well defined by angular margins, and concave; foramen rather narrow, its height exceeding its base. Dorsal valve sometimes more convex than the other; its greatest convexity a little above the middle of the valve, from where it slopes in gentle curves to lateral and anterior margins; the central-anterior portion of the valve is slightly elevated, forming a broad, low, and undefined mesial fold, whose starting point is at, or somewhat in front of middle of valve; beak of medium size, arched, but not incurved; cardinal area of about half the height of the ventral, and slightly curved. Surface of both valves ornamented by distinct, rather prominent, radiating ribs, of which from thirty-six to forty-four may be counted on the margins of shell, most all of which extend from beak to front. Bifurcation is very seldom noticed, and then only in old and very large specimens. With the exception of a few imbricating lines of growth, no other surface-markings are visible. This species resembles Orthis plicatella, but is more convex, and has more numerous and smaller costae; it is also less transverse, and its mesial depression and elevation are more marked.

Formation and Locality.—Found at Frankfort, Ky., in the Trenton limestone, in great abundance, and in excellently preserved specimens.

Orthis elegantula. Dalman.

Plate XXXII., figures 52 to 57.

Orthis elegantula, Dalman. K. Vet. Acad. Handl., p. 117—1827.
Orthis canalis, Sowerby. Murch. Sil. Syst., p. 631—1839.
Orthis canalis, Hall. Geol. Rep. 4th dist. N. Y., p. 107—1843.
Orthis elegantula, Hall. Pal. N. Y., Vol. III., p. 252—1852.
Orthis elegantula, Hall. 11th Rep. of Indiana, p. 285—1881.

Shell small, semi-oval, plano-convex, sometimes even somewhat concavo-convex; length usually exceeding width. Hinge-line less than greatest width of shell, cardinal extremities rounded.

Ventral valve gibbous, greatest convexity about the middle of the valve, from where it slopes in regular curves gently to front, more abruptly to lateral margins, umbo prominent, beak narrow, elevated and incurved over cardinal area, which latter is depressed triangular, not reaching to cardinal extremities; foramen of medium size, its base to height as two to three; in the center of the valve is sometimes a slight linear elevation, which extends from beak to front, visible; lateral margins regularly but gently curved; anterior margin forms a regular semi-circle, seldom showing in its center a slight sinuosity. Dorsal valve either flat or even a little concave, rarely being slightly convex, often showing a gentle linear depression in the center line of the valve from beak to front; hinge-area narrow, almost linear; beak small and incurved. Surface marked by fine radiating striae, which increase towards the margins by bifurcation; the lateral ones are strongly curved outwards. This beautiful species is closely allied to Orthis testudinaria, and, perhaps, more nearly to O. parva, both of which are Lower Silurian fossils. In our specimens the shell is generally more elongated, and the beak more extended, while the surface is more finely striated. Orthis elegantula is easily distinguished. In regard to size, it is impossible to give any dimensions, inasmuch as we find the shells from the size of a small pea to that of an average hazelnut.

Formation and Locality.—This elegant shell is found abundantly and well preserved in the Niagara rocks east of the city of Louisville, where it, however, occurs of very small size; the specimen represented on plate XXXII. is about the largest individual ever found. At Waldron, Indiana, it has attained its largest size. Average specimens from there measure about five-eighths of an inch in width, and somewhat more in length.

Orthis flabellum. SOWERBY.

Plate XXXIV., figure 30.

Orthis flabellum, Hall. Rep. 4th Geol. Dist.—1843.
Orthis flabellum, Sowerby. Murch. Sil. Syst., p. 639—1839.
Orthis flabellum, Var? Hall. Pal. N. Y., Vol. II., p. 254—1852.

Shell of medium size; semi-oval or semi-elliptical; hinge-line equal to greatest width of shell; cardinal angles rectangular or slightly acute; lateral margins sometimes slightly contracted below extremities; balance of the lateral margins and base form a regular curve; shell plano-convex. Ventral valve depressed convex, almost flat. The shell before me has, in its central line, a gentle depression, beginning at about one-third of whole length of shell from base, and extending to front, forming a kind of mesial sinus, but I am not able to find out with certainty whether this sinus is really a natural character of shell, or whether it is the result of distortion. I am inclined to take it for a real sinus, inasmuch as balance of shell does not show any signs of having been subjected to any violence. The dorsal valve is moderately convex in its marginal portion, but almost flat in its central part or in the umbonal region.

The cardinal extremities are slightly deflected, incurving the surface between them and the umbo somewhat. The cardinal area of the ventral valve is of moderate size, forming a low triangle; it is divided by a triangular fissure, partly closed; the area of the dorsal valve is narrow, almost linear; the dorsal beak incurves into ventral foramen.

The surface of the shell is ornamented by about twenty-four to thirty simple, prominent, sub-angular radii, which increase in number by interpolation. These radii are crossed by several marked, concentric lines of growth, which divide the surface in several concentric zones, and give the shell, wherever they become crowded, which is mostly the case at the margins, a rugose appearance.

Formation and Locality.—The only specimen which I ever have seen, and which belongs to my own collection, I found in the strippings of one of the quarries east of the city of Louisville; it was surrounded by Niagara clay, and belongs undoubtedly to the Upper Silurian formation.

Orthis goodwini. N. SP.

Plate XVII., figures 30, 31 and 32.

Shell small, sub-circular or sub-quadrate ; moderately convex in both valves ; hinge-line short, equal or less than half width of shell ; cardinal extremities rounded ; lateral margins almost straight, or very slightly curved; they diverge towards base, in consequence of which greatest width of the shell is close to base or front; the basal margin is broadly curved, with its central portion either straight or slightly inflected.

Ventral valve is somewhat more convex in its umbonal region than dorsal, but in its basal half it is the reverse. Its greatest convexity is just below umbo, from where it slopes in a very gentle curve to lateral and basal margins, but more rapidly, even almost abruptly, to the cardinal lines ; umbo moderate, beak a little elevated above opposite valve, sharp-pointed and slightly arched, but not incurved. Cardinal area short, but comparatively high, limited by sharp margins, and divided by an open, triangular foramen, which is partly closed at its base by the cardinal process of the dorsal valve.

Dorsal valve moderately convex ; point of greatest convexity a little above middle of valve, from where it slopes in a gentle curve to all the margins and to the beak, giving the valve over its whole surface an even convexity, with the exception of a narrow strip in the middle, which extends from beak to base, and which is slightly depressed. This mesial depression is deepest in its middle portion; it is only faintly marked upon the umbo, and it becomes shallower but wider towards the base. The surface of both valves is ornamented by fine, thread-like radiating striae, which increase in number, partly by bifurcation, but mostly by intercalation ; these radii are crossed by several concentric lines of growth, which become more numerous towards basal margin. In regard to size, the specimen illustrated on plate 17, figures 30, 31 and 32, is of about the average size, though a few specimens have been found which are considerably larger.

Formation and Locality.—Found mostly in the rotten hornstone in upper strata of the Devonian formation at the Falls of the Ohio. This species I name in honor of Prof. A. C. Goodwin, formerly of Charlestown, Indiana, an ardent collector.

Orthis hybrida. SOWERBY.

Plate XXXII., figures 32 to 35.

Orthis hybrida, Sowerby. Murch. Sil. Syst., p. 630—1839.
Orthis hybrida, Hall. Geol. Rep. 4th dist., page 107—1843.
Orthis hybrida, Hall. Pal. N. Y., Vol. III., p. 253—1852.
Orthis hybrida, Hall. 11th Rep. of Indiana, p. 284—1881.

Shell small, lenticular or depressed spheroidal, wider than long, valves nearly equal; the ventral one depressed from center to base, while the other one is regularly convex; beak a little elevated above the other and slightly incurved; hinge-line much shorter than width of shell; cardinal extremities rounded; hinge-area small. Dorsal valve slightly convex; beak and hinge area small.

Surface covered by fine radiating striae, which increase towards the front by interpolation and bifurcation. The interpolated striae start at anterior part of umbo, the bifurcation commences at the middle of the valves; sometimes the bifurcation is repeated or double; concentric lines of growth divide the surface of each valve into different concentric zones, which are more prominent in younger than older individuals. In young shells the shape is more ovate, in old ones more circular, besides the smaller specimens are more gibbous than the large ones.

This species is as variable in size as Orthis elegantula; it ranges from the size of a pea to that of a silver half-dime and more.

Formation and Locality.—Niagara group east of the city of Louisville, Ky., where very perfect, but also very small specimens are pretty abundantly found. The largest shells of this species are found at Waldron, Indiana. The individual represented on plate XXXII. is of the average size found near Louisville.

Orthis livia. BILLINGS.

Plate XVI., figures 23 and 24; Plate XVII., figures 33, 34 and 35.

Orthis livia, Billings. Can. Jour. of Ind. Sci. and Art, No. 27—1860,
Orthis livia, Billings. Can. Jour., Vol. 5, p. 267—1860.
Orthis livia, Hall. Pal. N. Y., Vol. IV., page 38—1867.
Orthis livia, Billings. Pal. Fossils, Vol. II., pt. I., p. 32—1874.

This species was established and first described by Mr. Billings, of the Canadian Geological Survey. I will, therefore, only copy his description; his figures correctly agree with mine.

"Shell sub-orbicular or sub-quadrate; length about eight-ninths of the width; greatest width usually a little in front of the middle; length of hinge-line one-half to two-thirds the width of shell; cardinal extremities rounded; sides in most specimens somewhat straight, often sufficiently curved to give a circular aspect to shell; front angles obtusely rounded; front margin in general broadly convex, sometimes, in a small central portion, nearly straight. Dorsal valve of medium convexity, most elevated about the middle; the outline forming an uniform arch from depressed beak to front margin; slope from umbo to cardinal angles gently concave; sometimes a barely perceptible mesial depression, commencing in a point at the beak, and becoming obsolete at one-half or two-thirds the length; area small, lying in plane of the lateral margins; beak minute, forming a small triangular projection, rising scarcely one-fourth of a line above edge of area. Ventral valve moderately convex, most elevated at between one-fourth and one-third the length from beak, thence descending with a flat or gently convex slope to the lateral margins, with a somewhat concave one to the front, and also to hinge-line and cardinal angles. The concavity towards the front is not found in all specimens; some shells have basal portion either flat or slightly convex. The ventral umbo is small and neatly defined; beak small, pointed, and some-what incurved, but scarcely overhanging edge of area; area triangular and somewhat larger than the dorsal one. Foramen not observed. Surface covered with small sub-angular radiating ridges or striae, of nearly uniform size, from eight to ten in the width of three lines, increasing by bifurcation, strongly curved outwards on lateral parts of shell; the interspaces sub-angular and equal in size with the striae.

"In very perfect specimens very fine concentric, sub-lamellar striae are visible, seven or eight to one line. In certain conditions of preservation, also, the radiating striae are seen to be sub-tubular, and exhibit numerous small oval or circular openings on their edges, each about the eighth or tenth of a line in width, and from one-fourth to two-thirds of a line distant from each other." (Billings.) The largest specimen which I have seen of this species is the one illustrated on plate 16, figures 23 and 24, though, according to Mr. Billings' statement, this species attains in some specimens a considerably larger size.

This species is allied to Orthis vanuxemi, but is more coarsely striated.

Formation and Locality.—Found in the rotten hornstone in the upper strata of the Devonian formation, in Jefferson county, Kentucky, and in Clark county, Indiana. It is rarely found in specimens of the size as shown in the illustration, while smaller shells, like those figured plate 17, figures 33, 34 and 35, are not so rare; with these latter there is, however, the trouble to distinguish them from smaller specimens of vanuxemi.

Orthis linneyi. n. sp.

Plate XXXIV., figures 7 to 13.

Shell of medium size; sub-circular or sub-elliptical; width exceeding length; hinge-line short, measuring little more than one-third the width of the shell; cardinal extremities broadly rounded; lateral margins regularly curved; basal margin broadly curved, showing in the dorsal view a slight emargination, and in ventral view a small basal extension in the central part of the front. (Figure 9, on plate XXXIV., shows a basal extension, where it should show a small sinus or inflection.) In regard to depth, it varies from moderately convex to gibbous.

Ventral valve is mostly less convex than the opposite one; its greatest con-vexity is at the umbo, from where it slopes in a more or less curved line to baso-lateral margins, and more abruptly to the cardinal borders; central part of valve is depressed, forming a mesial sinus, which extends from beak to base, and increases rapidly in depth and width towards front; it has a lingui form basal extension, which, however, does not deflect from the regular curve of the sinus, to meet the dorsal indentation. Ventral umbo is more or less prominent in different specimens, the beak elevated, pointed and arched, but not incurved; hinge-area is short but high, forming in some individuals almost an equilateral triangle; the larger portion of the hinge-area is occupied by a comparatively large, open, triangular fissure. The dorsal valve is varying from moderately convex to gibbous, having its greatest convexity just below the umbo, from where it slopes in a more or less stronger, regular curve to the baso-lateral margins, and abruptly to the apex and the cardinal borders; it has a mesial fold of moderate elevation, which commences to rise above the general surface just below the umbo, from where it extends to the base, only slightly increasing in width and depth. The dorsal umbo is somewhat inflated, and the beak small and incurved. The dorsal hinge-area is small, about one-half the size of the ventral. The surface is covered by simple, rounded or sub-angular radiating plications, of which usually three, but sometimes four, occupy the sinus, and generally four, but sometimes five, are placed on the mesial fold, while from four to seven or eight are seen on each side of the mesial fold or sinus. In some specimens of this species there exists a decided inequality in the lateral parts, consisting not so much in size as in the number of plications. I have, for instance, one shell before me, where the right side of the dorsal valve has only four ribs, while the left side contains six. On the ventral valve is the same difference between the number of the ribs of both sides. This inequality exists in a good many, though not in all specimens. There is an indication of very fine radiating lines on and between the plications. Fine concentric lines cross the plications, which become lamellose and imbricating towards the front.

Formation and Locality.—This species is named in honor of W. M. Linney, the able Assistant Geologist of our State, who collected this shell in the shales of the Hudson River or Cincinnati group, near Danville, Kentucky. It is found in excellent, almost perfect specimens, and seems to be somewhat abundant It also occurs in the base of the Lower Hudson, in Fayette and Franklin counties, Kentucky.

Orthis nisis. HALL.

Plate XXVII., figures 4 and 5,

Orthis nisis, Hall. 24th Rep. on N. Y. State Museum, page 161—1872.
Orthis nisis, Hall. 27th Rep. on N. Y. State Museum, pl. 9., figs. 1–8—1875.

Shell depressed-pyramidal when resting on the dorsal valve. Dorsal valve semi-elliptical, flat or slightly concave in middle, and gently convex on each side. Length and width about as two to three; area about one-quarter as wide as that of the ventral valve. Ventral valve depressed-pyramidal; the apex projecting backwards over the area. The elevation about equal to half the length of the dorsal valve; area twice as wide as high, fissure very narrow and slender, and reaching to the apex. Surface marked by strong angular striae, which are increased by interstitial additions, to the number of twenty-eight or thirty, on the margin of the shell; striae crossed by distinct lines of growth.

Length, five lines on the dorsal valve; width, seven lines. This species is of the type of Orthis tricenaria, of the Trenton group, but its beak is much more elevated, its area higher, and its striae more angular, and these are increased by interstitial additions, while in O. tricenaria and its congener O. pectinella the striae are simple.

Formation and Locality.—Found in the upper strata of the Niagara formation in the quarries east of the city of Louisville, Ky., where well preserved specimens are, however, rather rare.

Orthis propinqua. HALL.

Plate XVI., figures 1, to 3, and 7 to 11.
Orthis propinqua, Hall. Tenth Rep. on St. Cab., p. 110—1857
Orthis propinqua, Hall. Pal. N. Y., Vol. IV., p. 43—1857

Shell of more than medium size; transversely elliptical or sub-quadrate; varying from moderately convex to gibbous; hinge-line about one-half the width of shell; cardinal extremities broadly rounded; lateral margins regularly curved beyond the front angles; basal margin broadly curved and truncated or even somewhat inflected in its central part.

Ventral valve less gibbous than the dorsal; very prominent at the umbo, sloping very abruptly towards the cardinal angles, but more gently towards lateral and baso-lateral margins; flattened in center; the lower half marked by a gradually increasing, broad and undefined sinus, which gives a strongly upward curved outline to basal or front margin; beak acutely pointed and slightly incurved; cardinal area elevated and concave, and divided by a triangular foramen, which is open, and twice as high as wide in its base. The dorsal valve is larger and more gibbous than the opposite one; its greatest convexity is a little above the middle of the length, curving abruptly to the cardinal and cardino-lateral margins, and somewhat more gently to the front and baso-lateral margins. The cardinal extremities are sometimes slightly deflected, and the surface at the cardinal angles a little concave. Cardinal area is inclined to that of the ventral valve, and about one-half or two-thirds as wide. Surface marked by fine, unequal, radiating striae, which increase in number by intercalation, and are crossed by fine concentric striae, and, at unequal intervals, by stronger imbricating, lamellose lines of growth.

This species resembles closely O. multistriata of the Lower Helderberg group, from which it differs only in internal characters. It is also closely allied to O. tulliensis, from which it can only be distinguished by characters of the interior.

Formation and Locality.—Occurs in the upper strata of the Devonian formation, in Jefferson county, Kentucky, and in Clark county, Indiana. Fair specimens are rather rare.

Orthis rugaeplicata. HALL.

Plate XXVII., figures 1, 2 and 3.

Orthis rugaeplicatas, Hall. 24th Rep. N. Y. St. Mus., p. 182—1872.
Orthis rugaeplicatas, Hall. 27th Rep. N. Y. St. Mus., pl. 9, figs. 1, 2 and 3—1875

Shell small, subquadrate, four-fifths as long as wide, gibbous; cardinal line nearly equal to the greatest width of the shell; cardinal angles obtuse, basal margin nearly straight. Dorsal valve convex, with a distinct median sinus extending from beak to base; cardinal area linear; length three lines, width four lines. Ventral valve depressed-pyramidal, marked along the center by a distinct angular plication or fold; beak projecting slightly backwards over the area; area moderate, less than one-third as high as wide, and divided in the center by a moderately wide fissure.

Surface marked by very strong, sharply angular plications, which are increased by interstitial additions, and of which there are about fifteen on the margin of each valve, with a few other incipient ones.

Formation and Locality.—Found in the Niagara formation in the quarries east of the city of Louisville, Ky. It is, when well preserved, an elegant little shell; but perfect, even fair specimens, are very rare; those of Dr. James Knapp, deceased, and my own, are all, so far found

Orthis subnodosa. HALL.

Orthis subnodosa, Hall. Trans. Alb. Inst., Vol. X.—1879.
Orthis subnodosa, Hall. 11th Geol. Rep. of Ind., p. 286—1881.

It appears from Prof. Hall's description and illustration in the above mentioned report of Indiana, that he was then in possession of only the ventral valve of this species, and the same is the case with me to-day. Prof. Hall describes this shell as follows:

Ventral valve sub-orbicular, length and width about as ten to fourteen; hinge-line much shorter than the greatest width of the shell; an undefined mesial depression in the lower half of the shell. (In this last feature my shell differs from Prof. Hall's, in having this depression extend all the way up to the apex, but it is possible that this extended sinus was caused by the breaking off of one of the adjacent ribs.) The umbo is comparatively prominent; beak small and slightly arched; area small, triangular, apparently not occupying more than half the width of the valve; foramen large, triangular, reaching to the beak, wider than high. Surface marked by sub-angular plications, of which three occupy the mesial sinus, the central one being interstitial, coming in below the umbo; there are about ten plications on each side of the mesial depression; some of them originate by bifurcation or intercalation. The radii are crossed by fine concentric lamellose lines of growth, which gives them a sub-nodose appearance. This species has some resemblance to Orthis fissicosta, of the Hudson River group, but its cardinal extremities are more rounded and its cardinal area is not as high.

Formation and Locality.—Prof. Hall's specimen was found at Waldron, Indiana, and that before me I collected in the quarries east of the city of Louisville. It was imbedded in the white Niagara clay.

Orthis vanuxemi. HALL.

Plate XVI., figures 4, 5, 6, 12, 12a, 13 and 14.

Orthis vanuxemi, Hall. Tenth Rep. on St. Cab., p. 136—1857.

Orthis vanuxemi, Hall. Pal. N. Y., Vol. IV., p. 47—1867.

Shell above medium size, sub-circular, or transversely sub-elliptical; upper part of the shell bi-convex; lower or front part generally concavo-convex; shell strongly compressed; hinge-line very short, little more than one-third the width of the shell; cardinal angles broadly rounded; lateral margins strongly curved, and the front in its central half inflected or emarginate. Ventral valve mostly concave or sometimes flat, with the exception of the umbonal region, which is slightly convex; beak small, seldom extending beyond that of the dorsal valve, but often even somewhat less elevated; it is pointed and gently arched, but not incurved; cardinal area small, forming a low triangle, which is divided in its center by a small triangular foramen, partly filled by the cardinal process of the opposite valve. Dorsal valve moderately, but even and regularly convex over the whole surface of the valve, with the exception of the umbonal region, which is slightly more convex; the beak is scarcely distinct from the cardinal border and not incurved; cardinal process prominent and partly closing the ventral foramen; cardinal area small, about two-thirds as wide as the ventral, flat and inclined towards that of the opposite valve.

Surface of both valves ornamented by fine, closely arranged, radiating tubular striae, which are perforate at intervals, increasing in number partly by bifurcation and partly by intercalation, and crossed by very fine indistinct concentric lines, and at greater intervals, by more distinct concentric, imbricating lines of growth; entire surface granulate or punctate under a magnifier. Striae from twelve to sixteen in the space of two lines near the beak, and from seven to nine in same space near margin.

This species resembles closely Orthis michelini, of Laveille, but shows several points of difference. The later species is here, in our Carboniferous rocks, greatly more compressed.

Formation and Locality.—The specimens figured show the general size. Occurs in the upper strata of the Devonian formation in Jefferson county, Ky., and in Clark county, Indiana.

Genus Tropidoleptus. Hall.

Tropidoleptus, Hall. Pal. N. Y., Vol. IV., p. 404—1867.
Etymology: tropis, a carina; and leptos, slender.

Shell transversely sub-oval or semi-elliptical, concavo-convex; hinge-line extended, not crenulate; articulating by teeth and sockets. Ventral valve convex, with a distinct area and wide fissure beneath the beak.   Dental lamellae distinct from the margin of the fissure; crenulate.

Dorsal valve concave, with crenulate dental fossets; a strong cardinal process with diverging lobes in interior, which support slender crura that converge to and unite with the median crest.   Surface plicate; shell structure punctate.

Type of the genus is T. carinatus.

Tropidoleptus carinatus. Conrad.

Plate XVII., figures 14 and 15.

Strophomena carinata, Conrad. Ann. Geol. Rep., p. 64—1839.
Leptaena laticosta, Hall, in 1883.
Leptaena laticosta, of Owen and others.
Tropidoleptus carinatus, Hall. Tenth Rep. on St. Cab., p. 151—1857.
Tropidoleptus: Genus described and illust. in 12th Rept. on St. Cabinet.—1859.
Tropidoleptus carinatus, Hall. Pal. N. Y., Vol. IV., p. 407—1867.

Shell of medium size, concavo-convex, semi-elliptical, length sometimes nearly equalling width; hinge-line variable in size, but generally a little less than greatest width of shell; cardinal extremities rarely rounded, generally forming with the lateral margins an obtuse or right-angle.   The lateral margins are of double curvature, starting from the cardinal extremities, they curve at first inward for about one-fourth of the length, thence they curve outwards, combining with broad curve of base to an almost regular semi-circle.

Ventral valve ventricose, sub-carinate in the center by a stronger and more elevated plication, forming a kind of mesial fold, from which the valve slopes in a gentle curve to lateral and basal margins; umbo small, and the beak somewhat encroached upon by the broad foramen; cardinal area narrow, extending to the extremities, its margins almost parallel with the hinge-line; the cardinal angles deflected.   The area is longitudinally striate, which feature is, however, obliterated in silicified specimens.

Dorsal valve moderately concave, sometimes nearly flat, often with a slight mesial depression or sinus, which is usually only noticeable in the basal half; apex small and projecting a little beyond the hinge-line, partly closing the triangular fissure of the other valve. There is a narrow, almost linear area, interrupted in the middle by a wide pseudo-deltidium which covers the extremity of the cardinal process. Surface marked by about eighteen to twenty broad, simple, rounded plications, which are wider than the spaces between them. The central one on the ventral valve is stronger and more elevated than the balance, while on the dorsal valve there is a corresponding wider and deeper groove. Bifurcation is only noticed in rare instances. Fine undulating, concentric striae ornament the surface, and some stronger imbricating lamellae mark the different stages of growth. It appears that our Kentucky specimens differ slightly from the New York ones, which latter have rounded extremities and almost straight lateral margins, while in the Kentucky specimens extremities and lateral margins are as before mentioned.

Formation and Locality.—In the upper strata of the Devonian limestone in Clark county, Indiana, and some few places south-east of the city of Louisville, Ky. The Indiana specimens are very fine and perfect, often showing the two valves separated, except at the hinge. Our shells are almost all silicified and have different sizes; the one represented on plate XVII. belongs to the larger ones.

Genus Anastrophia. Hall.

Anastrophia, Hall. Pal. N. Y., Vol IV., p. 373—1867.

Etymology: ana, with; *strophe,* a turning round, alluding to the valves having reverse relation; the dorsal valve is larger than the other, and its beak overlaps the ventral beak.

Shell rotund or gibbous, with the valves, as in ordinary Pentamerus, reversed. The ventral valve is the smaller, gibbous in its upper part, depressed or sinuate below, with the V-shaped pit sessile for nearly its entire length; a small flattened space on each side of the fissure. The dorsal valve is ventricose, larger than the ventral, with prominent umbo. The hinge-plate is extended in gradually converging vertical lamellae, which are joined to the shell throughout their length, while the crura are extended into the cavity in thin free lamellae. The species: Pent. verneuilli, P. internascens and P. reversus are the types of this new genus.

Anastrophia internascens. Hall.

Plate XXXII., figures 17 to 20.

Anastrophia internascens, Hall. 11th Geol. Rep. of Indiana—1881.

See list of synonyms in said 11th Rep. of Indiana.

Shell transversely sub-elliptical, ovoid or sub-globose in different stages of growth; the length and width are sometimes nearly equal. Valves of young specimens nearly equal in convexity, in older individuals the dorsal valve becomes the more gibbous. Ventral valve moderately convex in young or medium sized specimens, and gibbous in the upper part of old ones; the anterior portion depressed, and marked by a broad, undefined sinus; beak short, acute, closely incurved over the umbo of the opposite valve, area small, short and sharply defined. Dorsal valve gibbous, and in old individuals the umbo projects beyond the beak of the ventral valve, with the apex incurved beneath the beak of the latter; central portion of the valve toward the front more elevated, and sometimes presenting a broad, undefined mesial fold. Surface plications abruptly elevated, rounded, angular or sub-angular, becoming depressed and sometimes obsolete on the cardinal slopes, usually simple, enlarging toward the front of the shell, rarely bifurcating or intercalating in a remarkable manner on the sides, where the folds bend abruptly outwards to the cardino-lateral margins; plications crossed by arching imbricating striae or lines of growth, which are sometimes very conspicuous. The dimensions of this species are very variable in different individuals. The figures on plate XXXII. show the average size of Louisville specimens.

Formation and Locality.—Occurs in the Niagara strata in the quarries east of the city of Louisville, Ky., in fine, well preserved specimens, which are, however, rather rare, and which never attain the size of individuals from Waldron. To avoid mistakes, I will here draw the attention of the students of palæontology to the fact that in this species the valves are easily confounded, inasmuch as the dorsal one is larger than the other, and its beak generally more prominent than the one of the ventral valve.

Genus Camarella. Billings.

Camerella, Billings. Can. Nat. and Geol., Vol. 4—1859.
Etymology: Kamara, arching chamber; ella, diminutive.

This genus was established by Mr. Billings in 1859, but I have never been able to see the description of his genus, which he should have repeated in his "Palæozoic Fossils" of the Geology of Canada, Volume I., 1861 to 1865, where he describes eight different species of this genus.

The different shells which he places in his new genus have the following characteristics: Shells sub-circular or ovate, unequivalve but equilateral; both valves more or less convex, having their greatest width below the middle of the length, usually close to the base or front. The surface is generally plicated but also smooth, and only marked by concentric lines of growth. The internal characters of this genus are not known.

Camerella congesta. Conrad.

Atrypa congesta, Conrad. Jour. Acad. Nat. Sci. Phil., Vol. 8—1842.
Atrypa congesta, Hall. Geol. Rep. 4th Dist. N. Y., p. 71—1843.
Atrypa congesta, Hall. Pal. N. Y., Vol. II., p. 67—1852.

Shell sub-orbicular, gibbous, often more or less ovate. Ventral valve much larger and more elevated at the beak than the dorsal valve, with a deep mesial furrow, which commences at the beak and gradually deepens and widens towards the base or front of the valve, where it forms a linguiform basal extension, which is strongly elevated to fit into a corresponding indentation of the dorsal valve. The mesial depression of the ventral valve is margined by a more or less obtusely carinated fold, produced by a depression of the shell on each side of the sinus. Dorsal valve with a strong, elevated mesial fold, and a depression on each side, beyond which is sometimes an obscure fold. Beak of the ventral valve elevated and strongly incurved over beak of opposite valve, while the dorsal beak is small and incurved. The entire surface is covered, in well preserved specimens, with fine concentric striae, and with a few imbricating lines of growth near the front. The specimen before me does not show any of these lines on account of its silicified condition. This species is subject to considerable variations in its form, but is, in spite of that, easily identified by its rotund and gibbous form.

Formation and Locality.—This species usually occurs in the lower strata of the Clinton group; but I found my specimen in the Niagara rocks near our city, from which it appears that the lower strata of our Upper Silurian rocks must belong to that group, as is also indicated by several other fossils of decidedly Clinton character.

Genus Pentamerella. Hall.

Pentamerella, Hall. Pal. N. Y., Vol. IV., p. 373—1867.
Etymology: Diminutive of pentamerus.

Shells ovate, more or less rotund, with a sinus on the ventral valve, and a mesial fold on the dorsal valve; internal structure of the ventral valve as in Pentamerus knighti. Dorsal valve with the crura or lamellae of the hinge-plate conjoined, so as to form a separate, trough-shaped cavity, which unites with the inner surface of the valve; a narrow area on each side of the fissure, and a flattened space or a false area along the cardinal margin of the valve. Pentamerella arata is the type of this genus.

Pentamerella arata. Conrad.

Plate XIII., figures 17 to 20.

Atrypa arata, Conrad. Ann. Rep. on Pal. of N. Y., p. 55—1851.
Atrypa octocostata, Id. Ib.
Pentamerus aratus, Hall. Tenth Rep. St. Cab., p. 120—1857.
Pentamerella arata, Hall. Pal. N. Y., Vol. IV., p. 375—1867.

Shell of medium size, ovate, more or less convex or gibbous, becoming arcuate-ovoid in old shells; proportion of length to width variable; in most cases both are equal, but in some individuals the width exceeds the length, and in others the length is the larger. Hinge-line is also very variable; in some specimens it is scarcely noticeable, in others of considerable size. Ventral valve regularly convex in young individuals, but becoming gibbous in old ones. The mesial sinus is regularly developed, but undefined and very shallow, even at the front; it starts below the umbo and forms a slight convexity in the basal margin, which is in most shells regularly curved; beak elevated and strongly incurved over the fissure, which it partly, sometimes wholly, closed; the foramen almost as wide in the base as its height; cardinal area sometimes scarcely visible, while again in some shells it forms a regular triangle; bounded by a faint but distinct elevation on each margin. Dorsal valve in young shells more or less convex, and sometimes gibbous in the upper part, and often only moderately convex in older shells; mesial fold starts below the umbo, never well-defined, and not much elevated, still distinctly developed. Surface ornamented by rounded or sometimes by somewhat angular plications, which, in rare instances, reach all the way back to the apex, but which are generally limited to the lower half or two-thirds of the valve; they increase by bifurcation. The interior of the ventral valve has an elongate spoon-shaped pit; the inner extremity of which is free for a considerable extent, and the upper part supported on a central septum, which usually extends less than half the length of the shell from the apex. In the dorsal valve, the crura or lamellae are conjoined at their bases, making a V-shaped trough or pit, which is attached to the valve in its upper part and continues sessile for about one-half the length of the shell. This species shows much variety in aspect and form, caused by age and the conditions under which it lived, which were either favorable or unfavorable to its development. Conrad's species, Atrypa octocostata, includes forms which are easily connected by intermediates with Pent. arata, and which, therefore, belong to this species. In size it differs greatly. The figures on plate XIII. represent an individual of more than average size.

Formation and Locality.—Occurs, not rarely, in the Corniferous limestone of Kentucky and Indiana, at and around the Falls of the Ohio, where fair and sometimes even very fine specimens are procured.

Pentamerella papilionensis. HALL.

Pentamerus papilionensis, Hall.   Geol. Rep. of Iowa, Vol. I., part II., cited on page 514—1860.
Pentamerus papilionensis, Hall.   Thirteenth Rep. on the State Cabinet, p. 86—1860.
Pentamerella papilionensis, Hall.   Pal. N. Y., Vol. IV., p. 377—1867.

Shell of medium size, ventricose, broadly ovate, often wider than long, more or less gibbous and arcuate in old shells.

Ventral valve gibbous or ventricose above, becoming depressed in the middle into a broad, shallow, undefined sinus, which scarcely reaches to the beak, and in some cases not much above the middle, and is little produced in front. I have a specimen before me, where the plication of the mesial sinus is even overreaching the general surface of the valve; sides curving abruptly to the margins; beak incurved, obtuse, arching over the broad fissure; cardinal area sloping on both sides down to about the middle of the valve, bounded by a sharp, somewhat curved line of demarcation, having a considerable size and being somewhat concave.

Dorsal valve moderately convex and regularly curving to the lateral and basal margins; mesial fold not much elevated, and limited to the lower half of the valve, where it is well defined. Surface plicated, the ribs rounded or sub-angular, becoming obsolete towards the beak, and prominent in the basal half. There are generally two, sometimes three plications in the sinus, and three, rarely four on the fold, while the lateral slopes of the valves contain from four to five. The plications are crossed by fine concentric lines of growth, which sometimes at irregular intervals are crowded into squamose, imbricating lines. The entire surface is finely papillose or punctate, and, when well preserved, might be mistaken for a punctate shell. The substance of the shell is lamellose-prismatic and brittle. The interior of the ventral valve shows a broad, short and deep spoon-shaped pit, extremity of which is bent abruptly to dorsal side. The septum, supporting the conjoined lamellae, extends from one-third to one-half the length of the valve, and in some examples may extend still further towards the anterior margin. This species bears much resemblance to P. arata, but its plications are less numerous on the whole valve; less numerous and stronger in the mesial depression and elevation, and its shell is less arcuate.

Formation and Locality.—Found in the Corniferous limestone in the neighborhood of the Falls of the Ohio in Kentucky and Indiana. Pretty abundant, but fair specimens rather rare.

Pentamerella thusnelda. N. SP.

Plate XXXI., figures 26, 27 and 28.

Shell of medium size, ovoid or sub-quadrate; cardinal extremities rounded, forming in the beak of the dorsal valve an angle of a little more than sixty degrees; length exceeding the width considerably, giving to the shell an elongate, somewhat slender appearance. Ventral valve ventricose, even gibbous; convexity regular from beak to front, and also transversely; greatest convexity a little above the middle of the valve; mesial sinus indicated by two very strong plications, and by a wide and deep groove on each side of them; the summit of these plications drops not at all, or at least very slightly, at the very front of the valve, below the regular surface; the two prominent grooves extend almost to the beak, forming on the umbo only one rib, which separates into two plications in front of the beak; these mesial ribs are considerably prolonged in front, producing a sub-quadrilateral extension; beak is prominent and incurved; cardinal area large, extending to the extremities, and bounded by a well-marked, regularly curved line of demarcation; fissure of moderate size, but partly closed by the beaks of both valves.

Dorsal valve depressed convex, curved slightly in the upper half of the valve; lateral portions of lower half almost flat; mesial fold formed by three strong plications, which are united into one single elevation on the umbo, where it is only faintly visible; below the umbo the three mesial ribs separate and extend to a little beyond the front, where they are considerably elevated; beak moderate and incurved into the foramen of the other valve; cardinal area only linear. Surface marked by about twelve sub-angular plications, of which those in the mesial depression and elevation are considerably stronger than those on the lateral slopes; the lateral ribs on the dorsal valve are single and of equal size; those on the ventral valve increase by bifurcation, and those nearest to the mesial furrows appear to be stronger than the more lateral ones.

This species resembles Pent. arata and Pent. papilionensis, also Pent. dubia; from Pent. arata it differs by its elongate form, its less numerous plications, and by its mesial ribs, which are here limited to three in the fold and two in the sinus, and which are of about double size of the lateral ones; while in Pent. arata the mesial plications are larger in number and of almost equal size with the balance. From Pent. papilionensis it differs in its elongate form, and in the peculiar character of the mesial plications, which in P. papilionensis have the same number, but do not differ from the lateral ones by size; and from Pent. dubia it differs also in form; while P. dubia has its greatest width about the middle of the shell, this one has its maximum breadth nearer to the front, at more than two-thirds from the apex; P. dubia has more plications generally, and also more on the fold and in the sinus.

Formation and Locality.—Found in the Corniferous limestone surrounding the Falls of the Ohio in Kentucky and Indiana. It is of rare occurrence here in the neighborhood of the falls; only two individuals of this species are known; they belong to my own cabinet.

Genus Pentamerus. Sowerby.

Pentamerus, Sowerby. Min. Couch., Vol. I.—1814.
Etymology: penta, five; *meros*, apartments.

This genus was proposed by Sowerby in 1813 to include all the shells allied to Pent. knighti, which he made the type of the genus Pentamerus. Dalman objecting to the name, on the ground that the shell was not five-chambered, proposed in its stead the name Gypidia, but this latter was never accepted.

This genus included for a while a large number of related species, but there existed differences which compelled the division into several genera, which Prof. Hall and Mr. Billings established. Prof. Hall gives the characteristics of Pentamerus as follows: Shells having rotund or gibbous forms, with the ventral valve prominent in the middle, and the dorsal valve flattened or depressed towards the front; lamellae of the dorsal valve distinct, as P. knighti, P. galeatus and P. pseudogaleatus. Or the form is elongate, with the valves sub-equally convex, lobed or sub-sinuate; internal structure like that of P. knighti, as P. oblongus and P. lens, etc.

Pentamerus complanatus. n. sp.

Plate XXVII., figures 14, 15 and 16.

Pentamerus nysius, var. tenicosta, Hall. 27th Rep. of N. Y. State Museum, plate 10, figures 1, 2 and 3.

Prof. Hall described, in the 24th Report on the N. Y. State Museum, pages 184 and 185, a new species, the Pentamerus nysius, and distinguished of the same the two varieties: Pent. nysius, var. crassicosta and Pent. nysius, var. tenuicosta. In the 27th Report on plate 10, he figured two different shells, one sub-figures 1, 2 and 3, and the other sub-figures 4, 5, 6 and 7, and placed both in his new species. The great diversity in their form Prof. Hall regards as the results of age, but not of specific importance. Only on account of the different size of their radii, he placed them into different varieties. Now I have before me more than fifty specimens, and find among them both forms, each one represented by specimens, from very young or small to very old or large, showing that the age did not cause the diversity of form, as shown in Prof. Hall's two shells. This difference in shape I consider of sufficient importance to base upon it a new species, and the only question is now, which of the two forms shall retain the original name, and which shall form the new species. The elongated and very gibbous shells represented by figures 4, 5, 6 and 7, show a marked difference in the size of their costae, which necessitates the separation of the species into two varieties, to be designated as crassicostus and tenuicostus; I, therefore, retain the original name for this form, while the shell, represented by the figures 1, 2 and 3, forms the new species with the following description: Shell of medium size, broadly triangular, with little gibbosity; both valves almost equal in size, form and convexity. The regular curve of the front margin is only slightly disturbed by a faint mesial extension; the lateral margins are nearly straight from the apex down to two-thirds of the length, and slightly curved towards the front. None of the shells show the least indication of a mesial depression or elevation; surface marked by fine radii; ventral valve a little more convex than the other, being depressed convex; greatest convexity below the umbo, from where it slopes in a slightly curved, almost straight line to the front; towards the lateral margins it slopes in a gentle, regular curve, but approaching the margins, it turns rapidly towards the dorsal valve, where it forms a smooth border; the beak is small, straight, and very little elevated above that of the dorsal valve, often touching the same at equal height. The dorsal valve is depressed convex, maximum convexity below the umbo, from where it slopes in a very gentle but regular curve to front and sides; only a very small strip of this valve at the lateral margins is rapidly and abruptly bent, to meet the smooth marginal border of the ventral valve; the umbonal part is strongly curved towards the other half of the shell; the beak strongly incurved beneath or against the other beak.

Surface is marked by fine radiating striae, single and rounded, and numbering from thirty to forty. The surface is generally divided by three prominent lines of growth into four zones, which are easily noticed on any fair specimen. The umbonal zone is always smooth, either the striae did not develop before a certain age, or if this portion was ever covered with radii, they became obliterated in the course of time.

Formation and Locality.—This beautiful species, of which my own cabinet possesses a few very fine and perfect specimens, is found in the Niagara rocks in the quarries east of Louisville, Ky. It is very rare.

Pentamerus globulosus. N. SP.

Shell very small; sub-globose; width exceeding the length; very ventricose or gibbous; ventral valve very convex; greatest convexity about the middle of the valve, from where it slopes, in a regular but strong curve, to the beak and to the lateral and basal margins; to the cardinal lines it slopes more abruptly, joining with the curved margins of the hinge-area; the cardinal area is small and not defined in its margins, which, as before stated, are curved and coalesce with the surface of the valve; umbo is very prominent; the beak is elevated and strongly incurved, but does not touch the beak of the opposite valve, from which it remains sufficiently distant to show a moderately sized, open, triangular foramen in the ventral hinge-area.

Dorsal valve is sometimes as convex as the ventral, though usually it is less so. It is most convex in the umbonal region, but flattens in the lateral parts. Below the middle of the valve its central part becomes depressed into a shallow sinus, which does not reach beyond the basal third of the valve; it is most perceptible in the basal margin, outside of which it is scarcely to be noticed. Corresponding with this mesial sinus the ventral valve shows a mesial elevation, which is also confined to the basal third of the valve, and outside of the front margin hardly observable. In some specimens these mesial depressions and elevation are not at all indicated. The surface of the larger portion of both valves is entirely smooth ; the basal margin shows, however, from eight to ten plications of different strength and extent on each valve ; the central ones are stronger and longer than the balance ; they diminish in size and length according to their distance from the central point of the base. None of these plications extend beyond the basal third ; most of them are confined to the border. An average-sized specimen measures five and one-half lines in width, four and one-half lines in length, and three and one-half lines in depth. This shell has some resemblance to P. sub-globosus of Meek and Worthen, from the Hamilton group, described in the Illinois Report, Volume III., but it differs from that species by its smaller size, less gibbosity and smaller number of plications.

Formation and Locality.—Found in the Niagara rocks, east of Louisville, in almost perfect specimens, but rather rare.

Pentamerus knappi. HALL.

Plate XXVIII., figures 1, 2, 3 and 4.

Pent. knappi, Hall. 24th Rep. N. Y. St. Museum, p. 184—1872.
Pent. knappi, Hall. 27th Rep. N. Y. St. Museum, pl. 10, figures 10, 11 and 12—1875.

Shell broadly elliptical, moderately gibbous above, compressed in front ; length about one-third greater than width, somewhat obscurely trilobate ; cardinal line equal to nearly one-half the width of the shell. Dorsal valve scarcely smaller than the ventral ; moderately gibbous in the upper part, broadly depressed-convex below the middle, and spreading at the latero-basal margins. Ventral valve a little more gibbous in the part above the middle than the opposite valve, and less depressed in the lower part ; the beak narrower below than the other beak, above which it is visibly elevated, pointed and only slightly arched. Prof. Hall in his description states the beak of the ventral valve to be closely incurved upon the other valve ; his figures on plate 10, in his report, show it the same way ; this is a mistake, caused by the imperfect condition of the specimen from which description and figures were made. At the time when I had my plates lithographed I had no good specimen of this species in my possession, and having then also no access to Dr. Knapp's shell, which was absent from Louisville, I was compelled to copy Prof. Hall's figures, carrying his mistake over on my plate. Since then I have acquired several almost perfect specimens of P. knappi, which prove without doubt the character of the beak as stated by me.

Surface is covered with strong plications, which become almost obliterated on the umbo, and which diverge and curve outward towards the front ; they are rounded, and bifurcate repeatedly with the growth of the shell, so that there are several times as many at the margins as at their starting. On most specimens the central plications form in their basal half, by double bifurcation, fascicles or bundles of ribs, such as mark so prominently the surface of Spir. camerata of the Carboniferous. These fascicles are only found on the middle lobe of the shell; the lateral lobes contain only single and much finer plications. The sides of the shell, along the cardinal line, and down to the point of maximum width of the shell, have a smooth surface.

Concentric lines of growth cover the shell. This species resembles somewhat Mr. Billings' Stricklandinia gaspensis, from which it differs by not having any mesial depression or elevation, and no straight hinge-extension and narrow area; while Mr. Billings' shell is covered, even on the sides, by plications, where P. knappi has a large, smooth lateral area.

Prof. Hall says that this shell resembles, in every feature except the strongly radiated surface, Pentamerus oblongus, and he does not doubt the possibility that intermediate forms may be found to connect the two species. It can not be disputed that this shell greatly resembles some of the broader forms of Pent. oblongus, from which it certainly branched off by evolution, and I feel certain that it will maintain its specific character.

Formation and Locality.—Found in the Niagara rocks in the quarries east of the city of Louisville, Ky., where it is not very rare, at least not in fractional shells; while perfect individuals are exceedingly seldom. Prof. Hall named this species in honor of the late Dr. James Knapp, of Louisville, Ky., who first discovered it, as he did so many other new species, belonging to the palæozoic fauna of Louisville's vicinity. Dr. Knapp was, for many years, almost the only collector of fossils of our city, thus having the rare opportunity of getting all the fine specimens which our many quarries around the city and the Falls of the Ohio afforded.

Pentamerus knotti. N. SP.

Plate XXXII., figures 9, 10, 11 and 12.

Shell below medium size; broadly ovate, sub-globose; length and width about equal; hinge-line shorter than the greatest width of the shell; cardinal extremities rounded; lateral and basal margins forming usually a regular curve, but sometimes the front is slightly straighter than the sides. Shell very gibbous and surface plicated. Ventral valve more gibbous than the other, having its greatest convexity about the middle of the valve, from where it curves regularly to the lateral and basal margins, but very abruptly to the cardinal area, with which it joins without any line of demarcation; about the middle of the valve, or, at least, below the umbo, the central portion for the extent of four plications becomes elevated above the adjacent surface, slightly increasing in height towards the front, thus forming a mesial elevation or fold; the umbo is prominent, and the beak elevated and strongly incurved, but not overlapping the umbo of the dorsal valve; the cardinal area is not defined in its margins, as it curves into the general surface of the valve; the triangular fissure is either open from cardinal line to apex, or partly closed by beaks of both valves.   Dorsal valve less convex than ventral; greatest convexity at the umbo, sloping from there in a gentle curve to the sides and front, but more rapidly to the cardinal line; about the middle of the valve a depression sets in, extending in width over three plications; it increases in depth but very slightly up to the front, where it forms a small basal extension, which deflects downwards to meet the small indentation of the other valve.   In some specimens no basal extension exists, or is so small as not to be noticed; umbo prominent, and beak strongly incurved below that of the other valve into the fissure of the latter.   Surface marked by from ten to twelve rounded or sub-angular plications, which are plainly visible at the lateral and basal margins, but become obsolete before reaching the umbo on both valves.   The specimen illustrated represents about the largest size which this species ever attains.

Formation and Locality.—Occurs in the upper strata of the Niagara rocks in the quarries east of the city of Louisville, Ky., where it is not very rare.   I name this species in honor of W. T. Knott, of Lebanon, Ky., the efficient Assistant Geologist of our State, who made us acquainted with the geology of his district.

Pentamerus knighti. Sowerby.

Plate XXIX., figures 1, 2 and 17.

Pentamerus knighti, Sowerby.   Min. Couch., Vol. I—1812.

Shell of medium size, sub-ovate and very gibbous; narrow, with its greatest width at the base, which is regularly curved.   Depth about four-fifths of its length.   Surface plicated.

Ventral valve about twice as deep as the other, very gibbous, and regularly arched from beak to front.   From the longitudinal center line on the summit of the valve it curves for a certain distance, about half way, gently and regularly towards the lateral margins, then it slopes very abruptly towards the cardino-lateral angle, where it forms on each side of the beak a large concave, smooth field.   The umbo is narrow but very prominent; the beak strongly arched over the umbo of the other valve, but not touching it.   Dorsal valve less gibbous than the other valve, regularly curved from beak to front, and also towards the lateral margins, except in a small strip at those margins, where the valve deflects abruptly downwards, joining the smooth concave field of the other valve by a similar but considerably smaller field.   This valve is wider than the other, except at the front, where both are of equal width.   The whole surface, with the exception of the above mentioned concave fields in the cardino-lateral angles, is covered by strong, simple sub-angular plications, reaching from beak to front, and increasing as the shell grows in strength or size and in distance,

There are from twenty to twenty-four ribs on each valve. Some concentric lines of growth are visible, but whether the shell possessed other surface-markings can not be found out in the silicified condition of the shells, inas-much as the silicification generally obliterates the finer striae. I have placed these shells, of which I possess only the two individuals figured on plate XXIX., as Pent. knighti, though I have never seen of that species any correct and detailed description, nor any reliable figure, except those in Lyell's Elements of Geology and in Woodward's Manual of the Mollusca. I hope my identification to be correct, but if there should be a specific difference, it will soon be found out by geologists, who have access to better libraries and muse-ums than the city of Louisville offers to her scientists.

Formation and Locality.—In the Corniferous rocks near Louisville, in Kentucky and Indiana; of exceedingly rare occurrence. The two specimens in my cabinet, as far as I know, are the only representa-tives of this species in the seven or eight collections of the Falls Cities, as Louisville, Jeffersonville and New Albany are often collectively named.

Pentamerus littoni. HALL.

Plate XXVII., figures 12 and 13.

Pentamerus littoni, Hall. Pal. N. Y., Vol. 3, page 262.
Pentamerus littoni, Hall. 24th Rep. N. Y. St. Mus., p. 186—1872.
Pentamerus littoni, Hall. 27th Rep. N. Y. St. Mus., pl. 10, figs. 8 and 9—1875.

Shell ovoid, somewhat elongate. Dorsal valve moderately and regularly convex from base to umbo; beak strongly incurved under the beak of the opposite valve. Ventral valve very gibbous; beak sub-attenuate, incurved.

Surface marked by about eighteen to twenty and more simple, sub-angular plications. There is a broad, concave, smooth space on each side below the beak of the ventral valve, and a much narrower space on each side of the dorsal valve. (Hall.) A large specimen of this species, in my cabinet, meas-ures eleven lines in length, about the same in width, and nine lines in thick-ness.

My figure is a copy of Prof. Hall's figure in the 27th Report. At the time when my plates were made I had no fit specimen to copy, and Dr. Knapp's shell was absent from the city. This species is associated with, and probably related to, Pent. nysius.

Formation and Locality.—It occurs in the Niagara rocks near Louisville, Ky., where it is one of the rarest species. At present my cabinet contains several fair specimens.

Pentamerus nucleus. Hall.

Plate XXVII., figures 25 26 and 27, and Plate XXXIII., figures 27, 28, 29, 31, 32 and 33.

Pentamerus nucleus, Hall. 24th Rep. N. Y. St. Mus., p. 200a—1872.

Pentamerus nucleus, Hall. 27th Rep. N. Y. St. Mus., pl. 9., figs. 30 to 32—1875.

Shell of medium size, sub-globose; in the typical specimens width and length about equal, but in the shells represented by figures 31, 32 and 33, on plate 23, the length exceeds the width considerably. Ventral valve considerably larger than the dorsal, and very ventricose; cardinal margins strongly rounded, forming, in most specimens, a regular curve, which joins the somewhat stronger curve of the lateral margins. In some shells, however, the cardinal margin is almost straight, equalling the greatest width of the shell, and making the cardinal extremities either only slightly rounded or obtuse angular, as may be seen in fig 31, plate 33. The umbo is very prominent, and the beak strongly incurved over a small triangular foramen. The middle of the valve, from below the umbo to the front, is slightly elevated, forming a small mesial fold, and which consists usually of two, but sometimes of three elevated plications. Dorsal valve transversely elliptical, or sub-oval, only moderately convex; umbo somewhat inflated. The middle of the valve, below the umbo, depressed, forming a mesial sinus, which contains one or two plications; the beak is small and strongly incurved into the opposite valve. Surface is marked by angular plications, usually two on each side of the mesial fold or sinus; these ribs do not reach very far back, never, or very seldom, extending beyond the middle of the valve, and in most specimens only noticeable at and near the margin of the base. This species resembles somewhat Pent. galeatus of the Lower Helderberg group, especially in those forms as represented by figure 31, plate 33, but it differs, in its shape and in the arrangement of its plications, sufficiently from that species to be distinguished from it at the first glance. It occupies an intermediate position between Pent. galeatus of the Lower Helderberg, and Pent. fornicatus of the Clinton group. In regard to the shells figured on plate 33, figures 31, 32 and 33, and even those figured on same plate, figures 27, 28 and 29, I was uncertain for some time whether to place them with this species or to refer them to Pent. galeatus. Since then I found specimens of intermediate forms, uniting said shells with the typical Pent. nucleus.

Formation and Locality.—These shells are found in the Niagara rocks of the quarries east of the city of Louisville. Several good specimens were found by different collectors.

Pentamerus nysius, var. crassicostus. HALL.

Plate XXVIII., figures 5, 6, 7 and 8.

Pentamerus nysius, var. crassicostus, Hall. 24th Rep. N. Y. State Mus., p. 184.

Pent. nysius, var. crassicostus, Hall. 27th Rep. N. Y. St. Mus., pl. 10, figs. 4 and 7—1875.

Shell large, at least above the medium size; sub-triangular or sub-quadrate, sometimes becoming obscurely trilobate; length always, or mostly, exceeding the width. Ventral valve gibbous; greatest convexity below the umbo, from where it curves gently to the front, and, at first slightly and later abruptly, to the lateral margins from apex to the front. This abruptly bent portion of the shell is always smooth. The beak is strong and pointed, and arched over a large open fissure; it is considerably elevated over the umbo of the other valve. This valve has its surface divided, by two prominent concentric lines of growth, into three zones, all of which are, however, covered by the radii. On some of the shells belonging to this species these zones are not noticeable. The dorsal valve is less convex than the other, it is depressed convex, with its maximum convexity at the umbo, from where it slopes in a gentle curve to the anterior and lateral margins. A strip on its lateral margins is abruptly bent towards the ventral valve, and is not covered by radii; the umbo is regularly curved and reaching into the fissure of the opposite valve.

The surface is covered by single, strong and rounded plications, numbering from twenty to twenty-five.

Formation and Locality.—Occurs somewhat abundantly in the Niagara rocks in the quarries east of the city of Louisville, Ky.; but well preserved specimens are rather rare. In my own cabinet there are some very perfect specimens of this species.

Pentamerus nysius, var. tenuicostus. HALL.

This variety agrees in every essential point with the preceding one, with the exception of the radii. These are strong and coarse in the latter, and fine and more numerous in the present variety. The number of costae never exceeds twenty-five in P. crassicostus, while in P. tenuicostus it is about forty.

Formation and Locality.—Found associated with the preceding variety in the Niagara rocks east of the city of Louisville, Ky.; somewhat rarer than the former.

Pentamerus oblongus. SOWERBY.

Plate XXXIII., figures 15, 16 and 17.

Pent. oblongus, Sowerby. Murch. Sil. Syst., p. 641—1889.

Pent. laevis, Ibrid. Iden, pl. 19, fig. 9.

Pent. oblongus, Hall. Geol. Rep. of 4th Dist. N. Y., p. 7—1843.

Pent. oblongus, Hall. Pal. N. Y., Vol. II., p. 79, pls. 25 and 26.

Shell sometimes very large, but very variable in size and form. It would be impossible to describe minutely every possible form of this species; I shall, therefore, limit myself here to the description of the forms occurring in the vicinity of Louisville, which are represented on plate XXXIII. Shell of medium size, longitudinally sub-elliptical or sub-quadrate ; somewhat gibbous in the upper portion, but depressed-convex towards the front ; trilobate, the middle lobe largely extending ; beak of the ventral valve elevated above and incurved upon the umbo of the dorsal valve ; both valves almost equally convex and their surface marked by concentric lines of growth, of which some are very fine and scarcely noticeable, others, however, very strong and dividing the surface into different zones. The beak of the dorsal valve incurves into the other valve below its beak. All the specimens in my cabinet are casts; some of them show undoubtedly, though only faintly, traces of longitudinal striae on the middle lobe of both valves.

An individual of average size has the following dimensions : length, two inches and one-quarter; width, one inch and three-fourths, and thickness about one inch.

Formation and Locality.—Found in great abundance in the lower strata of the Niagara and in the Clinton group, in Jefferson county, Ky., eastward from the city of Louisville. Though fractional shells of this species are numerous, well preserved or even fair specimens are rare.

Pentamerus oblongus, var. cylindricus. HALL AND WHITFIELD.

Plate XXX., figures 2, 3 and 4.

Pent. oblongus, var. cylindricus, H. and W.   24th Rep. N. Y. State Museum, pl. 188—1872.

Pent. oblongus, var. cylindricus, H. and W.   27th N. Y. State Museum, pl. 10, figs. 13 and 14—1875.

Shell of medium size, sub-cylindrical in form; length exceeding the width almost three times; very gibbous in the upper portion, gradually decreasing towards the front. Ventral valve a little more convex than the other; beak elevated above and arched over the umbo of the other valve; greatest convexity a little above the middle, from where it curves regularly towards beak and front, but sloping abruptly, almost in a straight line, to the lateral margins. The trilobate character of Pent. oblongus is very slightly noticeable. Dorsal valve less convex and more regularly curved gently to beak and front, more rapidly to the lateral margins ; beak incurved into the fissure of the other valve below its beak. Surface of both valves is divided into different zones by strong concentric lines of growth. The specimen figured measures in length three inches; in width one inch and three-eighths; and in thickness a little less than the width.

Formation and Locality.—Found in the Niagara and Clinton groups in Jefferson county, Ky., east of the city of Louisville ; somewhat rare.

Pentamerus pergibbosus. HALL AND WHITFIELD.

Plate XXIX., figures 23 and 24.

Pentamerus pergibbosus, Hall and Whitfield. Pal. of Ohio, Vol. II., p. 139, pl. 7, figures 10 and 11—1875.

Shell of medium size, extremely and extravagantly gibbous; proportionally very elongate from beak to base, and very narrow; the greatest width being near the front, and equal to only about two-thirds the depth of the two valves when united in the broader specimens, and in some extravagant cases even less, while the depth of the united valves almost equals the length of the dorsal valve. Beaks distant and strongly incurved, that of the ventral valve the most prominent and narrower than the opposite. Ventral valve more than twice as deep as the dorsal valve; most prominent at the umbo, from where it slopes somewhat gradually towards the front margin; triangular foramen large, higher than wide, partially filled by the beak of the opposite valve. Dorsal valve more regularly arcuate than the ventral, almost evenly so, except for the constrictions of the surface by lines of growth; beak wide, strongly incurved into the foramen of the other valve. Surface of the internal casts, in which condition the specimens occur, strongly constricted by concentric lines of growth, which are placed at irregular distances, and often dividing the surface into several strongly marked transverse zones. The interior of the shell has been characterized by large longitudinal septa, as seen by the cavities left in the casts; that of the ventral valve extending fully to or beyond the middle of its length, while those of the dorsal valve reach about two-thirds of the length of the valve, in all the specimens examined, and in one example almost to the front margin, and vertically to the entire depth of the valve. The surface of the shell, in its original condition, has been marked by fine radiating striae, which are still visible on the casts of some individuals near the front of the valves, although the most of them appear to be smooth except for the concentric constriction. This species is most nearly related to Pent. occidentalis, Hall, from the Onondago salt group, Galt, Canada West; it differs, however, very materially from that one in the much greater depth of the dorsal valve, and also in the relative thickness of the longitudinal septa, that one having them very thick and strong; also in the finer striation of the surface. From Pent. littoni, another closely allied species, it differs in being more extravagantly gibbous, and narrower, and in being more finely striated. Copied exactly from Hall & Whitfield's description in the Ohio Report, Vol. II.

Good specimens in my possession show also faint radiating striae in the front, still I doubt that the original shell was covered with radii. I have, for instance, some specimens of Spir. radiata, which, on the larger portion of the surface, retain the shell, while the front part is exfoliated. The shell-covered portion shows no plications nor traces of them, while the exfoliated front is plainly plicate, showing that striae or radii may have been obliterated from the surface of the shell, even when internal casts bear undoubted evidence of their existence. Pent. pergibbosus, as found in our quarries, a specimen of which is copied on plate XXIX., can not be confounded with other species; it must be recognized at the first glance.

Formation and Locality.—Found in the middle strata of the Niagara rocks, in our quarries east of the city of Louisville, where it is, however, exceedingly rare. I am not aware that, outside of the specimens in my cabinet, and those formerly owned by Rev. H. Herzer, but afterwards acquired by Prof. Hall, of Albany, N. Y., any others are in existence.

Pentamerus uniplicatus. N. SP.

Plate XXXIII., figures 25 and 26.

Shell below medium size; sub-triangular; width exceeding the length; greatest width below middle of shell.

Ventral valve very convex or gibbous, having its greatest convexity a little above middle of valve, from where it slopes in a moderate but regular curve to the beak, and to the baso-lateral margins, but very abruptly to the cardinal borders, which are broadly rounded; the baso-lateral margins are regularly curved, and the front is slightly sinuate. The central portion of the ventral valve is somewhat elevated, extending from beak to front, and forming a mesial fold, which is narrow, and, in fact, not at all elevated above the general surface of the valve; its apparent elevation is due to two broad furrows, between which it is situated. This mesial fold is flat on top, and has below the umbo a shallow central depression. Umbo is prominent, and beak elevated and incurved. The dorsal valve is moderately convex in the umbonal region, sloping from there rapidly to the cardinal lines, near which it is slightly depressed; towards the baso-lateral margins dorsal valve becomes flat. The middle portion of the valve from beak to front is depressed, forming a mesial sinus, which increases in depth and width towards the front, and which is bounded on each side by an obscurely marked plication; this marginal rib is, however, only in the basal half of the valve separated from the balance of the surface by a faint depression. The bottom of the mesial sinus is occupied by a low rounded plication, which extends to umbo. The umbo is small, and the beak pointed and incurved. Outside of the ribs already mentioned, and some faint concentric lines of growth, there are no other surface-markings indicated. Size of shell is shown in illustration.

Formation and Locality.—The specimen here described and figured is the only one so far known to me. I found it in the Niagara rocks east of the city of Louisville, Ky.

Pentamerus ventricosus. Hall.

Plate XXXIII., figures 12, 13 and 14.

Pentamerus ventricosus, Hall. Geol. Rep. Prog. Wis., p. 2—1860.
Pent. (Pentamerella) ventricosus, Hall. 20th Reg. Rep., p. 374—1868.
Pent. (Pentamerella) ventricosus, Hall. Ohio Pal., Vol. II., p. 138—1875.

Shell of medium size, globose; width and length about equal, sometimes a little wider than long; hinge-line short, and cardinal extremities rounded. Ventral valve greatly more convex than the dorsal, with a very prominent umbo, and a strongly incurved beak; the middle of the valve marked by a broad, moderately deep sinus, extending from beak to base, where it forms a basal extension, deflecting upwards to meet a mesial indentation in the dorsal valve. Dorsal valve most prominent at the umbo, from where it runs in a straight line along the summit of the mesial fold to the front ; on both sides of the mesial elevation there is a marked depression, formed by the mesial fold and the markedly upwards turned lateral margins ; beak small and strongly incurved into the opposite valve.

Surface of the shell is marked by concentric undulations of growth, which, according to Prof. Hall's statement, are visible on the internal casts, but which the specimens in my possession, being casts of the interior, do not show. In my shells the surface is entirely smooth. Medium septum of the ventral valve is very short. This species is easily recognized by its strong umbo and its trilobed appearance in a front view. It differs from the ordinary forms of Pentamerus in having the middle of its dorsal valve elevated in the form of a mesial fold, while, in true Pentamerus, the middle of the dorsal valve is depressed, forming a dorsal sinus, with a corresponding elevation on the other or ventral valve.

Formation and Locality.—Found very rarely in the Niagara rocks of the quarries east of the city of Louisville, Ky.

Genus Stricklandinia. Billings.

Stricklandia, Billings. Can. Nat. and Geol., Vol. 4—1859.
Etymology: Named in honor of Prof. Strickland.

The name Stricklandia having been previously applied to a genus of fossil plants, the author abandoned it and substituted Stricklandinia for it. This genus includes such shells as Pentamerus lens, P. liratus, and P. laevis. They differ from the real Pentamerus in having the valves usually sub-equal, and no longitudinal septa or triangular chamber in the interior of the dorsal valve. Both valves have an area, but in the dorsal it is usually linear, or slightly exceeding the thickness of the shell in height, The ventral valve has usually a concave mesial sinus more or less developed, and the dorsal valve a mesial fold corresponding thereto. Some of the species, as S. laevis and S. microcamera have the hinge-line straight and much extended.

Stricklandinia louisvillensis. N. SP.

Plate XXXIV., figures 31, 32, 33 and 34.

Shell of medium size, sub-circular or sub-elliptical; width greater than length; maximum width, below middle of shell, nearer to base than shown in the figures 31 and 32; cardinal line straight on each side of beaks, but deflecting somewhat to front; shorter than the width of the shell, and its extremities rounded; lateral margins almost straight, or only slightly curved; at their basal termination the shell attains its greatest width; basal margin broadly curved, with the exception of its central half, which is somewhat produced, and forming a broad but short linguiform basal extension, giving the shell a somewhat trilobed aspect; both valves are about equally convex, ventral umbo a little more than dorsal; umbones and beaks are so slightly developed as to give only a very moderate angulation to cardinal line at its center. The hinge-areas are almost concealed by the close approximation of the beaks; that of ventral valve shows a narrow, almost linear strip along its rounded margins. Neither of the valves shows the least indication of either mesial fold or sinus, and the only point of distinction between the two valves is the umbo of the ventral valve, which is slightly more convex than the dorsal, and which is also a little elevated above the opposite beak. The surface is ornamented by seven low, rounded plications on each valve, which start below the umbones and extend, gradually increasing in strength and distance, to basal margin; transversely they are limited to middle lobe of shell; lateral lobes and umbones are entirely smooth or free from ribs; this feature, and the three-lobate character in the basal margin, are not sufficiently expressed in the figures, which also show one rib too much. Of the seven plications on each valve, the central three are considerably stronger than the lateral ones. The whole surface of the shell is covered by fine, closely set, concentric striae of growth, of which a few are slightly stronger than the balance, dividing the surface into several concentric zones; there are also radiating lines visible which are still finer than the concentric striae. This shell bears some resemblance to Stricklandinia davidsoni of Billings, as figured and described by him in his "Palæozoic Fossils, Vol. II.," but it differs from that species by having its greatest dimension transversely, while the other shell measures *most* longitudinally; in our specimen the middle lobe, or the basal extension, is broader in proportion to the whole width of the front, but considerably shorter than that of Str. davidsoni; and the most prominent points of distinction are the plications, which in S, davidsoni are only faintly developed, but covering the whole surface, while in our specimen the ribs are well marked and limited to the central lobe. The specimen from which the illustrations are made is the only one so far known to me ; it is a well preserved, beautiful shell.

Formation and Locality.—I found it in the strippings of one of the quarries east of the city of Louisville, in clay belonging to the Niagara group, and associated with other well known Upper Silurian shells; I feel, therefore, fully assured that it belongs to the Niagara fossils.

Genus Chonetes. Fischer.

Chonetes, Fischer. Oryckt. Moscow—1837.
Etymology : chone, a little cup.

Shell semi-oval or transversely oblong, with a wide straight hinge-line. External margin of area of ventral valve furnished with a row of tubular spines. Surface radiately striated, often spinose. Foramen in the ventral area distinct, but partly closed by a pseudo-deltidium. Valves articulated by teeth and sockets. Dorsal valve with a cardinal process, which is simple at the base, but bifid or grooved at the extremity. Interior of the shell pustulose or papillose. The genus Chonetes is nearly allied to Productus, from which it is distinguished by its articulated valves and row of tubular spines on the margin of the ventral area, as well as by other characters of less importance. Unfortunately the spines are often missing, having become obsolete by wear and rubbing. Even in the absence of these spines, Chonetes may be distinguished from Producta by their less gibbous and ventricose ventral valve, and by their finer surface striation. On the other hand, Chonetes, in form and external appearance, makes an approach to the genera Strophomena and Leptaena, and may be regarded as connecting link between the Strophomenidae and Productidae,

Chonetes acutiradiata. HALL.

Plate XVIII., figures 18, 19 and 20.

Strophomena acutiradiata, Hall. Geol. Rep. 4th dist. N. Y.—1843.
Chonetes acutiradiata, Hall. Tenth Rep. on St. Cab., p. 117—1857.
Chonetes acutiradiata, Hall. Pal. N. Y., Vol. IV., p. 120—1867.

Shell of large size in its genus ; semi-circular ; sometimes more than twice as wide as long ; the cardinal extremities produced and sometimes very mucronate. Ventral valve moderately convex, sometimes a little gibbous in the upper part, and frequently flattened or depressed at and below the middle; greatest convexity a little above the middle, from whence it curves gently to the front, somewhat abruptly depressed towards the cardinal extremities, which are sub-auriculate and flat or slightly concave; umbo moderate, and beak small and pointed, little elevated above the hinge-line, but perceptibly incurved over 'the latter; hinge-area small, but increasing towards the beak, and concave. Dorsal valve concave, corresponding in its general form with the convexity of the other valve; hinge area, small and narrow, almost linear; no beak perceptible.

The surface of the ventral valve is covered by peculiar radiating striae, which are strong, rounded or subangular, and simple in the umbonal region, outside of which they bifurcate and increase also by implantation, but all the striae on the marginal part are greatly finer than the umbonal ones; within the cardinal angles and along the cardinal margins the striae becomes very irregular and often entirely obsolete. Hinge-line marked on each side of the beak by four or five strong, tubular spines, which are directed obliquely outwards. In the specimen before me, which completely agrees in all other points with Prof. Hall's description, neither these spines nor any marks of their former existence are seen; it is possible they became obliterated by the process of silicification.

Formation and Locality.—Found in the rotten hornstone in the upper strata of the Devonian formation, at the Falls of the Ohio, on the Indiana shore of the river. Good or perfect specimens are extremely rare.

Chonetes subquadrata. n. sp.

Shell as chonetes of medium size ; sub-quadrate, hinge-line somewhat shorter than the greatest width of shell ; cardinal extremities rounded ; lateral margins slightly curved, almost straight, except in their basal part, which is regularly curved into the basal margin ; central half of front is straight or only slightly curved.

Ventral valve only moderately convex in its central portion, which curves regularly from its middle to apex and base ; the slope towards the lateral and cardinal margin is more abrupt, causing a flattening of the valve along the lateral borders, and producing between the cardinal extremities, which are a little deflected, and the umbo, a shallow concavity ; umbo sharply defined, and moderately elevated ; the beak small, pointed, and incurved over the hinge-area ; the area is small, forming a low triangle, which is divided by a small triangular fissure ; the foramen is partly closed by the cardinal process of the opposite valve. The margins of the cardinal area are provided with two round, tubular spines on each side of the beak, which appear from their stumps to have an outward direction. The dorsal valve is concave, corresponding in its depression with the convexity of the ventral valve ; its hinge-area is narrow or linear.

The surface of both valves is covered by fine rounded, or sub-angular radiating striae, which increase partly by intercalation but mostly by bifurcation on the ventral valve, while it is the reverse on the dorsal valve, where very few of the striae dichostomize, but a great many short ones are implanted. The specimen before me, the only one so far known, measures seven and one-half lines in width, five and one-half lines in length, and two lines in depth. It differs from the other shallow Chonetes by its greater size, and from the larger species by its shallowness.

Formation and Locality.—Found in the rotton hornstone in upper strata of the Devonian formation, at the Falls of the Ohio, on the Indiana shore of river.

Chonetes yandelliana. HALL.

Plate XVII., figures 16, 17, 18 and 19, and Plate XXXI., figures 20 and 30.

Chonetes yandelliana, Hall. Tenth Rep. on State Cabinet, p. 118—1857.

Compare: Chonetes lineata, ut sup., page 121.

Chonetes yandelliana, Hall. Pal. N. Y., Vol. IV., page 123—1867.

Shell very small, semi-oval, more or less gibbous; hinge-line equalling the greatest width of the shell; cardinal extremities angular, but sometimes rounded.

Ventral valve regularly convex, having its greatest convexity below the umbo of the valve, from where it slopes in a regular curve to the lateral and basal margins, but more abruptly to the cardinal angles, which are slightly deflected, forming there a faint incurvation or concavity; beak small and little curved.

Dorsal valve corresponding in its concavity with the convexity of the ventral, but owing to the internal cavity of the shell being somewhat less than the ventral convexity. Cardinal area of the ventral valve parallel with the longitudinal axis of the shell, nearly twice as wide in the middle than at its extremities; foramen comparatively large, with margins projecting and the opening filled by the cardinal process of the opposite valve. Dorsal area extremely narrow, being barely a defined line. Surface marked by fine, almost equal striae, which increase by bifurcation and intercalation till there are from sixty to seventy on the margin of the shell. The ventral valve has on its cardinal margin three to four short, oblique spines on each side of the center. The interior of the ventral valve shows strong, dental lamellae, and the muscular impressions are pretty well defined. The dorsal muscular impression, are also well marked, and between them there is a strong mesial ridge, which is extended in a bidentate cardinal process. The lower half of the surface is strongly papillose. This species bears a close resemblance to C. lineata, but it is less gibbous, and not flattened on the middle of the ventral valve; while the interior presents more strongly defined markings. Generally three spines are noticed on each half of the cardinal margin, but this is subject to variation, as the number may differ from two to four. Figure 19, plate 17, is enlarged, and figures 19 and 20, on plate 31, show an elongate form.

Formation and Locality.—Occurs in the hydraulic limestone, in Jefferson county, Ky., and in Clark county, Indiana, and is somewhat abundant in well preserved specimens. Prof. Hall named this species in honor of the late Dr Lunsford Yandell, Sr., of Louisville, Ky., who was one of the first collectors of fossils from the Falls of the Ohio.

Genus Productella. Hall.

Productella, Hall. Pal. N. Y., Vol. IV., page 153—1867.
Etymology. Productella, diminutive of Productus.

Shell having the general form of Productus, but uniformly, with a narrow area on each valve, a foramen or callosity on the ventral area, small teeth, and more or less distinct teeth-sockets. The reniform vascular impression, rising from between the anterior and posterior muscular impressions, curves gently outwards, and following a curvature [somewhat parallel with the margin of the shell to below the middle of its length, is abruptly recurved and the extremity turned a little backwards, terminates about half way between margin and anterior extremity of mesial septum. The cardinal process, seen from the inner side, is bilobed, and from the exterior side each of these divisions is usually bilobed. These shells differ from Stropholosia in the extremely narrow, linear cardinal area, greater extension of hinge-line, more extreme arcuation or ventricosity of ventral valve in many or most of the species, and especially in the direction and termination of the reniform vascular impressions, which resemble those of Aulosteges, and of some of Productus. It differs from Productus by the constant presence of an area, hinge-teeth and sockets.

Productella subaculeata var. cataracta. HALL AND WHITFIELD

Plate XVII., figures 5 to 9.

Productella subaculeata var. cataracta, H. and W. 24th Regent's Report, p. 198—1872.
Productella subaculeata var. cataracta, H. and W. 27th Regent's Rep., pl. 9—1875.

Shell small, semi-globose, rounded; hinge-line straight and about equal to width of shell; length and width of shell about equal. Ventral valve very gibbous, regularly curved from umbo downward, and also transversely; umbo is considerably elevated above hinge-line, and the beak is small and incurved. The lateral margins form with the cardinal line nearly right-angles; they are a little contracted below the extremities, forming small ears; below the ears the sides are regularly curved, and the front is broadly rounded. The dorsal valve is deep concave, as shown in the specimen illustrated on plate 17, figures 5 and 6. Said specimen is nearly perfect in both valves, and entirely free from rock. In this shell the dorsal valve shows a regular deep concavity, into which the beak of the ventral valve overlaps.

The greatest depth of the dorsal concavity is about equal to half the length of the hinge-line ; below the beak there is a slight impression into the umbo of the other valve. The surface is ornamented by low, rounded, radiating striae, reaching almost to the beak. My specimen, before alluded to, shows real continuous plications, not mere isolated elevations above and near the bases of each spine. Even the dorsal valve has faint indications of corresponding striae. On these radii are placed at irregular intervals the long, slender, round spines, with which the ventral valve is closely covered. These spines are only indicated on the silicified internal casts by their scars, and on better preserved shells, by their bases and short stumps ; they are only preserved in full length, where even the surrounding matrix became silicified at the same time with the shell. Concentric lines of growth are seldom noticed on our shells.

Formation and Locality.—Occurs rather abundantly in the cherty layers superimposed upon the hydraulic limestone of the Devonian formation around the Falls of the Ohio, in Jefferson county, Kentucky, and in Clark county, Indiana, where it is usually found as silicified casts of the interior. Well preserved shells, like that illustrated, showing both valves in perfect condition, with the exception of the spines, are extremely rare.

Productella semiglobosa. N. SP.

Plate XXVI., figure 7.

Shell of medium size, semi-globose or sub-circular ; hinge-line somewhat shorter than greatest width of shell; cardinal extremities rounded. Ventral valve very gibbous, regularly curved from umbo to front, and also transversely ; umbo only moderately elevated above surrounding surface ; beak incurved upon hinge-line, not overlapping it into dorsal valve. Width and length of shell about equal, but sometimes the width exceeding the length. Dorsal valve apparently deep concave, but its other characters are not known. Surface does not show any markings, except the stumps of a few isolated spines placed at irregular intervals; the figure 7, on plate 26, shows about twice as many as in reality exist. I am unable to identify it with any of the species of Devonian Productella known to me, and I, therefore, place it in the above named new species. This shell has some similarity with some middle-sized, but very ventricose forms of Strophodonta demissa, from which it is, however, easily distinguished by its smooth surface, which shows only a few spine-bases, while the Strophodonta demissa is covered by radiating striae, and never becomes fully as ventricose as our shell. The specimen illustrated is of about average size.

Formation and Locality.—Occurs in the Corniferous limestone at and around the Falls of the Ohio, in Kentucky and Indiana. Only a few specimens are so far found.

Genus Leiorhynchus. Hall.

Leiorhynchus, Hall. 13th Regent's Report—1860.
Etymology: leios, smooth; *rhynchos*, a beak.

Shell ovate, circular or transverse, with valves unequally convex, and marked by mesial sinus and fold in the ventral and dorsal valves respectively. The surface is plicated by rounded, bifurcating ribs, which are always more conspicuous on the mesial fold and sinus, whilst they often become obsolete on the lateral portion of the shell; concentrically marked by strong lines of growth. Substance of the shell fibrous, usually thin. Valves articulated by teeth and sockets; the apex of the ventral valve perforate at some period of its growth, the lower side being closed by deltidial plates. On the interior of the ventral valve, two short diverging dental lamellae extend into and are joining the sides or bottom of the rostral cavity; the muscular impression occupies a narrow triangular or ovate triangular space, below the dental lamellae. The dorsal valve has a well-defined septum, often reaching below the middle of the valve, and divided above, leaving a triangular or spoon-shaped depression. The hinge-plates are narrow, strong processes, with sockets embracing the teeth of the opposite valve. (Hall.) This genus is closely allied to that of Rhynchonella.

Leiorhynchus quadricostatus. Vanuxem.

Orthis quadricostata, Vanuxem. Geol. Rep. 3d dist. N. Y., p. 186—1842.
Orthis quadricostata, Hall. Geol. Rep. 4th dist. N. Y., p. 223—1843.
Leiorhynchus quadricostata, Hall. 13th Rep on St. Cab., p. 86—1860.
Leiorhynchus quadricostata, Hall. Pal. N. Y.,·Vol. IV., p. 357—1867.

Shell of medium size; broadly ovate; from moderately convex to somewhat gibbous; with distinct mesial fold and sinus.

Ventral valve a little gibbous towards the beak; side nearly flat, with a mesial sinus commencing below the umbo and extending to the front; it increases gradually in width and depth towards front; umbo is of medium size, and beak elevated and pointed, and slightly arched but not incurved; place of the apex appears to be occupied by a round perforation. Dorsal valve is more convex than the opposite, having its greatest convexity in the middle of the valve, from where it slopes in a light curve to the baso-lateral margins, and in a stronger curve to the beak and cardinal margins. A mesial fold commences to rise above the surface in front of the umbo, from where it slightly increases in height and width towards the front. The dorsal umbo is low, beak small and incurved. The surface is partly plicated. On the mesial elevation and in the mesial sinus are generally four plications plainly visible in the basal half.

It appears that in the umbonal half of the shell only two plications existed before they became obliterated, and that by bifurcation the four ribs were produced, which now occupy sinus and fold. Some individuals have five ribs instead of four. The lateral parts of this shell are often covered with several faintly visible plications, but in most of the specimens these lateral ribs become entirely obsolete, and the surface outside of sinus and fold is free from any markings whatever.

Specimens of this species are seldom in a fair condition; they are found in the Genesee shale, and their shell being very thin, they become generally distorted and compressed. The inclosing shale or slate did not possess sufficient density and hardness to resist the pressure of the superimposed rocks, but became compressed itself, and thus the imbedded shells suffered the same fate as their matrix. I have found in the shales at the Falls of the Ohio, on the Kentucky shore of the river, an almost perfect specimen of this species, with a very slight distortion, and on the Indiana side I picked up another shell belonging to L. quadricostata, not distorted at all, but a little defective at the front, which, however, was easily restored; and thus I possess two specimens which show exactly the form and surface-markings of this species. Prof. Hall states in his description of this shell, in Pal. N. Y., Vol. IV., page 358, that on account of the compressed and crushed condition of the fossil, its real form and its correct proportions could not be determined. The specimen before me measures nine lines in length, nine and one-half lines in width, and five and one-half lines in depth. Another specimen found at Lexington, Indiana, measures thirteen lines in length, one inch in width, and seven to eight lines in depth. These dimensions show that, in most instances, this shell has its width and length about equal, while its convexity may vary somewhat; its greatest width is either at the middle of the shell or a little below it.

Formation and Locality.—Found mainly in the Genesee shales, being the top strata of the Devonian formation, at the Falls of the Ohio, in Kentucky, and at Lexington, Indiana, but some specimens are also found in the rotten hornstone just below said shales.

Genus Rhynchonella. Fischer.

Rhynchonella, Fischer. Mem. Soc. Imp., Mosc.—1809.
Etymology: rhynchos, a beak; ella, little.

Shells trigonal, acutely beaked, usually plicated, dorsal valve elevated in front, depressed at the sides. Ventral valve flattened or hollowed along the center; hinge-plate supporting two slender curved lamellae; dental plates diverging.

The foramen is at first only an angular notch in hinge-line of the ventral valve, but the growth of the deltidium usually renders it complete in adult shell; in the cretaceous species it is tubular. In some species the beak is so closely incurved upon the other as to allow no space for a pedicle.

The Rhynchonella loxia is made the type of the genus Rhynchonella.

Rhynchonella acinus. HALL.

Plate XXVI., figures 6, 13 and 14, and Plate XXXII, figures 13 to 16.

Rhynchonella acinus, Hall. Trans. Alb. Inst., Vol. IV., p. 215—1863.
Rhynchonella acinus, Hall. 28th Rep. N. Y. St. Mus. Nat. Hist., Mus. edit., p. 163, pl. 26, figs. 7-11—1879.
Rhynchonella acinus, Hall. 11th Geol. Rep. of Ind., p. 306—1881.

Shell very small, longitudinally ovate, sub-attenuate towards the beak and truncate in front, valves sub-equally convex. Ventral valve sub-arcuate, flattened in the middle, below which it is sinuate; beak incurved. Dorsal valve somewhat flattened in the middle, and sometimes a little depressed in upper part of median line, two of the plications becoming elevated towards the front, corresponding to an abruptly depressed sinus in ventral valve, in the bottom of which is a single plication; there are three and rarely four plications on each side of mesial fold of dorsal valve, and four on each side of the sinus of the ventral valve. Concentric lines of growth usually only faintly marked. Length to width usually about as four to three, and depth about equal to width, giving a sub-quadrate transverse section; average size of the shell as represented in the figures on plate 26.

This species differs from Rhyn. bidentata of Hisinger, in being larger, more robust and ventricose, and proportionally more elongate; the plications are more rounded, and the whole aspect of the shell less angular. It approaches in form the Rhyn. bialveata of the lower Helderberg formation, but it is more robust, and the plications are more rounded. (Hall.)

Formation and Locality.—Found in the lower strata of the Niagara group in the quarries east of the city of Louisville, Ky., but of rare occurrence. On some of the plates the two lower figures of this species have no numbers. The side view should be number 13, and the front view number 14. This front view shows in the mesial elevation three plications; there should be only two.

Rhynchonella bellaforma. N. SP.

Shell of medium size; sub-triangular or sub-pentagonal; moderately convex, rather somewhat compressed; cardinal margins sloping down to the middle of shell, and forming at the beaks an obtuse angle of about one hundred degrees; lateral margins short and strongly curved; base only curved at the front angles, the balance, about four-fifths of the whole front, almost straight, with a slight emargination or inflection of its middle part. Width to length as three to two; greatest width below the middle.

Ventral valve moderately convex at the umbonal region, and near the cardinal and lateral margins; in front of the umbo the central portion of the valve becomes depressed, which depression increases in depth, but more rapidly in width, towards the base or front, which it occupies almost to the full extent of basal length ; umbo is small, and the beak elevated and slightly incurved. The dorsal valve is somewhat larger than the ventral, and also more convex; it is divided into two halves by a central depression, which extends from the beak to a point below the middle of the valve, and which is most prominent in umbonal region ; it is occupied by six single strong plications which reach entirely back to apex.

The two outside of these six plications form the lateral limit of the depression, which ceases a little below the middle of valve, where the said six plications become elevated above surface, and all six rising to the same level extend to the front, where they form a mesial fold, which is entirely flat on top ; the lateral ,portion, of the valve outside of this mesial combination of sinus and fold, is regularly and gently curved from beak to the lateral and baso-lateral margins, while it slopes abruptly towards the cardinal lines, along which, in both valves, the borders are inflected, meeting under a very obtuse angle, but with its apex outward ; these inflected borders are entirely smooth ; the umbo is small, also the beak, which is incurved into the other valve. The surface is ornamented by strong, rounded, simple, radiating plications, of which the ventral valve has seven in its mesial sinus, and five on each side of it; while the dorsal valve has six on its mesial fold and six on each side of the same. All these ribs reach back to the beak, and are of about equal strength, with the exception of the two outside ones on each side of the mesial fold and sinus, which are smaller, and extend only for some distance back into the shell, becoming obliterated by the smooth cardinal borders. No other surface-markings are observable. The specimen here described measures : length, six lines ; width, nine lines ; depth, three lines. This is one of the most beautiful Rhynchonella, as far as its shape is concerned, and for that reason I have named it bellaforma. I do not know any species of its congeners to compare it with, except, probably, Rhyn. tennesseensis of Roemer, but not with that form of said species which Prof. Hall has, in late years, placed in the species of Rhyn. stricklandi. To Rhyn. tennesseensis it has some resemblance, but differs from it by its small depth, its being more transverse, its smaller and more numerous plications, its cardinal borders, which are not as much inflected as in that species ; in our shell the marginal angle at said borders has its apex outward, while the same angle in Rhyn. tennesseensis has its apex inward. But the most characteristic feature of our shell is its peculiar combination of mesial sinus and fold on its dorsal valve, by which it is easily distinguished from any other Rhynchonella.

Formation and Locality.—I found this interesting shell, finely preserved, in the Niagara clay, east of our city. So far this one specimen only is known to me.

Rhynchonella carolina. HALL.

Plate XIII., figures 1, 2 and 3, 34 and 35,

Rhyn. carolina, Hall. Pal. N. Y., Vol. IV., p. 337, pl. 34, figs. 14-19—1867.
Rhyn. carolina, Meek. Pal. of Ohio, Vol. I., p. 196, pl. 18, figs. 8a-c—1873.

Shell of medium size, trigonoid-subovate in general outline, moderately gibbous, a little produced or widened in front. In an old shell of unusual size belonging to my cabinet, the widening of the front portion is very considerable, so that the lateral margins, from beak to a little below the middle of the shell, become strongly concave, while in younger specimens, those as figures 34 and 35, said margins are almost straight.

Ventral valve a little less convex than the other; greatest convexity at the umbo, from where it curves gently towards the front, and more abruptly to the cardinal margins; beak prominent, little curved or nearly straight, and elevated a little above umbo of other valve.

Mesial sinus starts a little above the middle of the valve, is broad, shallow and flat at the bottom; its margins are not well defined. Dorsal valve more convex, moderately gibbous and regularly arcuate from summit to base, the sides more abruptly curved; mesial fold, beginning a little above middle of valve, is broad, slightly convex, mostly flat, without well defined margins; beak strongly incurved into the other valve.

Surface is marked by from twenty-four to thirty simple, sub-angular, radiating costae, of which from six to eight occupy the mesial sinus, and about the same number the mesial elevation; the ribs in the sinus and on the fold are stronger than the lateral ones. The plications increase from the beak towards the front in size and distance, and the lateral ribs are curving more or less outwards. No other surface-markings are visible, not even concentric lines of growth, on the most perfectly preserved shells in my cabinet. This species differs from all other rhynchonelloid forms of the Corniferous limestone, by its broad, shallow and poorly defined sinus, as well as by its broad, flat and also poorly defined mesial elevation, and by its more extended beak. Prof. Hall is of the opinion that a larger material may hereafter prove its generic distinction from Rhynchonella.

Formation and Locality.—Occurs in the Corniferous limestone at and near the Falls of the Ohio, in Kentucky and Indiana. It is rather rare, though I possess in my cabinet a few exceedingly well preserved specimens retaining the shell entirely.

Rhynchonella gainesi. N. SP.

Plate XXXI., figures 6, 7, 8, and 9.

Shell very small; sub-triangular; length equal to greatest width, which latter is near the base; the cardino-lateral margins run in almost straight lines from beak to point of greatest width; basal margin broadly curved, nearly straight. Shell concavo-convex, and surface smooth except near the margins, where faint plications are noticed. Ventral valve moderately convex at its umbo, and in its upper one-third; the balance deeply depressed to a sinus, which occupies the whole width of the valve, and which is margined on each side by the lateral margins of the shell, which deflect here downwards to a sharp prominent point; sinus is flat in the bottom and extends considerably beyond the base, forming a quadrilateral basal extension, which deflects at right-angles upward to fit into a corresponding indentation in the dorsal valve; the height, measured between the highest point of the basal extension and the apex of the pointed margins of the sinus, is almost equal to the width of the shell; the beak is elevated and slightly curved. Dorsal valve is somewhat gibbous, with its greatest convexity at the middle of the valve, from where it slopes in strong curves to the cardino-lateral and basal margins; its central portion runs in a straight line from the beak to the base, forming the mesial fold, which becomes visible at a little above the middle of the valve, and increases rapidly to the front or base, where it is very prominent; umbo is inflated, and the beak incurved into the opposite valve. The surface is entirely smooth in its upper half, while the lower one shows some plications, which are plainly visible at the basal margin, but do not extend far into the shell. There are two faint indication, of plications on each side of the mesial fold and sinus, while the mesial fold has three and the sinus two ribs on its summit or bottom respectively. No other surface-markings are observable on account of the silicification of the shell.

Formation and Locality.—Found in the rotten hornstone of the Devonian formation exposed in several washes in Jefferson county, Ky. This pretty little shell is not very rare. This species is named after Prof. J. T. Gaines, of Louisville, Ky., who, as ardent student and collector of fossils, deserves such a recognition.

Rhynchonella indianensis. HALL.

Plate XXXIII., figures 18, 19 and 20.

Rhyn. indianensis, Hall. Trans. Alb. Inst., Vol. IV., p. 215—1863.
Rhyn. indianensis, Hall. 28th Rep. N. Y. St. Mus. Nat. Hist., Mus. edit., p. 163, pl. 26, figs. 12-22—1876.
Rhyn. indianensis, Hall. 11th Geol. Rep of Indiana, p. 306—1881.

Shell small, broadly ovate or sub-triangular; length and width nearly equal, or the former is sometimes slightly exceeded by the latter. Cardinal slopes in the more gibbous specimens flattened. Ventral valve with the beak pointed and incurved, depressed-convex in the middle, and gradually becoming depressed and sinuate in front, two or three of the plications included in the sinus. Dorsal valve a little the more gibbous, somewhat flattened in front of the umbo. Three or four of the plications run straight from beak to front and form a mesial elevation, the lateral plications are curving outwards to the lateral margins. Each valve marked by from nine to twelve rounded or sub-angular plications, which sometimes obsolete toward the beak. The concentric lines are very obscure.

This species resembles the Rhyn. neglecta of the Niagara group of New York, but it is larger and more robust, with stronger and more rounded plications. (Hall.)

Formation and Locality.—Found rarely in the Niagara strata in the quarries east of the city of Louisville, Ky. Our specimens are smaller than the Waldron shells, and the plications on the Kentucky individuals are less marked. They even become sometimes almost obsolete on the lateral slopes of the shell, and seldom extend as far back as the ribs on Waldron specimens.

Rhynchonella louisvillensis. N. SP.

Plate XXXI., figures 1 to 4.

Shell of less than medium size among the Rhynchonellidae ; longitudinally sub-oval or sub-trigonal ; length and width about equal, the latter rarely exceeding the former slightly ; both valves about equally convex.

Ventral valve moderately convex; mesial sinus beginning in front of the umbo, is broad and flat, deepens at the base, and has a considerable quadrilateral extension, fitting in a corresponding indentation of the other valve ; it contains five plications ; beak small and pointed, and only slightly arched. Dorsal valve somewhat more convex than the other ; mesial fold starting below the umbo, and becomes prominent at the front, and contains, like the sinus, five plications ; beak small, narrow, and incurving into the other valve beneath the ventral beak.

Surface is ornamented by four or five rounded ribs on each side of the mesial depression or elevation ; those on the lateral slopes of the dorsal valve are abruptly curving outwards and downwards. In regard to measurement, the figures on plate 31 give the dimensions of an average-sized specimen.

Formation and Locality.—Found in the Corniferous rocks surrounding the Falls of the Ohio, in Kentucky and Indiana, where it is, however, of rare occurrence. As far as my information goes, only three individuals of this species are known. This species has some resemblance to Hall's Rhyn. indianensis of the Niagara group, but it is easily distinguished from that species, differing from it by its larger number of plications in the sinus and on the fold, by the greater extension of its mesial fold, and also by its greater convexity or gibbosity.

Rhynchonella pisa. HALL AND WHITFIELD.

Plate XXXII., figures 24 to 27.

Rhynchonella pisa, H. and W. Pal. of Ohio, Vol. II., p. 135—1875.

Shell small, globular in full-grown specimens, but varying from depressed lenticular to highly gibbous at different stages of growth. General outline of the shell broadly ovate, widest near the front or below the middle of the length. Ventral valve less gibbous than the dorsal; beak small, pointed and slightly curved, usually projecting but moderately beyond that of the opposite valve, though sometimes rather extended; body and sides of the valves regularly rounded, becoming broadly but not deeply sinuate in front, where it is prolonged and bent upward in the middle. Dorsal valve regularly convex, center of the valve most prominent, becoming slightly elevated in front, forming a not very prominent mesial elevation. Surface marked by from twelve to sixteen rounded plications, which are distinctly marked on sides and in front, but becoming obsolete soon after reaching the middle of the valve on the dorsal side, but are continued somewhat further on the ventral valve, and in some specimens those bordering the sinus extend to near the beak. On the dorsal valve there are usually four plications elevated to form the mesial fold, and three depressed in the ventral sinus, though in some cases there are only three elevated on the dorsal valve. This species resembles Rhyn. neglecta, with which it is associated, but differs in its general convexity of the valves and want of angularity in the plications, which do not extend to the beak as in that species. The more elongate forms have some similarity to Rhyn. acinus, but have not the flattening of the sides and surfaces of the valves, as in that species, and have, moreover, a greater number of plications. The more ventricose forms resemble, very closely, small specimens of Rhyn. nucleolata, but, besides being more elongate, with a more projecting beak, the plications are never flattened on their surfaces, and are destitute of the groove along the middle, as in that one. (Hall and Whitfield.)

Formation and Locality.—Occurs in the Niagara rocks of the quarries east of the city of Louisville. It is a rather rare species. The specimen illustrated on plate 32 is of about the largest size this species ever attains.

Rhynchonella rugaecosta. N. SP.

Plate XXXII., figures 48, 49, 50 and 51.

Shell of medium size, sub-triangular or sub-pentagonal; compressed or very moderately convex; width to length as three to two.

Ventral valve moderately convex in the umbonal region, sloping from there in a straight line to the baso-lateral margins, but rapidly, almost abruptly, to the cardinal borders; in the middle part of the valve is a mesial depression, which extends from beak to base, and increases in depth and width only moderately towards the front; the umbo is inflated, and the beak elevated, pointed and only slightly arched.

Dorsal valve moderately convex only at the umbo, balance only slightly curved, almost flat; middle of valve is elevated from beak to front, forming a well defined, but narrow and little elevated mesial fold, at the base of which the front-margin is slightly sinuate.

The surface is ornamented by simple sub-angular radiating striae, of which four to five on each side of the mesial fold and sinus are more prominent, and reach from the baso-lateral margins back to the beak; they are, however, only faintly marked in the umbonal region of each valve; above these principal ribs there are about four short ones on each side of the mesial fold and sinus, terminating in the cardinal margins, the uppermost not more than about a line from the dorsal beak. The illustration does not show this peculiar feature, except in the side-view, where it is faintly indicated. These radii are crossed by concentric lamellose, imbricating striae, which become crowded towards the front, and which produce the rugose appearance of the shell. The specimen before me measures six lines in width, four in length, and three in depth. There are no plications on the fold nor in the sinus. This species is easily distinguished from all other Rhynchonella.

Formation and Locality.—Found in the upper strata of the Niagara group, in the quarries cast of the city of Louisville. It is of rare occurrence.

Rhynchonella saffordi. HALL.

Plate XXVII., figures 22, 23 and 24, and Plate XXXIII., figures 4, 5 and 6.

Rhynchonella saffordi, Hall. Can. Nat. and Geo., Vol. V., Niag. group—1860.
Rhynchonella saffordi, Hall. 27th Rep. N. Y. State Mus., pl. 9, figs. 27-29—1875

Shell somewhat below medium size, varying from ovate to spherical, sub-pentagonal, having the five sides almost equal, the front or base generally a little larger than the lateral margins and the slopes of the beak; shell very gibbous. Ventral valve convex or depressed-convex, greatest convexity a little below the umbo, from where it curves gently towards the lateral margins, but before reaching these, it deflects very abruptly, almost forming here a right-angle; beak small and little arched, and slightly elevated above the one of the other valve; umbo scarcely noticeable. In the upper part of the valve, from apex to one-third of its length, there is a slight elevation in the middle; from the point where this elevation ceases, some of the central plications become depressed, which depression is only very slight but increases towards the front; here the depressed part of the valve makes a sudden and abrupt, almost angular bend, in the dorsal direction. The number of depressed plications is very variable, running from three to nine; the deflected front part of the valve is quadrilateral, its length sometimes exceeding its width; its deflection amounts, usually, to ninety degrees, but it sometimes exceeds the right-angle a few degrees.

The dorsal valve is very gibbous, having its greatest convexity a little below the middle of the valve, from where it curves regularly and gently to the front and rear, but very abruptly to the lateral margins; there is a slight depression in the middle of the valve from apex almost half-way down or even a little further. Where this depression terminates some of the central plications, from five to ten in number, commence to rise, increasing in elevation towards the front, forming here a kind of mesial elevation. This valve has in its front part a quadrilateral indentation, corresponding in form and size to the front extension of the ventral valve, which fits into it exactly. The base of the shell forms a regular quadrangle. The surface is covered by fine radiating plications, rounded or somewhat flattened, some of which bifurcate; they differ in size and number, which latter runs from twenty to thirty. Two some-what different forms of this species are found, as represented by the figures in the two different plates; the group represented on plate 27 is somewhat longer than wide, and its plications are less in number, and markedly coarser, while the shells figured on plate 33, are wider than long, with finer and more numer-ous plications; but there are so many specimens of intermediate forms con-necting the two groups, that I feel not justified to separate them as different species or varieties.

This species differs greatly in size in different specimens; one of average size has the following dimensions: width, seven lines; length, eight lines, and thickness, from six to seven lines.

Formation and Locality.—Occurs somewhat abundantly in the Niagara rocks in the quarries east of the city of Louisville, Ky., where even well preserved specimens are not rare. This species was named by Prof. Hall after Prof. Safford, of Nashville, Tennessee, formerly State Geologist of Tennessee.

Rhynchonella saffordi var. depressa. N. VAR.

Plate XXXIII., figures 1, 2 and 3.

Although this shell agrees in so many points with Rhyn. saffordi, to place it with that species, it, on the other hand, possesses some very important features which separate it from saffordi, and which I think justify me to make a new variety out of it. These features are as follows:

1. This shell is very flat or compressed, more so than any other Rhyncho-nella of its size, while Rhyn. saffordi is generally very ventricose,

2. The elevation and depression of the central plications are scarcely noticeable in this shell.

3. The beak of the ventral valve is more pointed, and elevated above that of the other valve. One of my specimens of this species shows faint traces of very fine radiating lines, also of fine concentric striae or lines of growth; both these lines, the radiating and the concentric, may also be found in more perfect specimens of Rhyn. saffordi, though none among the many shells of that species in my collection show them.

Formation and Locality.—Associated with Rhyn. saffordi in the Niagara rocks in the quarries east of the city of Louisville, Ky., but of rare occurrence.

Rhynchonella stricklandi. Sowerby.

Plate XXVII., figures 9, 10 and 11, and Plate XXIX., figures 3 to 6.

Terebratula Stricklandi,, Sowerby. Sil. Syst., pl. 13, fig. 19—1839.
Rhyn. Tennesseensis (Roemer), Hall. Trans. Alb. Inst., Vol. IV.
Rhyn. Stricklandi, Hall. 28th. Rep. N. Y. State Museum—1876.
Rhyn. Stricklandi, Hall. 11th Geol. Rep. of Ind., p. 308, pl. 26—1881.

Shell one of the large-sized Rhynchonellidae, sub-ovate or sub-trigonal; width sometimes equal, but mostly exceeding the length; sides and front rounded; shell almost concavo-convex. Surface plicate.

Ventral valve regularly curved from beak to front; the mesial sinus, which commences below the umbo, occupies, from that point to the front, the largest portion of the valve; it is shallow at the beginning, but deepens approaching the front. On each side of the sinus are five plications smaller than those occupying the mesial depression; in the most lateral plication the margin of the valve makes a very abrupt bend, equalling or exceeding ninety degrees towards the dorsal valve, forming here a smooth, vertical border; beak small and incurved over the umbo of the other valve. The sinus contains usually nine strong, simple and rounded plications; the whole valve has from eighteen to twenty of these ribs, which increase in size and distance from beak to front; most all of them reach to the front, only a few appear to be somewhat shorter. Dorsal valve is very gibbous or ventricose, slightly flattened at the umbo; mesial fold not defined on the umbo; from there it becomes gradually more elevated as it approaches the front, where it is more or less prominent. The fold has generally four plications on top and three on each of its slopes; outside of the mesial elevation, each side of the valve contains four plications, thus covering the whole valve with about eighteen ribs; those on the fold are somewhat stronger than the lateral. In the last lateral plication the surface of the valve bends abruptly towards the ventral valve, forming here, like the latter, a smooth border of considerable size. All the ribs are rounded and simple, and increase in size and distance from beak to front. The ventral valve has its mesial depression greatly produced in front, and abruptly turned upwards, which extension fits exactly in a corresponding indentation in the base of the dorsal valve. There are no radiating striae visible, but a few concentric lines of growth may be noticed. The shells of this species were originally identified with Rhyn. tennesseensis, a species described by Prof. F. Roemer, of Germany, from the Silurian of Tennessee, and they are, therefore, generally known under that name. A closer examination and comparison showed the former identification as erroneous, and placed our shells in their present species.

Formation and Locality.—This species occurs in great abundance and in fine and well preserved specimens in the Niagara rocks at Waldron and St. Paul, in Indiana; in the Niagara strata of Kentucky, near to and east of the city of Louisville, this species is also found, but very rarely, and then in defective and distorted specimens. The best individual, so far as I know, ever found in our quarries, is figured on plate 27; it is considerable smaller than the Waldron shells, but has their exact form and markings. Another specimen which I found associated with the former, has the same shape in its outlines, but shows only faint traces of the plications; its surface appears almost smooth.

Rhynchonella tenuistriata. N. SP.

Plate XVII., figures 27, 28 and 29.

Shell rather small, sub-triangular or sub-pentagonal; cardinal line forms a right-angle at the beak; its two sides, which are somewhat concave or incurved, slope down below the middle of the shell; here they meet the lateral margins, with which they form again an almost right-angle; lateral margins short, about one-third the length of the shell, almost straight or very slightly convex; basal margin straight, with a slight concavity.

Ventral valve less convex than the dorsal, with its greatest convexity at the umbo, from which it slopes in almost straight lines to the lateral margins; the cardinal margins deflect abruptly upwards to meet the margin of the dorsal valve in one and the same plane; below the umbo the central portion becomes depressed, which depression increases in depth and width towards the front, where it occupies the valve to the full extent of the basal margin. This mesial sinus is rounded, its margins are not well defined, and its depth becomes only somewhat prominent at or near the front; the umbo is small, the beak elevated above that of the other valve, and very little arched. The dorsal valve very little convex, almost flat in the umbonal region and below it to the basal margin, where a part of the front is elevated into a mesial fold. On each side of this mesial fold the valve slopes down very abruptly to the baso-lateral margins. The mesial fold is only observeable at or near the front; the umbo is inflated, and the beak small and incurved into the opposite valve. The surface of both valves is covered by slender, sub-angular or rounded radii, of which there are five or six on each side of the mesial fold and sinus; the fold is occupied by about seven, while the sinus only contains about six. These striae increase by intercallation, but not by bifurcation. Other markings of the surface are not observed.

Formation and Locality.—Occurs very rarely in the Corniferous rock of the Devonian formation in Kentucky and Indiana.

Rhynchonella tethys. BILLINGS.

Plate XIII., figures 25 to 33, and Plate XXXI., figures 22 to 25.

Rhynchonella tethys, Billings. Canadian Journal, p. 270—1860.
Rhynchonella tethys, Hall. Pal. N. Y., Vol. IV., p. 335—1867.

Shell of medium size among ths Rhynchonellidae, sub-trigonal ovate, usually wider than long, but sometimes length and width equal. Ventral valve depressed convex in the upper part, nearly flat at the sides; sinus, beginning above the middle, moderately depressed in young shells, and in older ones becoming deep in front and abruptly curving towards the dorsal valve. Dorsal valve moderately convex in young shells, more convex and finely gibbous in old shells; the broad mesial elevation becoming distinct about the middle of the length. Surface marked by from fifteen to eighteen angular plications, of which four to six are upon the mesial fold, and three to five in the median sinus, while about five or six cover the lateral slopes of each valve on each side of the mesial fold or sinus; plications outside of fold on dorsal valve curve very abruptly outwards as well as downwards. Fine concentric striae, which are undulated in crossing the plications, mark surface of shell, but this feature is rarely preserved.

Formation and Locality.—Found abundantly and in well preserved specimens in the Corniferous rock at and around the Falls of the Ohio, however, all the shells found are in a silicified condition, by which, generally, the finer surface-markings become obliterated. If we compare the shell figured on plate 31 with those on plate 13, it appears to us that it does not belong to the same species. The shell on plate 31 has its plications finer and rounded, and its mesial elevations and depressions less prominent; it has six ribs on the fold and five in the sinus. The shells on plate 13 show four to five plications on the fold, and three to four in the sinus; all the ribs are coarse and angular. But if we compare the different shells in a large lot of from fifty to sixty individuals, as are now before me, it is impossible to draw a dividing line; there are numerous intermediates connecting the two extreme forms, which must, therefore, be classed in one and the same species.

Rhynchonella increbescens. HALL.

Plate XXXIV., figures 26-29.

Atrypa increbescens, Hall. Pal N. Y., Vol. I., pl. 33, p. 146—1843.

Average shell small, ovate-trigonal, full-grown specimens quite convex, with slightly greater width than length. Cardinal slopes nearly straight in young examples, slightly curved in adult specimens, anterior margins rounded to the front.

Dorsal valve greatly convex, particularly towards the front, approaching which the mesial ridge is greatly elevated (especially in more globose specimens), and is gathered into four plications. The sides radiate from beak in five or six plications, strongly curved towards the anterior lateral margins.

Ventral valve is depressed from beak to anterior central region, where it curves more strongly. A mesial sinus begins at beak, has sloping sides, three plications, and diverges to a great width at the front, where it terminates in an extended, half-circular, marginal projection corresponding to elevation in the front of the dorsal valve. The sides radiate to the anterior margins in five or six plications rounding towards the front.

The beak of the ventral valve is curved so as to hide the apex of the dorsal valve. The angular plications and furrows give the margins a distinct zigzag outline; the larger specimens show several lines of growth, more distinct towards the front, crossing the plications and furrows.

In the specimens before me the plications in the lateral slopes vary; some are imperfectly developed and almost indistinct. The plications in the mesial sinus and elevation never vary. The smaller specimens are generally more compressed and the larger more rounded in outline than the typical forms.

Formation and Locality.—This shell seems to be confined to the Upper Trenton, where it is found quite abundantly, and associated with Orthis borealis. It occurs in most of the blue-grass counties of the State. The specimens figured are from Frankfort, Ky.

Genus Rhynchotreta. Hall.

Rhynchotreta, Hall. 28th Regent's Report—1879.
Etymology: rhynchos, beak; *tretos*, with a hole in it.

Type: Rhynchonella cuneata, Dalman.

Shell triangular; surface with angular plications. Ventral beak straight, produced beyond the dorsal beak, extremely perforated; foramen with an elevated margin; space between the foramen and hinge-line occupied by a deltidium in two pieces, being divided by a longitudinal suture, and transversely striated. Valves articulated by two slender, curving teeth, proceeding from a broad curving hinge-plate in the ventral valve, which fit into corresponding sockets in the dorsal valve. Crurae rising from near the dorsal beak, and curving into the ventral cavity, and thence recurved towards the dorsal side, and probably uniting. Structure fibrous, and apparently very minutely punctate.

Rhynchotreta cuneata, var. americana. HALL.

[Plate XXXII., figures 58, 59, 62 and 63.

Rhynchotreta cuneata, var. americana, Hall. 28th Rep. N. Y. State Museum, Nat. Hist. Mus., p. 167—1879.
Rhynchotreta cuneata, var. americana, Hall. 11th Geol. Rep. of Indiana, p. 310, pl. 25, figs. 29-38—1881

Shell triangular, cuneiform, longer than wide, greatest width near the front and tapering posteriorly into an angular beak. Valves moderately convex, the dorsal sometimes gibbous, ventral beak elongated, foramen sub-circular, formed by the extremity of the beak, and a portion of the area below, which is separated from the hinge-line by a deltidium in two pieces; sides of the beak compressed, flat or concave. Sinus wide, deep or shallow, according to development of shell, commencing at one-third the length of shell from beak, and becoming very conspicuous in front.

Dorsal valve the more convex, the mesial fold beginning as a depression just below the beak, and becoming very prominent on lower half of shell. Surface marked by nine or ten strong angular plications on each valve, of which three are depressed in the sinus, and four are elevated on the mesial fold, the two central ones being much the more prominent; the plications are crossed by numerous regular thread-like striae. The entire surface is minutely papillose. (Hall.)

Formation and Locality.—Found in the Niagara strata east of the city of Louisville, Ky. There it is, however, extremely rare, and the few specimens found are not well preserved, and show, besides, that the condition of our Niagara ocean did not favor their development, which appears to have been poor. Numerous, originally well developed, and afterwards well preserved specimens of this species come from Waldron, Indiana. In that locality the Niagara sea must have afforded conditions most favorable to the development of its rich molluscan fauna. If we compare this species with its European congener, we find our shell more robust and larger, and its surface is marked by fewer and stronger plications; while the transverse striae are a little finer and less distant, and the sinus is much deeper and more abrupt. The figures on plate 32 are copied from Hall's 28th Report. My own specimens from our locality were not sufficiently preserved to be used for figures.

Genus Ambocoelia. Hall.

Shell bivalve, inequivalve, equilateral, plano-convex or concavo-convex; valves articulated by teeth and sockets; cardinal line equalling the greatest width of the shell. Area common to both valves; foramen triangular, extending also to the area of the dorsal valve. Dorsal valve flat, depressed convex or concave; cardinal process bifurcate. The foveal plates are straight, longitudinal, pointed at their inner extremities, and from their center on the outside extends a callosity curving around the dental sockets, which open towards the cardinal line. Muscular impressions four, and distinctly marked in the middle of the valve or below. Ventral valve arcuate, with or without a distinct sinus;

beak arching over the area; dental lamellae strong, extending in short, obtuse teeth. The impressions of the cardinal muscles form two semi-oval pits near the middle of the concavity between the beak and base of the shell. Surface very finely cancellated by obscure, radiating striae and fine concentric lines of growth. Shell-structure fibrous or fibro-punctate; luster pearly. The typical species is Ambocoelia umbonata of Conrad.

Ambocoelia umbonata. Conrad.

Plate XVII., figures 25 and 26.

Orthis umbonata, Conrad. Jour. Acad. Nat. Sci., Phil., Vol. 8.
Orthis umbonata (Conrad), Hall. 10th Rep. on State Cab., p. 167—1857.
Ambocoelia umbonata, Hall. 13th Regent's Rep., p. 71—1860.
Orthis nucleus, Hall. Geol. Rep. 4th dist., pp. 180 and 181.
Ambocoelia nucleus, Hall. 13th Regent's Rep., p. 71.
Ambocoelia umbonata, Hall. Pal. N. Y., Vol. 4, p. 259—1867.

Shell very small, plano-convex, sub-circular; length and width in our specimens about equal; hinge-line equal to the greatest width of the shell; cardinal extremities either obtuse-angular or rounded.

Ventral valve gibbous, with the umbo extremely elevated, and a comparatively large incurved beak; mesial sinus distinct, extending from the beak to the front; it is shallow and rounded at the bottom; its margins are also rounded and not defined; the cardinal area is rather large in proportion to the small size of the shell; its margins are sharply defined; it is strongly concave, and has a large triangular fissure in its center; the beak is prominent and strongly incurved into the upper portion of the foramen.

Dorsal valve semi-elliptical, depressed convex in the upper central portions, concave below the middle and at the sides; apex scarcely elevated above the hinge-line; area very narrow and almost linear; there is no indication of any kind of a mesial fold.

Surface marked by very fine radiating and concentric striae, the latter sometimes becoming crowded, lamellose and imbricating towards the front of the valves. In the shells of our rocks these surface-markings are not visible, they became obliterated by the silicification of the specimens.

Formation and Locality.—Occurs in the rotten hornstone of the Devonian formation, in Jefferson county, Ky., and is mainly found in some washes east of the city of Louisville, where it occurs in great abundance, but of considerably smaller size than eastern specimens of the same species.

Genus Athyris. McCoy.

Athyris, McCoy. Carb. foss. Ireland—1844.
Etymology: a, without; *thuris*, a small door, in allusion to the absence of a deltidium or door.

Shell variable in shape; valves unequally convex, with or without a mesial sinus and fold; articulated by teeth and sockets. Beak of ventral valve incurved, usually overlying and in contact with beak of the dorsal valve, and perforated by a foramen, or, when old, the foramen fully concealed. In the interior of ventral valve the dental plates are fixed to and along the sides of a longitudinal prominence or convex arch-shaped place, which extends to less than a third of the length of the shell, with its narrow end fitting into the extremity of the beak, and its lateral diverging edges to bottom of valve. The interior of the dorsal valve is partly divided by a large, deep, longitudinal septum, which extends from the extremity of the umbo to about two-thirds of the length of the shell, supporting at its origin the hinge-plate, which is divided into two portions by a narrow, gradually widening channel. To the socket ridges are affixed the spiral cones, the extremities of which are directed towards the lateral margins of the shell; on either side of the septum are seen two muscular scars formed by the adductor.

Athyris vittata. HALL.

Plate XVI., figures 25-32.

Athyris vittata, Hall. Thirteenth Rep. on State Cab., p. 89—1860.
Compare Athyris concentrica; A. spiriferoides.
Athyris vittata, Hall. Pal. N. Y., Vol. IV., page 289, plate 46—1867.

Shell sub-circular or sub-quadrate; gibbous; hinge-line short, with cardinal extremities rounded; front conspicuously sinuate.

Ventral valve gibbous above, more convex than dorsal valve; umbo prominent; the beak incurved and truncated in the plane of the longitudinal axis by a round foramen; curving very abruptly to the cardinal and lateral margins; the center, marked by a mesial sinus which extends nearly or quite to beak; it is shallow, deepening and widening towards the front; its margins are not defined but rounded and coalesce with the surface of the valve; it has a considerable basal extension, which is abruptly bent upwards and fits into a corresponding indentation of the other valve. Dorsal valve a little less gibbous than the ventral one; sides regularly curving from the umbo; about the middle of the valve an elevation commences, which increases towards the front, where it is of considerable height, thus forming a conspicuous mesial fold; the beak is strongly incurved into the other valve below its beak,

Surface marked by regularly imbricating lamellose lines of growth, which, on the surface of well preserved specimens are finely crenulate on their edges and the intermediate spaces striate. In most of the specimens found the surface is entirely smooth, with the exception of a small strip around the lateral and basal margins, where the lines of growth are not obliterated by the silicification.

Formation and Locality.—Found in great abundance and in well preserved specimens in the Corniferous limestone at and around the Falls of the Ohio, in Kentucky and Indiana. In some washes of the fields around Charlestown the ground is, after some hard rains, literally covered with these pretty little shells. This species bears in its outlines the greatest resemblance to Athyris concentrica of Europe, with which it is undoubtedly nearly related, but it may be easily distinguished from that species by not having the fine concentric lines which are so conspicuous in the European species. From Athyris spiriferoides it differs partly in shape, and, according to Prof. Hall's statement, mostly in internal features. Specimens are found showing the internal spiral coils splendidly preserved. The figures 25 and 31, on plate 16, do not show plainly enough the round foramen or perforation in the beak of the ventral valve.

Genus Atrypa. Dalman.

Atrypa, Dalman. Vet. Acad—1827.
Etymology: a, without; *trypa*, a hole. Dalman supposed that this shell had no foramen beneath the beak, which it has; A is, therefore, a misnomer.

Shell inpunctate and fibrous ; surface often or usually ribbed, and often furnished with imbricating lines of growth, often produced into foliaceous expansions ; valves articulated by teeth and sockets ; the ventral valve often depressed in front, with or without a mesial sinus ; its beak incurved and perforated at the apex by a minute foramen, which is sometimes bounded in front by a deltidium. Dorsal valve convex and often very ventricose, with or without a mesial fold ; the hinge-plate divided and supporting two large conical spires, which are directed into the hollow of the dorsal valve.

Atrypa aspera. SCHLOTHEIM.

Plate XIV., figures 1 to 11.
List of synonyms, see Hall's Pal. of New York, volume 4, page 322.

Shell of medium size ; sub-circular or oval, moderately convex ; length and width almost equal ; hinge-line shorter than width of shell ; cardinal extremities rounded ; lateral margins gently curved ; basal margin somewhat more arcuate in some specimens, while in others the curvature is less. The central part of the base is, in some shells, slightly extended, while in others this feature does not exist. Ventral valve depressed convex, gently and regularly curving from beak to base ; lateral margins slightly elevated over adjacent portion of valve ; beak moderate and incurved over umbo of opposite valve.

Mesial depression broad but very shallow, and not extending back beyond the basal third of the valve ; in some instances no depression is observable.   Dorsal valve more or less convex, according to age; in young shells nearly flat, in old ones, on the contrary, even gibbous.   Mesial fold only faintly indicated in very old specimens; in all others not the slightest trace of it is visible.   Surface marked by strong angular plications, which increase towards the margins by bifurcation, and by lamellose, imbricating concentric striae, which give the shell a rugose appearance.

This species is easily distinguished from its congener, Atrypa reticularis, by its stronger radii, and by its rugose surface ; also by its smaller size ; its largest specimens seldom exceed in length and width one-half of cardinal dimensions of the larger A. reticularis.

Formation and Locality.—Found in the upper strata of the Devonian limestone, in Jefferson county, Ky., and in Clark county, Indiana. The steep banks on the Indiana side of the Ohio river, opposite the Falls, have furnished a considerable number of very fine specimens of this species. It is a peculiar appearance, that in the rotten hornstone of those banks, the ventral valves of this species occur very abundantly, weathered out and silicified, while very seldom a single dorsal valve is found. I have, for instance, collected there more than twenty-five single ventral valves, but did not find a single dorsal one. In some of the specimens there found, both valves are perfect and at the same time separate, showing exquisitely the interior arrangement of the shell.

Atrypa calvini. N. SP.

Plate XXXII., figures 64, 65 and 66.

Shell below medium size ; sub-circular or sub-elliptical ; moderately convex ; hinge-line less than greatest width of shell ; cardinal extremities rounded or forming a very obtuse angle; width greater than length.   Surface plicated.

Ventral valve depressed convex ; greatest convexity below the umbo, from where it slopes very gently toward the cardino-lateral margins; both margins of the valve, from the cardinal extremities down to the front of the mesial extension, are abruptly and prominently turned downward, forming a flange of considerable size in proportion to the shell, and establishing on the valve two lateral depressions, which are separated from the sinus by its elevated margins ; the sinus begins at the beak, is well defined, curves regularly and gently towards the front, where it deflects abruptly upward, and forms a large quadrilateral extension, which fits in a corresponding indentation in the base of the dorsal valve ; beak prominent and elevated above the beak of the other valve; only slightly arched, and having a small, round perforation in the apex.   Dorsal valve more convex, almost gibbous ; greatest convexity at the middle of the valve, from where it slopes abruptly to the lateral basal margins ; the mesial fold is well defined from beak to base, becoming prominent at the front ; beak very small and incurved into the fissure of the opposite valve ; umbo almost depressed.

Surface is marked by strong, rounded plications. The sinus is bounded by a strong rib on each side; this rib bifurcates below the umbo, and the branch next to the sinus drops into it, and at the front coalesces with the elevated flange of its extension; another rib starts in the bottom of the sinus in front of the umbo, and extends to the termination of the sinus, having sometimes bifurcated at about the middle of its length. The mesial fold has generally two plications on its summit and one on each of its lateral slopes, but the top ribs are often increased by bifurcation before they reach the front. On each side of the mesial fold and sinus there are about five or six plications, of which only two reach the apex; the others were added, partly by bifurcation, partly by interpolation. Other surface-markings are not visible.

Formation and Locality.—Found in the Niagara group in the quarries east of the city of Louisville, Ky. Although rare, some very fine specimens may be seen in some of the Louisville collections. This species has in its general outline some resemblance to Rhynchonella whitii, of the Niagara rocks from Waldron, Indiana, but it differs from it by its peculiar plications, and by the marginal flange of its ventral valve, which two features are sufficient to distinguish it at the first glance from that species. A still greater resemblance has it to Atrypa nodostriata, as figured by Prof. Hall in Pal. of Ohio, Vol. 2, plate 7, figures 12, 13 and 14, and described in same volume, page 133. Differences between these figures and our shells exist only in one or two minor points, which are easily accounted for by the fact that the Ohioan illustrations were made from an exfoliated cast, while my specimens are perfect shells. In consequence of this great resemblance, which amounts almost to indentity, I placed my shells, at first, in the species of A. nodostriata. But when I examined Prof. Hall's original description and figures of that species, in Pal. N. Y., Vol. 2, page 272, and plate 56, figures 2a-n, I could not identify my specimens by either. It appears to me that the description and illustrations in the New York Report are entirely different from those of the Ohio Report. By the New York description and figures the species is established. The Ohio shell, which is only an exfoliated cast, belongs, undoubtedly, to one and the same species with my specimens, but not to Atrypa nodostriata of the New York Report. For these reasons I have to establish a new species for the reception of my specimens and the cast figured in the Ohio Report, and I name this species in honor of Prof. Samuel Calvin, of Iowa City, Iowa, who ranks as scientist with the foremost of this country, and whose labors in Geology and Palæontology have greatly contributed to the wonderful progress made by those sciences in the latter half of the present century.

Atrypa ellipsoida. N. SP.

Of this beautiful shell I have two specimens in my collection, and if I am not mistaken, I have seen one or two in some other cabinets. It took me some time before I could come to a conclusion, whether to leave it with Atrypa reticularis, which it resembles in every feature, except the form, or to place it into a new species. I have decided to take the latter course, and I hope future developments in regard to this shell will prove my decision to be correct. The description of this new species is as follows:

Shell, in proportion to the common size of our A. reticularis, rather small; longitudinally sub-elliptical, the shell forming almost a regular ellipsoid; length about one and one-half its width, while its depth, measured at the points of greatest convexity, equals the width; hinge-line short and sloping from the beaks with a forward deflection to the cardinal extremities, which are rounded ; lateral margins slightly curved or almost straight; basal margin strongly curved and sometimes even forming a pointed basal extremity.   Surface covered with plications.

Ventral valve less convex than the other; greatest convexity at the umbo, from which it slopes in a gentle curve to the front, and to the basal half of the lateral margins, but more rapidly, almost abruptly, to the cardino-lateral margins.   The umbo is prominent, and the beak somewhat elevated above, but incurving closely upon the umbo of opposite valve.   No hinge-area nor a perforation in the beak are visible.   The dorsal valve is more gibbous, it slopes in a regular, light curve to the base, but in a considerably stronger curve to the lateral and cardinal lines ; its umbo is prominent, and its beak is closely incurved into the opposite valve.   It is only near, almost at the base, where the dorsal valve shows a faint elevation, indicating a mesial fold, and the ventral valve a slight impression in place of a mesial sinus.   The dimensions of an average-sized specimen are: length, nine-tenths of an inch ; width and depth, six-tenths of an inch.

Formation and Locality.—In the Corniferous limestone at the Falls of the Ohio, on the Indiana shore of the river.

Atrypa reticularis.   Linnaeus.

Plate XIV., figures 12 to 23, and Plate XV., figure 1.   -
Atrypa reticularis, Linnaeus. 'Syst. Nat. ed. XII., p. 1132—1767.
Atrypa reticularis, Hall. Pal. N. Y., Vol. IV., p. 316—1867.
See list of synonyms in last cited report.

Shell large, sub-circular or ovoid, convex-concave, but mostly plano-convex ; length and width almost equal, sometimes width a little greater than length; surface plicated; hinge-line less than width of shell ; cardinal extremities rounded, lateral margins gently and regularly curved ; basal margin forming a somewhat stronger curve, which is sometimes interrupted by a small extension of the mesial sinus, but oftener by a slight inflection, caused also by sinus. Dorsal valve very ventricose, sometimes gibbous, having greatest convexity either at the umbo or in front of it, from where it slopes abruptly to the cardinal and lateral margins, but more gently to the front.   In some shells there is a slight elevation in the center line of the valve from beak to base, indicating a kind of mesial fold, but in most specimens this feature does not exist; the umbo is prominent and regularly rounded ; beak strongly incurved into the fissure of the other valve.   Ventral valve depressed convex in the upper part near the umbo, but becoming concave on the sides and in front of it.   A broad shallow depression on both sides of the umbonal region extends from the cardinal line towards the front, where it connects with the mesial sinus ; the sinus begins at the middle of the valve and forms a slight extension in front.

In a few instances this extension bends abruptly upwards, and fits in a corresponding inflection in the dorsal valve ; beak moderate and closely incurved upon the umbo of the other valve, showing a slight, rounded perforation in the apex, which leads into the broad triangular fissure ; cardinal area scarcely visible. Surface ornamented by strong, rounded or sub-angular plications, which increase towards the margins by bifurcation as well as by interpolation, and by lamellose, imbricating concentric striae or lines of growth, which often give the shell a very rugose appearance, as may be seen in figure 1, plate 15. The size of the specimens in this species differs greatly among the individuals illustrated ; the larger may be considered as of maximum size, while the smaller are of average size.

Formation and Locality.—This species, together with Spirifera oweni, with which it is associated, belong to the most common fossils of the Corniferous limestone, at and around the Falls of the Ohio in Kentucky and Indiana. In the washes of the fields around Charlestown, Indiana, a collector can pick up, after some hard rains, in a day's hunt, more than a hundred fair specimens of this species; they are mostly silicified, and often contain the spiral coils, as may be seen in figures 18, 20, 21 and 22. There is a pretty little shell in the Niagara rocks, which is placed also in this species, though the difference in the exterior features of the Devonian and Silurian shells is so conspicuous, that nobody can overlook it. For what reason these two fossils are kept in the same species I can not understand, and I shall, therefore, separate the Niagara specimens from the Devonian, at least as a variety.

Atrypa reticularis, var. niagarensis. N. VAR.

Plate XXXII.; figures 5 to 8, and 44 to 47.

Shell small, at least below medium size ; longitudinally sub-elliptical or sub-ovate, plano-convex; hinge-line less than the width of the shell ; cardinal extremities rounded ; length somewhat greater than the width ; base regularly curved, sometimes slightly inflected in the center; lateral margins gently curved.

Ventral valve slightly convex in the umbonal region ; all around this and to the base there exists a slight depression, which forms at the front the mesial sinus; beak moderate and incurved upon the umbo of the other valve. In some specimens the sinus is produced beyond the front, and the extension, thus formed, often rapidly and abruptly bends upward, as may be seen in figure 7, plate 32; in others there is scarcely a sinus noticeable. Dorsal valve very ventricose or gibbous, sloping abruptly from the middle, where the greatest convexity is, toward the cardinal and lateral margins, but less abruptly towards the front. No mesial elevation is indicated, except in those specimens where the frontal extension of the ventral valve makes an abrupt upward turn ; here the dorsal valve is also deflected upward at the base and in the basal quarter. Surface covered by fine thread-like striae, which increase towards the margins by bifurcation; there are, also, fine concentric lines of growth.

Formation and Locality.—Found abundantly and as well preserved specimens in the Niagara rocks in Jefferson county, Ky., and in Clark county, Indiana. It differs from its Devonian cousin by its considerably smaller size, which seldom exceeds that of the specimens illustrated on plate 32, and also by the finer and elegant ornamentation of its surface.

Genus Cyrtia. Dalman.

Cyrtia, Dalman. Kongl. Vet. Acad. Handl.—1827.
Etymology: Kyrtia, a fishing basket.

This genus includes certain spiriferoid forms, possessing semi-conical or semi-pyramidal ventral valves, high, flat areas, with a narrow fissure closed by a convex pseudo-deltidium. Some of the species have a round perforation in the upper part of the pseudo-deltidium; but this feature is not constant; it may be present or absent, and has not been considered of generic significance. The types of Dalman's genus, Cyrtia, are C. exporrecta and C. trapezoidalis, which are now considered identical. In 1858, Mr. Davidson separated several species, which were then classed with Cyrtia, from it, because they did not correspond with the types in several important points, and placed these in the genus Cyrtina. Both genera differ in the shell structure, which in Cyrtia is impunctate, while it is punctate in Cyrtina. The dental plates of the ventral valve in Cyrtia are similar to those of Spirifera, while those in the ventral valve of Cyrtina are greatly different and show a peculiar modification.

Cyrtia exporrecta. WAHLENBERG.

Plate XXVII., figures 6, 7, 8 and 20.

Cyrtia exporrecta, Wahlenberg. Nova. Acta. Regiae. Soc. Sci., Vol. 8, Niagara group—1821.
Spirifera (Cyrtia) *trapezoides.* Hall. 24th Rep. N. Y. State Museum, p. 183—1872.
Cyrtia trapezoides, Hall. 27th Rep. N. Y. State Museum, pl. 9, figures 19, 20 and 21—1875.

Shell below medium size, pyramidal when resting on the dorsal valve; hinge line longer than the greatest width of the shell, but sometimes a little less. Cardinal extremities mostly acute, sometimes obtuse, but never rounded. Surface smooth without plications. Ventral valve regularly pyramidal, forming at the apex an almost right-angle triangle. Mesial sinus extending from apex to front, where it forms a medium-sized quadrilateral extension, well defined, but shallow and rounded or flattened in the bottom, and rather narrow in front. Cardinal area greatly elevated, sharply defined in its margins, more or less concave, being mostly vertical, but sometimes leaning a little either to the front or rear. Beak arching over a high but very narrow fissure, which is generally closed, and shows a foramen a little above the middle, as may be seen in figure 35, plate 34.

Dorsal valve semi-elliptical, depressed ventricose; greatest convexity about the middle, from where it slopes with a gentle curve to the front and sides, but flattened at the cardinal angles; mesial fold well defined, extending from beak to front, low and flattened, or even depressed in the middle; beak incurved over a very narrow or linear area.

Surface marked by fine radiating striae, which increase in size and distance from apex to front; there is neither bifurcation nor interpolation of striae.

Size of this species is somewhat variable; a specimen of average size has the following dimensions: length, six lines; height, seven lines, and width, nine lines and one-half. In figure 6, plate 27, the dorsal valve is represented with rounded cardinal angles, which is a mistake, caused by defects in the specimen copied. The angles should be obtuse.

Formation and Locality.—Occurs in the upper strata of the Niagara formation, in the quarries east of the city of Louisville, Ky. It is not very rare, though well preserved specimens are seldom found.

Cyrtia exporrecta, var. arrecta. HALL.

Plate XXVII., figure 21, and plate XXXIV., figure 35; plate XXXII., figures 60 and 61.

Spirifera (Cyrtia) exporrecta, var. arrecta, Hall. 24th Rep. N. Y. State Museum, page 183—1872.
Cyrtia trapezoidalis, var. arrecta, Hall. 27th Rep. N. Y. Museum, pl. 9, figures 22 and 23—1875.

This shell resembles in most important points the preceding species, from which it, however, differs in the following features:

1. The cardinal area of its ventral valve is more elevated, narrower in its base, and never curved, but always straight, and generally leaning a little towards the front. In several specimens before me, the cardinal area shows, even in its upper part, a marked convexity, the beak curving really a little into the mesial sinus; but this feature may be the consequence of distortion, though the shells in question do not show any indications of being subjected to any compression or other violence.

2. The excess of its height over its length is in these specimens considerably greater than in the foregoing species.

3. Its mesial sinus appears to be somewhat more angular, and proportionably deeper than that of Cyrtia exporrecta.

It is obvious that specimens exist which may, with equal right, be placed in either species, but usually the species are easily separated.

Formation and Locality.—Found associated with the former in the upper strata of the Niagara formation, in the quarries east of the city of Louisville, Ky. Is rather rare.

Genus Cyrtina. Davidson.

Cyrtina, Davidson. Monog. Brit. Carb. Brachiopoda—1858.
Etymology: Kyrtia, a fishing basket.

Shell small and resembling that of Spirifera in its general form. Shell structure punctate. Valves very unequal; ventral valve elevated and pyramidal in shape; area very high, with a long narrow foramen, closed by a pseudo-deltidium; dental lamellae converging from margins of foramen, and uniting to form a mesial plate or septum, which divides the cavity of the ventral valve into two compartments. Dorsal valve nearly flat or moderately convex. Spires well developed, and resembling those of Spirifera and Spiriferina. The genus Cyrtina is closely allied to Cyrtia, of Dalman, and Spiriferina, of D'Orbigny, and has, also, near relationship with the genus Spirifera.

Cyrtina crassa. Hall.

Plate XIII., figures 21, 22, 23 and 24.
Cyrtina crassa, Hall. Pal. N. Y., Vol. IV., p. 267, pl. 27—1867

Shell depressed pyramidal, semi-elliptical in a dorsal view; hinge-line about equal to greatest width of shell, with the extremities slightly rounded; surface plicate; shell of medium size.

Ventral valve depressed pyramidal, convex regularly arched from beak to front, and also from sinus to margins of cardinal area; sinus broad and rounded in bottom; beak extended and slightly incurved over area, which has a height equal to one-half the width of shell, and which is almost straight in its lower half, and regularly curved in the upper part; fissure prominent, twice as high as wide in the base.

Dorsal valve slightly convex, little curved from front to rear or in lateral direction; flat or even a little concave at cardinal-extremities; mesial fold broad, moderately elevated, rounded on top and strongly defined; cardinal area linear.

Surface marked on each side of the mesial fold and sinus by about four strong, low, rounded plications, which are crossed by fine, thread-like concentric striae, and a few imbricating folds. (Hall.) Size of the only specimen in my possession is as follows: length, nine lines; width, fourteen and one-half lines; and depth, nine lines and one-half.

Formation and Locality.—Occurs in the Corniferous limestone around the Falls of the Ohio, but is exceedingly rare. So far as I know, only three specimens of this species were ever found; two of them belonged to the cabinet of the late Dr. James Knapp, and the third one was found by myself; it is copied on plate 13,

Cyrtina hamiltoniae. HALL.

Plate XIII., figures 4 to 12.

Cyrtia hamiltonensis, Hall. Tenth Rep. on St. Cab., p. 166—1857.
Cyrtia hamiltonensis, Billings. Dev. Foss. of Can. West., p. 263—1861.
Compare *Cyrtia acutirostra*, Shumard, Geol. Rep. Missouri, part 1, p. 204—1854.
Cyrtina hamiltonensis, Nicholson. Pal. of Ontario, p. 83—1874.
Cyrtina hamiltoniae, Hall. 24th Rep. N. Y. St. Mus., p. 198—1872.

Shell small, more or less triangular, sub-pyramidal; hinge-line equal to greatest width of shell; proportions of length, width and depth variable, but frequently width is equal to length of ventral valve, and height of area is equal to length of dorsal valve. Surface plicate.

Ventral valve quadrilateral in outline, obliquely sub-pyramidal, most prominent at beak, which is very variable in elevation, and straight or a little arched over cardinal area, and not unfrequently attenuate and distorted or turned to one side; mesial sinus wide and strongly defined, rounded or sub-angular in bottom; area variable, large and elevated, plane or arcuate in different degrees, with its lateral margins angular, distinctly striate in both directions; fissure narrow, closed by a convex, pseudo-deltidium, which is perforated above by an oval foramen. Dorsal valve depressed convex, with a broad, more or less prominent mesial fold, which is bounded by broader furrows than those between the plications, and is sometimes extremely elevated in front; beak scarcely rising above hinge-line; area narrow, almost linear, but quite distinct.

Surface marked by about six to eight (rarely one or two more) simple, rounded plications on each side of mesial fold or sinus, and these are crossed by very fine concentric lines of growth, which, at intervals, become crowded and sub-imbricate, especially towards margins of shell. The finer surface-marking is minutely granulose or papillose and shell structure distinctly punctate. In some of the larger individuals there is an obscure elevation on each slope of sinus, resembling an obsolete plication. The longitudinal medium septum extends for more than half the length of the ventral valve, and is continued into the cavity beneath pseudo-deltidium. These features are shown in casts and in transverse sections of valve. The dorsal valve shows a double or bilobed cardinal process with the strong crural bases supporting spiral arms, which are directed into the two compartments of the ventral valve, and, making numerous turns, terminate in the rostral part of the shell.

Formation and Locality.—This species is found in the Hamilton group in different localities. At Widder Station, in Canada West, it occurs in great abundance, and in most perfectly preserved specimens. In the Corniferous group around the Falls of the Ohio it is also somewhat abundant in good but silicified specimens.

Cyrtina hamiltoniae, var. recta. HALL.

Plate XIII., figures 13 to 16.

Cyrtina hamiltonensis, var. recta, Hall. Pal. N. Y., Vol. IV., p. 270—1867.

Prof. Hall separates this shell from the species Hamiltoniae, and makes a variety of it, which is based upon two points: first, upon the plane, flat area and straight beak, and second, upon the angular plications. If only the extreme forms were in existence, those points would suffice to maintain the new variety; but inasmuch as the species Cyrtina hamiltoniae is very variable in shape, we find individuals which gradually lead from one form to the other. Three groups may be distinguished among these shells; in the first we find specimens with very arcuate or concave cardinal area, such as shown in figure 11, plate 13; in the second group the cardinal area is only slightly curved near the beak, and the latter is always somewhat twisted or turned to one side; and in the last group we find the forms, separated by Prof. Hall from the main species, and put in the variety recta. In these shells the cardinal area is always plane or flat, and leaning generally towards the front, and the beak is without any curvature. Intermediate forms connect the first with the second group, and others lead from the second to the third group.

Formation and Locality.—Found associated with the preceding species.

Genus Meristella. Hall.

Meristella, Hall. 13th Regent's Report—1860.

Etymology: a diminutive of Merista.

The shells of this genus are oval, ovoid or sub-orbicular, elongate or rarely transverse; valves unequally convex, with or without a median fold or sinus; beak of the ventral valve often with a circular foramen and incurved over the umbo of the dorsal valve. Area none; valves articulating by teeth and sockets; surface smooth or with fine concentric lines of growth, and with very fine, indistinct or obsolete radiating striae.

The interior of the dorsal valve is marked by the presence of a strong hinge-plate or cardinal process, and from the base of this proceeds a thin, longitudinal septum, which often extends for half the length of the valve. The interior of the ventral valve shows a triangular fissure below the beak, which joins a semi-circular perforation at the apex. At the base of this fissure are two strong teeth, which extend in thickened or slender plates to bottom of cavity, and curve around upper part of the muscular area, which is broadly triangular or ovate. There is sometimes a thickening of the shell at the base of the rostral cavity, which abruptly limits the muscular impression; but there is neither septum nor rudiment of one as in Merista,

Meristella nasuta. Conrad.

Plate XV., figures 2 to 8.

Atrypa nasuta, Conrad.   Ann. Rep. on Pal. N. Y., p. 18.
Meristella nasuta, Hall.   Thirteenth Rep. on St. Cab., p. 93—1860.
Meristella elissa, Hall.   Fourteenth Rep. on St. Cab., p. 100—1861.
Meristella nasuta, Hall.   Fifteenth Rep. on St. Cab., p. 160—1862.
Athyris clara, Billings.   Canadian Journ., p. 274—1860.
Athyris clara, Geology of Canada, p. 373—1863.
Meristella nasuta, Hall.   Pal. N. Y., Vol. IV., p. 299—1867.

Shell large, sub-oval, ovate or sub-rhomboidal; the greatest width near or a little below the middle; length equalling or slightly exceeding width. Both valves convex, the ventral one rather gibbous. A nasute or linguiform extension of the front in old shells.

Ventral valve exceeding the other one considerably in convexity; point of greatest curvature being a little above the middle, from where it slopes in strong curves towards the lateral margins and to the cardinal lines, but in somewhat gentler curves to the front.

Umbo extremely prominent; beak regularly rounded and closely incurved. The anterior portion of the valve is produced into a nasute or linguiform extension; no depression for a mesial sinus is noticeable. In young or half grown individuals no basal extension exists. Dorsal valve less convex than the opposite, moderately and regularly convex in young shell, becoming in old shells gibbous above, curving regularly to the sides, and often a little flattened at the baso-lateral margins; at about the middle of the length, or sometimes above, the central portion of the valve becomes more gibbous, and towards the front is abruptly elevated into a rounded prominent fold, corresponding to the linguiform extension of the opposite valve. The beak is moderately incurved, lying close beneath that of the opposite valve.

The general aspect of the surface is that of a smooth shell with a few concentric lines of growth; in perfect individuals, however, the entire surface is ornamented by very fine concentric lines, and usually by indistinct radiating striae, which are often more conspicuous in the partially exfoliated shell, and still more distinct in some of the casts. The interior of the ventral valve preserves the generic characters in a marked degree, in the open fissure beneath the beak, which is terminated by a sub-circular perforation; in the strong dental plates, and deeply marked muscular impression. The inner surface, surrounding the muscular impression is covered by radiating striae. The interior of the dorsal valve shows a strong cardinal process, with a shallow, spoon-shaped depression in center, margined by deep teeth sockets. The muscular area is elongate-ovate, broader above, and divided through the center by a thin elevated septum.

This shell is described by Mr. Billings, of the Canadian Geological Survey, under the name of Athyris clara, but, inasmuch as Mr. Conrad's name of Atrypa nasuta preceded that of Mr. Billings, his species has priority, while that of Billings must be dropped.

Both in general exterior, form and internal characters, this species bears much resemblance to Meristella (Atrypa) tumida of Dalman, but in Dalman's species there is a distinct sinus in the ventral valve, while the umbo is more gibbous, the beak larger and more incurved, and the entire shell is comparatively more ventricose. The muscular area in the ventral valve is of the same shape, but narrower than the prevailing form in our species.

Formation and Locality.—Found in the upper strata of the Devonian group at and around the Falls of the Ohio in Kentucky and Indiana. It is of rather rare occurrence, and fair specimens still more so.

Meristella unisulcata. Conrad.

Plate XV., figures 9 to 16.

Atrypa unisulcata, Conrad. Ann. Rep. on the Pal. of N. Y., p. 56—1841.

Rhynchonella unisulcata (Conrad sp.), Hall. Tenth Rep. St. Cab., p. 125—1857.

Atrypa unisulcata, referred with doubt to Meristella, and name Goniocoelia proposed in Fourteenth Rep. St. Cab., p. 101—1861.

Compare: Pentagonia peersii, Cozzens. Ann. of N. Y. Lyc., Vol. III., p. 158—1846.

Meristella unisulcata, Hall. Pal. N. Y., Vol. IV., p. 309, pl. L.—1867.

Shell of medium size, sub-trigonal, quadrilateral or sometimes sub-pentagonal in outline; wider in front, with the sides sometimes sloping from the beak, but in others the hinge-line is extended nearly straight, and the sides rectangular to it. A wide mesial depression on one side with prominent elevation.

Ventral valve, with a broad, deep mesial sinus, which occupies nearly whole width of valve, and is bounded on either side by an angular elevation, which extends from beak to baso-lateral angles. The portion of the valve, outside of limitation sinus, is abruptly inflected upwards or towards the dorsal valve, often nearly at right-angles. Umbo is prominent, and beak is incurved over umbo of dorsal valve.

Dorsal valve gibbous in the middle; the center occupied by a prominent mesial fold, from which the surface slopes abruptly to the lateral angles, becoming more or less concave within the lateral and cardino-lateral margins. The mesial fold is marked along the center by a single deep groove, which extends to the beak of the valve. Surface marked by fine concentric striae, and sometimes by strong imbricating folds; there are also slight indications of interrupted radiating striae. The specimens of our limestone are either exfoliated or silicified; in both cases the finer markings are obliterated. The interior of the ventral valve, specimens of which are found in an excellent state of preservation, shows a perforation in the beak, opening below into an angular space, which has been occupied by the beak of the other valve, and thence communicating with the main cavity of the valve. The base of the fissure is margined on each side by a strong tooth, which extends in strong dental plates to bottom of cavity, and these are often continued in a thickened ridge bordering the muscular impression. The imprints of the adductor muscles are opposite the base of the dental plates, and below and on either side are the imprints of the broad divaricator muscle. In dorsal valve, cardinal process is broad and strong ; crural bases somewhat widely diverging and center abruptly depressed. The teeth sockets are large, and supported by strong lamellar callosities, which extend along inner side of the valve nearly parallel to the exterior margin. The muscular imprints are divided by a low distinct septum. This shell presents considerable variation in its form and general aspect, though always preserving its unmistakable character. In young and half grown shells, where the hinge-line is but little extended, it has a general triangular form. When the hinge-line becomes extended, and the sides nearly straight, with a moderately curving base, it is quadrangular. Some specimens assume the shape of a hexagon, others of a pentagon. In some individuals there is a slight elevation in center of sinus, but this is of rare occurrence, oftener the sinus contains a central rounded depression, margined by a slight elevation, which extends from beak to front. The beak of the ventral valve is sometimes *not* closely pressed upon the dorsal umbo, but in most specimens is such the case, and oftentimes to such a degree that the apex is incurved into the groove of the mesial fold. On the dorsal valve we find two considerable elevations, one on each side of the mesial fold ; they start from the cardinolateral margins, near to which they have their maximum elevation, gradually decreasing until they disappear in the surface of the valve a little above its middle; their direction is not quite parallel to the mesial groove, but is deflecting outwards. (Copied from Hall's description, with many alterations of my own.)

Formation and Locality.—Found in the upper strata of the Corniferous group surrounding the Falls of the Ohio, in Kentucky and Indiana, where fractions of this species are pretty abundant in some localities, but fine and well preserved specimens of the whole shell, as well as of single valves, which are found, are exceedingly rare. My cabinet contains some exquisite examples of this species. The fossils of the Corniferous strata, from the neighborhood of the Falls, are, on the Indiana side of the river, generally more numerous, and in the average better preserved, than those found in Kentucky. The little town Charlestown, in Clarke county, Indiana, two or three miles off the river, is about the center of one of the richest fields of the Devonian formation, which has furnished a great many cabinets with very choice specimens. A day's rambling in the washes of the fields around Charlestown, after several days' hard rain, is a real treat to any geologist, and never fails to fill his basket with fine shells, beautiful corals, and sometimes, but not very often, with rare crinoids.

Genus Meristina. Hall.

Meristina, Hall. 20th Regent's Report—1867.
Etymology: Merista, a genus of shells; *inus*, implying resemblance.

The shells of this genus resemble in shape and general aspect those of Meristella ; they differ only from the latter by internal arrangement of the loops. The lamellae of the shells of this genus are united by a single loop only. This interior arrangement is observed in Meristina maria and M. nitida, both of the Niagara group. In neither of these species is there any indication of accessory lamellae, as in Athyris, nor evidence of the extension of the loop beyond a certain point. The simple character of the spires in these forms are of sufficient value to constitute a new genus, that of Meristina.

Meristina maria. HALL.

Plate XXIX., figures 7, 8, 9 and 10.

Meristella maria, Hall.   Trans. Alb. Inst., Vol. IV., p. 212—1863.
Meristina maria, Hall.   Pal. N. Y., Vol. IV., p. 299—1867.
Meristina maria, Hall.   28th Rep. N. Y. St. Mus., Mus. Edit., p. 159—1879.
Meristina maria, Hall.   11th Geol. Rep. of Ind., p. 299—1881.

Shell of large, at least of more than medium size, ventricose, broadly ovate or subquadrangular ; length and width usually equal ; greatest width at one third of length from base or front.   Ventral valve gibbous in the upper half, having a slight elevation from beak to middle of valve, where it becomes depressed and sinuate, and abruptly deflected upward into a linguiform basal extension, from the point of greatest convexity, which is a little above middle of valve; it slopes gently to lateral and basal margins, but more abruptly to the cardinal margins, at which the cardinal borders are inflected.   Umbo is prominent, and beak strongly incurved upon the umbo of other valve.   Dorsal valve gibbous, greatest convexity below umbo, from where it slopes abruptly to cardinal margins, but in a gentle curve to the lateral and basal margins ; a sub-angular ridge extends from beak to front, near which it increases rapidly in width and elevation, thus forming a prominent but undefined mesial fold ; umbo moderate, and beak strongly incurved under that of other valve.

Surface marked by strong, concentric lines of growth.   Interior of ventral valve marked by two strong diverging dental lamellae, which extend to near the middle, limiting a deep, triangular muscular cavity.

This species is most nearly related to Meristella (Merista) tumida of European authors, but is less rotund, while that species does not possess the peculiar flattening of the cardinal half of the ventral valve, and its accompanying subangular ridge. It differs from all other species of the Niagara and Lower Helderberg groups, but approaches in some characters to Meristella (Atrypa) crassirostrata of the Niagara group. From Meristina nitida, with which it is usually associated, it differs greatly, and is therefore easily distinguished.

Formation and Locality.—Found in the Niagara strata in the quarries east of the city of Louisville, Ky., where it is, however, somewhat rare, at least in well preserved specimens, while at Waldron, Indiana, it occurs in great abundance, and of great beauty and perfection.

Meristina nitida. DALL.

Plate XXXIII., figures 10 and 11.

Atrypa nitida, Hall.   Geol. of N. Y., Geol. Sur. 4th dist., Tab. of Org. Remains, p. 11—1848.
Atrypa nitida, Hall.   Pal. N. Y., Vol. II., p. 268, pl. 55—1852.
Merista nitida, Hall.   12th Rep. St. Cab. Nat. Hist., p. 78—1859.
Meristella nitida, Hall.   Trans. Alb. Inst., Vol. IV., p. 226—1863.
Meristina nitida, Hall.   Pal. N. Y., Vol. IV., p. 299—1867.
Meristina nitida, Hall.   28th Rep. N. Y. St. Mus., Nat. Hist. Edit., p 100—1879.
Meristina nitida, Hall.   11th Geol. Rep. of Indiana, p. 300—1881.

Shell, as found in the neighborhood of Louisville, of small size; those found at Waldron, Indiana, of medium size, sub-triangular, with a sinuate base and largely extended beaks; most of the shell only moderately convex, but some becoming very gibbous, even, in isolated instances, per-gibbous; lateral and basal margins broad and square, owing to the fact that in both valves the marginal borders inflect almost rectangularly. Only in few individuals do both valves slope regularly without inflection to their edges, and meet under an acute angle (see figures 10 and 11, plate 33). Ventral valve usually of equal convexity with dorsal, showing in its basal third a slight depression, which terminates in basal inflection or emargination; the beak is much elevated above and incurving over beak of the opposite valve.

Dorsal valve has no indication of a mesial elevation; its beak is strongly incurved into ventral valve. There are no surface-markings except a few concentric lines of growth.

Formation and Locality.—It occurs usually associated with Meristina maria in the Niagara strata east of the city of Louisville, Ky.; it is, however, not as rare as that species, but is found pretty abundantly and also in very small but well preserved specimens. Shells of this species from Waldron, Indiana, are often of more than double size of even our largest individuals. This species is easily identified, inasmuch as it differs considerably from all other species of the Upper Silurian formation. The shells figured are different from the usual forms.

Genus Nucleospira. Hall.

Nucleospira, Hall. Pal. N. Y., Vol. III., page 219—1859.

Etymology: nucleus, a kernel; *spira*, a spire, alluding to the internal spire of these shells.

Shell spheroidal or transversely elliptical, more or less gibbous or ventricose, furnished with internal spires, as in Spirifer. Hinge-line shorter than width of shell; cardinal extremities rounded. Valves sub-equal, articulating by teeth and sockets. Ventral beak extended beyond the dorsal, and beneath it a triangular depression or area, which sometimes terminates in a shallow, spoon-shaped pit, on each side of which, at the base, is a strong tooth. A narrow ridge or septum extends along the center of inner side of valve from beak to base.

Dorsal valve furnished with a strong, spatulate, cardinal process, which, rising vertically from cardinal margin, is closely grasped at its base by the cardinal teeth of other valve, and thence bending abruptly upwards, and expanding, is projected into the cavity of other beak, lying close upon under side of false area. This process is grooved or depressed in the center of the upper side, so as to leave between it and the arch of the ventral beak a narrow space for the passage of a pedicle, for protrusion of which a minute foramen is sometimes observed in beak. From the sides of this process, above the junction of teeth of other valve, and at the point where it bends upward, originate the brachial processes, which support the spires. A deep cavity beneath the cardinal process extends to dorsal beak, from which originates a thin elevated septum, running to base of shell. Muscular imprints confined to a narrow, oval space. Surface smooth; shell structure punctate, and, when perfect, covered with minute hair-like spines.

Nucleospira concinna. Hall.

Plate XXXII., figures 1, 2, 3 and 4.

Atrypa concinna, Hall. Geol. Rep. 4th Dist. of N. Y., p. 200—1843.
Nucleospira concinna, Hall. Twelfth Rep. on St. Cab., p. 25—1859.
Nucleospira concinna, Hall. Pal. N. Y., Vol. IV., p. 279—1867.

Shell small, depressed, sub-spheroidal, nearly circular in outline; width being usually a little greater than length; valves sub-equal. Ventral valve regularly convex, greatest convexity a little above middle, and curving regularly to the sides and front; umbo prominent; beak neatly pointed and incurved over apex of dorsal valve, leaving a space between which sometimes exposes the narrow area. There is usually a narrow depressed line from beak to base of valve; but this is often absent, or so faint as not to be readily observed. Dorsal valve regularly convex, sometimes gibbous, becoming a little depressed towards base; the greatest convexity a little above middle of valve. The hinge-line is about one-third and sometimes one-half as long as width of shell. Surface usually smooth or very finely papillose; but in perfect specimens the surface is covered by numerous fine setae, which are matted together, and the interstices being filled with clay, it has a rough appearance while under a lens; these setae give a finely striate aspect. Beneath the fine papillose surface the texture of the shell is minutely punctate.

Formation and Locality.—Found occasionally in the Corniferous limestone at and around the Falls of the Ohio, in Kentucky and Indiana. It is a rather rare shell.

Nucleospira elegans. HALL.

Nucleospira elegans, Hall. Pal. N. Y., Vol. III., p. 222—1859.

Shell sub-orbicular, wider than long. Lateral margins strongly curved, basolateral margins very slightly curved, almost straight. Central third of the base somewhat prolonged or produced, and straight. Ventral valve moderately convex, except in the umbonal region, which is somewhat gibbous. There is sometimes, on the elevated center, a flattened or faintly depressed mesial line from umbo to base; beak elevated above that of the opposite valve and closely incurved upon it. Area usually covered by the incurved beak, but sometimes visible. Dorsal valve depressed convex, but sometimes almost as convex as the ventral; more elevated in the umbonal region; beak small, strongly incurved beneath the beak of the opposite valve. Surface of the shell finely and beautifully punctate, and sometimes preserving remains of its former pilose covering. Some specimens of this species, showing the cardinal area, might be mistaken for Orthis.

Formation and Locality.—Occurs in the Niagara limestone east of the city of Louisville. A large specimen measures eight lines in width by seven in length, while a smaller one has a width of six lines by a length of five.

Nucleospira pisiformis. HALL.

Plate XXXIII., figures 7, 8 and 9.

Orthis pisum, Hall. Pal. N. Y., Vol. II., p. 250—1852.
Nucleospira pisiformis, Hall. Pal. N. Y., Vol. III.—1859.
Nucleospira pisiformis, Hall. Trans. Alb. Inst., Vol. IV., p. 226—1863.
Nucleospira pisiformis, Hall. 28th Regent's Rep., p. 160—1879.
Nucleospira pisiformis, Hall. 11th Geol. Rep. of Ind., p. 302—1881.

Shell small, sub-globose; valve nearly equal, each valve with as light depression down the center. Ventral valve somewhat more convex, and beak more elevated than in the dorsal. Area narrow, small, scarcely extending beyond width of beaks at their base. Surface marked by fine concentric striae, usually obscured by the covering of minute, hair-like spines, which, when removed, leave a punctate surface.

Formation and Locality.—Occurs abundantly at Waldron, Indiana, and rarely in the quarries east of Louisville; in the Niagara limestone of both places.

Genus Spirifera. Sowerby.

⸗*Spirifera*, Sowerby. Min. Couch., Vol. II.—1815.
Etymology: spira, a spire; *fera*, to bear.

Shell structure fibrous and impunctate ; form very variable, but typical; more or less three-sided or quadrate, sometimes oval or sub-circular. Hinge-line straight, mostly as long as, or longer than greatest width of shell, sometimes shorter. The cardinal angles sometimes obtusely rounded, more commonly produced and extended, sometimes greatly so. Surface usually with radiating ribs, or smooth or striated. Generally an elevated fold in one valve, and a corresponding sinus in the other. Valves articulated by teeth and sockets. Ventral valve the larger, with a more or less prominent beak, a well marked area and a triangular foramen, which is sometimes closed by a pseudo-deltidium. Dorsal valve with a narrow area, and a wide triangular foramen. Interior more or less occupied by two spirally rolled lamellae, forming two cones, the apices of which are directed towards the cardinal angles.

Spirifera acuminata. Conrad.

Plate VIII., figures 1 to 8.

Delthyris acuminata, Conrad. Ann. Rep. of Pal. of N. Y., p. 65—1839.
Spirifera acuminata, Conrad. Hall in 10th Rep. on State Cab., p. 135—1857.
Spirifera acuminata, Hall. Pal. N. Y., Vol. IV., p. 198, plate 29.

Shell large, ventricose, transverse, with the hinge-line usually less than width of shell ; cardinal extremities rounded or truncate, having a sub-elliptical or sub-quadrate outline ; mesial fold and sinus extreme. Surface plicated. Ventral valve variably convex on two sides, with a wide mesial sinus, which is well defined in the upper part, becomes wider and deeper and less distinctly defined in middle of shell, and is produced in front into a long triangular extension, curving abruptly from the greatest convexity to sides and cardinal angles ; umbo prominent, with the apex incurved over the wide triangular fissure ; area extending to cardinal angles, with margin rounded except towards the extremities.

Dorsal valve gibbous, highly elevated in middle into a strong angular mesial fold, and curving from sides of fold to margin of shell, except at the cardinal

angles, where it is a little flattened and projecting, so as to give a minute artic-
ulate appearance; summit of mesial fold regularly arcuate from beak to base:
apex lightly incurved over the narrow, nearly vertical area.

Surface on either side of the fold or sinus marked by from sixteen to twenty
plications, about four or five of which, nearest to the center, are dichotomous
from below the middle of their length; plications low and rounded above and
flattened below middle, those towards the margin very slender; first ten or
twelve ribs on each side of the fold or sinus occupy greater part of shell. The
entire surface is marked by delicate concentric striae, which are often crowded
into imbricating lamellose lines towards front of shell. In very perfect specimens these concentric striae are papillose or fimbriated by fine radiating striae.
These fine surface-markings, however, are usually nearly or quite obliterated.

The interior of ventral valve shows but a partial thickening of the shell in
rostral cavity; teeth are strong and short, dental plates spreading and margin-
ing the upper part of the ovate muscular area, which is broader above, and
sometimes very much resembles this feature in S. striatus.

The casts preserve strong and prominent marks of the muscular impressions,
and sometimes vascular markings outside of the muscular area, while in other
individuals the papillose ovarian markings are very distinctly preserved. In
the cast of the dorsal valve there are sometimes strong impressions of the oc-
clusor muscular markings, and the apex also show the striae of the cardinal
muscular attachment. (Hall.)

This species has some similarity with Spir. macrothyris, but is easily distinguished from this and all the other Spirifera of our strata by its extremely
elevated angular mesial fold and deep sinus, which are bounded by the dichotomous plications. The size of this species is very variable; it measures from one
inch to two and a quarter inch in width, and from three-fourths of an inch to
an inch and seven-eighths in length.

Spir. acuminata is considered by the European geologists, Dr. F. Roemer
and M. de Verneuil, as identical with the Spirifera cultrijugata of Europe;
but Mr. Davidson, the eminent English Palæontologist, has pointed out the
fact that the American species has bifurcating plications, which are not seen
in Roemer's figures of the European species, and also that the European shell
has less plications than the American. Here again the figures are used to determine the similarity and dissimilarity of two shells. The figures may not
be correct, or it is also possible that the specimen from which Mr. Roemer drew
his picture, like many of our species, did not show dichotomous ribs. Even
Mr. Conrad, who first described Spir. acuminata, did not mention the bifurcated
plications, showing that either his specimens did not possess them at all, or
only in such a faint condition that Mr. Conrad did not notice them. Mr.

Roemer's species is very rare in Germany, making it difficult to procure specimens showing the exact features of perfect shells. From these facts we must draw the conclusion that both species are either identical, or that one is only a variety of the other. In this case Mr. Conrad's species has the priority over Roemer's and Spir. acuminata would be maintained, even if its similarity with Sp. cultrijugata were admitted. Figures 7 and 8, plate 8, show a very fine internal cast of this species.

Formation and Locality.—Found abundantly and in good condition in the Devonian limestone of Kentucky and Indiana, around the Falls of the Ohio.

Spirifera atwaterana. S. A. MILLER.

Plate IX., figures 1 to 7.

Spirifer pennatus and *Spirifer ligus,* Owen. Geol. Rep. of Wisconsin, Iowa and Minnesota, p. 585, pl. III., figs. 8, 4 and 8—1852.

Spirifer pennatus, Hall. Geology of Iowa, Vol. I., Part II., p. 510, pl. 5—1858.

Spirifer atwaterana, S. A. Miller. Proc. Davenport Acad. Sci.—1878.

This species is generally known under the name of Spir. pennata; but this specific designation was used already in 1820 by Atwater for another Spirifera, and, therefore, another name had to be adopted for this shell. S. A. Miller, Esq., of Cincinnati, Ohio, named it *atwaterana.*

This species belongs to the large sized Spirifera; in width it is not exceeded by any other kind; it is very variable in form, from sub-globose to transverse and broadly triangular semi-circular, or semi-elliptical, sometimes inequilateral; hinge-line always more or less extended into wing-like expansions, resembling in this feature Spir. mucronata; valves mostly equally convex.

Ventral valve most convex in the middle and on the umbo; beak much elevated above the hinge-line, more or less pointed and slightly incurved. Mesial sinus strongly defined at margins, rapidly widening towards base, and produced in an angular extension in front. Area large and extending to cardinal extremities; concave and striated vertically and longitudinally; foramen large and open to apex, and forming an equilateral triangle.

. Dorsal valve also most gibbous in the middle and on the umbo; beak markedly incurved; valve curves from the point of the greatest convexity regularly to anterior and lateral margins, and is more or less compressed at cardinal angles; mesial fold is strongly elevated, sometimes a little flattened on top, and often sub angular towards front.

Surface marked by from fifteen to twenty-five, or even more simple, rounded plications on each side of mesial fold and sinus; central ribs are much stronger than lateral ones; of the former only about six to eight on each side reach apex, all others run out on the margins of the cardinal area. In well preserved specimens the entire surface is ornamented by slender radiating striae, which, however, are not visible in most specimens. Concentric lamellose, imbricating lines of growth are numerous in some specimens, while others show very few or even none at all.

Formation and Locality.—Found rarely, and seldom well preserved, in the upper strata of the Devonian limestone around the Falls of the Ohio, in Kentucky and Indiana.

Spirifera arctisegmenta. HALL.

Plate XII., figures 14 and 15.

Spirifer arctisegmentus, Hall. Tenth Rep. on State Cab.—1857.
Spirifer arctisegmenta, Hall. Descript. of New Pal. Fossils, p. 91—1857.
Spirifer arctisegmenta, Hall. Pal. N. Y., Vol. IV., p. 208, pl. 31.

Shell transversely semi-oval; length equal or less than one-third of width; hinge-line equal to greatest width of shell, and terminating in salient angles or mucronating points. Ventral valve the more convex; most convex at the umbo, from which it slopes regularly to anterior and lateral margins; mesial sinus angular and distinctly defined quite to apex of shell; beak not incurved; area flat and straight and a little inclined towards the front. The lateral view given of this shell in figure 15, plate 12, is incorrect, by showing the area concave and inclined towards the rear. Fissure narrow and open to apex.

Dorsal valve depressed convex, scarcely flattened towards the cardinal extremities; beak and central portion of the shell, together with the linear area, slightly incurved.

The surface is marked by from five to eight or nine angular plications on each side of the fold or sinus, which on the ventral valve are slightly curved towards the front, and of which only about three reach the beak, while the balance run out along the margins of the cardinal area, where they coalesce with an elevated ridge, which borders the area. The plications on the dorsal valve are pretty direct; fine, close, concentric, undulating striae mark the entire surface.

This shell may be distinguished from Sp. segmenta, as well as from other allied forms, by its larger and more angular, as well as less numerous plications, and in having a distinct linear ridge along margin of area of ventral valve; its foramen is likewise narrower, and its sinus deeper and more angular than in Spir. segmenta. (Hall.)

Formation and Locality—Found in the Corniferous limestone at and around the Falls of the Ohio in Kentucky and Indiana, where it is, however, of rare occurrence, especially in well preserved specimens.

Spirifera byrnesi. N. SP.

Plate X., figures 1-5, 31-34 and 36-39.

Shell sub-quadrate, semi-circular and gibbous in outline; hinge-line equalling greatest width of shell and terminating in salient angles. Surface plicate.

Ventral valve ventricose and only little more gibbous than other valve; regularly arcuate from beak to front; greatest convexity in the upper part a little above the middle, from where it curves regularly to the front and sides; beak much elevated above hinge-line, and slightly arcuate. Cardinal area high, concave, and extending to cardinal angles, where it never forms an acute angle, but shows always a height of from one-quarter to one-half of a line, a feature which is not sufficiently expressed in the figures on plate 10; mesial sinus sharply defined, forming a deep triangular groove, with an acute angle at the bottom, much produced in front; fissure of medium size.

Dorsal valve gibbous, with a greatly elevated mesial fold, which is edged in its upper part and rounded below; beak little elevated and slightly inclined over a narrow hinge-area. Surface marked by from eight to ten very prominent and angular plications on each side of the mesial fold and sinus, which are crossed by strong imbricating concentric lines of growth, showing more prominently in front than in upper portion of shell. Of the plications, the lateral ones do not reach to the beak, but run out on the margins of the cardinal area.

The dimensions of this species are as follows: it measures from one-half to three-fourths of an inch in length, and from three-fourths to seven-eighths of an inch in width; its width always exceeds its length.

This species takes an intermediate position between Spir. gregaria and Spir. varicosa; it is more transverse than the former, and less so than the latter; its umbo is less elevated and curved than that of gregaria, and more so than that of varicosa; its deeper and sharply angular sinus, and its more elevated fold, distinguish it from both of its relations. It is a well marked and easily recognized species.

Formation and Locality.—Found in the upper strata of the Devonian limestone around the Falls of the Ohio, in Kentucky and Indiana. Very fine specimens I found in considerable numbers in the quarries at Lexington, Indiana. I dedicate this species to Dr. R. M. Byrnes, of Cincinnati, Ohio, who devotes all his spare time to the study of geology and palæontology, and who greatly contributed to our knowledge of the Cincinnati fossil fauna.

Spirifera conradana. S. A. MILLER.

Plate VII., figures 11, 12 and 13.

Delthyris fimbriata, Conrad.   Jour. Acad. Nat. Science, Philadelphia, Vol. VIII., p. 263—1842.
Spirifera fimbriata, Conrad.   Billings in Canadian Jour., p. 259—1861.
Spirifera fimbriata, Hall.   Pal. N. Y., Vol. IV., p. 214, pl. 33.

Shell transversely sub-elliptical, gibbous; hinge-line less than width of shell ; cardinal extremities rounded.

Ventral valve gibbous in upper half, regularly curving to front and sides; sinus well defined, usually shallow and rounded, sometimes deep and angular, and much produced in front. Beak small and incurved over the area, which is high and concave, and extending about half the entire width of the shell; foramen often limited by a sharp elevated border, which appears to be a projection of the dental plates.

Dorsal valve gibbous, regularly convex on the sides, a little flattened at the cardinal extremities ; mesial fold abruptly elevated in the lower part, often but little elevated or scarcely defined in the upper part; beak small, slightly arched over the sub-linear area, which is somewhat concave.

Surface marked by from three to nine low, rounded, often obscure plications on each side of the mesial fold and sinus ; these are crossed by imbricating, lamellose striae, which are sometimes wide or distant, and often crowded. The concentric striae are studded with elongated nodes or tubercles, which are thus arranged in parallel bands, more or less contiguous, according to distance of the concentric striae.

The elongate tubercles may, perhaps, more properly be regarded as interrupted radiating striae, which, in the perfect condition of the shell, have, doubtless, extended in slender spines or setae ; they are termed by Mr. Conrad short longitudinal striae.

The cardinal area is strongly striated vertically. This species begins its existence, so far as we know, in the Oriskany sandstone, where it has been so rarely observed. It occurs in the Schoharie grit, and reaches its greatest dimensions in the Corniferous limestone, where it not seldom attains a width of nearly two inches by a length of an inch and a quarter. It is often found well preserved in the Hamilton formation, but does not here attain the size it has in the Corniferous limestone.   (Hall.)

The Sp. conradana is not found in strata younger than the Hamilton, but it is represented in later periods by forms showing great similarity to it.

Formation and Locality.—Under this heading I give only the places and groups in which the species in question is found in Kentucky. Sp. conradana is found in the Devonian limestone of Kentucky and Indiana, near and at the Falls of the Ohio, but is not abundant This species has been known ever since Mr. Conrad's first description of the same as Spir. fimbriata, but it can not retain its specific designation, inasmuch as Mr. Morton pre-occupied the name Spir. fimbriata, in 1836, for a different Spirifer of the Coal Measures. Conrad's first description of this species and its naming date only back to 1842. Mr. Morton's right to the name can not be disputed; Mr. Conrad's species must, therefore, be dropped. Mr. Miller has proposed the name "Conradana" as a substitute, which I hereby cheerfully accept. Mr. Miller named the species in honor of Mr. Conrad, former geologist of the State of New York.

Spirifera crispa, var. simplex. HALL.

Plate XVII., figures 36 and 37.

Spirifera crispa, var. simplex, Hall. 11th Rep. of Ind.—1881.

Shell small, semi-circular or semi-elliptical, more or less gibbous or ventricose; both valves about equally convex; hinge-line somewhat less than the greatest width of the shell; cardinal extremities obtuse or rounded. Surface plicate.

Ventral valve ventricose, with its greatest convexity about the middle of the valve, from where it curves regularly towards the anterior and lateral margins; mesial sinus well defined from apex to front, deep and angular in the bottom, and widening towards the front, where it forms a strong triangular projection; cardinal area high, but not defined in its margins, which are rounded, and gradually extend into the surface of the valve; foramen or fissure long and narrow; beak arched, but not incurved.

Dorsal valve nearly as ventricose as the other, having its greatest convexity about the middle of the valve, from where it curves regularly towards front and sides. Mesial fold well defined, strong and angular; beak small and curving over a linear area.

Surface marked on each side of mesial depression and elevation by two or three plications, of which only the first one near fold or sinus is mostly strong and well marked, while the others are either only slightly elevated or sometimes entirely obsolete. The whole surface of the shell is covered by strong, thread-like concentric striae.

These specimens are considerably smaller than those used by Professor Hall for his figures and description in the Indiana Report, which came from Waldron, Indiana. Even some slight differences exist between our Kentucky shells and those from Indiana, but these differences do not justify a further specific separation.

Formation and Locality.—Occurs in the upper strata of the Niagara formation, in the quarries east of the city of Louisville, Ky., where it is somewhat abundant, but well preserved specimens are rather rare.

Spirifera davisi. n. sp.

Plate XII., figures 1, 2, 3 and 4.

This shell was given to me by one of the collectors around the Falls of the Ohio as a Spirifera raricosta, with which it has some similarity, but from which it is easily distinguished by its form and surface-markings.

The shell is semi-circular or sub-quadrate and gibbous. Hinge-line equal or larger than the greatest width of the shell. Cardinal extremities acute and mostly somewhat acuminate. Surface strongly plicated.

Ventral valve considerably more gibbous than dorsal valve, regularly arcuate from beak to front; greatest convexity at or a little above middle, and curving gently to the sides and front, except at the cardinal angles, which are somewhat flattened; beak much elevated above that of the opposite valve, and arching over that fissure, but scarcely incurved. Cardinal area high and concave, and reaching to the cardinal extremities. Mesial sinus is broad and rounded and reaches quite to the apex. Dorsal valve gibbous, most convex in the middle, flattened or a little concave towards the cardinal extremities. The mesial fold is very prominent, rounded, and regularly arcuate; it has a faint impression extending from beak to middle of valve.

The beak is small and arched over the linear area. Surface is marked by six to eight rounded or sub-angular plications on each side of the mesial fold and sinus. The shell is smooth, with the exception of front part, which is marked by from five to seven strong concentric imbricating lines of growth, which reach to the cardinal angles, and which give to the shell its peculiar beautiful front view. Such imbricated front is only noticed in Spir. gregaria and in Spir. mucronata, in both of which it is less regular and less prominent. Interior of shell is unknown. The specimens so far found show a great similarity in form and also in size; they measure from one inch to one inch and a quarter in width, by from three-fourths to seven-eighths of an inch in length. This species is related to Spir. raricosta and to Spir. gregaria. From the former it differs in its greater number of plications; its somewhat acuminate cardinal extremities; its larger and more elevated hinge-area, and by its peculiar imbricated front. From Spir. gregaria it is distinguished by its larger size, by its smooth shell, by its greater width, and by its less prominent umbo, and also by its more marked imbricated front.

Formation and Locality.—Spirifera davisi is found associated with Spir. gregaria in the upper strata of the Devonian limestone in Kentucky and Indiana, in the neighborhood of the Falls of the Ohio; it is not abundant, and only found in a few limited localities, where it occurs in well preserved specimens I have named this species in honor of my friend and co-laborer, W. I. Davis, the author of "Kentucky Fossil Corals," who devoted his attention and study mostly to the fossil corals, in which the Falls of the Ohio and its surrounding quarries are so exceedingly rich.

Spirifera divaricata. HALL.

Plate XI., figures 6 to 11, and Plate XII., figures 5 to 11.'

Spirifer divaricatus, Hall. Tenth Rep. on the State Cab., p. 130—1857.
Spirifer venstus, Hall. Thirteenth Rep. on State Cabinet, p. 82—1860.
Spirifera divaricata, Hall. Pal. N. Y., Vol. IV., p. 213, plate 32.

Shell ventricose, somewhat rhomboidal or quadrilateral (looking upon the ventral valve). Dorsal valve semi-elliptical; hinge-line less than width of the shell; cardinal extremities obtuse or rounded; area large.

Ventral valve most convex above the middle, extremely arcuate from umbo to base; abruptly curving to the sides; beak abruptly arching over the area; sinus plicated, shallow above and becoming rapidly expanded below, with the margin undefined and terminating in a broad, triangular extension in front. Area high, flat below, but abruptly arcuate above, and reaching to the cardinal extremities; foramen large.

Dorsal valve regularly and strongly convex, with an angular mesial fold, which is narrow above and expands towards the front, with bifurcating plications; sides regularly curving and sometimes a little flattened towards the cardinal extremities. Area rather wide, with the beak and central portion of the valve arching over it. The surface is marked by numerous fine bifurcating rounded or sub-angular plications; mesial sinus having on each side a stronger plication, which bifurcates on one or both sides. At the beak there is a single plication in the bottom of the sinus, which sometimes continues simple nearly or quite to the base; while the accessions take place mainly from those on the sides of the depression, till they reach the number of ten, eleven or twelve within the limits of the sinus near the base. In a specimen of ordinary size, where the surface is well preserved, there are, sometimes, sixty and more plications with their divisions at the margin of the shell. In some specimens from the Corniferous limestone, where the surface is partially or entirely exfoliated, the bifurcating character of the striae is not observed, and in some specimens the plications appear to have been simple throughout. The plications are crossed by fine imbricating lamellose striae, which are abruptly arched backwards. (Plate 12, figure 11.) A cast of the ventral valve shows a large oval muscular area, which is deeply divided by a rounded median crest, and strongly striated on the lateral portion. (Hall.)

The shells represented on plate 12, figures 5 to 11, I was, at first, inclined to consider as specifically different from Sp. divaricata. They appeared more robust, and their plications were fewer and stronger. Instead of a simple bifurcation, as in divaricata, these specimens show some instances where a single plication divided towards the base into three and even four branches, forming a kind of fascicle, which are so characteristic in Spirifera camerata of the Coal Measures. The true character of the plications of these shells is not shown exactly in the drawings.

This shell, when well preserved, is one of the finest Spirifera of our palaeozoic fauna; it is easily distinguished from the others by its form, by its bifurcating plications, and by its sharp zigzag, concentric striae.

Its size differs from two to three inches in width, and from one and three-fourths to two inches in length, by a depth of one inch and one-eighth.

Formation and Locality.—Found in the Hamilton group and in the Corniferous limestone of Kentucky, around Louisville, and near Lebanon, Kentucky, where W. T. Knott, Esq., found some very fine specimens, which are figured on plate 11. This species is not very rare, though it is very difficult to procure good specimens.

Spirifera duodenaria. HALL.

Plate XII., figures 12, 13 and 16. ·

Delthyris duodenaria, Hall. Geol. Rep. 4th Dist. N. Y., p. 171, figure 5—1843.
Spirifer duodenaria, Hall. Catalogue in Rep. on State Cabinet.
Spirifera duodenaria, Hall. Pal. N. Y., Vol. IV., p. 189, pl. 27 and 28.

Shell transverse, semi-circular; hinge-line equal to greatest width of shell; cardinal extremities obtuse or acute, rarely acuminate; valves sub-equally convex; area very narrow. . Surface plicated.

Ventral valve moderately gibbous; arcuate, compressed towards the cardinal extremities. Mesial sinus of moderate width and depth; rounded or slightly flattened on the bottom; umbo prominent; beak small, neatly curved over a wide triangular fissure, and reaching to within half a line of the umbo of the opposite valve; area concave, sub-linear, a little wider on each side near the center.

Dorsal valve regularly convex, a little gibbous in the middle and flattened or sometimes slightly concave at the cardinal extremities. Mesial fold rather narrow, rounded, prominent and strongly defined, sometimes a little flattened on the middle. The surface is marked by six and rarely seven strongly rounded ribs on each side of the mesial fold or sinus. The ribs gradually decrease in size and prominence from the center; and the outer ones are often scarcely elevated in young or medium-sized individuals. The entire surface is marked by lamellose, concentric striae, giving a papillose or sub-fimbriate aspect at their junction; it usually happens, however, that the surface is smooth from partial exfoliation. (Hall.)

This species has usually a width of one inch to one inch and a quarter, and a length of one-half to three-fourths of an inch. Younger individuals, such as are figured on plate 12, are smaller in size, and generally contain less plications.

Formation and Locality.—This species is found in the Corniferous limestone of Kentucky and Indiana, around the Falls of the Ohio, but is very rare. During ten years of collecting I have found only two or three specimens, and these not even in very good condition.

Spirifera dubia. N. SP.

Plate XXXIII., figures 23 and 24.

This shell I found in the strippings of a quarry east of the city of Louisville, where the top rocks belong to the Devonian, and the lower strata to the Silurian; it is, therefore, impossible to state to which of these formations it belongs. It further has in form and outline great similarity with Spir. crispa, var. simplex, from which it, however, differs greatly in other points. Concerning this shell there is, therefore, doubt in regard to its formation, and also whether or not it should form a new species, and for these reasons I think it fully deserves its specific name.

Shell small, semi-circular or semi-elliptical and ventricose. Convexity of both valves almost equal; hinge line less than greatest width of shell; cardinal extremities rounded. Surface without plications.

Ventral valve ventricose, having its greatest convexity a little above the middle of the shell, from where it curves regularly and markedly to the anterior and lateral margins. Mesial sinus extends from beak to front, shallow in the upper part, deepening and widening towards the base; angular in the bottom, but its margins not at all defined; in front it forms a pretty strong triangular extension. Cardinal area elevated, with undefined rounded margins; beak arcuate, but not incurved over a high and narrow fissure.

Dorsal valve almost as convex as the other, having its greatest convexity a little above the middle, from where it curves regularly towards the front and sides. Mesial fold not at all noticeable on the umbo; little elevated and subangular towards the base; beak incurved over a narrow area.

Surface having not the least trace of plications, but covered by lamellose, imbricating, concentric striae, similar to those in Spir. var. simplex. Size of shell is three-eighths of an inch in length, and a little less than one-half of an inch in width.

Formation and Locality.—The formation from which it comes uncertain as above stated; found in a quarry east of the city of Louisville. This one specimen the only one so far known.

Spirifera euruteines. OWEN.

Plate VI., figures 1 to 7; 9, 11 to 17.

Delthyris (Spirifer) *euruteines*, Owen. Report of Geological Exploration in Iowa, Wisconsin and Illinois.
Spirifer euruteines, Owen. Geol. Surv. of Wisc., Iowa and Minn., p. 586, Tab. III., figs. 2 and 2a, and 6, 6a, b.
Spirifera euruteines, Hall. Pal. of N. Y., Vol. IV., page 209, plate 31, figures 14 to 19.

This species was first described and figured by Prof. David Dale Owen, in his report on the Geological Survey of Wisconsin, Iowa and Minnesota, from specimens found on Pine creek, Iowa. Owen states that this is the same shell found in great abundance in the hydraulic limestone at the Falls of the Ohio, near Louisville. The figures given by him in said report can not belong to one and the same species; those marked 2 and 2a are by far too large and robust; the cardinal view in figure 2 measures, between the cardinal extremities, two and one-fourth inches, while the breadth of euruteines was given by Owen to be one and a half inches. The figures 6, 6a, 6b, must be taken as the correct representation of Owen's Sp. euruteines.

Prof. Hall described in Pal. N. Y., volume 4, pages 209, 210 and 211, Sp. euruteines and Sp. euruteines, var. fornacula; the difference of these consists only in the greater curvature of the cardinal area in fornacula. Owen's side view of euruteines shows the cardinal area considerably concave; the curvature equal through the whole area from hinge-line to the apex of the beak; while Hall's side view of euruteines marks the cardinal area as straight, with the exception of a little offset near the beak. Among Hall's figures no side view is given of fornacula; we are, therefore, left uncertain as to the amount of curvature required to place a euruteines among the var. fornacula. The hinge-area in this species is exceedingly variable; in some it is straight, and leans forward, in others it is also straight, but leans backward; then, again, it leans forward but is curved a little near the beak, while in others it leans backward and is bent either only near the beak or throughout its entire height. Spirifera euruteines is described by Prof. Hall in Pal. N. Y., volume 4, page 209, as follows:

Shell semi-elliptical; length and breadth about as six to ten; hinge-line equal to greatest width of shell. Surface plicate.

Ventral valve sub-pyramidal, the elevation being nearly equal to half the width, curving abruptly and equally to the front and lateral margins; the distance from the apex to the cardinal extremity, and to the front of the shell, being about equal. Apex sometimes projecting slightly over the area; mesial sinus shallow, well defined, and reaching to the apex; sometimes a little flattened in the bottom. Area extremely elevated, nearly flat or slightly concave above; fissure large and open to the apex, the length of its sides being about once and a half the width of its base.

Dorsal valve moderately and evenly convex, with a well defined, low rounded mesial fold; beak and margin of the valve in the middle slightly arched; area narrow at the sides, but having the width of a line in the middle. Surface marked by from 16 to 20 plications on each side of the mesial fold or sinus; these plications are rounded and well defined; about eight of them reach the apex on the ventral valve, and the remainder coalesce with the angular border of the area. In perfect specimens, the entire surface has been covered by fine concentric undulating striae, which are crossed by fine radiating striae; the remains of these on some of the silicified specimens give a granulose surface.

The length of a full grown individual is a little more than three-fourths of an inch, its width about one inch and three-eighths, and its height also about three-fourths of an inch. (Hall.)

After the foregoing description Prof. Hall makes the following statement: "I have before me more than a dozen specimens from near the Falls of the Ohio, or from Charlestown Landing, among which there is very little variation in the general features."

If those specimens did not show *great* variations, they must have formed a *picked* lot. I have before me more than an hundred shells of this species, which I could easily divide into at least five different groups. The extreme form of each group is so pronounced in its features, and so greatly different from the extreme form of other groups, that they, by themselves, would constitute good species; but the intermediate forms connect all these groups to one single species.

Formation and Locality.—Found in great abundance, and well preserved, in the Devonian limestone in Kentucky and Indiana, near and at the Falls of the Ohio. Some of the specimens have preserved the internal spiral coils in almost perfect condition, as may be seen by plate 6, figures 21 and 22.

Spirifera euruteines, var. fornacula. Hall.

Plate VI., figures 8, 10, 18, 19 and 20.

Spirifera euruteines, var. fornacula, Hall. Pal. N. Y., Vol. IV., page 211, pl. 31, figures 11, 12 and 13.

Prof. Hall, in describing this variety, remarks that it possesses the essential characters of Spir. euruteines, and points out, as the only difference from that species, that its area is a little more arcuate in the upper part. Those figured by me here are of the type which is generally considered as fornacula by all the geologists living in the cities around the Falls of the Ohio. The strong curvature of the whole cardinal area is their only marked characteristic.

Formation and Locality.—Associated with the preceding species in the Devonian limestone in Kentucky and Indiana, around the Falls of the Ohio.

Spirifera foggi. n. sp.

Plate XXXII., figures 28, 29, 30 and 31.

Shell of medium size; sub-circular sub-oval or sub-elliptical; very ventricose or gibbous; hinge-line greatly less than width of shell; cardinal extremities rounded. Surface plicated.

Ventral valve ventricose in young specimens, becoming gibbous in old ones; greatest convexity a little above the middle of the valve, from where it slopes in a gentle regular curve to the front, but abruptly to the cardino-lateral margins; a mesial sinus extends from beak to front, well defined in its whole course, moderately widening, but not, or very little, increasing in depth towards the front; flat at the bottom, and having only a small basal extension, which is not deflected; umbo more or less prominent, according to age, and beak strongly arched over the umbo of opposite valve; hinge-area small and undefined in its margins, which are rounded and coalesce with the surface of the valve; triangular fissure of moderate size, with its base to its height as two to three.

Dorsal valve of equal convexity with the ventral, both in young and old shells; greatest convexity below the umbo, from where it slopes very abruptly to the cardinal margin, but in a gentle and regular curve to the lateral and basal margins; a mesial fold of moderate elevation and moderate width, but well defined in its whole course, extends from beak to front, with a flat or broadly rounded summit; umbo moderate, and beak strongly incurved into the foramen of the opposite valve. Surface ornamented by five to six broadly rounded plications on each side of the mesial fold or sinus, of which only the first one, adjacent to the median elevation or depression, is of moderate size and plainly marked from beak to front, while the others diminish in size and distinctness more and more toward the lateral margins. In well preserved specimens retaining the shell, the surface is covered with fine, thread-like, radiating striae, which increase greatly towards the front by bifurcation; these striae are crossed by fine imbricating lines of growth, which become somewhat crowded near the front. This species is generally found as exfoliated casts, which do not show these radiating and concentric lines, or at least indicate them only very faintly.

Professor Hall has repeatedly, but always with the expression of doubt, referred this species to Spirifera niagarensis, but it appears to me that it differs too much from that shell to be associated with it. Spir. niagarensis shows in all of Hall's figures large cardinal dimensions; it has a hinge-line as large as the width of the shell; it also has a considerable hinge-area, which is well defined, and its plications are numerous and plainly marked; all these points are greatly different in our shell; its hinge-line is very short, not exceeding one-half the width of the shell; the cardinal area is small, and not defined by sharp, angular, but by broadly rounded margins, and the plications are few, and only faintly marked. These differences are certainly sufficient to separate our shell specifically from Spir. niagarensis. Nearer related is this species to Spirifera radiata, from which it differs only by its small cardinal area, which, however, occurs in some specimens of that species also, but mainly by its plicated surface. It certainly occupies an intermediate position between Spir. niagarensis and Spir. radiata, of which it presents the transition-form in the process of evolution.

Formation and Locality.—It occurs in the Niagara group so prominently exposed in the quarries east of the city of Louisville, where it is rare, generally, but more so in well preserved individuals; only a few specimens of this species are to be found in the different cabinets of the Falls Cities. It affords me great pleasure to name this species in honor of my friend, the noble-hearted and venerable Mr. Fogg, of Jeffersonville, Indiana.

Spirifera gregaria. CLAPP.

Plate VIII., figures 9 to 13, and Plate X., figures 6 to 10.

Spirifer gregaria, Clapp. MS.
Spirifer gregaria, Hall. Tenth Rep. on the State Cab., p. 127—1857.
Spirifer gregaria, Clapp. Billings in Canadian Jour., p. 128—1857.
Spirifera gregaria, Hall. Pal. N. Y., Vol. 4, p. 195, plate 28.

Shell ventricose, sub-globose, semi-oval or sub-quadrate in outline; hinge-line usually equal, but sometimes less than width of shell ; cardinal extremities truncate or somewhat rounded.   Surface plicated.

Ventral valve very gibbous, and more so than the dorsal valve; it is regularly arcuate from beak to front.   Its greatest convexity is at or a little above the middle, from where it curves somewhat abruptly to the sides, but more gently to the front ; beak much elevated, and apex closely incurved over the fissure; area high, concave and extending to the cardinal angles, where it is sometimes more than half a line high, often distinctly striated ; mesial sinus rounded or sub-angular and much produced in front.

Dorsal valve very convex with a strong mesial fold, either angular or some-what flattened along the summit, and sometimes marked by an indistinct groove; beak often considerably elevated, and slightly inclined over the hinge area, which is narrow except in the center, where it widens perceptibly Surface marked by from six to ten strong rounded ribs on each side of the mesial fold and sinus.   The entire surface is covered with undulating con-centric striae, which, towards the front, become strong zigzag imbricating lines of growth, resembling somewhat the front ornamentation of Spirifera davisi.

The interior of the ventral valve presents a well defined, oval, muscular impression, with a low crest in the center.   The dental plates are often much thickened, filling the entire rostral cavity, and encroaching upon the muscular area.

The width of this species ranges from one-half to seven-eighths of an inch, and the length is usually a little less than the width; but there are some speci-mens in which the length equals or even exceeds a little the width, as may be seen in the one figured on plate 8.   In very gibbous specimens the beak of the ventral valve is so extremely elevated, that almost one-half of the ven-tral valve is above the cardinal line.   In the majority of specimens there are six or seven plications on each side of the mesial fold or sinus.   The variable gibbosity of the shell gives an apparent variation in the height of the area; the beaks of the two valves sometimes approach very close to each other. (Hall.)

Formation and Locality.—This species is found abundantly in the Corniferous limestone at and around the Falls of the Ohio in Kentucky and Indiana. It appears here silicified, in well preserved specimens of the whole shell, as well as of the separated single valves. Specimens still inclosed in the limestone are of the same material. From observations made by me at the Falls of the Ohio, and which, undoubtedly, were also made by other geologists, who visited and examined that world-renowned storehouse of Devonian fossils, but of which I never found any notice in print, I am forced to the conclusion that the silicification of the shells and corals is produced by their exposure to water and weather, and that this process requires only a comparatively short time. Whenever, at low stages of the water, the bed of the falls becomes dry, we find it entirely covered by fossil shells and corals, partly exposed above the solid rock and partly inclosed in the same. All the exposed fossils which have been acted upon by water and weather for some length of time are silicified, as far as they are above the matrix, while the inclosed parts are still limestone, or, if a change in their material has already commenced, the silicification has not sufficiently advanced to resist the dissolving power of muriatic acid, which has not the least influence upon the exposed parts. In the same condition are the fossils found in the fields near the falls in Kentucky and Indiana. Those which are entirely weathered out, and the parts of others freed from the matrix, are silicious, while the inclosed parts have retained their original material.

Spirifera grieri. HALL.

Plate IX., figures 8 to 14.

Spirifer grieri, Hall. Tenth Rep. on State Cab., p. 127—1857.
Spirifer grieri, Hall. Pal. N. Y., Vol. 4, p. 194, plates 27 and 23.

Shell gibbous, transversely oval or sub-quadrilateral, sometimes longitudinally ovate, the proportion of length and breadth being very variable; hinge-line considerably shorter than the greatest width of the shell; cardinal extremities rounded. Valves sub-equally convex.

Ventral valve gibbous or ventricose; most convex above the middle, and nearly opposite the center of the hinge-line, and sloping somewhat abruptly to the lateral margins, but more gently to the front; sometimes regularly arched from beak to front, and often arcuate in the upper part and straight in the lower portion. Umbo prominent and much elevated above the hinge-line; beak more or less incurved over the fissure of the high and arcuate area, which has a length of one-half to nearly two-thirds the width of the shell. Mesial sinus wide and deep, sub-angular in the lower portion.

Dorsal valve regularly arcuate; the greatest convexity near the middle, and regularly curving to the lateral margin; mesial fold prominent, sometimes rounded, but usually more or less distinctly angular; beak small, slightly incurved over a nearly vertical narrow area. Surface marked by from six to ten more or less rounded, simple plications on each side of the mesial fold or sinus, while there are three or four distinctly bifurcating or dichotomous plications upon the fold or sinus, giving six to eight at the margin of the shell. I have before me a specimen of grieri, in which the first rib on each side of the mesial fold and the second one on each side of the sinus are plainly dichotomous. In perfect specimens the surface is covered by fine concentric lamellose striae, which are crossed by delicate, radiating striae. This species is distinguished from most of the allied forms by its simple, strong plications on each side of the mesial fold and sinus, while those occupying the latter are smaller and bifurcating.

Sometimes the middle plication on the mesial fold is simple, in which case the fold is quite angular, while in other instances it bifurcates, leaving a longitudinal depressed line on the middle, giving it a more rounded outline. It is only on specimens which have suffered no injury by wearing or exfoliation, that the fimbriate appearance of the concentric markings is visible. In some of the larger and older individuals the plications are low and gently rounded, in others they are more prominent, while from exfoliation they often become angular and more conspicuous, and the same appears to be true of the dichotomous plications of the mesial fold and sinus. The interior of the shell is so far unknown. (Hall.)

The size of the shell differs considerably in the different specimens; its width is from less than three-fourths of an inch to an inch and a half, and its length measures from less than three-fourths of an inch to an inch. The specimen figured on plate 9, figures 8 to 12, has a width of one inch and five-eighths, by a length of an inch and a quarter, but specimens of these dimensions are of unusually large size, and of rare occurrence.

Formation and Locality.—This species occurs in the Corniferous limestone at and near the Falls of the Ohio, in Indiana and Kentucky; it appears in some strata pretty abundantly, though good and well preserved specimens are somewhat rare. This species was named in honor of Judge Grier, of Dayton, Ohio, who presented Prof. Hall with good specimens from that locality.

Spirifera hobbsi. N. SP.

Plate X., figures 21, 22, 26 to 30, and 35 and 40.

Spirifera varicosa var., Hall. Pal. N. Y., Vol. 4, p. 206, pl. 31, fig. 28.

Shell transverse, semi-oval; width exceeding the length considerably, sometimes having its double size; hinge-line equalling the greatest width of the shell, and terminating in salient, mostly mucronate angles. Surface plicate.

Ventral valve much elevated, sub-pyramidal; most prominent at the beak or a little in front of it. The beak is not incurved, or at least only slightly so; mesial sinus well defined and forming a deep triangular groove, with an acute angle in the bottom, resembling that of Spir. byrnesi, but not so much produced at the front. Cardinal area straight and large, with sharply angular margins, vertical and extending to the cardinal extremities, where it does not form an acute angle, but still maintains a visible height, which is not sufficiently shown in figure 29, plate 10.   Triangular fissure of moderate size.

Dorsal valve very little convex, and flattened towards the cardinal extremities, and of equal size with the ventral valve. The mesial fold elevated, rounded in the upper part, but somewhat flattened towards the front.

Surface marked by about twelve prominent and rounded or sub-angular plications on each side of the mesial fold and sinus, which are crossed by strong, lamellose, imbricating, concentric striae and lines of growth, which give the shell a rugose appearance.   Only the plications next to fold and sinus reach to the apex, the lateral ones run out along the margins of the area. Length of shell about half of an inch and even less; its width measures from one inch to one inch and one-eighth.

Prof. Hall has given in Pal. N. Y., vol 4, plate 31, subfigure 23, the ventral valve of a shell which he calls, on page 206 of the same volume, *Spirifera varicosa, variety*.   His description is short and incomplete.   His figure shows some similarity with the present species, but it differs in its enlarged sinus towards the front, and also by the area, which, in Hall's specimens, is partly concave, while that of mine is always straight.

Formation and Locality.—Found in the upper strata of the Devonian limestone around the Falls of the Ohio, in Kentucky and Indiana.   It is rare, and seldom found in well preserved specimens.   I named this species after Orlando Hobbs, Esq., of Jeffersonville, Ind., who is an ardent student and collector.

Spirifera knappiana.   N. SP.

Plate VII., figure 14.

Shell sub-circular, gibbous; hinge-line shorter than width of shell; cardinal extremities rounded.

Ventral valve gibbous in the upper part, and regularly curving to the front and sides.   Mesial sinus well defined from front to apex of beak, somewhat shallow and rounded; it contains two faintly marked plications.   Beak of medium size and curved over the area, which is high and concave, extending over about two-thirds of the entire width of the shell; fissure of medium size.

Dorsal valve gibbous, regularly convex on the sides, a little flattened at the cardinal extremities; mesial fold prominent and well defined to apex of beak, containing on its middle a well marked depression; beak small, slightly arched over the sub-linear area, which is somewhat concave.

Surface marked by from six to eight rounded plications on each side of fold or sinus; they are crossed by imbricating lines or striae, which have irregular distances in the upper part, but become regular and close set in the front part. The whole surface is covered with very fine closely set radiating striae, but there are no elongated nodes or tubercles, as in conradana.

The cardinal area is densely covered with fine vertical striae. Any one comparing the description of this species with that of conradana, will see that both species agree in a great many essential characters, but, in spite of that, there are several points of difference of sufficient value to entitle Sp. knappiana to the full rank of a species. These points of difference are :

1. The plications in the mesial sinus and the depression of the mesial fold found in knappiana are wanting in conradana.

2. The elongated nodes or tubercles of conradana are not possessed by knappiana.

3. The difference between width and length is greatly less in knappiana than in the other species.

4. The plications in knappiana are more prominent than those of conradana.

5. The knappiana has fine regular radiating striae instead of the tubercles of conradana.

Some more differences might be pointed out, but I consider those enumerated here fully sufficient to enable anybody, even the beginners in geological science, to distinguish this new species from the preceding one without the least doubt or trouble. With no other Devonian Spirifer could Sp. knappiana be confounded ; it is, therefore, easily identified.

Formation and Locality.—This elegant species is associated with conradana, with which it is undoubtedly nearest related, in the Corniferous limestone of Kentucky, but it is of rare occurrence, at least it is not represented in any collection of the Falls Cities but my own and that of Major Wm. J. Davis. I have named it in honor of the late Dr. James Knapp, who collected, during his life-time, one of the finest geological, or rather palæontological cabinets, not only of Louisville, but of the whole south and west. He furnished many of the eastern prominent palæontologists with valuable material for their palæontological writings. and, in this manner, rendered great services to science. His collection contained a great number of very valuable specimens of Devonian and Silurian crinoids, shells and corals, which were not to be found in any cabinet outside of Louisville.

Spirifera macconathii. N. SP.

Plate XI., figures 1 to 5.

Shell transverse, sub triangular or semi-elliptical ; hinge-line much extended ; extremities often mucronate ; valves unequal in depth ; area large ; surface plicate.

Ventral valve elevated at the beak ; abruptly sloping to the front and lateral margins, but with little convexity. Area one-third as high as long, and only slightly concave ; fissure about twice as high as wide, and reaching to apex of valve; beak minute. Mesial sinus well defined, but shallow, and flattened at the bottom, with sub-angular margins rapidly widening towards the front, where it is somewhat produced.

Dorsal valve depressed, convex, most convex above the middle; cardinal extremities often inflected; beak not prominent, incurving over the linear area. Mesial fold well defined and rounded, but flattened on top towards the front. Surface marked by from eighteen to twenty simple rounded plications on each side of the mesial fold and sinus; only few of these ribs reach to the beak, the others run out on the margins of the cardinal area.

This species agrees in many points with Prof. Hall's description of Spirifera macronata, in Pal. N. Y., volume 4, page 231, but it differs by its smaller number of ribs, which in this species never exceeds twenty, while macronata has from twenty-five to thirty-five. The area of macronata is straight, while that of mcconathii is always concave, and the surface of this last species is generally smooth, while the surface of the former is covered by several lamellose imbricating lines of growth.

Formation and Locality.—Found in the upper strata of the Devonian limestone, at and near the Falls of the Ohio, in Kentucky and Indiana. It is somewhat rare, at least in well preserved specimens. Named after Prof. W. J. McConathy, of Louisville, Ky., who has gathered a very valuable collection of the Devonian and Silurian fauna from the Falls of the Ohio.

Spirifera marionensis. Shumard.

Spirifer marionensis, Shumard. Geol. Rep. of Mo., p. 203—1855.
Spirifer marionensis, Hall. Geol. Rep. of Iowa, p. 511—1858.

Shell of medium size, nearly semi-circular, moderately gibbous; length about equal to two-thirds of the greatest width; valves almost equally convex; hinge-line longer than greatest width of shell; cardinal extremities pointed, and sometimes mucronate. Ventral valve broadly semi-elliptical or semi-circular, greatest convexity above the middle; umbo gibbous; beak pointed and incurved; sinus well defined, angular and narrow at the beak, becoming broad and shallow below, and marked by two or three dichotomizing plications; area narrow; sides nearly parallel and extending to the hinge-extremities, striated transversely; foramen broadly triangular; base greater than the height.

Dorsal valve regularly convex; flattened towards the cardinal extremities; mesial elevation very moderate, marked by two or three plications above, which bifurcate below. Surface marked by from twelve to twenty rounded and little elevated plications on each side of the mesial fold and sinus. Plications increasing by bifurcation either near umbo or near base.

Concentric lines of growth cover the surface, also fine radiating striae, both of which give the shell a granulose appearance.

This species is subject to some variations in different localities; but its narrow, almost linear area, its mucronate cardinal extremities, its shallow sinus and slightly elevated fold, both of which are covered by dichotomizing plications, serve to distinguish it from all other Spirifera with which it is associated. It might be confounded with Spir. parryanus, which has its sinus and fold also covered by dichotomizing plications, but which has only single ribs on its lateral parts.

Formation and Locality.—Found in the rotten hornstone in upper portion of the Devonian formation, at and around the falls, in Kentucky and Indiana. It is an exceedingly rare species; the only specimen known as found in our rocks was found by Major Wm. J. Davis, on the Indiana shore of the river, just below the Falls of the Ohio.

Spirifera medialis. HALL.

Plate XXVI., figures 2 to 5.

Delthyris medialis, Hall.   Geol. Rep. 4th Dist. N. Y., p. 208—1843.
Spirifer medialis, Hall.   Tenth Report on State Cab., p. 164.
Compare Delthyris audacula, Conrad.   Jour. Acad. Nat. Sci. Phil., Vol. VIII., p. 262.
Spirifera medialis, Hall.   Pal. N. Y., Vol. IV., p. 227—1867.

Shell of medium size or larger; sub-triangular, semi-circular or semi-elliptical; hinge-line longer than greatest width of shell below; cardinal extremities extended, often mucronate; shell moderately convex or ventricose. Surface plicated.

Ventral valve somewhat more convex than the dorsal; beak prominent, elevated above the hinge-line, and only slightly incurved at the apex; cardinal area in our specimens of medium size, having the shape of an irregular pentagon, of which the two sides at the cardinal extremities, in the specimen before me, measure about two lines; its margins, sloping down from the beak, are almost straight, but sharply defined; the area is almost flat except near the beak, where it is slightly curved; it is covered by longitudinal striae, and divided in the middle by a triangular fissure, which is twice as high as wide at its base, and which reaches to the apex of valve. Mesial sinus is of moderate width, but rather deep; it reaches to the apex, and' is generally rounded but sometimes flattened at the bottom; its margins are angular and well defined.

Dorsal valve moderately convex or gibbous; the greatest convexity above the middle, from where it slopes in a gentle curve to the lateral and basal margins, except at the cardinal angles, where it deflects a little, and forming a slight depression; beak small and slightly incurved; area linear and well defined. Mesial elevation prominent and sharply defined, rising abruptly at its sides, rounded or slightly flattened on top. Surface ornamented by about twenty-five rounded, simple plications on each side of the mesial fold or sinus, of which the principal ones are sometimes marked by a small thread-like groove along their center, a feature most common on the ventral valve. Near the lateral and basal margins there are several strong concentric lines of growth, which give to that part of the surface a strongly imbricate character. This shell is subject to many and extreme variations in the extent of the hinge-line, convexity of the valves, height of area, and the incurving of the beak.

Formation and Locality.—Occurs in the Corniferous limestone at and around the Falls of the Ohio in Kentucky and Indiana. It is an exceedingly rare species in our rocks; only few specimens have been found in Clark county, Indiana.

Spirifera mucronata. Conrad.

Plate XXXI., figures 10 and 11.

In the collection of the late Dr. James Knapp was a Spirifera showing the closest resemblance to Spirifera mucronata. The Doctor claimed that he found it somewhere between Watson's Station 'and Charlestown, in Clark county, Indiana. When he found it, he directly identified it as Spir. mucronata, and being aware of the fact that this species had never been found here, he marked it as soon as he reached home. I am fully convinced that the Doctor found the specimen as he stated, but it is possible that the specimen was not a Spir. mucronata.

The Doctor loaned the shell to me for illustration, but he took it away before I had time to examine it more carefully. Thus I had no opportunity to gain access to the specimen in question, and I am, therefore, not able to give a description of said shell. If it is really a Spir. mucronata, it is certainly the first one ever found in our rocks.

Spirifera oweni. Hall.

Plate VII., figures 1 to 10.
Spirifera oweni, Hall. Pal. N. Y., Vol. IV., page 197, pl. 29, figures 1 to 8.

Shell more or less ventricose in its different stages of growth, somewhat transversely oval, semi-elliptical or sub-quadrate; hinge-line about equal to width of shell; cardinal extremities rounded or angular. Surface plicated.

Ventral valve scarcely as gibbous as the dorsal valve, its greatest convexity above the middle of its length, and curving regularly to the margins; beak much elevated above that of the opposite valve, and arching over the fissure, but scarcely incurved; mesial sinus shallow, concave, usually well defined, and reaching distinctly to the apex. Area high, concave, elevated and continuing to the hinge-extremities; foramen or fissure large, reaching to the apex, and sometimes partially filled by the thickening of the dental plates.

Dorsal valve the more gibbous, the greatest convexity in the middle, and curving regularly to the front and lateral margins, and usually a little flattened or sometimes concave towards the cardinal extremities; mesial fold prominent, rounded, with a longitudinal depressed line along the middle. Area narrow, vertical, or in plane of the longitudinal axis.

The surface is marked by from fifteen to seventeen rounded or sub-angular plications on each side of the mesial fold and sinus, and these are crossed by distinct concentric striae, which become strongly imbricating, or are marked in strong imbricating lines of growth towards the margins. In well preserved specimens there are distinct radiating striae. In many of the silicified specimens, however, both the radiating and concentric striae are partially or entirely obliterated. The interior of the ventral valve shows two short and rather strong teeth, with the rostal portion quite solid. The dental plates, reaching to the bottom of the cavity of shell, curve slightly outwards and partially inclose an oval muscular area, which in its upper part is divided by a short medium crest. In some silicified specimens the conical spires are partially and sometimes entirely preserved. The crura are widely separated at their bases, and converging somewhat abruptly, curve into the dorsal valve, making twelve or more turns, and producing a short strong spire. In well preserved specimens the mesial fold and sinus are usually well defined, but in some of the more gibbous forms the sinus is very broad, and one or two of the plications on each side are involved in the sides of the depression, at the same time the mesial fold is very prominent, rounded, and sloping almost imperceptibly into the general contour of the convexity of valve.

This species has been generally referred to *Spir. laevicosta* of Lamarck, from which it differs in being less gibbous, having a greater number of plications, and having also a depressed line along the middle of the mesial fold of the dorsal valve. It may be easily distinguished from Spir. euruteines, with which it is associated, by its narrower and much more arcuate area and less angular plications. Some specimens show remains or traces of a faintly impressed line along the center of each plication. (Hall.)

Formation and Locality.—Found in great abundance and beauty in the Devonian limestone in Kentucky and Indiana, around the Falls of the Ohio. Specimens showing the internal spiral coils well preserved in silicified shells are not very rare. This species was named by Prof. Hall in honor of D. D. Owen, the former State Geologist of Kentuc'

length, reaching to the apex of the beak, the others are interpolations and considerably shorter, they reach only to the umbo. The bifurcations on the dorsal valve, and the interpolations on the other one, are so plainly marked that they must be observed at the first glance. The fine radiating striae cover fold and sinus as well as the other part of the valves; towards the. front their number is increased by interpolation, not by bifurcation. Prof. Hall mentions concentric striae, of which I have not noticed the slightest trace, though I possess a specimen showing the surface-markings most perfectly.

' This species has some similarity with Spir. eudora of the Niagara formation, but it is easily distinguished from the latter by its elevated beak, its peculiar plications, and less gibbosity.

Formation and Locality.—Occurs in the upper strata of the Niagara rocks, in the quarries east of Louisville, Ky., where it is found in well preserved specimens; but it is extremely rare. Less than a dozen of specimens are so far found, which belong either to my own cabinet or to that of the late Dr. James Knapp, of Louisville, Ky., who furnished Prof. Hall with the types for his figures and descriptions. I have never heard of its occurrence at any other place.

Spirifera radiata. Sowerby.

Plate XXIX., figures 13, 14, 15 and 16.

Spirifer radiatus, Sowerby. Silurian System, p. 637, pl. 12.
Delthyris radiatus, Hall. Geol. Rep. 4th Dist. N. Y., p. 105—1843.
Spirifer radiatus, Hall. Pal. N. Y., Vol. 2, pp. 66 and 265—1852.
Spirifera radiata, Hall. Ind. 11th Rep. of State Geologist, page 296, plate 24, figures 20 to 30—1881.

Shell variable in form, sub-triangular, rotund or sub-globose; valves almost equally convex; hinge-line considerably less than the greatest width of the shell; cardinal extremities rounded.

Ventral valve gibbous, and curving regularly towards the anterior and lateral margins; greatest convexity above the middle of the valve; mesial sinus shallow and flat at the bottom, and, extending to the apex, it is rapidly widening towards the front, where it forms a broad extension, the termination of which is only faintly curved. The specimen figured on plate 29 shows, in figures 13 and 14, the termination of the mesial depression and elevation too much curved; this is not the fault of the draughtsman, but is caused by the form of the specimen, of which said figures are correct copies. Generally the mesial fold is flattened in front, causing the straight termination; but this specimen had the fold rounded to the front, which produced the strongly curved extension.

The margins of the sinus are pretty well defined in the umbonal region, but from there downwards they are only faintly indicated. The beak is sometimes considerably elevated above the hinge-line, and only slightly curved, as in the specimen figured, while in others the cardinal area is scarcely visible, and the beaks of both valves almost touching each other.   The length of the hinge line is so variable that in some specimens it almost equals the greatest width of the shell, while in others it is so much reduced that it, in connection with the rounded extremities, and beaks touching each other, leaves its generic position doubtful.   Such specimens show nearer relation to Atrypa than to Spirifera. The triangular fissure is also variable; sometimes it is broad in the base, sometimes long and narrow; in some specimens it is open, in others partially or entirely closed by a pseudo-deltidium.

Dorsal valve is almost as gibbous as the other valve; its greatest convexity is below the umbo, from where it regularly but gently curves to the anterior and lateral margins.   The mesial fold is arcuate from beak to front, pretty well defined in its upper portion, but very slightly or not at all towards the front; it is rounded above the middle of the valve, but flattened and sometimes even a little depressed in the basal half; beak incurved over the linear area.

Surface marked by regular fine radiating striae, which cover also the mesial fold and sinus, some of which bifurcate or dichotomize towards the front. Prof. Hall, in his description of this species in the Indiana Report, states, that of these striae, eight or more occupy the space of a line, that the radii are flattened, and that the interspaces are only about half as wide as the striae. The specimen before me, the same figured on plate 29, which I found in the quarry near the new water-works, east of Louisville, and which shows the surface-markings as perfect as possible, agrees as to the number of striae in the space of a line, but it differs as to the balance of Prof. Hall's observation. In my specimen the striae are not flattened, but plainly rounded, and the interspaces are certainly as wide, if not wider, than the radii.   It appears to me that the Waldron specimens differ in some respects slightly from those of our strata.   I have a good many Waldron shells before me; they show finer and closer set striae than the Kentucky specimens.

In size this species is as variable as any other Spirifera, or even more so.

In the quarries near our city we generally find the Spir. radiata of small dimensions, some measuring only three-eighths of an inch in length and one-half of an inch in width, while the specimen figured is about one of the largest found near Louisville, and specimens of this size are extremely rare. In the Niagara limestone near Waldron, Ind., we find specimens of an inch and a quarter in length by a width of an inch and a half.

Formation and Locality.—Found in the Niagara limestone east of the city of Louisville, and on the opposite bank of the Ohio river in Indiana.   But the finest and most perfect specimens of this species are found, even abundantly, near Waldron, Indiana.

Spirifera sculptilis. Hall.

Plate XXXI., figure 13.

Delthyris sculptilis, Hall. Geol. Rep. of 4th Dist. N. Y., p. 202—1843.
Spirifera sculptilis, Hall. Pal. N. Y., Vol. 4, p. 221, pl. 35—1862-1866.

Shell gibbous; valves sub-equally convex, semi-elliptical or sub-triangular; hinge-line longer than greatest width of shell, and prolonged into mucronate extensions; length about one-half the width on the hinge-line. Surface coarsely plicated.

Ventral valve regularly convex, arcuate; beak arcuate over a sub-linear area of moderate height, extending to the limits of the cardinal line; mesial sinus strongly defined, sub-angular.

Dorsal valve regularly convex, the greatest convexity in the middle, and regularly arcuate from beak to base; mesial fold abruptly and strongly elevated, with the summit flattened or grooved; beak incurved; area very narrow.

Surface strongly marked by three, four or five abruptly elevated angular, plications on each side of the mesial fold and sinus, leaving a somewhat wide corrugated space at the cardinal angles. The plications bordering the sinus are stronger, more elevated, and continuing distinct quite to the apex. The shell is concentrically marked by strong, imbricating lamellose striae, which are abruptly bent backwards, and much elevated in crossing the plications, giving them a sub-nodose character. In the bottom of the sinus these striae have often a distinct backward bend, with a slight elevation indicating an incipient plication, which corresponds with the depression in the mesial fold. This species is readily recognized by its few strong plications, and the wide space at the cardinal extremities marked only by the concentric striae. (Hall.)

Formation and Locality.—Found in the upper strata of the Devonian formation, around the falls, in Kentucky and Indiana, where it is of very rare occurrence. My figure is taken from a very fine and well preserved ventral valve, showing the inside and the hinge in perfect order. This specimen I found at the Falls of the Ohio, in the so-called rotten hornstone, which furnishes the best preserved fossils.

Spirifera segmenta. Hall.

Plate XIII., figures 36, 37 and 38.

Spirifer segmentus, Hall. Tenth Rep. on the State Cab.—1857.
Spirifer segmentus, Hall. Descript. of New Pal. Fossils, p. 91—1857.
Spirifera segmenta, Hall. Pal. N. Y., Vol. 4, p. 207, plate 31.

Shell transverse, semi-oval; length less than half the width; hinge-line equalling the greatest width of shell, and terminating in salient angles. Surface plicate.

Ventral valve much elevated, sub-pyramidal, most prominent at the beak, which is not, or at least very seldom, incurved ; mesial sinus strongly defined, shallow and nearly flat in the bottom ; its sides are straight, which give it a triangular form, in which the sides are about once and one-half as long as the base. Area very large, with sharply angular margins, and greatly inclined forward, and nearly of the same size as the exterior of the valve ; the fissure is high and large, almost equalling in size the mesial sinus.

Dorsal valve depressed, convex and flattened towards the cardinal extremities, larger than the ventral valve, semi-elliptical in form, with a low but sharply defined mesial fold, which is barely flattened upon the summit. The proportions in height of area, length of ventral and length of dorsal valves, is about as five, six and seven.

Surface marked by twenty or more simple, rounded or sometimes sub-angular plications on each side of the mesial fold or sinus, the lateral ones of which do not reach the beak, but run out along the margins of the area. In its perfect condition the shell has been marked by fine concentric striae, traces of which are still preserved, together with stronger imbricating lines of growth. (Hall.)

This species is associated with Spir. varicosa, and its younger and smaller specimens may sometimes be mistaken for those of that species ; but Spir. segmenta differs from Spir. varicosa in the following points :

1. In Spir. segmenta the area is always straight and greatly inclines towards the front, which easily distinguishes it from almost any other species of Spirifera, except some forms of euruteines. In Spir. varicosa the cardinal area is markedly concave and stands at right-angles to the margins.

2. Spirifera segmenta has twenty and more plications on each side of the mesial fold and sinus, while Spir. varicosa has only from eight to ten ribs in each half of each valve ; then, again, the plications of segmenta are always smoother than those of varicosa.

3. In Spir. segmenta the dorsal valve exceeds in size the ventral valve, which is not the case in Spir. varicosa.

Besides these, there are several other differences which the student of palæontology will soon find, whenever he closely examines numerous specimens of both species.

The older and larger specimens of this species resemble some Spir. euruteines, but it is easily distinguished from euruteines by the frontward inclination of its area, by its greater transversity, by its smaller size and more numerous plications, and by its dorsal valve exceeding in size the ventral one. All three species are found associated, and the Spir. segmenta forms a kind of connecting link between the two other species.

Prof. Hall states that Spir. segmenta finds its nearest analogue in Spir. augusta of the Hamilton group, and indicates that both species might be identical. Specimens in the collection of the late Dr. James Knapp, marked by Prof. Hall himself as Spir. angusta, can not be distinguished from Spir. segmenta. If his original Spir. angusta are really identical with those marked by him as of the same species in Dr. Knapp's cabinet, we must consider segmenta and angusta as belonging to one and the same species. Both are originally described by Prof. Hall in his tenth report on the State Cabinet, in 1857, and it is therefore difficult, if the identity of segmenta and angusta should be proved, to decide which of them ought to be placed among the synonyms. Inasmuch as Spir. segmenta is described in said report on page 131, while the description of Spir. angusta appears on page 164, the name segmenta has precedence over angusta.

But those specimens marked by Prof. Hall do not at all agree with his figures in the 4th volume of the Pal. of New York, and it is, therefore, possible that he made a mistake in his identification. I have never found a Spirifer in our strata that agreed fully with Hall's figures of Spir. angusta, where the cardinal area inclines so much forward, and where the cardinal extremities are so mucronate. If Spir. angusta holds good as a species, it has, as far as I know, not been found near the Falls of the Ohio.

Formation and Locality.—Spir. segmenta is found in abundance, and as well preserved specimens, in the Corniferous limestone of Kentucky and Indiana, at and around the Falls of the Ohio river.

Spirifera varicosa. HALL.

Plate X., figures 11 to 20, and 23 to 25.

Spirifer varicosus, Hall.   Tenth Rep. on the State Cab., p. 130—1857.
Spirifer varicosus. Hall.   Description of New Pal. Fossils, p. 90—1857.
Spirifera varicosa, Hall.   Pal. N. Y., Vol. 4, p. 205, pl. 31.

Shell somewhat semi-circular or semi-elliptical; length equalling or less than half the width; hinge-line equal to greatest width of shell, and terminating in salient angles or mucronate extensions. Surface plicated.

Ventral valve much the more convex; greatest elevation at the umbo, and regularly curving to the front and to the lateral margins; mesial sinus strongly defined, rather flat in the bottom; beak slightly arcuate; area high, nearly flat below, and slightly concave towards the apex.

Dorsal valve moderately convex, with a prominent, abruptly elevated mesial fold, which is flattened on the summit, and sometimes slightly depressed along the center; the beak projecting a little above the hinge-line, and over a narrow area gently incurved.

The surface is marked by from eight to ten simple and somewhat abruptly elevated plications on each side of the mesial fold or sinus; they are crossed by strong lamellose, imbricating lines of growth, which give a varicose character to the surface, and where the shell is exfoliated the plications are nodose. In some specimens, distinct, fine radiating striae can be observed, but this is of rare occurrence. There is often a retrorse curving of the concentric striae in the center of the mesial sinus, and sometimes a slight elevation on that line. (Hall.)

Prof. Hall, who first described this species, compares it with Spirifera euruteines of Owen. In regard to size, the euruteines is almost twice as large as the varicosa, at least we find plenty specimens of the former species which have double the width of the latter one. Spir. varicosa is always more transverse, that is, the excess of its width over its length is considerably greater than the excess of the width over the length in Spir. euruteines. In Spir. varicosa the plications are more angular, and the concentric lines of growth greatly stronger than in Spir. euruteines. It differs from the latter also by its abrupt and angular mesial fold. This species shows very little variations in the more than one hundred specimens before me.

Formation and Locality.—Found in great abundance, and in most perfectly preserved specimens, in the Corniferous limestone around the Falls of the Ohio, in Kentucky and Indiana.

Genus Trematospira. Hall.

Trematospira, Hall. Pal. N. Y., Vol. 3, page 207—1859.
Etymology: trema, a foramen; *spira*, a spire; alluding to the perforation in the beak of the ventral valve.

Shell transverse, elliptical or sub-rhomboidal, furnished with internal spires (arranged as in Spirifera); hinge-line shorter than width of shell; cardinal angles rounded. Valves articulated by teeth and sockets; beak of ventral valve produced or incurved, and truncated by a small, round perforation, separated from the hinge-line by a deltidium. A deep triangular pit or foramen, beneath the beak of ventral valve, which is filled by beak of the dorsal valve. False area sometimes defined. Surface marked either with strong, simple plications or finer fasciculate or bifurcating striae, which cover also the mesial elevation and depression. Shell structure punctate. (Hall.)

In the extension of the hinge-line, the mesial sinus, the internal spires, and, partly, in the exterior markings, this genus resembles Spirifera and Spiriferina. In the perforate beak, false area and incurving of the dorsal beak beneath that of the other valve, it resembles Atrypa, while one species has the general aspect of Rhynchonella. The broad triangular foramen for the reception of the dorsal beak is a constant and conspicuous feature of this genus.

Trematospira hirsuta. HALL.

Plate XVI., figures 15 to 19.

Atrypa hirsuta, Hall. Tenth Rep. on State Cabinet, p. 108—1857.
Trematospira hirsuta, Hall. Thirteenth Rep. on State Cab., p. 101—1860.
Athyris (?) *chloe*, Billings. Canada Journal, p. 282—1860.
Trematospira hirsuta, Hall. Pal. N. Y., Vol. 4, pp. 274 and 275—1867.

Shell of medium size; sub-elliptical, in very old specimens sub-circular or sub-quadrate; moderately convex when young; increasing in convexity with increasing age, and finally becoming gibbous; sinus and fold wanting in young shells, appearing at a certain age, and becoming prominent in old individuals, which assume in outline the exact shape of Athyris vittata.

Ventral valve moderately convex, with greatest convexity at the umbo, from where it slopes somewhat abruptly to the cardinal margins, and gently to the lateral and basal margins; the umbo is prominent and the beak incurved; a mesial sinus is indicated in young shells; it becomes more definite with age, but remains, even in very old specimens, shallow; this sinus is undefined in its margins, which are rounded, and which coalesce with the general surface of the valve, and it does never extend further back than to a little behind the middle of shell.

Dorsal valve of about equal convexity with the ventral, except in old specimens, in which it is considerably less; greatest convexity above the middle of the valve, from where it slopes in a gentle curve to the sides and front; umbo flat, but becoming more prominent with age, and the beak strongly incurving into the other valve beneath its circular foramen; a mesial fold is only indicated in young specimens, it becomes somewhat more prominent in older shells, but never attains more than a moderate elevation, and is undefined in its margins, which are rounded, and run gradually into the general surface of shell.

Surface ornamented by from thirty to forty simple, low, rounded, radiating striae, which increase from beak to front in size and distance; these radiating striae are crossed by fine, concentric lines of growth, and more distant imbricating lamellae. The surface of the specimens, as they are usually found, is granulose; but in perfectly preserved shells it is covered by minute setae or spinules, the bases of which remaining, give the papillose character. The entire shell structure is punctate.

The specimen illustrated is of more than average size; in its proportion of width to length, it is more transverse than the usual form; but at the time when the drawings were made it was the only specimen at my disposal.

Formation and Locality.—Found in the rotten hornstone of the Corniferous group, in a quarry in the eastern portion of the city of Louisville. Formerly very rare, but of late a good many very good specimens have been found, so that my collection embraces now, at least, a dozen fair individuals,

Trematospira helena. N. SP.

Plate XXXII., figures 40 to 43.

Shell very small, broadly ovate or sub-globose, very gibbous; somewhat longer than wide; greatest width below the middle of the length, but not as near the base as shown in the figures 40 and 41. Surface plicated.

Ventral valve regularly curved from beak to base; greatest convexity at the middle of the valve, from where it slopes in a regular curve to lateral and basal margins, but rather abruptly to cardinal lines; beak in proportion to the size of shell prominent, elevated and incurved over that of the opposite valve; the place of the apex is occupied by a round, plainly visible foramen; lateral and basal margins form a regular curve, with a slight emargination in the central portion of the base, which is not shown in figures 40 and 41; from the umbo to the front a mesial depression is marked.

Dorsal valve equal in convexity to the other; most prominent at the middle, and curving regularly to side and front margins, but more rapidly to the cardinal line. This valve has also a mesial depression indicated; its umbo is prominent, and its beak strongly incurved into the opposite valve below the foramen of the same.

Surface is marked, in proportion to the size of the shell, by very strong, rounded plications, all of which, with the exception of those in the mesial depressions, reach to the beak; the ventral valve has five and the dorsal valve four on each side of the sinus. The sinus of the ventral valve has in its bottom a greatly smaller plication, which starts at the lower side of the umbo, and bifurcates at about the middle of its length; in some shells the mesial rib does not dichotomize. The plication in the mesial depression of the dorsal valve is also somewhat smaller than the others, but the difference in size is not so marked as in the ventral valve, and consequently the mesial sinus of the dorsal valve is not as conspicuous as that of the ventral. This mesial rib of the dorsal valve starts at the beak, and bifurcates below the umbo; both prongs attain at the base almost the same strength as the adjacent ribs, thus leaving in a front view of the shell only a faint indication of the dorsal sinus. All these radiating plications are crossed by fine, closely set, lamellose concentric lines of growth, which give the surface a somewhat rugose appearance. The figures, which are very defective in not representing important features of this beautiful little shell, are enlarged to about double size.

Formation and Locality.—Found in the lower strata of the Niagara group (which by some geologists are placed in the Clinton group), in the quarries east of the city of Louisville, Ky. It is exceedingly rare, only three, but very fine specimens, are in my collection, while I have never seen it in any other cabinet. This shell has a close resemblance to Trem. globosa, Hall, from the Lower Helderberg group.

from which it differs, however, by its smaller size and smaller number of plications; our shell has only ten ribs on each valve, while that species has, according to Prof. Hall, from twelve to sixteen; then, again, our specimen has only one rib, which bifurcates below in the depressions, while Tr. globosa has always two, often three, in said depressions.

Genus Zygospira. Hall.

Zygospira, Hall. 15th Regent's Report, 1862.
Etymology: zygos, a yoke; *spira*, a spire.

This genus was established by Prof. Hall to receive such forms as Zygospira modesta, Z. cincinnatiensis and Z. headi.

Z. modesta is made the type of the genus, which has great similarity to Z. kentuckiensis, and which latter, therefore, presents the main characteristics of the genus. The original description of this genus, by Prof. Hall, is cited from his 15th Regent's Report. It is to be regretted that Prof. Hall's valuable writings are scattered through such a great number of scientific periodicals and State reports.

Zygospira kentuckiensis. N. SP.

Plate XXXIV., figures 21 to 25.

Shell rather large, as compared with other species of Zygospira; sub-circular or sub-elliptical; from moderately convex to gibbous; cardinal lines sloping towards the front, forming a very obtuse angle at the beaks; lateral margins regularly curved; front broadly rounded, with a straight or sinuate central part. Ventral valve larger than the dorsal; central part elevated, and forming a mesial fold, extending from beak to front, not defined at its margins, and of moderate elevation. The middle line of this fold is marked by a somewhat broader and deeper furrow, towards which both sides of the fold slightly incline, thus forming a small mesial sinus on the top or summit of the fold; this central depression on the fold extends also from the beak to the front. The lateral slopes of the mesial fold are more or less abrupt, and the surface between fold and sides becomes flat and even somewhat concave; the umbo is prominent and the beak pointed, and, in most shells, closely incurving upon the beak of the opposite valve, concealing entirely the hinge-area and its foramen.

In a few specimens in my collection the beaks of both valves are sufficiently apart to show a small ventral hinge-area, with a small triangular fissure.

The dorsal valve is moderately convex in its lateral parts; its central portion is depressed, forming a mesial sinus, which extends from the apex to the front, and increases gradually in depth and width towards the base; the umbo is inflated, and the beak minute and incurved. The surface is covered by simple, rounded or sub-angular, radiating plications, all of which, with the exception of a few near the lateral margins, extend back to the beak; they increase gradually in strength and in the size of their interspaces towards the front. The size and number of these plications is variable in different specimens.

The two shells illustrated on plate 34, of which one is shown in figures 21, 22 and 23, and the other in figures 24 and 25, are so different in form and in the size and number of the ribs, that I would be justified to put them in distinct species; but there are so many intermediate forms connecting these two extremes, which compel me to place them both in the above named species. These shells have a somewhat close resemblance to Zygospira modesta, and are considered by some geologists to be merely a larger and robust form of that species; but it differs from that little shell not only by its size, which is often more than twice that of Z. modesta, but also by its convexity, which often increases to gibbosity, and also by its general aspect. I have collected several hundreds of this shell; I found them of all sizes; some very large, as shown in the illustrations, and again others very small, not exceeding the Z. modesta in size; but even these small or young shells differed so much in their whole appearance from Z. modesta, that I think it necessary to separate our shell from Z. modesta and place it in a new species to be named Z. kentuckiensis.

Formation and Locality.—I collected this fine shell in different places in Oldham county, Ky., but I found it in great abundance at Taylor's Station, in said county, on the Shelbyville railroad, in the shales of the Hudson River or Cincinnati group.

Genus Streptorhynchus. King.

Streptorhynchus, King. Monogr. of Perm. Fossils—1850.
Etymology: *strepto*, I bend or twist; *rhynchus*, a beak.
Copied from Hall's Pal. N. Y., Vol. 4, page 64—1867.

The shells of this genus are semi-circular or semi-elliptical, concavo-convex or plano-convex, and sometimes bi-convex. They are externally striated, with rounded bifurcating striae, which are crossed by fine concentric lines; and in some forms the stronger striae are distant, with finer radiating and concentric striae cancellating the intermediate spaces. The ventral beak is sometimes produced and bent or twisted, and the fissure beneath the beak is closed or partly closed by a solid deltidium, while the area is subject to great variations. A narrow area often exists on the dorsal valve, but this is not a constant character. This genus is very closely allied to Strophomena, the most obvious external character by which the former is distinguished being the irregular twisting of the beak of ventral valve.

Streptorhynchus arctostriata. HALL.

Plate XXXI., figures 31, 32 and 33.

Orthisina arctostriata, Hall. 13th Reg. Report—1860.
Streptorhynchus arctostriata, Hall. Pal. N. Y., Vol. 4, p. 71—1867.

Shell of medium size, semi-circular or semi-elliptical, frequently unsymmetrical; the proportion of length to width differs in different specimens; hinge-line straight, differing in length in different individuals, but in the average about equal to the greatest width of the shell; lateral margins meet the cardinal line usually at right-angles; they have generally a compound curve, concave in the upper, and convex in the lower half. Ventral valve more or less convex towards the umbo, and sometimes in the middle, being more or less flattened towards the sides and front of the shell; beak often distorted; area straight, triangular and well defined in its margins; inclines sometimes forward, and again, in other specimens, backwards; it is often unequal in its two sides as divided by the triangular fissure, which is closed by a strong convex deltidial plate.

Dorsal valve depressed convex, but in some shells, partly in consequence of distortion, markedly ventricose, with a narrow or linear area. Surface ornamented by sharp, close, radiating, crenulated striae, which increase mainly by interpolation or interstitial addition.

This shell is very variable in its main characters; its beak, generally distorted, is sometimes exactly straight; the cardinal area, unequal in most specimens, is, in some individuals, fully symmetrical; the ventral valve is, in most of our shells, crushed, and consequently does not show its original form; while the dorsal valve of our specimens is, even in individuals not distorted, considerably convex, instead of the flat or slightly concave dorsal valve of eastern shells of this species.

Concentric lines of growth are more or less shown on different shells.

Formation and Locality.—Found in the upper strata of our Devonian formation, which by Prof Hall are considered as belonging to the Hamilton group; it is a rare shell, and to my knowledge, so far, never found undistorted. The specimen illustrated on plate 81, figures 32 and 33, represents about the largest size attained by this species, at least in our rocks.

Streptorhynchus subplanus. CONRAD.

Plate XXIX., figures 11 and 12.

Strophomena subplana, Conrad. Jour. Acad. Nat. Sci. Phil., Vol. 8—1842.
Leptaena subplana, Hall. Pal. N. Y., Vol. 2. p. 259—1852.
Streptorhynchus subplana, Hall. Trans. Alb. Inst., Vol. 4, p. 226—1863.
Streptorhynchus subplana, Hall. 11th Indiana Report, p. 288—1881.

Shell of medium size ; plano-convex, semi-elliptical; length and width often equal, but sometimes the latter exceeds the former considerably ; hinge-line is generally longer than the width of shell below ; cardinal extremities are always somewhat produced, but in some instances they become even mucronate.

Ventral valve moderately convex ; its greatest convexity a little above the middle, from where it slopes gently to the lateral and basal margins ; the cardinal extremities are deflected and forming a slight depression, extending from the cardinal line obliquely to the lateral margins, intersecting these about one-third the length of the shell from the cardinal extremities ; beak is small and not incurved. The foramen is closed by a deltidium. The area extends to the extremities, but is narrow.

Dorsal valve is less convex than the other ; it is in our specimens almost plane, with the exception of the umbonal region and the cardinal angles, both of which are slightly convex, the umbonal region by a natural elevation, and the cardinal angles by a downward deflection of the extremities.

Cardinal area narrow, but about as large as the area of the other valve. Both valves meet under an angle of about sixty degrees.

The surface is covered by numerous single thread-like radii, which increase by intercalation but not by bifurcation. The intercalated striae are smaller than the original; they become equal at the margin. These radii are crossed by fine concentric striae, and by a few marked concentric lines of growth, generally two in number, dividing each valve into three concentric zones. Our specimens differ somewhat in shape from those found at Waldron, Indiana. Ours are somewhat wider in proportion to length, and the extremities are more produced. The size of different specimens differs greatly; the one illustrated is of about maximum size, as found in our rocks.

Formation and Locality.—Occurs in the Niagara rocks in the quarries south-east of the city of Louisville, Ky., where it is a rather rare species. Very fine specimens are found abundantly in the Niagara rocks of Waldron, Indiana.

Streptorhynchus tenuis. HALL.

Streptorhynchus tenuis, Hall. Trans. Alb. Inst., Vol. 4, p. 210—1863.
Streptorhynchus tenuis, Hall. 28th Regent's Rep., p. 150—1879.
Streptorhynchus tenuis, Hall. 11th Geol. Rep. of Ind., p. 287—1881.

Shells found at Waldron, large; those found in the rocks near Louisville of medium size; semi-circular or broadly semi-elliptical; cardinal line less than greatest width of shell; cardinal extremities rounded.

Ventral valve moderately convex at the umbo and the umbonal region, extending over about one-third of the whole surface of the valve; balance slightly concave; cardinal area narrow, but increasing in height at the beak and near it; beak elevated and straight; triangular fissure of moderate size and closed by a deltidium.

Dorsal valve moderately convex; umbo very small; surface depressed near the cardinal extremities, and also near front margin.

Surface ornamented with radiating striae of ·different size, all fine and rounded, but alternately large and small, which are strongly curved on the lateral portion of shell. These radii are crossed by fine concentric striae, which give surface of shell, under lens, a beautiful rugose character. The substance of the shell is very thin. Large specimens of this species are found at Waldron, Indiana, of which one individual, according to Prof. Hall's statement, measures forty millimeters in length, by fifty millimeters in width. The specimen before me being the only one found in our rocks, measures nine lines in length by fourteen lines in width.

Formation and Locality.—Found in the Niagara limestone at Waldron, Indiana, and in the quarries east of the city of Louisville, Ky. It is very rare; only few specimens are so far found at Waldron, and but one at Louisville; this last one belongs to my collection.

Genus Strophodonta. Hall.

Strophodonta, Hall. Pal. N. Y., Vol. 2, p. 63—1852.
Etymology: strophos, bent; odous, tooth.

Shell with general form and characters of Leptaena; one valve convex, the other one concave; the concave one following the general curve of the other, and being nearly parallel with the same. Cardinal area continuous, nearly linear, mostly occupied by the dorsal valve, striated transversely; foramen decidedly closed; ventral valve with the hinge-line uninterrupted; margins of the hinge-line crenulated; area strongly striated in the transverse, and more slightly in the longitudinal direction. Muscular impressions somewhat bilateral.

The crenulated hinge-line is a very strong distinctive character, since in

Leptaena this margin is smooth. In true Leptaena, also, the area is striated only longitudinally, that is, in the direction of the hinge-line, and the foramen is in part occupied by a projection of the ventral valve, which fills it, while in Strophodonta the foramen, if it ever existed, is entirely closed by the growth of the dorsal valve, and the hinge-line of the ventral valve is straight and continuous. The striae of the shell in many species of Strophodonta differ from those of Leptaena, and some of the species are readily distinguished by this character alone.

The chief peculiarity of the shells belonging to Strophodonta is the absence of a foramen in area of the ventral valve ; otherwise, they do not differ from Strophomena, which may hereafter take the place of Strophodonta.

Strophodonta demissa. CONRAD.

Plate XVIII., figures 10 to 16, Plate XXXIII., figure 22.

Strophodonta demissa, Conrad. Journ. Acad. Nat. Sci. Phil., Vol. 8—1842.
Strophomena (Strophodonta) demissa, Hall. 10th Reg. Rep., p. 137—1847.
Strophodonta demissa, Hall. Rep. Geol. Sur. of Iowa, p 495—1859.
Strophomena demissa, Billings. Canadian Journal—1861.
Strophomena demissa, Billings. Geology of Canada, p. 367—1863.
Strophodonta demissa, Hall. Pal. N. Y., Vol. 4, page 101—1867.

Shell semi-elliptical, usually somewhat wider than high, but in some specimens both dimensions are equal ; hinge-line about equal to greatest width of shell, sometimes differing from it by being either a little larger or smaller. The shell is often a little contracted below the cardinal extremities, which are sometimes auriculate. In some of the specimens, the lateral margins are nearly straight and parallel for more than half the length of shell, while the lower parts of the sides and the base form a regular curve.

Ventral valve regularly convex ; greatest convexity a little above middle of the length, from where it slopes in a regular curve to the lateral and basal margins ; between the umbo and the cardinal extremities is a slight depression, which only runs a short distance from the cardinal line into the body of the valve, and which is sometimes confined to the mere deflection of the cardinal extremities ; umbo is small, but well expressed, and the beak is slightly incurved, and reaches somewhat beyond the plane of the ventral area.

Dorsal valve is moderately concave, and corresponds in the general form of its depression with the convexity of the ventral valve. The area of the ventral valve is very variable in specimens from different localities, but in our shells it is of moderate size, forming a low triangle, and being curved below and on both sides of the beak ; it is covered by fine transverse, and still finer longitudinal lines ; no foramen or fissure is indicated ; the inner margin of the area is crenulated in its whole extent. The dorsal area is considerably smaller than the ventral; it is very narrow, almost linear. The planes of the two cardinal areas are inclined to each other in such a manner as to form an angle of more than ninety degrees; this angle of the areas is, however, different in one and the same specimen according to the distance from the cardinal extremities; near the latter it is smallest and increases gradually, sometimes rapidly, towards the beaks, below which, in some individuals, they form no angle at all, but fall in one and the same plane.

The surface of both valves is ornamented by radiating and concentric striae. Of the radii, some ten to twelve are much stronger and more elevated than the balance, but they maintain their prominence only inside of the umbonal region; leaving this, they bifurcate directly, which process is repeated about half-way between umbo and front; in addition to this increase by bifurcation, a further enlargement in the number of finer radii is attained by the intercalation of radiating striae, some of which reach even into the umbonal region, between the before mentioned prominent costae, while others set in a little above the second bifurcation; thus the marginal portion of the valve is covered by numerous fine striae.

The dorsal valve is covered by a similar system of striae, with the only exception, that in this valve, between the first and second bifurcation of one and the same radius, is only a short distance. In well preserved specimens the entire surface of both valves is covered by fine concentric lines of growth, some of which are more prominent, and divide the surface into concentric zones. In most of the shells these concentric lines, with the exception of the most marked ones, are obliterated by either silicification or exfoliation. Shells from different localities show considerable variation in form and size. Our shells, although differing in size, are uniform in shape and in the ornamentation of their surface. With very few exceptions, they have all a brownish-red color, which is entirely superficial, not penetrating into the body of the shell to any extent.

* **Formation and Locality.**—Occurs rather abundantly in the upper strata of the Devonian formation, in Jefferson county, Ky., and in Clark county, Indiana. Very fine and well preserved specimens are found, lacking only the fine concentric lines of growth. The illustrations on plate 18 represent the different sizes of the shell as found in our rocks, and figure 22, plate 33, a very young specimen.

Strophodonta hemispherica. HALL.

Plate XVIII., figures 4, 5 and 6.

Strophomena (Strophodonta) *hemispherica*, Hall. Tenth Report on St. Cab., p. 113—1857.
Strophodonta hemispherica, Hall. Pal. N. Y., Vol. 4, p. 90—1867.

Shell of large size, sub-hemispheric, semi-elliptical in outline; hinge-line equal or greater than maximum width of shell; cardinal extremities always angular, sometimes salient and auriculate ; length smaller than the width, their proportion about as four to five. The largest specimens measure about two inches in length, by two inches and a half in width. Ventral valve is very gibbous ; its depth is sometimes equal to half of its length. The point of greatest convexity below the middle of the length, from which it slopes rapidly or rather abruptly to the front, and to the basal half of the lateral margins, while it curves gently to the cardinal lines.

The umbo is more or less elevated, and the beak incurved. The cardinal area is narrow, and its margin crenulated.

Dorsal valve shallow, concave in its larger portion, and only more abruptly deflected in a marginal strip surrounding basal half of the valve, which strip becomes sometimes even geniculated.

Surface is ornamented by fine radiating striae, which are somewhat unequal on the upper and middle portions of the ventral valve, but are fine and regular towards the margins. In some specimens of the dorsal valve the striae show a tendency to the alternation of three or four finer ones with a distinctly stronger one between ; but this feature is not prevalent ; most shells have the striae or their dorsal valve fine, close, and nearly equal in strength. Fine concentric lines cross the radii in well preserved specimens, but they are usually obliterated. Four or five marked wrinkles extend obliquely from the cardinal extremities into the body of the valve, but reach only to the base of the umbo. This species differs from St. inequiradiata by its larger size and greater gibbosity ; while, according to Prof. Hall's statement, it is so nearly allied to Stroph. concava, that it probably belongs with that shell in one and the same species.

Formation and Locality.—Occurs in the Corniferous limestone of the Devonian formation in Jefferson county, Ky., and in Clark county, Indiana. The specimens for the figures 7, 8 and 9, on plate 18, seem to be an internal cast of Strophodonta hemispherica.

Strophodonta inequistriata. CONRAD.

Plate XVII., figures 10 and 11.

Strophomena inequistriata, Conrad. Jour. Acad. Nat. Sci. Phil.—1842.
Strophomena inequistriata, Hall. Geol. Rep. 4th Dist., p. 290—1843.
Strophomena (Strophodonta) inequistriata, Hall. 10th Reg. Rep., p. 142—1857.
Strophodonta inequistriata, Hall. Pal. of N. Y., Vol. 4, p. 106—1857.

Shell semi-oval or somewhat semi-elliptical or semi-circular in outline ; hinge-line extended beyond width of shell below ; cardinal extremities acute, sometimes mucronate. In the specimen before me, which is illustrated on plate 17, figure 10, the lateral margins below the mucronate extremities, and the basal margin, form a regular curve,

Ventral valve moderately convex, becoming more gibbous in its center portion from umbo to front ; greatest convexity a little above the middle of the valve, from where it slopes in a regular curve to the front or base, and to the basal half of the lateral margins; to cardinal line and to the rear half of the lateral margins it slopes more rapidly ; the cardinal angles are reflected, by which a shallow concavity is formed between them and the umbo; the beak is little elevated above the hinge-line and slightly incurved ; the cardinal area is narrow, extending to the extremities, and striate vertically.

Dorsal valve concave, differing greatly in its depth in different individuals ; but usually its concavity corresponds in general form with the convexity of the ventral valve; hinge-area very narrow, almost linear, and of not more than half the height of the ventral one ; no beak is observed in this valve.

Surface is ornamented by radii of different size and character, as may be seen in figure 11, plate 17. Some of these striae are more prominent, most of which extend to the beak, but some are added by intercalation ; the interspaces between these stronger striae are filled by finer ones, which are scarcely visible to the naked eye ; all the radii are crossed by fine concentric striae. The general surface character of the convex valve is much like that of good specimens of Strophomena alternata, of the Trenton limestone, but it does not appear to be subject to such extreme variations in respect to the striae. It also resembles greatly in its surface-markings Strophodonta textilis, but it is always smaller, has a more extended hinge-line, and is never so flat as that species. It is often confounded with Strophodonta inequiradiata, which is a much larger species, with different internal characters. Its surface striae are more delicate than any of the other species.

Formation and Locality.—Occurs in the Corniferous limestone at the Falls of the Ohio, in Kentucky and Indiana.

Strophodonta nacrea. Hall.

Strophodonta nacrea, Hall.   Tenth Rep. on St. Cab., p. 144—1857
Strophomena lepida, Hall.   Geol. Rep. of Iowa, Vol. 1, pt. 2, p. 493—1858.
Strophodonta nacrea, Hall.   Pal. N. Y., Vol. 4, p. 104—1867.

Shell below medium size ; semi-elliptical, having a brilliant nacreous luster ; hinge-line crenulated, equalling, or a little less, than the greatest width of shell below ; cardinal extremities angular. Ventral valve regularly and moderately convex ; depressed or slightly concave within the cardinal angles, caused by a slight deflection of the cardinal extremities ; umbo depressed and the beak very small, scarcely elevated above the hinge-line, and not incurved ; cardinal area very small and without foramen.

Dorsal valve concave, corresponding in its depression with the form of the ventral convexity; its hinge-area is very narrow, almost linear; no beak perceptible.

Surface smooth, with a few concentric lines of growth. Prof. Hall states, that in well preserved specimens, traces of very fine concentric, as well as radiating striae have been observed. Our shells of this species are all entirely silicified, in which condition the finer surface-markings are usually obliterated.

Formation and Locality.—Found in the Corniferous limestone at the Falls of the Ohio, on the Indiana shore of the river.

Strophodonta perplana. CONRAD.

Plate XVIII., figure 17.

Strophomena perplana, Conrad. Jour. Acad. Nat. Sci. Phil., Vol. 8—1842.

Strophomena pluristriata, Conrad. ut. sup., p. 259.

Strophomena crenistria, Hall. Rep. 4th Geol. Dist. N. Y., p. 171—1843.

Strophomena (Strophodonta) *fragilis,* Hall. 10th Rep. on St. Cab., p. 143—1867.

Strophodonta fragilis, Hall. Rep. Geol. Surv. of Iowa, p. 496—1858.

Shell semi-elliptical; length varying from two-thirds to three-fourths the width, which is from half an inch to two inches; slightly concavo-convex, and often nearly flat; hinge-line equal, or often a little greater, than width of shell below; the cardinal extremities usually somewhat salient, except in extremely old shells. Margins of the shell often a little concave just below the cardinal extremities, making the width there less than below. From this incurvation downwards, the lateral and basal margins form usually a regular curve.

Ventral valve very little convex, the greatest convexity above the middle of its length, from where it slopes in a gentle curve to the lateral and basal margins; towards the cardinal angles it slopes a little more rapidly, and as the extremities are somewhat deflected, the valve becomes slightly concave between them and the umbonal region; the apex is scarcely rising above the hinge-line, and slightly incurved.

Dorsal valve is gently concave, but often almost flat. Area of the ventral valve is usually less than a line in width, and covered with vertical striae. Area of the dorsal valve about half as wide as that of the ventral.

Surface covered by fine sub-equal striae, those of the ventral valve being finer than the striae on the dorsal, extremely sharp, and often gently undulating, increasing both by bifurcation and by intercalation, and crossed by fine, even, concentric striae. Prof. Hall states, that in some specimens the longitudinal striae rise at frequent and regular intervals into minute granules, which he considers the bases of minute spines, formerly covering the ventral valve. This feature is not indicated on any of our specimens as far as I know. The dorsal valve is marked by fine, even, rounded striae, which are cancellated by close concentric striae, and the same obscure concentric undulations, which are often noticed on the ventral valve near the umbo. In general the shell is readily recognized by its nearly flat form and by its fine, nearly equal striae.

Formation and Locality.—Occurs in the upper strata of the Devonian limestone at the Falls of the Ohio, in Kentucky and Indiana, where the ventral valves are somewhat abundant.

Strophodonta profunda. HALL.

Plate XXIX., figure 26, and Plate XVII., figures 20 and 21.

Leptaena pr ofunda, Hall. Pal. N. Y., Vol. 2, p. 61, pl. 21, figures 4 and 5—1852.
Strophodonta profunda, Hall. 20th Regent's Rep., p. 369—1867.
Strophodonta profunda, Hall. 28th Regent's Rep., p. 151—1879.
Strophodonta profunda, Hall. 11th Geol. Rep. of Ind., p. 289—1881.

Shell large, broadly semi-oval ; width larger than length ; hinge-line greater than greatest width of shell ; cardinal extremities slightly extended and sub-auriculate, in casts often obtuse or rounded ; shell concavo-convex. Ventral valve, according to Prof. Hall's description, very convex ; this is not the case with our shells. In our specimens the ventral valve is only moderately convex ; in some individuals the central portion around the umbo is most convex, while the balance is depressed, or even somewhat concave ; in other shells the central portion is flat, or even somewhat concave, while the marginal portion of the valve all around, from one extremity to the other, is strongly curved ; and, again, in some specimens the whole valve, with the exception of the cardinal angles, is regularly and prominently curved ; in these shells, the cardinal extremities are slightly deflected, and the surface between them and the umbo gently depressed or concave.

Hinge area narrow ; foramen triangular, of moderate size, and covered by a strong deltidial callosity.

Dorsal valve corresponding in its concavity with the convexity of the ventral valve. Hinge-area narrower than that of the ventral valve ; foramen covered by a callosity. Surface marked by strong, large, radiating striae, which alternate with four or five smaller striae, all of which, the smaller as well as the larger, increase by intercalation. These radii are crossed by fine concentric lines. In some specimens the smaller striae become stronger, forming the larger and less regular striae. The specimen illustrated on plate 17, figure 20, is one of the largest found near our city.

Formation and Locality.—Occurs in the Niagara rocks in the quarries east of the city of Louisville. It is not abundant.

Strophodonta plicata. Hall.

Strophodonta plicata, Hall. 13th Rep. on St. Cab., p. 90—1860.
Strophodonta plicata, Hall. Pal. N. Y., Vol. 4, p. 114, pl. 63, figs. 30-32—1867.

Shell of medium size; semi-oval or semi-elliptical; concavo-convex; hinge-line somewhat shorter than the greatest width of shell; cardinal extremities rounded; lateral margins almost straight or slightly curved; basal margin broadly curved. Shell resembling closely, as far as form is concerned, specimens of Strophodonta demissa, of medium size and medium convexity.

Ventral valve moderately convex, with greatest convexity at about the middle of the shell, from where it slopes gently to the cardinal and lateral margins, and somewhat more rapidly to the front. The umbo is small; beak little elevated and incurved; cardinal area small, with a triangular fissure, closed by the beak of opposite valve.

Dorsal valve moderately concave, nearly following the contour of ventral valve; its cardinal area very narrow, almost linear; its beak closing the ventral foramen.

The surface is ornamented by strong, sub-angular or rounded radiating striae, which increase in number by bifurcation and intercalation, and which are crossed by a few concentric lines of growth near the margin. This shell resembles, as before stated, Stroph. demissa, from which it is, however, easily distinguished by its strong and prominent striae; there is about the same proportion in strength between the striae of St. plicata and Stroph. demissa, as between the striae of Atrypa aspera and Atr. reticularis.

Formation and Locality.—Occurs in the Corniferous limestone of the Devonian formation at and around the Falls of the Ohio, in Kentucky and Indiana, where it is, however, a very rare shell.

Strophodonta striata. Hall.

Strophomena striata, Hall. Geol. Rep. of 4th Dist. N. Y.—1843.
Leptaena striata, Hall. Pal. N. Y., Vol. 2, p. 259—1852.
Strophodonta striata, Hall. 28th Regent's Rep., p. 152—1879.
Strophodonta striata, Hall. 11th Geol. Report of Ind., p. 290—1881.

Shell semi-elliptical; hinge-line equal or a little longer than the greatest width of the shell below; dorsal valve slightly convex; ventral valve flat or somewhat concave. Surface covered by unequal, radiating striae, of which the stronger ones have large interspaces, which are occupied by one, mostly by two, finer radii, all of which increase in number by intercalation, and not by bifurcation. There are, sometimes, fine concentric lines of growth crossing the radii, but these are often obsolete. The specimens of this species found in our rocks differ somewhat in form from those found at Waldron, Indiana.

Our shells are more transverse, and show a somewhat geniculated base like Strophodonta rhomboidalis, and besides, are considerably smaller; but these differences are only the results of local conditions.

Formation and Locality.—Found in the Niagara limestone in the quarries east of the city of Louisville, Ky.

Genus Strophomena. Rafinesque.

Strophomena, Rafinesque.   Manuel de Malac. of Blainville—1825.
Etymology: strophos, bent; *mene*, a crescent.

The Genus Strophomena was established by Rafinesque, and has for its type the S. rugosa, which is identical with Strophomena rhomboidalis of Wahlenberg, a species which ranges from the Lower Silurian to the base of the Carboniferous system.   This species has some little differences in shape and markings, according to the formations in which it appears.   I have not been able to see Rafinesque's original description; but whatever this may be, it covers all the shells which are now included in this genus and those of Hall's genus, Strophodonta, which latter will certainly be discontinued.

Strophomena rhomboidalis. Wahlenberg.

Plate XVIII., figures 1, 2 and 3.
Strophomena rhomboidalis, Wahlenberg.   Acta. Soc. S. Upsaliensis, Vol. 8—1821.
Strophomena rhomboidalis, Hall.   Pal. N. Y., Vol. 4, p. 76—1867.
See list of synonyms in last named report.

Shell of more than medium size; semi-elliptical or sub-quadrate; varying greatly in its proportions of length and breadth; hinge-line straight, and equal to greatest width of shell; cardinal extremities mostly rectangular, sometimes salient.   The valves are geniculated, and the proportions of the flattened part of the disc and the recurved part of the shell are very variable, insomuch that the geniculation is sometimes little more than one of the strong concentric wrinkles.   (Hall.)

In the specimens of this species, found in our rocks, there is not so much variation as stated in the foregoing description of Prof. Hall.   Our shells have almost all the form, as shown in the illustrations.   They are sub-quadrate; their lateral margins are parallel and almost straight, and the basal margin is broadly curved.   The geniculation is usually found in both valves, although in some specimens the dorsal valve does not possess any, but is entirely plane. The deflected portion of the lateral margins is triangular, with its apex at the cardinal extremity; it increases gradually towards the base, where it equals

in width the deflected basal margin ; the height of this basal deflection measures from one-third to one-half of the length of disc.

The ventral valve is slightly convex at and around the umbo, but flat or even
somewhat depressed between the umbo and the geniculation; its beak is small
and only slightly curved.

Dorsal valve generally corresponding in its concavity with the convexity of
the ventral, only differing in the depth of the valve ; but in some shells there
is an exception to this rule, inasmuch as the dorsal valve is entirely straight
from the cardinal line to the level of the lateral and basal geniculation.

The surface is ornamented on the flattened portions of the shell by concentric, undulating, strong elevations, which are parallel with the curve of
the geniculation, and deflect outwards at the cardinal margin ; they are most
prominent in the portion parallel with the base, decrease in strength in their
lateral course, and become almost obsolete in some shells near the hinge-line ;
their number is variable, according to size and shape of the shell.   The entire
surface is covered by radiating thread-like striae.   The triangular fissure of the
ventral valve is partially closed by a deltidium and the apex of the ventral
valve.

Formation and Locality.—Occurs in the upper strata of the Devonian rocks in Jefferson county,
Ky., and in Clark county, Indiana.   It is met with very often, but seldom found in fair, undistorted specimens.   The individual illustrated is one of the largest found here, though there is little difference in the
size of our shells belonging to this species

Strophomena rhomboidalis.   Wahlenberg.

This species has been described from the Devonian formation, in which the
conditions for the development of the shell appear to have been more favora-
able, inasmuch as the animal attained a considerably larger size.   Outside of
this difference we find no distinction between the shells from both formations,
and there are no reasons for a new description here.

Formation and Locality.—Occurs in the Niagara limestone in the quarries east of the city of Louisville, where it is, however, rare, and where it attains not even half the size of those found in the Devonian
rocks in Clark county, Indiana.

Genus Leptocoelia.   Hall.

Leptocoelia, Hall.   Rep. on the St. Cab. of Nat. Hist.—1856.
Copied from Hall's Pal. N. Y., Vol. 3, page 447—1859.
Etymology: leptos, minute; *koilia,* belly, in allusion to the shallow visceral cavity.

Shell inequivalve ; variable in form, usually semi-oval or sub-circular,
transverse or elongate, plano-convex or concavo-convex ; hinge-line sometimes

equal to greatest width of shell. Ventral valve convex or sub angular in the middle, with beak more or less extended; moderately incurved. Foramen terminal, the lower side formed by two deltidial pieces.

Dorsal valve flat or concave or depressed convex. A mesial fold and sinus existing, but not often prominent. Structure of the shell lamellose or fibrous, not punctate. Valves articulating by means of two strong teeth in the ventral, inserted into the sockets in the dorsal valve, which are mainly excavated in the base of a strong cardinal process. Teeth converging. Muscular impression marking a large ovate or flabelliform area, with a thin medium septum. Adductor imprints small.

Leptocoelia hemispherica. SOWERBY.

Plate XXXII., figures 21, 22 and 23, and 36 to 39.

Atrypa hemispherica, Sowerby. Sil. Syst., p, 639—1839.
Atrypa hemispherica, Hall. Pal. N. Y., Vol. 2, p. 74—1852.
Atrypa hemispherica, Nicholson. Pal. of Ontario, p. 47—1875.

Shell rather small; hemispheric or sub-circular; plicated. Hinge-line in some specimens extended and straight; in others short and deflected towards the front. Both valves in the specimens before me somewhat convex. Surface ornamented by about ten to twelve strong, rounded, simple radii, which increase in strength and in size of their interspaces from apex to front. The two shells illustrated, sub-figures 21 to 23, and sub-figures 36 to 39, agree in every feature except in the size and direction of their cardinal lines.

Formation and Locality.—Found in the lower strata of the Niagara group, which may possibly belong to the Clinton, in the quarries east of the city of Louisville, Ky., where it is, however, a rather rare species, of which fair specimens are very seldom found.

Genus Centronella. Billings.

Centronella, Billings. Can. Nat. and Geol., Vol. 4—1859.
Etymology: a little point.

Shells having the general form of Terebratula. Dorsal valve with a loop consisting of two riband-like lamellae, which extend about one-half the length of the shell. These lamellae at first curve gently outwards, and thence approach each other gradually, until at their lower extremities they meet at an acute angle; then becoming united, they are deflected backwards towards the beak, in what appears to be a thin, flat, vertical plate. Near their origin, each bears upon the ventral side a single triangular crural process. This genus appears to stand between Terebratula and Waldheimia. In the former the loop is short, not exceeding greatly one-third the length of the shell, and not reflected. In the latter it extends nearly to the front, and is reflected, but the laminae are not united until they are folded back. (Billings.)

Centronella glans-fagea. HALL.

Plate XXXI., figures 14, 15, 16 and 17.

Rhynchonella glans-fagea, Hall. Tenth Rep. on St. Cab., p. 125—1857.
Centronella glans-fagea, Billings. Canadian Nat. and Geol., p. 131—1859.
Centronella glans-fagea, Hall. Sixteenth Rep. on St. Cab.—1863.
Centronella glans-fagea, Hall. Pal. N. Y., Vol. 4, p. 399—1867.

Shell small, ovate or sub-triangular, concavo-convex, with rounded base and very unequal valves.

Ventral valve much larger than dorsal, greatly elevated in its center line from beak to front, thus making the valve sub-carinate, or its transverse section triangular. From the sub-carinate middle line it curves very abruptly to the lateral margins, while longitudinally there is almost no curvature in the whole valve except at the umbo; the beak is much extended beyond that of the opposite valve, and arched dorsally far enough to extend to the level of dorsal valve.

Dorsal valve sub-angularly concave from beak to front, the depression corresponding to the angular elevation of the other valve; the beak not incurving into the opposite valve; the mesial sinus widening rapidly towards the front, extending in the basal third to the lateral margins. With the exception of some concentric lines of growth, there are no other surface-markings. The specimen illustrated is one of the largest found in Kentucky; it also shows the usual proportion between width and length. Comparing our shells of this species with Prof. Hall's figures, we find them differ from most of his forms in size and shape; still they have the specific aspect and characters.

Formation and Locality.—Found in the rotten hornstone of the Devonian group in Jefferson county, Ky., and Clark county, Indiana, where it is, however, rarely met with, especially in well preserved or even fair specimens.

Genus Terebratula. Llhwyd.

Terebratula, Llhwyd. Lith. Brit. Ichn.—1696.
Etymology: diminutive of *terebratus,* perforated.

Types: T. maxillata and T. vitrea.

Shell minutely punctate, smooth and convex, usually round or oval. Ventral valve with a prominent beak, which is truncated and perforated; foramen circular.

Dorsal valve with a depressed umbo; a prominent cardinal process between the dental sockets; deltidium of two pieces, frequently blended; loop very short, simple, attached by its crura to the hinge-plate.

GEOL. SUR.—20

Terebratula harmonia. Hall.

Plate XVII., figures 1, 2, 3 and 4.

Terebratula harmonia, Hall. Pal. N. Y., Vol. 4, p. 388—1867.

Shell of more than medium size; ovate or sub-spatulate; tapering somewhat abruptly to the beak, compressed at the margins, but convex in middle; base regularly curved.

Ventral valve regularly arcuate from beak to front, moderately convex in the middle; a little gibbous above, and depressed convex or slightly concave towards the front; the upper part narrowing; the beak much extended, attenuate and arcuate, but not closely incurved; apex perforated, the slope to the cardinal margin scarcely concave; deltidial plates large.

Dorsal valve moderately convex, sometimes a little more prominent along the middle in the upper part, and depressed towards the front and sides.

Surface marked by fine concentric lines of growth; the substance of the shell finely punctate.

This species resembles to a certain degree Ter. sullivanti, but it is more regularly arcuate from beak to front of the ventral valve, and has a regularly rounded base, while Ter. sullivanti has a truncate or sinuate front. Its well marked regular form in larger specimens will easily identify it.

Formation and Locality.—Found in the corniferous limestone at and around the Falls of the Ohio, in Kentucky and Indiana. It is a somewhat rare species. Prof. Hall received the original specimens, from which he made his description and illustrations of this species, from the late Dr. James Knapp, who collected the same at the Falls of the Ohio.

Terebratula jucunda. Hall.

Terebratula jucunda, Hall. Pal. N. Y., Vol. 4, p. 390—1867.

Shell of medium size; sub-circular or very broadly ovate; length and width about equal; regularly rounded in the margins of the basal half, but abruptly converging to the ventral apex in upper half.

Ventral valve moderately convex; gibbous in the umbonal region, sloping in a gentle, regular curve to the base and baso-lateral margins, showing a faint mesial depression; beak obtuse and arched over the umbo of the opposite valve; apex truncated by a rounded foramen.

Dorsal valve less convex than the ventral, but regularly arched all over the surface, with the exception of the cardinal angles, which are somewhat inflated. The specimen before me shows a faint elevation in the basal half, corresponding with the sinus of opposite valve.

Surface is marked by fine concentric striæ or lines of growth. My specimen measures in length and width a little more than three-eighths of an inch.

Formation and Locality.—Occurs in the corniferous limestone in Jefferson county, Kentucky, and in Clark county, Indiana.

Terebratula lincklaeni. Hall

Plate XVII., figures 22, 23 and 24.

Terebratula lincklaeni, Hall. 13th Regent's Report—1860.
Terebratula lincklaeni, var., Hall. Pal. N. Y., Vol. 4, p. 418—1867.

Shell of medium size; sub-ovate or sub-triangular, with broadly curved or slightly truncated base; moderately ventricose; length somewhat exceeding width.

Ventral valve larger, and slightly more ventricose than the dorsal; greatest convexity at the umbo, from where it slopes in a gentle regular curve to the lateral and basal margins, but abruptly towards the cardinal margins, whose borders are somewhat inflected; the umbo is prominent, and the beak elevated and incurved above the beak of the other valve; at the front there is a slight depression noticeable, but this feature is often wanting.

Dorsal valve smaller, and less convex than the ventral; greatest convexity at the umbo, from where it slopes in an almost straight line to the front, in a gentle curve to the lateral margins and abruptly to the cardinal lines; umbo moderately prominent, and the beak strongly incurved under that of the opposite valve.

The surface is covered with concentric lines of growth, some of which are more prominent, and divide the surface of some individuals into different zones. No other surface-markings are visible on our specimens, which are all in a silicified condition.

Formation and Locality.—Found in the rotten hornstone of the Devonian formation, in Jefferson county, Ky., and in Clark county, Ind.; it is of rather rare occurrence. This species resembles Ter.roemingeri, with which it is associated, but differs by having its greatest width near the base, while Ter.roemingeri has its maximum width above the middle, and the latter species is generally more gibbous and stronger umbonated.

Terebratula roemingeri. Hall.

Plate XVI., figures 20, 21 and 22.

Terebratula roemingeri, Hall. Sixteenth Rep. on St. Cab., p. 48—1863.
Terebratula roemingeri, Hall. Pal. N. Y., Vol. 4, p. 389—1867.

Shell ovate, more or less gibbous; truncate or slightly sinuate in front.

Ventral valve gibbous above the middle; umbo gibbous, inflated; beak prominent, incurved over that of the opposite valve, and truncated by a round foramen, which is often mainly anterior to the apex, and completed on the lower side by two deltidial plates; cardinal slopes rounded, often depressed in the middle towards the front.

Dorsal valve extremely gibbous, little longer than wide; the greatest convexity at the middle or above.

Surface marked by fine concentric lines of growth, which are often crowded into prominent wrinkles towards the front. Shell structure finely punctate.

The interior shows a short terebratuliform loop, which is abruptly recurved at its lower extremities.

This species resembles Ter. lincklaeni, from which it differs, however, by its greater gibbosity, by having its greatest width above the middle, while that species has its maximum width near the base, and by its truncated or sinuate base.

Formation and Locality.—Found in the rotten hornstone of the Devonian formation in Jefferson county, Ky., and in Clark county, Ind. A rather rare species.

MOLLUSCA.

PTEROPODA.

Genus Tentaculites. Schlotheim.

Tentaculites, Schlotheim. Petrefacten—1820.
Etymology: tentaculum, a feeler; *lithos,* stone.

The shells belonging to this genus are easily distinguished by their exterior appearance; they form very elongated, slender cones, marked by prominent annulations and fine transverse striae.

The place which these shells had to occupy in the great sub-kingdom Mollusca, was for a long time doubtful, until in 1845 Mr. Austin assigned them to the Pteropoda, which position is accepted by all the naturalists up to the present day, though doubts are sometimes expressed as to their relation with the thin hyaline shells of most of the existing forms of Pteropoda.

Tentaculites scalariformis. Hall.

Plate XXXI., figure 12.

Tentaculites scalaris, Hall. Geol. of N. Y., 4th Dist., p. 172—1843.
Tent. scalariformis and *T. sicula,* Hall. Illust. of Dev. Fossils—1876.
Tentaculites scalariformis, Hall. Pal. N. Y., Vol. 5, pt. 2, p. 167—1885.

Shell elongate-conical, straight, somewhat more cylindrical in approaching the aperture; the apex in well preserved specimens extremely attenuate, and quite solid for one-fourth to one-third of the entire length of the shell. Annulations prominent, sub-angular, sometimes rounded on the larger part of the cone; closely arranged and sharply angular near the apex, gradually increasing their distance; becoming less angular with the increase of the size of the shell and obtuse and rounded towards the aperture. On the outer half of the shell, the spaces between the annulations are greater than the annulations themselves. The interspaces, as well as the annulations, are covered in well preserved specimens with fine, even, transverse striae; the number of which differ greatly. In some specimens there is much irregularity in the distance and development of the annulations towards the aperture. The extreme point of the apex is rarely or never preserved in our specimens.

Our specimens of this species are always silicified, and maintain their original cylindrical form; they never suffered compression.

The shells of this species attain a length of one inch—rarely more, but usually somewhat less. The largest individual before me, and of which the illustration—figure 12, plate 31—was made, measures one-half of an inch; the figure is enlarged to double size.

Formation and Locality.—Found in the rotten hornstone of the Devonian formation, in Clark county, Indiana, on the northern shore of the Ohio river, opposite its falls, and in the cherty layers superimposed upon the hydraulic limestone at Watson's Station, on the Ohio and Mississippi Railroad.

Genus Styliola   Lesueur.

Etymology: stylos, a pillar.

Prof. Ludwig gives the following translation of a description of this genus from M. Barrande: Shell small; transverse section circular; closed below, and thicker than in the upper part; conical. Surface without annulations; smooth, but with fine striae of growth, and sometimes with fine longitudinal striae; without longitudinal slit, but sometimes with one or two longitudinal grooves, which do not penetrate the shell; without operculum, and without interior partitions, but having a persistent point sometimes curved backward. The greatest width is at the opening, which is oblique or normal to the axis of shell.

Styliola fissurella.   HALL.

Tentaculites fissurella, Hall. Geol. Surv 4th Dist. N. Y.—1843.
Not. Tentaculites fissurella, Hall. Ill. of Dev. Fossils—1876.
Styliola fissurella, Hall. Pal. N. Y., Vol. 5, pt. 2, p. 178—1885.

Shell an extremely slender, elongate cone. Apical portion of shell solid. Apex extremely minute, often bulbiform, and very gradually enlarging to the aperture.

Surface often smooth and without any visible ornamentation, so far as can be ascertained, or with fine striae or lines of growth, which are often unequally developed on different parts of the shell; and also with fine longitudinal striae, which may be present with or without the transverse striae. Length different in different individuals. Prof. Hall gives their length from two to five millimeters.

The specimens before me, which have all the characters mentioned in the foregoing description, are considerably larger ; they are only fragments, without apex and aperture, but all indications point at least to a length exceeding half an inch.

Formation and Locality.—Occurs in the upper strata of the Devonian formation, at and around the Falls of the Ohio, in Kentucky and Indiana. This little shell is rather rare.

MOLLUSCA.

GASTEROPODA.

Genus Bellerophon. Montfort.

Bellerophon, Montfort. Conch. Syst., Vol. 1—1808.
Etymology: a mythological name.

The type of this genus is Bellerophon bicarinatus. The shells of this genus are symmetrically convoluted, globular or discoidal, strong, few-whorled ; the whorls are often sculptured ; dorsally keeled. The apereture is sinuated and deeply notched on the dorsal side ; its shape is variable, sometimes triangular, and sometimes reniform or sub-orbicular. The surface is usually marked by fine concentric striae, and sometimes by fine revolving striae also.

This genus extends from the Lower Silurian to the Carboniferous, inclusively.

Bellerophon leda. Hall.

Plate XVII., figures 12 and 13.

Bellerophon leda, Hall. Descpt. of New Sp. of Foss. p. 30—1861.
Bellerophon leda, Hall. Fifteenth Rep. N Y. St. Cab., p. 58—1862.
Bellerophon leda, H. and W. 29th Regent's Rep., p. 200—1872.
Bellerophon leda, H and W 27th Regent's Rep., pl. 13—1875.
Bellerophon leda, Hall Illust of Dev. Foss., pl. 24—1876.
Bellerophon leda, Hall. Pal. N. Y., Vol 5, pt. 2. p. 110—1879.

Shell sub-globose, often a little flattened upon the dorsum ; body-whorl ventricose, very rapidly expanding ; aperture very wide ; peristome abruptly spreading, broadly sinuate in front, and sometimes with a deep notch in the middle. The margin gently recurved, joining the volution a little on the ventral side where it is thickened, somewhat abruptly curving over and partly inclosing the small umbilicus, and extending in a callus over the columellar lip, which is sometimes distinctly striato-pustulose.

Surface marked by strong longitudinal or revolving striae, which alternate in size; are sometimes fasciculate, and often finer and more numerous on each side of the dorsal band than on the lateral portions of the shell. The revolving striae are cancellated by finer, sub-equal, thread-like, transverse striae. The dorsal band is narrow, rarely elevated, or sometimes scarcely raised above the surface, and usually flat or slightly concave; the concentric striae making an abrupt retrorse curve upon it in crossing. The band is likewise usually marked by two, three or more revolving striae, finer than those on the sides of the shell, and sometimes quite obscure.

This species is very variable in size and form as well as in surface-markings, which are, however, mainly due to the distortion of the shell. A specimen without distortion is a very rare occurrence. The average size of this shell is about three-fourths of an inch. The specimens found in our rocks seldom exceed the one illustrated on our plate.

Formation and Locality.—Occurs in the rotten hornstone of the upper strata of the Devonian formation, in Jefferson county, Ky., and in Clark county, Ind., where it is not rare, but fair specimens are seldom found.

Genus Bucania. Hall.

Bucania, Hall   Pal. N. Y., Vol. 1--1847.
Etymology : bukane, a trumpet.

Shells convolute; spire equally concave on either side; volutions in the same plane, all visible, outer one ventricose, inner ones usually angulated on the edge, concave on the ventral side; aperture rounded oval, somewhat compressed on the inner side by contact with the next volution, laterally and dorsally abruptly expanded.

This genus is established for the reception of several species of shells of a peculiar form, which were formerly placed with the Bellerophons, but from which they differ by having all their volutions visible, which is not the case in Bellerophon proper. Bucania differs from Porcella in being symmetrical, the volutions in the same axis being equally expanded on either side, both sides presenting the same aspect, and the aperture corresponding to the axis of the shell.

Bucania devonica. HALL AND WHITFIELD.

Plate XXVI., figure 9, and Plate XXII., figures 8 and 4.

Bucania devonica, H. and W. 24th Regent's Rep., p. 195—1872.
Bucania devonica, H. and W. 27th Regent's Rep., pl. 13—1875.

Shell discoid, widely and equally umbilicate on the two sides; remaining volutions about four; slightly embracing, vertically compressed, giving the transverse diameter a little more than twice the vertical diameter. Lateral margins of the volutions obtusely angular towards the dorsal side.

The surface has apparently been marked by several (three or four) revolving ridges or carina on each side of the center or dorsum, which is greatly concave. Finer surface-markings, and also the form and size of the aperture, are unknown.

Formation and Locality.—Occurs in the Corniferous rock of the Devonian formation in Jefferson county, Ky., and in Clark county, Ind. It is always found in an exfoliated condition as internal casts, which seldom show any surface-markings at all.

Genus Platyceras. Conrad.

Platyceras, Conrad. Ann. Geol. Rep. of N. Y.—1840.
Etymology: platys, broad; keras, a horn.
Copied from Hall's Pal. N. Y., Vol. 3, page 309—1859.

Shell depressed sub-globose, sub-ovoid or obliquely sub-conical. Spire small, volutions few, sometimes free and sometimes contiguous, without columella. Aperture more or less expanded, often companulate, and sometimes with the lip reflected. Peristome entire or sinuous.

Surface striated or cancellated, often spirally ridged or plicated, and sometimes strongly lamellose transversely, nodose or spiniferous.

Platyceras bucculentum. HALL.

Plate XXIII., figures 9 and 11, and Plate XXV., figure 3.

Platyceras bucculentum, Hall. Desc. of New Sp of Foss., p. 5—1861.
Platyceras bucculentum, Hall 15th Regent's Rep., p. 33—1862.
Platyceras bucculentum, Hall. Illust of Dev. Fossils, pl. 3—1876.
Platyceras bucculentum, Hall. Pal. N. Y., Vol. 5, pt. 2, p. 10—1885.

Shell ventricose, obliquely sub-ovoid; apex extremely attenuate, the spire making one or two closely enrolled volutions, with a gently enlarging diameter, and below this abruptly expanding; very ventricose in the middle and lower part, spreading more upon the right side than upon the left. The shell near the posterior side swells out into a distinct pouch-like projection, with two or three rounded folds or semi-plications, which give a deeply sinuous outline to the margin. Aperture sub-ovate and sinuate on the right posterior side. Peristome sinuous, and on the posterior side spreading partially over the preceding volution.

Surface marked by fine, closely arranged concentric striae, which are undulated towards the margin of the aperture, and sometimes over the greater part of the surface, the irregularity having commenced during the earlier stage of growth. In well preserved specimens there are revolving striae or fascicles, rising in little bands of obsolescent striae, giving a waved aspect to the surface.

This species resembles somewhat P. ventricosum, of the lower Helderberg group, but the first volution is more slender, the spire less closely enrolled, while the pouch-like expansion and the revolving bands are distinctive features. In size it differs greatly in different specimens, as may be noticed in the different figures.

Formation and Locality—Occurs in the Corniferous limestone of the Devonian formation in Jefferson county, Ky., and in Clark county, Ind.

Platyceras conicum. HALL.

Plate XXV., figures 2 and 11.

Platyceras conicum, Hall. Descript. of New Foss., p. 3—1861.
Platyceras conicum, Hall. 15th Reg. Report, p. 31—1862.
Platyceras conicum, Hall. Illust. Devon. Fossils—1876.
Platyceras conicum, Hall. Pal. N. Y., Vol. 5, pt. 2, p. 3—1885.

Shell above medium size, erect conical, the minute apex closely incurved but mostly missing, at least in the specimens found in our rocks. Body-chamber entirely straight, with broad, undefined, longitudinal ridges and depressions, which are faint or obsolete at or near the apex, but become more distinct approaching the aperture. The height of the shell is usually greater than the width of the aperture, which is somewhat elliptical in shape; its length exceeding its width.

The surface is covered by concentric undulating striae, which become sublamellose towards the aperture, and are sometimes closely crowded and wrinkled with numerous knots or nodes. Peristome deeply sinuous. The length of the shell varies in different specimens, and can not be exactly ascertained on account of the missing apex; but it is certain that the shell illustrated in figure 11, plate 25, if complete, would certainly measure not less than two inches and a quarter.

This species resembles P. pyramidatum of the Lower Helderberg group, but is less elongate; the peristome more sinuous, and the longitudinal ridges and depressions are more distinct; besides, the crowded, wrinkled and nodose striae of our shell are missing in the Silurian species.

Formation and Locality.—Occurs in the Corniferous limestone of the Devonian formation at the Falls of the Ohio, on the Kentucky side of the river, and in different other places in Jefferson county, Ky., and Clark county, Ind. It is not very rare, but fair specimens are not abundant.

Platyceras compressum. N. SP.

Plate XXV., figures 8 and 9.

Shell of medium size or below it; very compressed in a lateral direction. Apex closely enrolled for one or one and a half volutions, which increase in size very gently; after this the body-whorl, measuring a little more than a half volution, expands very rapidly in the post anterior direction, while its lateral extension remains almost the same throughout the whole length of the body volution. The right side of the shell is moderately convex in the apical half, but becomes concave in the lower half, the center line of the concavity running at right-angles to the peristome. The left side is throughout concave, but the center line of the concavity is parallel to the peristome, or at least nearly so. The aperture is very elongate and narrow, and expands more or less at the posterior end of its right side. The surface is marked by fine concentric lamellose striae, which are closely arranged, especially in the lower half, and by somewhat obscure, shallow, radiating plications, only noticed in the lower part.

A smaller specimen, of about half the size of the one illustrated, does not show any indications of those plications. The size of the larger specimen is shown in figures 8 and 9, on plate 25.

Formation and Locality.—This beautiful little shell was loaned to me for description and illustration by Major Wm. J. Davis, who found it at the Falls of the Ohio, in the Corniferous limestone, imbedded in the rock, which he removed, without the least injury to the shell, by the use of muriatic acid and paraffine. The smaller specimen he found in the same strata, but already weathered out, in Clark county Indiana.

Platyceras dumosum. CONRAD.

Plate XXIII., figures 1 to 6 and 12.

Platyceras dumosum, Conrad. Third Ann. Rep. of 4th Dist. N. Y.—1840.
Platyceras dumosum, Hall. 12th Regent's Report, p. 19—1859.
Platyceras dumosum, Hall. Descript. of New Spec. of Fossils—1861.
Platyceras dumosum, Hall. 15th Regent's Report, page 37—1862.
Platyceras dumosum, Hall. Illust. of Dev. Foss., pls. 5 and 6—1876.
Platyceras dumosum, Hall. Pal. N. Y., Vol. 5, pt. 2, page 14—1885.

Shell above medium size; sub-ovoid; extremely ventricose in full grown specimens. Its length, from the apex to the anterior margin of the aperture, greater than the height. Apex minute, closely enrolled for a single volution or more, then the body-whorl becomes free and rapidly expanded, spreading more upon the right side, which is sometimes depressed-convex, while the left side is more abruptly rounded. The aperture is sub-rhomboid-ovate, with the peristome making a sinus on the left side, the posterior margin widely separated from the preceding volution.

The surface is marked by strong concentric striae, which are interrupted and irregular from the numerous nodes projecting from the shell, and extended into long tubular spines.

This shell, in full grown specimens, attains sometimes a length of two inches and a half, and its entire surface is covered with strong, tubular spines, which are sometimes two inches long, as may be seen in the inclosing rock. In the specimen figured on plate 23, figure 2, all the spines are preserved to a certain extent; some measure more than half an inch. These shells were found at the falls, imbedded in soft limestone; the shells themselves were entirely silicified. By the use of muriatic acid, the limestone envelope was gradually removed, and any portion of the shell or spines, whenever it was sufficiently freed from the matrix, was then carefully coated with paraffine, to prevent the acid from further acting upon these cleared portions. By this process, in which very diluted acid must be used, and which requires often several days close watching, in order to protect the exposed parts in time from the further action of the acid, the most excellent specimens in shells, crinoids, and especially in coral, are obtained. In the collection of my co-laborer and friend, Major Wm. J. Davis, the author of "Kentucky Fossil Corals," the most exquisite and valuable specimens of which that cabinet is so rich, and, therefore, unparalleled by any other collection in this country, are produced by the careful application of muriatic acid and paraffine. The specimens of this species, found in the clay, are mostly exfoliated, and show the places of the spines by moderately elevated nodules, as may be seen in the figures 5, 6 and 12; the last one is that of a young specimen.

Formation and Locality.—Occurs in the upper strata of the Corniferous limestone, just above the hydraulic cement rock, at the Falls of the Ohio, on the Kentucky side of the river; the layers containing them are only exposed at a very low stand of the river. In the clay, exfoliated shells are found in different places in Jefferson county, Ky., and in Clark county, Ind.

Platyceras dumosum, var. rarispinum. HALL.

Plate XXIII., figures 7 and 8.

Platyc. dumosum, var. rarispinum, Hall.   Desc. of New Sp. of Foss.—1861.
Platyc. dumosum, var. rarispinum, Hall.   15th Reg. Rep., p. 38—1862.
Platyc. dumosum, var. rarispinum, Hall.   Illust. of Dev. Foss., pl. 5—1876.
Plat. dumosum, var. rarispinum, Hall.   Pal. N. Y., Vol. 5, pt. 2, p. 16—1885.

Shell only of medium size or below it; sub-ovate; apex closely incurved and enrolled for about one and one-half volutions, and in some shells the volutions are contiguous nearly to the aperture, as seen in figure 8, plate 23. For one volution and a half or three-fourths the shell is slender and only gently enlarging; after that the body-whorl expands more rapidly and becomes moderately ventricose, depressed on the dorsum, and the left side sometimes marked by a strong fold, indicating a sinus in the margin of the peristome commencing at an early stage of growth. Aperture somewhat oval, longest in the dorsal-ventral axis.

Surface marked by wrinkled, concentric striae, which are strongly undulated at the base of the spines, and often abruptly bent backward at other places. Spines scattered, comparatively strong and few in number, from five to fifteen on the whole shell. The specimen before me, a most perfect one, with the exception of a few broken spines, is a complete hollow shell from apex to aperture, without defect; it shows eleven spines.

Formation and Locality.—This shell was presented to me by Major Wm. J. Davis, who found it in the upper strata of the Devonian formation, in Clark county, Indiana. I have no doubt that this shell is related to P. dumosum, but it differs sufficiently from it to constitute a distinct species, and not merely a variety. It is certainly as far removed from P. dumosum as P. multispinosum, and if that is considered a good species, I think our shell has the same claim. It ought to be called simply Platyceras rarispinum. It differs by the smaller number of spines, and by its different shape from P. dumosum, and besides, it is never found with the latter in the same strata, but occupies a higher horizon.

Platyceras echinatum. Hall.

Plate XXXI., figure 21.

Platyceras echinatum, Hall.   Descript. of New Foss.—1861.
Platyceras echinatum, Hall.   15th Rep. N. Y. St. Cab.—1862.
Platyceras echinatum, Hall.   Illust. of Dev. Fossils—1876.
Platyceras echinatum, Hall.   Pal. N. Y., Vol. 5, pt. 2, p. 13—1885.

Shell small; apex closely incurved for about one and one-half volution; the body-whorl occupying about one volution, very ventricose; rapidly expanding from the first volution, giving the shell an obliquely conical form. Aperture nearly circular or broad oval; peristome sinuate; the lines of growth and fine striae conforming in direction to the outline of the margin. Remains of revolving lines are sometimes traceable when the shell is not exfoliated. Besides the concentric and obscure revolving striae, the surface is studded with numerous nodes or fine spines, which are as much crowded as the figure 21, plate 31, shows, but they are not quite so regularly arranged as in the illustration. The specimen before me has preserved the shell, but of the spines only short stumps are visible; the spines perished by the process of silicification. In regard to size, this species varies from half an inch to an inch and a quarter in length, and in large specimens the greatest diameter of the aperture is one inch. This form could be the young of P. dumosum, and would probably be considered as such if it occurred with that species in the same strata or horizon, but this is not the case. It is never found associated with P. dumosum, but occurs at a much higher horizon, and for that reason must be considered as a distinct species.

Formation and Locality.—Found in the upper strata of the Devonian formation, in Clark county, Indiana. It is not often met with.

Platyceras erectum. HALL.

Acroculia erecta, Hall.   Geol. Surv. of 4th Dist. of N. Y.—1843.
Platyceras erectum, Hall.   Desc. of New Sp. of Foss., p. 4—1861.
Platyceras erectum, Hall.   15th Regent's Report, p. 4—1862.
Platyceras erectum, Hall.   Illust. of Devon. Fossils, pl. 2—1876.
Platyceras erectum, Hall.   Pal. N. Y., Vol. 5, pt. 2, p. 5—1885.

Shell erect and slender.   The spire at the apex is closely enrolled, for about one volution and a half, beyond which the body-volution becomes somewhat rapidly expanding, with the aperture often spreading.   The specimens are often more arcuate than their name indicates.   The aperture is oblique, with the peristome sinuate.

The surface is marked by closely arranged, revolving, lamellose striae, which, upon the lower half of the body-volution, are abruptly arched along narrow bands, corresponding with former sinuosities of the aperture.

Formation and Locality.—Occurs in the Corniferous limestone of the Devonian formation, at the Falls of the Ohio, on Kentucky shore of river.

Platyceras milleri. N. SP.

Plate XXV., figure 1.

Shell very elongate, forming a slender cone.   Apex very minute, and closely incurved for about one or one and a half volution; after this the shell is free for about one and one-half volution.   The whole shell increases very gradually in size from apex to aperture.   The different volutions are separated from each other by very large interspaces.   The aperture is nearly circular, and the lip is entire without sinus, but with very slight undulations.   The real shell is very thin.   The surface is marked by fine, undulating concentric striae or lines of growth, and, in well preserved specimens, with numerous slender, tubular spines, which are seen when part of the matrix remains attached to the shell.   To a specimen of that kind before me are spines attached which measure more than three-fourths of an inch in length.

This species resembles, in regard to the number and size of the spines, Platyceras dumosum, but its elongated form distinguishes it from that species at the first glance.   There is, in fact, no other species of Platyceras known to me with which this one might be compared.

Formation and Locality.—I found three very fine specimens of this species in the Corniferous limestone of the Devonian formation, at the Falls of the Ohio, on the Kentucky side of the river.

It affords me great pleasure to name this elegant fossil in honor of S. A. Miller, Esq., of Cincinnati, Ohio.   There are very few palæontologists in this country whose labors are of equal importance with those of S. A. Miller.   His catalogue of fossils is an invaluable guide to all his co-laborers.

Platyceras multispinosum. MEEK.

Plate XXV., figure 4.

Platyceras multispinosum, Meek. Proc. Acad. Nat. Sci. Phil.—1871.
Patyceras multispinosum, Meek. Pal of Ohio, Vol. 1, page 210—1878.

Shell attaining a large size, considerably larger than its near relative, the P. dumosum; it has a very thin shell, is depressed sub-ovate and very oblique. Its apex is free in the casts—may not be so in the perfect shell; comparatively stout, and obliquely coiled for about one and one-half volution; after this the body-whorl expands very rapidly to the aperture, occupying in this part of the shell less than half a volution.

Aperture very large and nearly round; lip entire; neither sinus nor undulated.

Surface without any surface-markings except the numerous closely arranged, slender, tubular spines on well preserved shells, or their small, depressed, smooth, undefined tubercles or nodules on the internal casts. In regard to general size, and the proportion of its different dimensions, this shell differs greatly. The illustration, figure 4, on plate 25, shows a large-sized specimen. This species differs from Platyceras dumosum by its considerably larger size, its more oblique, depressed and more rapidly expanding form, and mainly by its more numerous and more slender spines. Specimens belonging to this species will be very seldom confounded with P. dumosum; their difference is noticed at the first glance, whether they are shells or internal casts. The spines are seldom attached to the specimens; they become separated by exfoliation, but are often preserved in the matrix.

Formation and Locality.—Occurs in the Corniferous limestone of the Devonian formation at the Falls of the Ohio, and in other places in Jefferson county, Ky., and Clark county, Ind. It is not rare, though fair specimens are not abundant.

Platyceras rictum. HALL.

Platyceras rictum, Hall. Desc. New Sp. of Foss., p. 7—1861.
Platyceras rictum, Hall. 15th Regent's Rep., p. 35—1862.
Platyceras rictum, Hall. Illust. of Dev. Fossils, pl. 4—1876.
Platyceras rictum, Hall. Pal. N. Y., Vol. 5, pt. 2, p. 13—1885.

Shell very depressed, arcuate or sometimes obliquely sub-conical; width equalling and often exceeding height. Apex or nucleus minute, the spire enrolled for about one turn and a half, when it abruptly expands, spreading more upon the right posterior side, and becoming greatly extended and expanded in front.

The dorsal line of the first volution is continued in an oblique angular ridge, extending on the left side, and often reaching to the front of the shell, giving a peculiar obliquity to the form. Aperture expanded, obliquely ovate ; peristome entire, or with a slight sinuosity on the left posterior side, and sometimes showing the effect of the undefined folds of the posterior margin usually contiguous to the preceding volution.

Surface marked by undulating concentric striae, and a few broad undulations longitudinally. Aperture a little greater in the diameter from front to rear than in the lateral one. Height reaching sometimes to an inch and a quarter.

Formation and Locality.—Occurs in the Corniferous limestone of the Devonian formation in Jefferson county, Ky., and in Clark county, Ind.

Platyceras symmetricum. Hall.

Plate XXIII., figure 10.

Platyceras symmetricum, Hall.   Desc. of New Sp. of Foss., p. 6—1861.
Platyceras symmetricum, Hall.   15th Reg. Rep., p. 84—1862.'
Platyceras symmetricum, Hall.   Illust. of Dev. Fossils, pl. 3—1876.
Platyceras symmetricum, Hall.   Pal. N. Y., Vol. 5, pt. 2, p. 9—1885.

Shell elongate, sub-ovoid, arcuate, incurved nearly in the same plane ; apex minute, making about one or one and a half volution before the body-whorl becomes free and rapidly or somewhat abruptly expanded ; spreading about equally on the two sides of the dorsum, which is more prominent and sometimes marked by a ridge. Aperture oblique, sub-quadrate or rhomboidal ; margin of the peristome sinuate, and on the posterior side distant from the spire.

Surface marked by concentric undulating striae, and longitudinally by obscure interrupted ridges, which, on some parts of the older shells, become regular and uniform, with a narrow groove between.

This species is well marked by the equilateral expansion on each side of the dorsum, and by the volution of the apex being nearly in the same plane. The posterior margin of the aperture is widely separated from the preceding volution. The longitudinal ridges are strongly marked, and of a different character from those of characteristic specimens of Plat. bucculentum ; it is not, however, improbable that we may find intermediate forms uniting the two species. It is also possible that a comparison of a larger number of specimens may prove that the forms included under P. thetis, symmetricum and bucculentum, are only varieties of one and the same species.

Formation and Locality.—Occurs in the Corniferous limestone of the Devonian formation at the Falls of the Ohio, and in different other places of Jefferson county, Ky., and of Clark county, Ind., where it is usually found already weathered out and entirely silicified.

Platyceras thetis. HALL.

Platyceras thetis, Hall.   Desc. of New Foss., page 4—1861.
Platyceras thetis, Hall.   15th Regent's Rep., p. 32—1862.
Platyceras thetis, Hall.   Illust. of Dev. Foss., pl. 3—1876.
Platyceras thetis, Hall.   Pal. N. Y., Vol. 5, pt. 2, p. 8—1885.

Shell oblique arcuate from base, with the apex incurved, nucleus making barely more than a single minute volution; gradually expanding from the apex to near aperture, which is sometimes more abruptly spreading. The beak of the body-whorl is prominent, and a little flattened on the left side, while right side, from one-third to one-half the length, is sometimes marked by two or three longitudinal folds, and often by more numerous, finer plications. Aperture a little oblique, nearly round or sub-quadrate, with the peristome sinuous.

Surface marked by fine, closely arranged lamellose striae, which are abruptly undulated on all parts of the body of the shell. This species resembles P. attenuatum, but differs in being arcuate from apex to base, in the gradual attenuation towards the apex, and the closely incurved nucleus and less abrupt expansion.

Formation and Locality.—Occurs in the Corniferous limestone of the Devonian formation at the Falls of the Ohio, on the Kentucky side of the river.

Platyceras unguiforme. HALL.

Platyceras unguiforme, Hall.   Pal. N. Y., Vol. 3, p. 322—1859.

Shell oblique, arcuate, sub-spiral; volutions one or two, more or less contiguous at the apex; last volution angular, extending in a straight or slightly curved direction towards the aperture. Aperture oblique, sub-ovoid; peristome sinuous·

Surface longitudinally plicate, and marked by fine, crowded, undulating lamellose striae. The plications are of unequal size; they are flat and broad on the dorsal side, and angular and smaller on the ventral side. These plications increase in number by bifurcation.

Formation and Locality.—Found in the Niagara limestone in the quarries east of the city of Louisville, Ky. It is a rather rare shell.

Platyceras ventricosum. CONRAD.

Plate XXV., figure 10.

Platyceras ventricosum, Conrad.   Ann. Rep. N. Y.—1840.
Platyceras ventricosum, Meek and Worthen.   Ill. Geol. Rep., Vol. 3—1868.

Shell obliquely sub-ovate; composed of two and a half to three very rapidly enlarging contiguous, volutions, the last one of which is very large and ventricose ; spire depressed below the upper side of the body-whorl. Aperture very large and circular ; inner lip usually in contact with the spire, so as to leave a moderately large umbilical cavity. Surface traversed by fine striae, and near the aperture coarser, somewhat undulated lines of growth, crossed by faint traces of extremely fine, revolving lines. General size differs in different individuals ; the illustration shows a specimen of average size.

Formation and Locality.—Found in the Corniferous limestone of the Devonian formation in Jefferson county, Ky., and in Clark county, Ind.

Genus Murchisonia. D'Archiac and DeVerneuil.

Murchisonia, D'Archiac and Verneuil. Bull. Soc. Geol. Fr., Vol. 12—1841.
Etymology : Named after Sir R. I. Murchison, of England.

This genus was proposed by D'Archiac and DeVerneuil, to include Buccinum spinosum and *B.* abbreviatum of Sowerby, Turritella bilineata of Goldfuss, and others. Shells spiral, with very elevated spire and many volutions, marked by a spiral band and bent striae; body very elongate, with a notch or slit in the outer lip of the aperture, or where this is wanting, the striae are bent, indicating the slit. Murchisonia are a sort of elongate Pleurotomaria. Type, Murchisonia bilineata.

Murchisonia desiderata. Hall.

Plate XXVI., figure 8.

Murchisonia desiderata, Hall. Descpt. of New Sp. of Foss.—1861.
Murchisonia desiderata, Hall. 15th Rep. N. Y. St. Cab.—1862.
Murchisonia desiderata, Hall. Pal. N. Y., Vol. 5, pt. 2, p. 89—1885.

Shell elongate, turretiform ; spire somewhat rapidly ascending. Volutions ten or more, and obtusely angular, flattened on their upper sides, and a little more convex below the spiral band. The volutions, from apex to aperture, are gradually enlarging. The greatest width of the last volution is about equal to the combined height of the second and third whorls, but scarcely more ventricose than the preceding one, except towards the aperture. Aperture somewhat elongate ; the columellar lip thickened and bounded by a well-marked callosity.

Surface marked by distinct, concentric striae, which are sometimes raised into fascicles above the general surface of the shell, and, bending gently back from the suture, reach the spiral band, crossing which, they bend forward more abruptly, making a gentle curve to the suture below. The spiral band, at about three-fifths of the width of the volution below the suture, is simple, flattened or slightly concave, limited by narrow, moderately elevated revolving lines, and marked by the retrorsely curving striae, which are less prominent upon it and the adjacent parts than near the suture. Suture close.

The dimensions and general size of the shells belonging to this species are given in the illustration, which shows the natural size of the specimen from which it was made.

The specimen before me is an internal cast, but it is covered by a thin coral bearing on its whole surface small tubercles, as shown in the illustration, but not placed with such a regularity as the draughtsman has given them in the figure. This incrusting, tuberculose coral was mistaken for the real shell of the fossil.

Formation and Locality.—Found in the cherty layers of the Devonian formation at and around the Falls of the Ohio, in Kentucky and Indiana.

Murchisonia petilla. Hall and Whitfield.

Plate XXXI., figure 5.

Murchisonia petilla, H. and W. 24th Regent's Rep., p. 186—1872.
Murchisonia petilla, H. and W. 27th Regent's Rep., pl. 13—1875.

Shell small, spire elevated, slender and regularly tapering from base to apex; volutions about twelve gently and regularly expanding from the apex; moderately convex, somewhat obtusely subangular below the middle; last one scarcely ventricose.

Aperture sub-rhomboidal. Surface not known, the specimen being an exfoliated internal cast. Length of the specimen one inch; diameter of last volution seven-twentieths, and height one-fifth of an inch.

Formation and Locality.—Occurs in the lower strata of the Niagara rocks in the quarries east of the city of Louisville. The specimen illustrated and described is, so far, the only one known; it belonged to the collection of the late Dr. James Knapp.

Genus Pleurotomaria. De France.

Pleurotomaria, De France. Dict. Sci. Nat., 41—1826.
Etymology: pleura, side; *tome*, cut or notch, having a deep cut or notch in the outer lip.

Shells spiral, trochiform, solid, few-whorled, with the surface variously ornamented; aperture subquadrate, with a deep slit in its outer margin. The part of the slit which has been progressively filled up forms a band round the whorls or volutions. This slit, in the outer lip of the aperture, on which the name has been founded, is seldom visible, as specimens are rarely found perfect; but the peculiar bending of the transverse striae, curved backwards to and marking the line of the slit, are always a prominent character of this genus. (Copied from Woodward's Manual and Portlock's Report on Londonderry.)

Pleurotomaria casii. MEEK AND WORTHEN.

Plate XXVI., figure 11.

Pleurotomaria casii, M. and W. Ill. Geol., Vol. 3, p. 359—1868.

Shell attaining a rather large size, higher than wide; spire conical, a little more than equalling length of lower half of body volution. Whorls about five and a half, very convex; those of the spire each showing three-fourths of its entire height above the next succeeding one ; upper ones (in casts) rounded, last one large and ventricose, and, like the next above, sub-angular around near the middle, below which it is somewhat produced, and rounds into a small, umbilical opening in the cast, probably entirely closed by the columella in specimens retaining the shell. Spiral band apparently of moderate breadth, occupying the obtuse angle a little above the middle of body-whorl, and passing around near the middle of the others. Suture deep in consequence of the great convexity of the volutions.

Aperture sub-circular. Surface of internal casts showing, on the upper convex slope of the body-whorl, and that of the next above it, obscure transverse ridges, curving backwards as they extend out from the suture, probably parallel to the lines of growth. Crossing these, there is an undefined, revolving ridge on the body-whorl a little more than half way out from the suture towards the spiral band. Other surface-markings are unknown. (Copied from Meek and Worthen's description in Vol. 3, of Geol. Rep. of Illinois.)

This species is easily distinguished by the transverse striae, on the upper side of its body-whorl, from all other Silurian Pleurotomaria.

Formation and Locality.—In the Niagara limestone of the quarries east of the city of Louisville, Ky. A rather rare species.

Pleurotomaria arabella. N. SP.

Plate XXVI., figure 12.

Shell rather large, turbinate, spire elevated ; apex minute, aperture sub-quadrate, apparently somewhat wider than high. Volutions five or six, prominently convex; rapidly enlarging, last one or body-whorl very ventricose. Shell wider than high.

Surface marked by three revolving carinae, of which one is above and the other two below the peripheral band ; the band itself is flat and narrow, and not limited by elevated carinae ; the upper part of the volution, at least in the two last ones, is gently sloping from suture to the first or upper carina; from this it curves to the spiral band, forming a moderately deep, rounded furrow.

The interspaces between band and second carina, and between this and the third or last carination, are also rounded depressions, of which only the one next to the band is of about equal depth with the furrow in the upper half; the second depression in the lower half is shallow. In consequence of the great convexity of the volutions the suture is deep. The character of the transverse striae is only indicated but not fully known.

Formation and Locality.—In the Corniferous limestone in Jefferson county, Ky., and in Clark county, Ind. My specimen is only an internal cast, from which the surface-markings, with the exception of the revolving carinae, are obliterated. I have compared this shell with all the different species of Pleurotomaria known to me, but can not place it with any one, and I am thus compelled to make a new species for its reception.

Pleurotomaria lucina. Hall.

Euomphalus? rotundus, Hall.   Geol. of N. Y., Surv. of 4th Dist.—1843.
Pleurotomaria lucina, Hall.   Descpt. of New Sp. of Foss., p. 14—1861.
Pleurotomaria lucina, Hall.   Fifteenth Reg. Rep., pl. 42—1862.
Pleur. rotunda and P. lucina, Hall.   Ill. of Dev. Foss. Gastrop, pl. 8—1876.
Pleur. lucina, Hall.   Pal. N. Y., Vol. 5, part. 2, p. 67—1879.

Shell sub-globose or obliquely ovoid-conical. Spire moderately elevated; apex minute; volutions about four, gradually expanding to the last one, which comes very regularly ventricose, with the aperture expanded and nearly round, extended on the lower side, with a shallow notch on the anterior margin; upper side of the volutions very symmetrically convex; suture neatly defined, slightly canaliculate; lower side of the body-volution convex in the middle, and abruptly curving into the umbilical depression.

Surface beautifully cancellated by concentric and revolving striae, which, in many specimens, are of equal strength. Periphery marked by a moderately wide band, on which the striae are turned abruptly backwards; this band is limited by stronger striae or narrow ridges on each side, sometimes with one or two slender revolving striae within the limits of the band, making a narrow space, which is often crenulated by the concentric striae.

This species is well marked by its symmetrically rotund form, with moderate elevation of the spire, and the regular convexity of the volutions, even in casts of the interior when not compressed. There is some variety in the surface-markings of specimens apparently belonging to this species. The concentric striae are sometimes much coarser than the revolving ones; and finer striae are implanted between the stronger ones, and do not reach the suture-line. In old specimens the revolving band is sometimes nearly a quarter of an inch wide. A very symmetrical specimen has a diameter of a little more than two inches, and is nearly an inch and three-fourths in height.

Formation and Locality.—Found in the Corniferous limestone, at and around the Falls of the Ohio, in Kentucky and Indiana, but generally as internal casts, which show only the general form, but not the surface-markings of the shell.

Pleurotomaria procteri. N. SP.

Plate XXI., figures 9, 10 and 13.

Compare Pleurotomaria capillaria, var. of Pal. N. Y., Vol. 5, Part 2, text, page 87, and Pleur. capillaria, var. rustica, of Pal. N. Y., Vol. 5, Part 2, Plates, Plate 30, figures 20, 21 and 22.

Shell trochiform; height exceeding width about one-fourth or more. Volutions from five to six, somewhat rapidly increasing in size, the last one ventricose; there is only one carina above and one below the peripheral band: the carina above the band gives to upper portion of the volution a sub-angular appearance, while the lower part is regularly rounded. The peripheral band is divided by a somewhat finer central carina, which is crossed rectangularly by strong striae, which only extend from margin to margin of the peripheral band, with interspaces of about four times their own size. These rectangular striae are entirely separated from the striae of the upper or lower half of the volution; they give the dividing carina a beautifully crenulated appearance. On both sides of the peripheral band, the surface is ornamented by strong transverse striae; in the upper half they start from the suture, and run in an almost straight line, with a backward deflection of about ten degrees, to the first carina, from where they curve slightly backward to the upper marginal carina of the peripheral band. This system of striae, interrupted by the band, continues at the lower marginal carina of the latter, from where the striae extend in slightly curved or nearly straight lines with a forward deflection, either to the sutures of the upper volutions, or to the lower carina of the body-whorl. From this lower carina, which forms the suture-line of the upper whorls, and which is, therefore, only visible on the last volution, the striae curve gently to the umbilicus and to the columellar lip; but a great number of them die out or become extinguished at different distances from the lower carina. All the volutions are, in their transverse section, extremely convex, which gives them very deep sutures, and separates them from each other in a very decided manner. The aperture of this shell is not known, inasmuch as in all the specimens in my collection the outer lip is missing.

This species stands between P. sulcomarginata and P. capillaria, both of which it resembles in some respect, but it is easily distinguished from the first by its more elevated spire, its larger size, and the difference in the number and arrangement of the revolving carinae; from the latter by the greatly smaller number of revolving carinae, and from both here named, and all other species of the genus Pleurotomaria, by the crenulated central carina in the peripheral band, which is very characteristic in P. procteri.

Formation and Locality.—Associated with P. sulcomarginata in the Corniferous limestone of Jefferson county, Ky., and of Clark county, Ind. It is a somewhat rare species. This beautiful shell I name in honor of Kentucky's State Geologist, Prof. John R. Procter, who has served his State with great distinction, and who has labored, more than any other man, to bring the great mineral wealth of Kentucky to the knowledge of the people at large.

Pleurotomaria sulcomarginata. Conrad.

Plate XXI., figures 11 and 12.

Pleur. sulcomarginata, Conrad. Jour. Acad Nat. Sc. Phil., Vol. 8—1842.
Pleur. sulcomarginata, Hall. Descript. of New Sp. of Foss., p. 18—1861.
Pleur. sulcomarginata, Hall. Fifteenth Rep. N. Y. St. Cab.—1862.
Pleur. sulcomarginata, Hall. Illust. of Dev. Foss. Gastr., pl. 19—1876.
Pleur. sulcomarginata, Hall. Pal. N. Y., Vol. 5, part 2, p. 69—1879.

Shell depressed trochiform ; spire moderately elevated ; apex minute. Volutions four or five, very depressed convex on the upper side, gradually enlarging to the last one, which becomes somewhat ventricose. Aperture subquadrate, somewhat wider than high, the columella much extended below.

Surface ornamented by two distinct, narrow, revolving carinae on each volution, one just below the suture and the other near the periphery, with finer intermediate striae, which are rarely visible ; the entire surface marked by strong, regular and even concentric striae, which crenulate the revolving carinae, and, passing over the lower one, bend backward to the concave peripheral band. Sutures sometimes sharply canaliculate. In entire specimens, the apex is very minute, and, when the outer carination is crenulated by the strong transverse striae, the shell has a coronate aspect. This carination, however, is often obsolete on the outer volution, and is more rarely noticed on the next above, and the striae then continue uninterruptedly, bending backward to the peripheral band, and continuing on the lower side, often very nearly of the same strength as above. There is frequently a narrow depressed band just below the peripheral band on the last volution, causing a slight deflection of the striae. The striae are usually finer, and sometimes become nearly obsolete below the outer carination, and more rarely on other parts of the shell, especially near the aperture.

Formation and Locality.—Found very abundantly in the cherty layers of the Corniferous limestone around the Falls of the Ohio, in Kentucky and Indiana, and very often in very fine and well preserved specimens.

Genus Callonema. Hall.

Callonema, Hall. Pal. N. Y., Vol. 5, pl. 2.
Etymology: kallos, beautiful ; *nema,* a thread.

Shell sub-globose, turbinate or ovoid-conical. Volutions rounded or sometimes sub-angular above and below ; outer lip apparently thin ; columellar lip thickened and spreading over the volutions above and extended below ; axis umbilicate.

Surface marked by fine, even striae, which extend equally over the volutions, rarely divided, and sometimes merging into the ordinary striae of growth, and extending into the umbilicus. The chief external characters of this genus being the sharply elevated, even, thread-like, concentric striae traversing the volutions above and below, a distinct columellar lip, and an umbilicate axis.

Callonema bellatula. HALL.

Plate XX., figures 4, 5, 6 and 7.

Laxonema bellatula, Hall. 14th Rep. N. Y. St. Cab., p. 104—1861.
Isonema bellatula, Meek. Proc. Acad. Nat. Sci. Phil., p. 252—1865.
Isonema bellatula, Meek. Geol. Surv. of Ill., Vol. 3, p. 443—1868.
Isonema bellatula, H. and W. 27th Regent's Rep., pl. 13—1875.
Isonema bellatula, Hall. Illust. of Dev. Foss. Gaster., pl. 14—1876.
Callonema bellatula, Hall. Pal. N. Y., Vol. 5, pt. 2, p. 51—1879.

Shell sub-ovoid-conical ; spire elevated and rapidly expanding below. Volutions about six or seven, the upper ones minute, and somewhat gradually expanding to the third or fourth whorl, and more rapidly below, the last one being very ventricose, regularly rounded or obtusely subangular towards the base. Aperture apparently transverse ; the specimen before me, and represented by figure 7, is perfect, with the exception of the peristome, of which the outer lip is missing ; I am, therefore, unable to state the exact form of the aperture ; columellar lip thickened, spreading above and extended anteriorly. In my specimen the umbilicus is partly open, and partly closed by the columellar lip.

Surface is covered by regular, even, sharply elevated striae, with about equal interspaces, which are slightly turned backwards from the suture, and gently curved to the base of the volution, and on the last one curving over the periphery with equal strength ; a portion becoming obsolete and others coalescing and becoming stronger as they enter the umbilical depression. Some specimens of this species show an obtuse angularity at the base of the last volution, as slightly indicated in figure 6 ; but most shells are regularly rounded and ventricose. There is no specific difference between these two forms. This species has a close resemblance to Callonema lichas, with which it may even be identical.

Formation and Locality.—Occurs in the Corniferous limestone at and around the Falls of the Ohio in Kentucky and Indiana, and belongs to the rarer forms.

Callonema clarki. N. SP.

Plate XXIV., figures 2, 3, 4 and 5.

Shell above medium size ; sub-hemispherical ; spire moderately elevated, more or less so in different shells, as shown by the two specimens illustrated, consisting of from three to five volutions. The volutions are regularly increasing from apex to aperture, which is sub-circular or subquadrate ; they are depressed convex on their upper side.

The columella is much extended below. Suture small and shallow, between the upper volutions scarcely noticeable. The surface appears, to the naked eye, entirely smooth, but under a magnifier shows fine, transverse striae, closely set between some stronger marked lines of growth. These striae and lines of growth extend from the suture down and backwards to the umbilical depression. The last volution, or the body-whorl, as it is also called, curves very abruptly at its middle, and slopes from there in a straight or slightly curved line to the inner lip of the aperture, making the lower half of the last volution either flat or only very little convex. The apex appears to be very minute in perfect specimens. Figure 4 I consider to be the normal form, while figure 2 is either an aberration or the result of a slight compression.

Formation and Locality.—This species occurs in the rotten hornstone of the Devonian formation and was found by Dr. K. S. Clark in the Devonian clay topping the Niagara rocks east of the city of Louisville. I name this heretofore undescribed species in honor of Dr. Clark.

Callonema imitator. HALL AND WHITFIELD.

Plate XX., figures 12 and 13.

Pleurotomaria imitator, H. and W. 24th Regent's Report, p. 195—1872.
Pleurotomaria imitator, H. and W. 27th Regent's Report, pl. 13—1875.
Callonema imitator, Hall. Pal. N. Y., Vol. 5, part 2, p. 52—1879.

Shell of large size, sub-hemispherical; spire moderately elevated, consisting of four or five rounded volutions, regularly increasing from the apex to the aperture, which is sub-circular; rounded below and broadly umbilicate; suture distinct, not channeled, situated at the periphery of the preceding volution. Surface of the upper sides of the volution marked by strong ridges, which have a slight bend just below the suture, and thence curve backward to the periphery, gradually increasing in strength from apex to outer volution, on the middle of which they are in the ratio of about twenty to an inch; on the outer half of the last volution they become gradually obsolete, or merge into the lines of growth, which also mark every part of the surface.

Below the periphery there are apparently none of the ridges existing. This species is very similar to Pleurotomaria lucina in form, being a little more depressed, and the volutions less rapidly increasing. The surface-markings are more nearly like those of Pleur. arata, while the volutions are more ventricose on the upper side, and the periphery is apparently destitute of a band or sinus, which is a distinguishing feature.

Formation and Locality.—In the rotten hornstone of the Corniferous group, in Jefferson county, Ky., and in Clark county, Ind. Rarely found. Only a few specimens are known outside of Dr James Knapp's collection. A good interior cast is in my own cabinet.

Genus Loxonema. Phillips.

Loxonema, Phillips. Palaeoz. Fossils—1841.

Etymology: loxos, oblique; *nema*, a thread—alluding to the oblique thread-like striae.

Shell spiral, turriculated; whorls or volutions convex, their upper edges pressed against the next above; without spiral band; mouth oblong, attenuated above, effused below, with a sigmoidal edge to the right lip; no umbilicus (?).

Surface covered by longitudinal threads, and ridges generally arched. (Geol. Rep. of Londonderry, by J. E. Portlock.)

Loxonema sinuata is the type of this genus.

Loxonema hamiltoniae. Hall.

Plate XXXI., figure 29.

Loxonema hamiltoniae, Hall. Descpt. of New Sp. of Foss.—1861.
Loxonema hamiltoniae, Hall. 15th Regent's Rep.—1862.
Loxonema hamiltoniae, Hall. Illust. of Dev. Foss., pl. 13—1876.
Loxonema hamiltoniae, Hall. Pal. N. Y., Vol. 5, pt. 2, p. 45—1885.

Shell elongate, subulate; volutions moderately convex, numbering from ten to thirteen; as many as the last number were counted in the largest specimen known. The volutions are gradually increasing in size from the very minute apex to the aperture; the last one becomes ventricose. Aperture ovate, narrowing below, columella extended.

Surface marked by longitudinal, sharp, curving striae, which bend gently backward from the suture, and forward to the base of the volution, having the greatest curve near the middle, those of the last volution curving abruptly backward to the columellar lip. Striae separated by distinctly defined grooves, which are a little wider than the ridges, the striae increasing in distance as the shell grows older. In the specimen figured, the apical volutions are missing; the draughtsman restored them, but he made the volutions too high, and not enough in number. The height of the figure would have been the natural size of the shell when complete; it should have shown twelve volutions instead of its present nine. It measures seventeen lines in length, and its body-whorl has a diameter of four lines. This species is associated with L. hydraulica, which it resembles in its surface-markings, but it may be easily distinguished from that shell by the different shape of the volutions and suture. In L. hydraulica the whorls are very convex, while in L. hamiltoniae they are only moderately curved; the suture in L. hydraulica is very deep and constricted, that of L. hamiltoniae comparatively very shallow. Besides, the spire in L. hamiltoniae is more elongate than that of L. hydraulica.

Formation and Locality.—Occurs in the chert bed which overlies the hydraulic cement rock at the Falls of the Ohio, on the Kentucky shore of the river, and also at Watson's Station, on the Ohio and Mississippi Railroad, in Clark county, Ind.

Loxonema hydraulicum. HALL AND WHITFIELD.

Plate XX., figures 8 and 9.

Loxonema hydraulica, H. and W. 24th Regent's Rep., p. 193—1872. .
Loxonema hydraulica, H. and W. 27th Reg. Rep., pl. 13—1875.
Loxonema hydraulica, H. und W. Illust. of Dev. Fossils, pl. 13—1876.
Loxonema hydraulicum, Hall. Pal. N. Y., Vol. 5, part 2, p. 44—1879.

Shell turreted; volutions rounded, from five to eight and more; greatest convexity about the middle of each; upper ones always missing, and, therefore, unknown. Sutures deep, giving a constricted aspect at the junction of the volutions.

Surface marked with distinct, angular striae, bending gently backward from the suture to the periphery, and with a longer forward curve to the base of each volution; those of the last volution bending more abruptly backward, and making a second abrupt retrorse curve to the columellar lip.

This species, in the rotundity of the volutions, and the constriction at the sutures, contrasts with all the other species of this genus here described.

Formation and Locality.—Found rather plentiful in the cherty layers overlying the hydraulic limestone of the Devonian formation, at and around the Falls of the Ohio, in Kentucky and Indiana, associated with Lox. laeviusculum and Lox. rectistriatum.

Loxonema laeviusculum. HALL.

Plate XXII., figures 8 and 9.

Loxonema laeviusculum, Hall. Pal. N. Y., Vol. 5, part 2, p. 131—1879.

Shell elongate, subulate; volutions from nine to twelve; rounded and somewhat rapidly expanding to the last one, which is moderately ventricose. Suture close and simple. Aperture ovate; the columellar lip much extended below.

Surface nearly smooth, or marked by faint, obsolescent striae, which are moderately curved over the convexity of the volution, and become fasciculate on the lower side of the last one as they approach the columellar lip.

This species has the general aspect of Loxonema hamiltoniae, but it is less rapidly tapering towards the apex, the volution somewhat less convex, and the last one not so ventricose as in well preserved specimens of that species. Usually the specimens have the appearance of being worn and macerated, and the general absence of striae upon the surface may be due in part to this cause; but they are associated upon the same surface with L. hydraulicum, which, in similar conditions, has retained its surface-striae in good preservation. This species is readily distinguished from L. hydraulicum by the less rounded volutions and slighter constriction at the suture. It is more rapidly tapering than

L. rectistriatum, with which it is also associated, and has no constriction of the upper part of the volution as in that species.

A specimen preserving nine volutions, including the last one, measures about one inch and a quarter.

Formation and Locality.—Occurs in the cherty layers above the hydraulic limestone of the Devonian formation, at and around the Falls of the Ohio, in Kentucky and Indiana. Not as abundant as its associate, the Lox. hydraulicum.

Loxonema rectistriatum. HALL.

Loxonema rectistriatum, Hall. Pal. N. Y., Vol. 5, pt. 2, p. 131—1879.

Shell elongate terete; volutions probably twelve and more in number; moderately convex, very gradually increasing in size; the last one being scarcely more ventricose than the preceding; each volution is distinctly contracted a little below the close suture, and then expanding, gives the greatest convexity near the lower third. Suture line close; aperture ovate, with the columella extending below.

Surface marked by slender, gently curving, longitudinal striae, which bend backward from the suture to bottom of constriction, and then continue to the base of the volution, those of the last one curving gently forward to the columellar lip. The spaces between the striae are from one and a half to twice the width of the ridges.

This species may be distinguished from any other described of the genus Loxonema, by the finer longitudinal striae, which are scarcely curved on the body of the volution, and also by the constriction of each volution just below the suture-line. The striae are stronger on the upper volutions, gradually becoming finer and less prominent on the lower ones, though continuing distinct throughout. A specimen, which preserves about eight volutions from the aperture, measures a little more than one inch in length.

Formation and Locality.—Found associated with Lox. hydraulicum and Lox. laeviusculum, in the cherty layers superimposed upon the hydraulic limestone of the Devonian formation at and around the Falls of the Ohio, in Kentucky and Indiana. Prof. Hall's descriptions and illustrations of this species, and of those just mentioned as its associates, were made from specimens belonging to the cabinet of the late Dr James Knapp, who collected them at the Falls of the Ohio on the former Corn Island.

Genus Macrocheilus. Phillips.

Macrocheilus, Phillips. Pal. Fossils—1841.
Etymology: macros, long; and *cheilos,* a lip.

Synonym: Polyphemopsis, Portlock.

Shell thick, ventricose, buccinoid; aperture simple, effuse below; outer lip thin, inner lip wanting; columella callous, slightly tortuous. Type: Macrocheilus arculatus of Schlotheim. (Copied from Woodward's Manual.)

Macrocheilus carinatus. N. SP.

Plate XX., figures 20, 21, 22 and 23.

Shell of medium size, turreted, sub-fusiform; length less than twice the diameter; volutions four or five, gradually increasing from the apex, last two ventricose, and the last one occupying one half the length of shell.

Aperture not known; indications point to its being elongate. No surface-markings are visible; they may have been obliterated by the process of silicification, to which our specimens were subjected. A peculiarity of this shell is the carina on the periphery of the last volution, as plainly shown in figures 20 and 23. It is in fact not a real carina, but produced by the elevation of the lower half of the volution above the surface of the upper half. This species has some resemblance to M. hebe, but differs from it by the peculiar feature of its lower volution.

Formation and Locality.—Found in the Corniferous limestone of the Devonian formation at and around the Falls of the Ohio, in Kentucky and Indiana.

Genus Polyphemopsis.˙ Portlock.

Polyphemopsis, Portlock. Geol. Rep. of Londonderry—1843.

Etymology: polyphemus, a genus of shells; *opsis,* appearance—having the appearance of Polyphemus.

Portlock does not give a definite description of the genus; but from his article on the subject, the following description may be formulated:

Shell free, univalve elongated, with a mammillated spire; mouth narrow; columella smooth and truncated; base notched; the last whorl greater than the balance together; base of the columella curved; outer lip is not marginated, and does not form on the whorls any suture or varices which might indicate the position of former apertures.

This is the description of Montfort's genus, Polyphemus, from which Portlock's Polyphemopsis differs by its sharp spire, while Polyphemus has a mammillated one, and by the want of a wave in outer lip of the aperture.

Polyphemopsis louisvillae. HALL AND WHITFIELD.

Plate XX., figures 16, 17, 18 and 19.

Polyphemopsis louisvillae, H. and W. 24th Reg. Rep., p. 193—1872.

Shell small, ventricose, consisting of about six rapidly tapering volutions, the last of which comprises about two-thirds the entire length of shell. Aperture large, ovate, widest below the middle, and pointed at the upper angle; a little more than half as long as the shell. Columella slight; suture scarcely impressed.

Surface smooth ; figures 16 and 17 are of natural size, while figures 18 and 19 are enlarged to two diameters. Figures and description made from specimens belonging to the collection of the late Dr. James Knapp.

Formation and Locality.—Occurs in the hydraulic limestone of the Devonian formation at the Falls of the Ohio, in Kentucky and Indiana.

Genus Euomphalus. Sowerby.

Euomphalus, Sowerby. Minn. Conch., Vol. 1—1814.
Etymology: eu, wide; *omphalos*, umbilicus,

The type of this genus is Euomphalus pentagonalis. Shell depressed or discoidal ; whorls angular or coronated ; aperture polygonal ; umbilicus very large ; operculum shelly, round, multispiral. The genus Euomphalus is nearly related to Straparollus of Montfort, and to Phanerotinus of Sowerby. It is difficult to mark out any features of importance in which these three genera differ. Prof. Hall uses the name Straparollus in a sub-generic sense for those shells with close rounded volutions, where the spire rises moderately above the plane of the outer volution, while those shells with disjointed volutions form the genus Phanerotinus.

Euomphalus decewi. BILLINGS.

Plate XXI. figures 1 and 2.

Euomphalus decewi, Billings. Can. Jour., p. 358—1861.
Euomphalus conradi, Hall. 14th Reg. Rep., p. 107—1861.
Euomphalus decewi. Meek. Geol. Rep. Ohio Pal., Vol. 1—1873.
Euomphalus decewi, Hall. Illust. of Dev. Foss., pl. 15—1876.
Euomphalus decewi, Hall. Pal. N. Y., Vol. 5, pt. 2, p. 55—1879.

Shell discoid, upper side moderately concave or sometimes nearly flat, the lower side broadly and deeply concave. Periphery moderately convex or nearly flat, and slightly oblique to the plane of the shell ; sometimes, in the casts of young shells, gently rounded from the upper margin to the edge of the umbilical depression. Volutions three or four (there are rarely more than two or three preserved in the casts), inner ones rounded, gradually becoming depressed on the upper and lower sides. The periphery, at first rounded and undefined, becomes more flattened and distinctly limited by a defined angularity above and below, becoming more flattened towards the aperture ; the upper side being gently depressed, while the lower side gradually assumes a more abruptly concave aspect, forming a broad umbilicus. Aperture unknown ; section of the outer volution sub-quadrilateral or triangular, with the inner angle truncated.

Surface, in young specimens, marked by fine elevated striae of growth. The fossils has a diameter of from one to four inches.

This species occurs usually as internal casts; in those of older specimens the apex is decollated, and the termination smoothly rounded, as if separated by a septum, no evidence of a continuation above being perceptible. The interior volutions being rounded, the angularity on the upper side is scarcely noticeable before the end of the second volution, and that of the lower side about the same time or a little later. In some of the casts of the interior there is a low, undefined angularity upon the back of the shell. This species appears to be nearly identical with Euomphalus wahlenbergii of Goldfuss (Petrefacta, vol. 3, p. 82, pl. 189, figs. 7, *a*, *b*), found in the limestone of the Eifel. That species also presents the same features in the decollation of the earlier volutions, and the rounded apical extremity. That European form is associated with Euomph. planorbis, a species much resembling our Euomph. clymenioides, which occurs in the same beds with Euomph. decewi, in western localities.

Formation and Locality.—Found abundantly in the Corniferous limestone in Jefferson county, Ky., and Clark county, Ind. A specimen containing the shell is figured in Geol. Ohio Pal., Vol. 1.

Euomphalus sampsoni. N. SP.

Plate XXI., figures 3 and 4.

Shell discoid, but generally, by apical decollation, receiving the shape of a horn; both sides considerably concave; the periphery broadly convex. Number of volutions unknown, probably only two. The outer volution rapidly increasing in size; its cross-section near the apex circular, near the aperture oval. The surface is ornamented by from twenty-five to thirty strong, simple plications, each of which extends over the whole length of the outer or last volution, and may probably reach back to the apex. These plications increase in strength from apex to the aperture; their interspaces are also gradually widening in their course towards the front; they are of unequal width; some are of four times, and others of double the size of the adjacent ribs. My specimens, being internal casts completely silicified into hornstone, no other surface-markings are retained.

Form and size of the aperture unknown. This species, with decollated apex, showing only a horn of not quite a whole volution, resembles somewhat Prof. Hall's Nautilus liratus, with which I confounded it, when I found the first specimen, but I soon discovered my mistake. Hall's Nautilus shows plainly the transverse lines of the septae, which do not exist in our shell; in the latter the curvature is greatly stronger than in the former, and the increase in the size of the outer volution is more gradual in my species than in the Nautilus.

The specimen illustrated on plate 21 is about of average size, and represents the general condition of most of the specimens so far found.

Formation and Locality.—Found in the cherty layers superimposed upon the hydraulic limestone of the Devonian formation, at Watson's Station, in Clark county, Ind., about six miles from the Falls of the Ohio. This species is named to honor a gentleman who cultivates, not only for himself, different branches of Natural Science, among which most prominently, Geology and Palæontology, but who also endeavors to popularize the same by forming scientific societies in his western home. It is named after the Hon. F. A. Sampson, attorney at law, Sedalia, Missouri

Genus Platyostoma. Conrad.

Platyostoma, Conrad. Jour. Acad. Nat. Sci. Phil., Vol. 8—1842.
Etymology: platys, broad ; *stoma,* mouth.

Mr. Conrad gives the following very meager description of this genus :

Shell sub-globose; spire short; aperture very large, sub-orbicular, dilated; labrum joining the body-whorl at right-angles to the axis of shell. The species, Platyostoma niagarensis or P. lineata, may be taken as the type for this genus. The shells of this genus are related to those of Platyceras, with depressed spire, but they differ by the larger number of their volutions and the more gradual increase in the size of the whorls.

Platyostoma lineata. Conrad.

Plate XXI., figures 7 and 8, and Plate XIX., figures 5, 6, 7 and 8.

. *Platyostoma lineata,* Conrad. Jour. Acad. Nat. Sci. Phil., Vol. 8—1842.
Platyostoma lineata, Hall. Illust. of Devonian Foss., Gast., pl. 9—1876.
Platyostoma lineata, Hall. Pal. N. Y., Vol. 5, part 2, p. 21—1876.

Shell above medium size, depressed spiral ; each volution elevated moderately above the succeeding one ; number of volutions seldom exceeding four ; apex being usually imperfect. The outer volution large and very ventricose ; it is regularly convex, with the exception of the portion near the suture line, which is generally a little depressed or concave. Aperture sub-rhomboidal, with thin outer lip and a sharp entire margin; columellar lip thickened, folded and reflexed over the umbilicus, which is entirely closed in adult specimens.

Surface marked by fine, nearly equidistant, thread-like revolving striae, as seen in figures 5 to 8, plate 19, which are cancellated by fine concentric striae of about the same strength, but of unequal distance ; the latter sometimes bend abruptly backward upon the back of the shell, indicating a sinus in the lip at some period of growth, and are frequently crowded in fascicles, giving a rugose appearance to the surface of the shell. In well preserved specimens the surface is beautifully cancellated ; and in worn and partially exfoliated specimens, some of the surface-markings remain visible; the revolving striae are generally the first which become obliterated. This species is very variable in size; we find specimens as small as half an inch or less, and, again, others measuring even more than two inches. The individuals illustrated on plates 19 and 21 are about of average size.

Formation and Locality.—Found abundantly, in even well preserved specimens, however, without the revolving striae, in the rotten limestone of the Corniferous group, in Jefferson county., Ky., and in Clark county, Ind.

Platyostoma lineata, var. callosa. HALL.

Plate XXI., figure 14; Plate XXII., figures 10 and 11, and Plate XXV., figures 5, 6 and 7.

Platyostoma lineata, var. callosa, Hall. Illust. of Dev. Fossils, Gasteropoda, pl. 9—1876.
Platyostoma lineata, var. callosa, Hall. Pal. N. Y., Vol. 5—1879.

This variety has the general form and also the surface-markings of specimens of the species Plat. lineata, with the exception that in this variety the spire is extremely depressed, scarcely extending above the upper level of the volution of habitation, which is generally called the body-whorl. The aperture is large, sub orbicular, with the peristome slightly sinuate on the upper side near its junction with the preceding volution. The inner lip is marked by a thickened callus, not observed in any other specimens; the callosity extending into the lip below, which thence assumes the ordinary features of the species.

Formation and Locality.—Found associated with Plat. lineata in the rotten hornstone of the Devonian formation, in Jefferson county, Ky., and in Clark county, Ind.

Platyostoma turbinata. HALL.

Plate XXI., figures 5 and 6.

Platyostoma turbinata, Hall. Fourteenth Rep. N. Y. St. Cab.—1861.
Platyostoma turbinata, Hall. Illust of Dev. Foss., pl. 10—1876.
Platyostoma turbinata, Hall. Pal. N. Y., Vol. 5, part 2, p. 27—1879.

Shell sub-turbinate, sometimes approaching a sub-globose form. Spire depressed, or more or less elevated above the outer volution, sometimes nearly on the same plane; volutions three or four rapidly expanding, the last extremely ventricose, with the lower part projected in the direction of the columella, which is much extended. Aperture sub-ovate, broader above, narrowing, and often extended below.

Surface marked by fine, sub-equal concentric striae, crossed by finer revolving striae; the former variously undulated upon the surface, indicating sinuosity in the lip of the aperture at former stages of growth. In older shells the striae become lamellose and often crowded in fascicles.

Formation and Locality.—In the Corniferous group around the Falls of the Ohio, in Kentucky and Indiana.

Platyostoma turbinata, var. cochleata. HALL.

Platyostoma turbinata, var. cochleata, Hall. Illust. of Devonian Fossils, Gaster., pl. 10—1876.
Platyostoma turbinata, var. cochleata, Hall. Pal. N. Y, Vol. 5, part 2, p. 28--1879.

Shell turbinate. Spire elevated, conical; volutions about four or five; periphery of the last volution obtusely rounded or distinctly sub-angular, with a sinus in the margin of the aperture; the last volution sometimes becoming free near the aperture, which latter is obliquely sub-ovate or ovate; peristome sinuous, often with a deep notch in the upper margin, and sometimes continued in a columellar extension below.

The specimens referred to this variety all agree in having an elevated spire, with rounded volutions above the last one, which is almost invariably subangular.

Formation and Locality.—Found associated with Plat. lineata in the rotten hornstone of the Devonian formation around Louisville, Ky.

Platyostoma niagarense. HALL.

Plate XXXIII., figure 30.

Platyostoma niagarensis, Hall. Pal. N. Y., Vol. 2, p. 287, pl. 60, figs. 1a-1v—1852.
Platyostoma niagarense, Hall. 28th Rep. N. Y. St. Mus. Nat. Hist., Mus. edit., p. 175, pl. 28, figs. 1-12; pl. 29, figs. 1-15—1879.
Platyostoma niagarense, Hall. Ind. Geo. Survey, 11th Rep., pl. 29, p. 318—1881.

The following description is quoted from Prof. Hall: Shell ovoid or subglobose; volutions three to four, the last one very ventricose; spire varying from the plane of the outer volution to an elevation of one-fifth or one-fourth the height of the shell above.

Apex minute, somewhat rapidly expanding, the first two volutions usually symmetrical; the outer volution often unsymmetrical, very ventricose and regularly rounded upon the back, but not unfrequently extended and becoming free towards the aperture, and marked on the upper or lower side, or upon both, by a groove, along which the striae are abruptly bent, indicating a sinus in the peristome during some period of its growth; peristome entire or undulated, sometimes distinctly notched in the margin, free or adhering on the columellar side, and sometimes expanded and presenting a thickened callosity or columellar lip.

Surface marked by fine undulating striae of growth, which sometimes become lamellose. In well preserved specimens, finer revolving striae cancellate the striae of growth, and sometimes the surface is marked by revolving ridges.

Formation and Locality.—Occurs in the Niagara near Louisville, Kentucky. The specimen figured is a very young one.

Genus Strophostylus. Hall.

Strophostylus, Hall. Pal. N. Y., Vol. 3, page 303—1859.
Etymology: strophe, turning around; *stylos*, a column.

Shell sub-globose or ovoid-globose; spire small, with a large ventricose body-whorl. Outer lip thin, not reflected, sometimes slightly expanded.

Columella twisted or spirally grooved within ; not reflected. No umbilicus. Aperture somewhat round-ovate or transversely broad oval.

Strophostylus varians. Hall.

Plate XXII., figures 6 and 7.
Strophostylus varians, Hall. Ill. of Dev. Foss., pl. 2—1876.
Strophostylus varians, Hall. Pal. N. Y., Vol. 5, pt. 2, p. 31—1879.

Shell of medium size, spiral, with moderately elevated spire; volutions about three or four; ventricose and regularly rounded above, and somewhat rapidly increasing, the last one becoming very ventricose, and extending downward and forward. Aperture ovate or sub orbicular ; peristome entire ; the columellar lip usually expanded, and spreading over the umbilicus, some-times free, and leaving the umbilicus exposed.

Surface covered by fine, closely set, transverse striae, the suture, owing to the great convexity of the volutions, deep and well exposed. Prof. Hall makes the following remarks about this species: " This species, in some re-spects, makes a wider departure from the typical forms of Strophostylus than any other of the genus known to me. The peculiar and characteristic form is preserved ; the symmetrical rounding of the volutions above, and the delicately formed spire, as well as the form of the aperture in some specimens, are all characteristic of the genus. The striae, however, have a tendency to become lamellose or interruptedly undulating ; and there are evidences of irregularity of growth and indentations in the margin of the peristome, both above and below the periphery. The form of the aperture is extremely variable, from narrow elliptical to broadly expanded. There is, though rarely, a tendency in the last volution to become free, and the characteristic plication of the colum-ellar lip is not often well preserved. In some of its variations it simulates Platyostoma, but in all phases it differs from that genus in the characteristic expression of the spire."

Formation and Locality.—Occurs in the Corniferous limestone at and around the Falls of the Ohio in Kentucky and Indiana; but it is a rather rare shell in our rocks.

Genus Cyclonema. Hall.

Cyclonema, Hall. Pal. N. Y., Vol. 2—1852.
Etymology: kuklos, a circle; *nema*, a thread.

Shells turbinate, thin; spire short, consisting of few volutions, which increase rapidly from the apex; aperture large, rounded anteriorly, and somewhat flattened on the columella side; umbilicus none; surface strongly marked by spiral, thread-like striae, which are cancellated by finer striae.

This genus includes shells which have been referred to Pleurotomaria, Littorina and others, but which have no slit or indentation in the outer lip or a band upon the volutions.

The surface is marked by elevated striae parallel to the direction of the volutions, and the spaces between these are marked by finer striae crossing the others obliquely; these latter, however, are often obsolete.

The Pleurotomaria bilix of Conrad is the type of this genus.

Cyclonema cancellata. Hall.

Plate XX., figures 10 and 11.

Littorina cancellata, Hall. Geol. Rep. 4th Dist. N. Y.—1843.
Cyclonema cancellata, Hall. Pal. N. Y., Vol. 2, page 90—1852.

Obtusely sub-conical or globose, with a short spire; volutions about four, rounded, rapidly increasing from the apex, so that the last one occupies almost the whole bulk of the shell; aperture scarcely expanded.

Surface marked by prominent thread-like lines, coincident with the spire, which are decussated by finer elevated striae in a slightly oblique direction.

The size of this shell varies greatly, from one measuring only a few lines to the size shown in the illustrations. In .young individuals, the decussating striae are usually well preserved, while they gradually become obsolete in older specimens, which are also often distorted by pressure.

Formation and Locality.—Occurs in the lower strata of the Niagara group in the quarries east of the city of Louisville, where, however, it is a very rare shell. The specimen from which this description, and the figures 10 and 11, on plate 20, were made, belonged to the collection of the late Dr. James Knapp; no others are known to me.

Cyclonema rugaelineata. Hall and Whitfield.

Plate XXXIII., figure 21.

Euomphalus (Cyclonema) *rugaelineata*, H. and W. 24th Rep. on N. Y. State Cabinet, p. 186—1872.
Euomphalus (Cyclonema) *rugaelineata*, H. and W. 27th Rep. on N. Y. State Cabinet, pl. 13—1875.

Shell of medium size, depressed turbinate, with four or five volutions, which increase very rapidly; they are rounded, very convex, and the last one is very ventricose. The surface is ornamented by ten to twelve strong, sharply elevated, revolving lines, having a smaller one between them. On the upper half of the body-whorl the stronger revolving lines have larger interspaces than those on the lower half, but the lines in the interspaces are smaller above the center of the volution than those below it. Between suture and the upper carina or strong revolving line, there are four very fine revolving lines, only indicated by the four rows of imbrications, which are there conspicuously marked. These revolving striae are crossed transversely by irregular lamellose lines of growth, to which the surface owes its finely ornamented, somewhat rugose appearance.

Suture, owing to the great convexity of the volutions in their cross-sections, deep and sharply marked.

Apex and the first one or two volutions not known on account of the decol-. lated condition of the shell. Aperture supposed to be round; form of base and columella unknown.

Prof. Hall states that this species bears considerable resemblance to Euomphalus carinatus of Sowerby, found in Europe in the Niagara group, from which it differs by the smaller number of revolving carinae, and in the possession of the intermediate lines, as also in the character of the transverse striae.

Formation and Locality.—In the Niagara strata of the different quarries east of the city of Louisville, Ky. My illustration of this shell is a copy of Prof. Hall's, who made his from a not very good specimen in Dr. James Knapp's collection. That specimen was, for some time, the only one known; but since then I have found several myself. One of my shells is not at all distorted, showing three volutions in their regular form, and with their surface ornamentation, except the markings on the lower half of the last volution.

Cyclonema multilira. HALL.

Plate XXII., figure 5.

Cyclonema multilira, Hall.   Descr. New Sp. of Fossils, p. 20—1861.
Cyclonema multilira, Hall.   Fiteenth Rep. N. Y. State Cab. Nat. Hist., p. 48—1862.
Cyclonema multilira, Hall.   Illustrations of Devonian Fossils, Gasteropoda, pl. 12—1876.
Cyclonema multilira, Hall.   Pal. N. Y., Vol. 5, pt. 2, pl. 12—1879.

Shell medium size, pyramidal in outline, gently turbinate, with four increasing volutions; suture line indistinct. On the surface of the volutions are regular, prominent plications, and very broad sinuous furrows, winding parallel to the suture-line. Volutions begin sharply, but increase in diameter, and become a little more ventricose.

The description is based upon a very imperfect cast, in which the lip and umbilicus are wanting.

Formation and Locality.—From the lower Devonian near Louisville, Ky.

Genus Trochonema. Salter.

Etymology: trochos, a wheel; nema, a thread.

This genus is never defined by any writer in this country. It includes spiral shells, having some relations to Pleurotpmaria, but differing from that genus by exterior characters.

Trochonema fatua. HALL.

Trochonema fatua, Hall. 20th Reg. Rep., page 345—1867.

Spire elevated ; shell turritiform, consisting of about four or five volutions, which gradually increase to the last one, which is moderately ventricose ; volutions biangular, leaving a flattened space upon the back about equal to flattened space between upper angle and suture line; lower half of last volution rounded ; aperture ovate-elongate.   The specimens from which this description was made by Prof. Hall were casts, and so is the one before me, which answers in every particular the above description. Prof. Hall states that the surface of the shell, as seen in an imprint in the rock, is finely striated, and that the flattened space on the back of volution is margined on each side by a slender carina, and is covered by coarser striae.

The size of different specimens varies greatly ; its height is from one to one and seven-eighths of an inch, while the diameter of its base is about four-fifths of its height.

Formation and Locality.—Found in the Niagara rocks, in the quarries east of the city of Louisville, Ky. It is very rare; the only specimen known to me belongs to the collection of Major Wm. J. Davis, of Louisville, Ky.

Trochonema rectilatera. HALL.

Plate XX., figures 1 and 2.

Trochonema rectilatera, Hall. 24th Regent's Rep., p. 193—1872.
Trochonema rectilatera, Hall. 27th Regent's Rep., pl. 13—1875.

Shell of medium size, turbinate ; breadth and height almost equal ; volution about five, carinated above with straight, nearly vertical sides ; outer one ventricose, with two carinae having a wide, vertical, slightly concave space between, which occupies more than one-third the height of the volution.   Upper side of the volutions convex for half the distance to the carina, and below this they are concave, giving the form of an ogee.

In another specimen, apparently the upper side of the volutions are slightly concave, and regularly sloping downward from the suture to the carina.   Lower side of the volution not carinate ; umbilicus small, or closed with a callosity

Surface marked by fine striae of growth, which are turned backward from the suture, and are vertical on the sides of the volution, and on the lower side curve backward to the umbilical area.

Formation and Locality.—In the upper strata of the Devonian limestone, at and around the Falls of the Ohio, where it is exceedingly rare. As Dr. Knapp's collection, which contained the original specimens, is sold, I don't think there exists a representative of this species in the Falls Cities.

Trochonema yandellana. Hall and Whitfield.

Plate XX., figure 3.

Trochonema yandellana, H. and W.　24th Regent's Rep., p. 194—1872.
Trochonema yandellana, H. and W.　27th Regent's Rep., pl. 13—1875.

Shell turbinate; volutions about five (three of which are shown in the illustration), rapidly increasing, carinated; the last volution becoming ventricose, and marked by seven revolving carinae, including the one bordering the somewhat channeled suture; four of the carinae are distinctly marked by thin, lanceolate nodes, which become more prominent with the increased growth of the shell, while the other three—one bordering the suture and two on the lower middle portion of the volution—are destitute of nodes in the specimen described, but it may be that it assumes this character only in an advanced stage of growth. The carinae are situated, one at the suture and one bordering the moderately large umbilicus, with five on the body of the volution, of which two are above the middle and three below. The spaces separating those bordering the suture and the umbilicus from those on the body of the volution, are considerably wider than the spaces between the intermediate carinae. Aperture rounded, slightly modified by the carinae.

Surface marked by fine transverse striae of growth, which turn backward as they cross the volution to the umbilicus.

The illustration on plate 20 is a copy of Prof. Hall's figure in the 27th Reg. Rep., and this description also a copy of Prof. Hall's in the 24th Reg. Rep. At the time when my plates were prepared there was only one specimen of this species known, which belonged to the cabinet of the late Dr. James Knapp, and which at that time was not accessible to me. Since then I came myself in possession of a very fine specimen of this species, which differs somewhat from Knapp's. Instead of having only four carinae with nodes, as is the case in Knapp's shell, mine has six. The only smooth carina in my specimen is that bordering the suture. There is also a marked difference in the interspaces between the carinae; while in Knapp's shell the distance from the carinae bordering the suture and the umbilicus, to their adjacent one, is larger than the distances between the other carinae, in my specimen the interspaces between the first carina, as which I count the one near the suture, and the second, and between this and the third, are almost twice as wide as any of the balance. Outside of these mentioned differences there is a complete resem blance between the two specimens.

Formation and Locality.—Found in the cherty layers of the Corniferous limestone, at and around the Falls of the Ohio, in Kentucky and Indiana. This beautiful fossil is exceedingly rare; as far as I know, Dr. Knapp's and my own specimen are the only representatives of this species. Prof. Hall, who first described and illustrated this species from Dr. Knapp's shell, named it in honor of the late Dr. Lunsford Yandell, Sr., of Louisville, Ky., who was one of the first collectors of the fossils at and around the Falls of the Ohio.

Genus Turbo. Klein.

Turbo, Klein. Tent. Moth. Ostr.—1753.
Etymology: turbo, meaning a top.

Type of this genus is Turbo marmoratus.

Shells turbinated, solid; whorls convex, often grooved or tuberculated; aperture large, rounded, slightly produced in front; operculum shelly and solid, callous outside, and smooth, or variously grooved and mammillated; internally horny and pauci-spiral.

This genus extends from the Silurian to the present time.

Turbo shumardi. De Verneuil.

Plate XIX., figures 1 to 4, and Plate XXII., figures 1 and 2.
Turbo shumardi. De Verneuil. Bulletin de la Soc. Geol. de France.

Shell large, gibbous, sub-globose. Spire moderately elevated; apex minute · volutions about five or six, gradually enlarging in the earlier stages of growth, while the last one increases in size very rapidly, and becomes very ventricose with an expanded aperture. The first two or three volutions are smooth and regularly rounded upon the exposed surfaces, gradually becoming nodose and flattened, or somewhat concave, on the upper or front side. The nodes increase in size and strength with the increase of the volutions. Suture close in the earlier volutions and becoming somewhat canaliculate in the later ones. Lower side of the outer volution very convex, even in the umbilical region, and much extended in the direction of the columella. Aperture broadly rounded; columellar lip obtuse, thickened, having a distinct broad opercular groove; callus covering the umbilicus and spreading outwardly; external margin of the aperture thin.

Surface marked by fine, comparatively even striae of growth, which are often crowded into fascicles, and in old shells are somewhat imbricated at irregular intervals.

The periphery of the outer volution is marked by a strongly elevated, obtusely angular carina, which is continued from the suture-line at the inner posterior angle of the aperture. The outer one or two of the volutions (depending on the size of the shell) are marked or ornamented by strong curving nodes, which, commencing just below the suture, are nearly vertical for a short distance, and then curving forward, are finally directed towards the aperture, and gradually become merged into the general surface.

The striae, originating at the suture, are first directed backward, and thence, gently curving over the nodes, become nearly vertical, and thus continue to near the peripheral carina, where they are turned a little backward, and, passing this elevation, they are directed with a light curve towards the columella.

This species possesses all the features of the Linnaean genus Turbo, to which it was originally referred by M. de Verneuil, who described and named it in honor of the late Prof. B. F. Shumard, of St. Louis. It is so very different from all other shells of our rocks, that it will be recognized at the first glance by any one, who has ever seen a correct illustration of it. The shell is usually silicified, and is rarely well preserved or occurs as internal casts, which bear only slight indications of the nodes, but none of the other surface-ornamentations.

Prof. Hall made his descriptions and illustrations from fine specimens belonging to the cabinet of the late Dr. James Knapp. One of Knapp's specimens was also used for my illustrations, sub-figures 1, 2 and 3, plate 19. The individual, of which figure 4, plate 19, and figure 2, plate 22, are copies, is in my own collection, presented to me by Miss Spangler, of Clark county, Indiana.

Formation and Locality—Found in the rotten hornstone of the Devonian formation in Jefferson county, Ky., and in Clark county, Ind. It is not a very rare species, although specimens like Dr. Knapp's and my own are extremely rare.

MOLLUSCA.

CEPHALOPODA.

Genus Gomphoceras. Sowerby.

Etymology: gomphos, a club; *keras,* a horn.

Gomphoceras oviforme. HALL.

Plate XXI., figures 17 and 18.

Gomph. oviforme, Hall. Thirteenth Rep. N. Y. St. Cab., p. 105—1860.
Gomph. oviforme, Hall. Illust. of Dev. Foss., Cephal., pl. 45—1876.
Cyrtoceras gibbosus, Hall. Illust. of Dev. Foss., Cephal., pl. 47—1876.
Gomph. oviforme, Hall. Pal. N. Y., Vol. 5, part 2, p. 344—1879.

Shell small, ovoid, sub-cylindrical, straight ; transverse section elliptical or sub-circular; longitudinal section sub-quadrate or sub-ovate. Plan of greatest transverse section at the bottom of the body-chamber. The specimens of this species found in our rocks have retained only a small section of the septate portion of the shell ; usually only one or two septae are preserved. Apex is truncated, apical angle about sixty degrees. Chamber of habitation comparatively large ; its length is about equal to three-fourths of its largest diameter ; aperture large and trilobate (the one shown in figure 18, plate 21, is incorrect, it is too narrow, and the third lobe, branching from the middle to the right, is not at all illustrated, owing to the faulty condition of the shell which served for illustration). Siphuncle near the ventral side, with a diameter of two millimeters at the last septum. Test strong, having a thickness of one and a half millimeters over the chamber of habitation.

Our specimens do not show any surface-markings ; if any existed on perfect and well-preserved individuals, they are obliterated on ours by the process of silicification and by exfoliation. Our shells being internal casts, the suture-lines are plainly shown. The specimen illustrated in figures 17 and 18, plate 21, is of average size of those here found. This species is easily distinguished by its cylindrical form, and by the trilobate shape of its aperture.

Formation and Locality.—Found associated with its congener, Gomph. turbiniforme, in the chert topping the hydraulic limestone of the Devonian formation, in Jefferson county, Ky., and Clark county, Ind., where it is somewhat abundant, but not in fair specimen.

Gomphoceras turbiniforme. Meek and Worthen.

Plate XX1., figures 15 and 16.

Gomph. turbiniforme, M. and W.　Proc. Acad. Nat. Sci. Phil.—1860.
Gomph. turbiniforme, M. and W.　Geol. Rep. of Ill., Vol. 3, p. 444—1868.

Shell rather small, turbinate or obovate, very slightly unsymmetrical; section circular, or nearly so; chambered part rapidly expanding, with sides slightly convex above. Non-septate part very short, or three times as wide as long, rounding in abruptly, above; aperture contracted, but exact form unknown. Septa only moderately concave, nearly equidistant at all points, except near the outer chamber and the apex, where they are more crowded; at about the widest part of the shell, separated by spaces equalling one-eighth its greatest diameter. Siphon small and marginal. Surface nearly smooth, or with only fine lines of growth.

This description is copied from Ill. Geol. Rep., Vol. 3, page 444. The specimen there described and figured on plate 12, figures 2a, b, came from the neighborhood of the Falls of the Ohio. The specimens figured on my plate, 21, are of the average size.

Formation and Locality.—Four ... .ue cherty layers superimposed upon the hydraulic limestone of the Devonian formation, in Jefferson county, Ky., and in Clark county, Ind.

Genus Goniatites. De Haan.

Etymology; gunia, an angle; *lithos,* a stone.

Goniatites discoideus. Hall.

Plate XX., figures 14 and 15.

Goniatites discoideus, Hall.　13th Rep. N. Y. St. Cab.—1860.
Goniatites discoideus, Hall.　27th Rep. N. Y. St. Cab.—1875.
Goniatites discoideus, Hall.　Illust. Dev. Foss., pl. 71—1876.
Goniatites sinuosus, Hall.　Rep. 4th Dist. N. Y., p. 246—1843.
Goniatites discoideus, Hall.　Pal. N. Y., Vol. 5, pt. 2, p. 441—1885.

Shell depressed orbicular in the young state, becoming discoid in its advancing growth. It differs in size, and in the proportion of its dimensions, according to its age.

The specimen illustrated shows the average size of shells found in our rocks.

A minute description can only be given by a geologist who has a large number of specimens before him, some of which he may break or cut up, in order to see the number of volutions, which are all inside of the last one, or to examine other internal features. The outside appearance of the shell offers few points for description which the illustration does not plainly show.

Formation and Locality.—Found in the Corniferous limestone of the Devonian formation, at and around the Falls of the Ohio, in Kentucky and Indiana.

Genus Lituites. Montfort.

Etymology: letuus, a trumpet.

Lituites marshi. Hall.

Plate XXX., figure 1.
Lituites marshi, Hall. 20th Regent's Rep., p. 362—1867.

Shell of medium size, consisting of four or more closely enrolled volutions, which increase in size gradually, but very slowly, from the apex; transverse or cross-section circular or sub-circular; slightly flattened on the dorsum, and marked on the sides by sharp, strong, oblique annulations, with regularly concave spaces between them. These ridges, rising on the ventral margin, are directed obliquely backward as they cross the sides of the volutions, reaching the center of the dorsum at a point opposite the origin of the second preceding one, having their greatest elevation on the sides of the shell, and making a somewhat abrupt retrorse curve, become almost obsolete on the dorsum. Septa moderately distant, deeply and regularly concave, the chambers regularly increasing in depth with the diameter of the shell. The space of three chambers, measured on the side of the shell, are equal to the dorso-ventral diameter of the volution. The dorsal margins of the septa are directed forward, giving a broad rectral curvature on the side of the volution. Siphuncle small and sub-central.

Surface of shell and form of aperture are unknown. This beautiful species is readily distinguished by its slender volutions, and the strong, oblique ridges, which, in the outer part of the shell, are a little more distant than the septa, while on the inner volutions they are nearer to each other, the increase in the distance of the annulations being a little more rapid than that of the septa. Owing to the retrorse curving of the annulations, and the advancing curvature of the septa, the ridges are cut by the latter near the dorso-lateral angle of the volution, throughout the greater part of the extent of shell.

In the specimen illustrated on plate 30, both termini of the shell are missing; it has preserved more than three complete volutions. The vacant central space indicates that, probably, two full volutions are obliterated there at the apex. How much there is destroyed at the other end can not be ascertained, but that there is a large part of a volution missing can not be doubted. Thus it appears that the illustrated specimen, in its perfect condition, had six full volutions. Prof. Hall named this species in honor of Prof. O. C. Marsh, the eminent geologist.

Formation and Locality.—Found in the Niagara rocks of the quarries east of the city of Louisville, where fragments of this shell are not rare, but fair specimens are not often found.

Genus Nautilus. Breynius.

Etymology : nautilos, a sailor or navigator.

Nautilus maximus. CONRAD.

Plate XXIV., figure 1.

Cyrtoceras maximum, Conrad. Geol. Survey of N. Y., Pal. Dept. First Ann. Rep.—1838.
Nautilus maximus, Hall. Illust. Dev. Fossils—1876.
Nautilus maximus, Hall. Pal. N. Y., Vol 5, pt. 2, p. 418—1875.

Shell very large, sub-discoid, gibbous, becoming very ventricose. Volutions about three, contiguous, not re-entrant. Umbilicus wide and deep, exposing all the volutions. Transverse section sub-circular, flattened on the concave dorsal side; tube regularly and gradually enlarging to a point near the aperture; apical angle about fourteen degrees. The body-whorl, or chamber of habitation, very large and ventricose, occupying half a volution and more. In the larger individuals it is free from the inner volution for about one-third its length.

Length of the grand chamber more than twice its greatest diameter, gradually contracting towards the aperture from a point about two-thirds of its entire length from the base. Aperture slightly oblique to the axis of the tube, opening upward. Air-chambers numerous, regular and very deep, gradually increasing from the apex, and measuring on the convex side sometimes more than thirty millimeters; the last one shallower than several of those preceding.

Septa regular, distant, very concave, the concavity greater than the depth of the air-chambers; strongly imbricating. The distance between the septa is variable in different specimens, but in the same individual is nearly constant, with a gradually increasing distance. Siphuncle large, sub-central, slightly expanding between the septa.

The ventral side of the shell is indicated by a sharp, narrow, longitudinal raised line on the outer face of the chambers, on the convex side of the volutions. Test seldom preserved.

Surface marked by fine and coarser, irregular, lamellose lines of growth, and fine, regular, undulating, elevated, thread-like striae, parallel to the lines of growth ; longitudinally marked by rounded, or sometimes sharper, undulating, revolving striae, of which there are five or six in the space of five millimeters.

These markings are visible on the macerated inner laminae of the shell, and often even on the internal cast. The internal cast is strongly marked by the suture-lines, which are deeply impressed from the solution and removal of the imbricating margins of the septa.

The largest known specimen of this species has a diameter of 360 millimeters, and the chamber of habitation of the same specimen, measured along the middle of the lateral face, has a length of more than 360 millimeters, and measured on the periphery, has a length of more than 450 millimeters. This species resembles N. oriens and magister, from both of which it is, however, easily distinguished.

Formation and Locality.—Found in the hydraulic limestone of the Devonian formation at the Falls of the Ohio, in Kentucky and Indiana. The figure on plate 24 is only one-half of the natural size of the shell from which it was taken.

MOLLUSCA.

LAMELLIBRANCHIATA.

Genus Limoptera. Hall.

Limoptera, Hall. Prelim. Notice Lam. Shells—1870.
Etymology : lima, a genus of shells; *pteron*, a wing.

Shell large, inequilateral, inequivalve ; the right valve the smaller ; ligamental area large, common to both valves ; longitudinally striate, and extending to the extremities of the wings. Margins of valves sinuate on the anterior border, forming an elongate byssal opening ; hinge edentulous (?). Anterior muscular impression situated within the umbones, very small and deep ; the posterior one large, and placed a little behind the middle of shell, and nearer to the hinge than to base of valve. Pallial line simple, formed of a series of small, deep pits (or, as seen in the casts, composed of a series of small nodes).

The general form of the shells, when well preserved, is broadly ovate or sub-quadrate in outline, strongly alate on the posterior side, and often more or less produced on the anterior end. The valves are convex in all species known; the left valve being strongly convex throughout, while the opposite one is but slightly elevated, and in one species is somewhat concave near the base. The surface is coarsely radiate in all but one species. The ligamental area is large, in both valves sub-equal, and without cartilage pits. Lima macroptera of Conrad may be considered as type of this genus.

Limoptera cancellata. HALL.

Plate III., figures 6, 7 and 8; Plate IV., figure 24.

Limoptera cancellata, Hall. Prel. Nat. Lam. Shells, pt. 2—1869.
Limoptera cancellata, var. occidens, H. and W. 24th Reg. Rep., p. 199—1872.
Limoptera cancellata, Hall. Pal. N. Y., Vol. 5, pt. 1, p. 244—1883.

Shell large; body sub-erect; general outline very variable, from broadly ovate to sub-elliptical; axis of the body nearly vertical to the hinge-line; proportion of height to length very variable; sometimes both dimensions are nearly equal, but mostly the height predominates over the length, and, as shown in our illustration, in some shells to a considerable extent. The prevailing form may be described as follows: Elongate oviform, almost erect, with a slight anterior inclination; plano-convex, with the left valve strongly convex in the umbonal region, and only moderately convex, almost flattened, in its basal half. The right valve is entirely flat, with only a gentle elevation in the umbonal region. Height exceeding the length; their proportion as four to three.

The margins in the lower or basal half of the shell regularly curved; in the upper half, the anterior margin of the body is only slightly rounded, while the posterior margin of the body forms an entire straight line.

The lateral slopes of the umbonal region are very steep, meeting the surface of the wings almost at right-angles, forming thus a demarcation line for the ears. The wings are unequal, the anterior considerably smaller than the posterior. The front wing forms only a small triangular deflection of the anterior margin, while the posterior wing has a considerable width on the hinge-line, and in its longitudinal dimension extends below the middle of the shell. The hinge-line is usually straight, but sometimes deflected in different directions, as our illustration shows; it is shorter than the height or length. The umbo of the left valve is prominent, and the beak straight, rounded and pointed, and overreaching a small triangular hinge-area, which has no foramen. The beak is situated about one-third the length of the cardinal line from its anterior end, and has a decided anterior direction. In the right valve the beak does not extend beyond the cardinal line. The posterior margin of the rear wing is concave, but deflects back near the cardinal extremity, which is angular.

Test is of moderate thickness, and is ornamented by rounded, abruptly elevated radii, with large, flat interspaces, which are sometimes occupied by one and even two finer, radiating striae; but in some shells these finer striae are obsolete. These radii are crossed, and the large interspaces cancellated by fine concentric lines of growth. Towards the margins, in the basal half of the shell, the radii become either entirely obsolete, or at least very obscure. On the wings the radiating striae are also obsolete, but the concentric lines of growth are there more prominent and crowded. On the anterior slope of the left umbo exists a curved line of small and low nodules, numbering from ten to twelve or more. This line starts at the beak and extends about an inch towards the front. These nodes indicate small pits in the interior surface of the shell, and served, probably, as attachment for some muscles. The right valve has a similar line of nodes. The specimen here described measures three inches in height, two inches and one-fourth in length, and its hinge-line one and three-quarters inches long.

Formation and Locality.—Occurs in the cherty layers superimposed upon the hydraulic limestone of the Devonian formation, in Jefferson county, Ky., and in Clark county, Ind., where it is found as a silicified internal cast. Not rare.

Genus Clinopistha.   Meek and Worthen.

Etymology : klino, I lean ; *opisthe,* backwards.

Clinopistha subnasuta.   HALL AND WHITFIELD.

Plate IV., figures 6, 7, 8 and 12.

Tellinomya subnasuta, H. and W.   24th Reg. Rep., p. 191—1872.

Dystactella (*Tellinomya*) *subnasuta,* H. and W.   27th Reg. Rep., pl. 2—1875.

Shell small, elongate, sub-elliptical, twice as long as high, with very ventricose valves, giving the shell in its middle part a sub-cylindrical appearance; posterior end very narrow, shorter than the anterior one, and pointed at the extremity; anterior end regularly rounded, longest above the center; basal line in its central half almost straight, sometimes a little inflected opposite the beaks, or slightly convex; its terminal parts turn in a gentle and regular curve upwards to the anterior and posterior extremities; beaks small and closely appressed, situated at two-thirds of the length of shell from the anterior end. Muscular impressions of moderate size distinctly marked, situated near the margin of valve; pallial line entire, composed of a series of radiating pustules, as seen on the cast.

Surface marked by distinct, rather strong, somewhat lamellose lines of growth. Prof. Hall expected that this species might not really belong to the genus Tellinomya, and proposed for it the name of Dystactella, but placed it afterwards with Clinopistha.

Formation and Locality.—In the chert beds overlying the hydraulic limestone in Jefferson county, Ky., and in Clark county, Ind.

Clinopistha antiqua. Meek.

Plate IV., figures 9, 10 and 11.

Clinopistha antiqua, Meek.   Proc. Acad. Nat. Sci. Phil.—1871.
Clinopistha antiqua, Meek.   Geol. of Ohio.   Pal., Vol. 1, p, 208—1873.

Shell transversely sub-oval, regularly and moderately convex ; height two-thirds of the length, and depth one-half of height; anterior end regularly rounded; posterior extremity only one-half as high as the anterior one, narrowly rounded, and most prominent below; basal margin almost straight, or a little inflated or slightly convex, and curving abruptly upwards at the extremities; beaks depressed nearly or quite to the dorsal outline, small and closely appressed, and placed at five-eighths of the whole length of the shell from its anterior end ; dorsal line near the beaks parallel with basal margin, but curving regularly into the anterior margin.

Surface shows fine concentric lines of growth, but no other markings. The specimen illustrated is of average size and form. I place this shell with Meek's species, though my specimens are more elongate and less gibbous than his.

Formation 'and Locality.—In the chert beds superimposed upon the hydraulic limestone of the Devonian formation, in Jefferson county, Ky., and Clark county, Ind.

Clinopistha striata. N. sp.

Plate IV., figures 1 and 2.

Shell of medium size, transversely sub-elliptical ; length not quite twice the width or height, and thickness about one-half the height; beaks small and closely appressed, in the level of dorsal margin, and situated about two-thirds of the whole length from anterior extremity ; basal margin slightly convex in its central half, but curving regularly but rapidly into the terminal margins. Dorsal margin straight and almost parallel with the central portion of the basal one; at its anterior end it curves down into the anterior margin, which appears to be regularly rounded; posterior end slopes down from the beaks to a somewhat pointed posterior extremity, which is most prominent a little below middle height of the shell ; both valves are moderately convex,

The surface is marked by very peculiar radii, which, apparently, run from the basal margin to the dorsal one, across the valves, but which make, near the dorsal line, a rapid deflection into the direction of the beaks. These radii are low and flat, and have a faint, but plainly observable depressed line in their middle, a feature which I have never noticed in any other shell. Their interspaces are large, from three to four times of their own width; in some of these interspaces there is a smaller intermediate line. This species has the general features as Clinopistha subnasuta and antiqua, except its peculiar surface-markings, and its greater size. I place it into the genus Clinopistha, on account of its general form agreeing with that of C. subnasuta; whether or not interior characters will leave it there or transfer it to another known genus, or make a new one for its reception, I can not say. The two specimens illustrated on plate 4 are of average size, and are, as far as I know, the only two shells of this species so far found. Both belong to my own collection.

Formation and Locality.—Found in the cherty layers overlying the hydraulic limestone of the Devonian formation, in Jefferson county, Ky., and in Clark county, Ind.

Genus Ptychodesma. Hall.

Ptychodesma, Hall. 24th Regent's Report—1872.
Etymology: ptychos, a folding; *desma,* a ligament or band.

Shell modioloid in form; valves equally convex; hinge with a wide ligamental area, the sides of which are sharply grooved in parallel lines, caused by the successive growth of the ligament, as in Pectunculus. The grooves and ridges are slightly arched beneath the apex of the valves, where they take their origin.

The internal hinge structure is unknown. In general form and characters this genus resembles Modiomorpha, but differs in having a ligamental area marked by fine striae parallel to the hinge-line, while this is parallel to the margin of the shell.

The type of the genus is Ptychodesma knappiana.

Ptychodesma knappiana. Hall.

Plate II., figures 13, 15, 16, 17 and 18.
Ptychodesma knappiana, H. and W. 24th Rep. N. Y.—1872.
Ptychodesma knappiana, Hall. Pal. N. Y., Vol. 5, pt 1, p. 353—1885.

Shell of medium size, obliquely sub-ovate; length usually more than one-third greater than the height; basal margin oblique, often nearly straight in the middle of its length. Posterior end broadly rounded.

Cardinal line straight, oblique, having a length posterior to the beaks of about one-half the length of the shell. Anterior end very short, curving downward into the basal margin without limitation. Valves convex in the lower and posterior portions ; gibbous in the middle and above.

Beaks sub-anterior, small, distant, closely incurved, rising but little above the hinge-line. Umbonal slope presenting an undefined ridge, which merges into the general convexity of the shell about the middle of its length. Test thick, marked by fine concentric striae, with distant imbricating lamellae.

Ligamental area deeply excavated, marked by numerous longitudinal striae, which are abruptly arched just beneath the beak. Hinge with two or more cardinal teeth. Anterior muscular impression strong.

Dimensions of the shells in this species do not vary much. Figure 16, plate 2, represents an individual of average size.

This shell bears some resemblance, externally, to some species of Modiomorpha and Nyassa, but its deeply grooved ligamental area is a distinctive feature. Figure 18, plate 2, shows the said area of a left valve once enlarged.

Formation and Locality.—In the cherty layers of the Devonian limestone, which Prof. Hall places among the Hamilton rocks, in Clark county, Ind., and in Jefferson county, Ky. It is found in well preserved, silicified specimens, but is a rather rare species; it is represented in only a few collections in the Falls Cities and elsewhere. Prof. Hall named this species in honor of the lamented Dr. James Knapp, of Louisville, Ky., who collected the first specimens of it, and loaned them to Prof. Hall for description and illustration.

Genus Conocardium. Bronn.

Conocardium, Bronn. Lethaea Geognostica, Vol. I., p. 92—1835.
Etymology: konos, a cone; *kardia*, the heart.

Type : Cardium hybernicum, Sowerby.

Shell equivalve, inequilateral, more or less fusiform or trigonal. Posterior end obliquely truncate, produced along the cardinal line into a siphonal tube, and sometimes the antero-inferior margin is also produced. Anterior end conical and gaping in front. Beaks prominent and strongly incurved. Ventral margins crenulated ; cardinal line straight; umbonal ridge prominent, and ornamented with an expansion of the test in continuation of the truncated posterior end.

Surface marked by concentric striae, and usually ornamented with strong radii. Hinge with anterior and posterior laminar teeth. Ligament external ; muscular impressions two in each valve, situated near the cardinal extremities ; pallial line simple. In the anterior end there is a thickening or internal process forming, apparently, a foot-sheath.

Conocardium cuneus. CONRAD.

Plate V., figures 10 to 19.

Pleurorhynchus cuneus, Conrad.   Geol. Surv. N. Y. Ann. Rep.—1840.
Pleurorhynchus trigonalis, Hall.   Geol. Surv. N. Y. Rep. 4th Dist., p. 171—1843.
Conocardium trigonale, Hall.   Pal. N. Y., Vol. 5, pt. 1, pls. and exp.—1883.
Conocardium cuneus, Hall.   Pal. N. Y., Vol. 5, pt. 1, page 409—1884.

Shell large ; shape very difficult to compare with any generally known form ; its side-view is more or less sub-trigonal, and its dorsal or ventral view angularly sub-ovate. The proportion of its length to its height varies considerably ; the length is always greater than the height, but never becomes twice as large as the latter.

The basal margin is gently curved from the posterior extremity to the anterior end. The ʹposterior extremity is abruptly truncated, and produced into a tubular extension along the cardinal line. This tubular extension attains, in some shells, a considerable length, and is supposed to serve as a siphuncle. The truncated rear end is very large in extent, and cardiform in shape ; it is usually concave, with the exception of the part near and around the siphuncle, which is more or less convex.

Cardinal line straight ; its margins, anterior to the beaks, are inflected. Anterior end more or less rapidly contracting, with the margins gaping before reaching the extremity. Valves entirely equal, and more or less gibbous. The beaks are prominent and closely incurved over the hinge-line; they are situated near the center.

The umbonal ridge is acutely angular, forming the line of demarcation between the lateral and posterior surfaces ; it extends from the beaks to the posterior extremity in basal margin. Test thick, composed of two distinct layers.

Surface marked by numerous radiating plications, and intermediate arching lamellose, concentric striae on the body of the shell. The posterior surface is ornamented by regularly curving radii, circling around the base of the siphuncle. From the entire periphery of the umbonal ridge extends an expansion of the shell, called the shield, increasing in extent from the beaks downward to the posterior extremity of the basal margin. This shield is covered with fine striae, running parallel with the basal margin. In some specimens, we notice at the extreme rear end of the body of the shell, where the shield has been removed, a long, slender, cylindrical tube in the extension of the basal line. What purpose it serves is not known. The valves are finely crenulated at the margins. Prof. Hall has united different forms, which were heretofore considered different species, into Con. cuneus ; he retains the abandoned species, however, as varieties, which are as follows :

Var. attenuatum, Conrad, which are apparently only the young of C. cuneus.

Var. trigonale, the forms found in our rocks, and formerly always known under that name.

Var. nasutum, Hall, a short, very ventricose, and abruptly truncated form.

Formation and Locality.—This shell is not rare in our Devonian rocks, at and around the Falls of the Ohio, where it is often found in the rotten hornstone; but fair or perfect shells are not often met with. I have figured on plate 5 a small individual which comes as near perfection as possible; it shows the whole shell with complete shield, and is a most beautiful but delicate fossil. I found it on the Indiana shore of the Ohio, opposite the falls.

Genus Cypricardinia. Hall.

Cypricardinia, Hall. Pal. N. Y., Vol. 3, page 266—1859.
Etymology · Resembling Cypricardia.

Shell being inequilateral, with a more or less distinctly defined oblique posterior ridge, the umbones anterior or sub-anterior, and little elevated. The surface is concentrically grooved, or more or less distinctly marked by prominent ridges or imbricating lamellae, and, on some of them, these lamellae are radiatingly striated or cancellated.

A single well-preserved specimen shows no external ligamental area. In some species the posterio-cardinal margin becomes alate or sub-alate. They bear some general resemblance to Modiolopsis, but the shell is apparently thicker, and is more strongly marked by concentric striae, and with a less conspicuous anterior muscular prominence, while the aspect and general expression of the shells are quite distinct.

Cypricardinia cataracta. Conrad.

Plate IV., figure 3.

The illustration of this species was made from the only specimen which I then possessed ; that shell was defective in several places of its margins, in consequence of which the figure does not show the exact shape or form of the perfect shell. I shall try to correct this in my description.

Shell of medium size, sub-rhomboid-ovate ; length one-half greater than height ; basal margin nearly straight, slightly concave anterior to the middle. Posterior extremity abruptly rounded below, and obliquely truncate above. Cardinal line straight, oblique. Anterior end very short, rounded below. Both valves about equally convex; the right one, apparently, little more than the left. The left valve is somewhat compressed in its middle portion near the basal margin, but it becomes very convex, almost gibbous, in its umbonal region.

Beaks nearly anterior, of moderate size, and somewhat elevated above the hinge-line; both incurved, and the right one below the other. The umbonal ridge extends from the beaks to the produced lower part of the posterior extremity. It is most convex at about the middle of the shell, from where it slopes in a gentle curve to its posterior extremity; towards the hinge it increases in gibbosity. On its dorsal side the umbonal ridge has a sharp, angular limitation, separating what may be called the dorsal incline from the lateral area of the valves. This umbonal line is acute-angular, and runs below the summit of the ridge, on its dorsal side, up to the middle of shell to the point of greatest convexity; from here it occupies the summit and becomes more or less rounded, losing its distinction entirely on the posterior third of the shell. The dorsal incline is strongly inflected at and near the beaks, but becomes convex for the balance of its extent. On the basal side of the umbonal ridge there is a shallow, broad depression, extending from the beaks obliquely across the valves to the middle of basal margin; this concavity is more pronounced on the left valve than on the right.

The cardinal line is straight, and measures about two-thirds the length of the shell. The surface is marked by several strong concentric lines of growth. This shell resembles C. indenta, but differs from it by its shape and surface-markings.

Formation and Locality.—Found in the Corniferous limestone at the Falls of the Ohio, on the Indiana shore.

Cypricardinia cylindrica. HALL AND. WHITFIELD.

Plate IV., figures 13, 14 and 15.

Cypricardinia cylindrica, H. and W.   24th Reg. Rep., p. 190—1872.
Cypricardinia cylindrica, H. and W.   27th Reg. Rep., pl. 11—1875.

Shell rather small, cylindrical; extremities rounded; height little more than the depth, and rather more than twice as long as high; beaks nearly terminal, rounded and incurved; left valve scarcely less convex than the opposite; umbonal slope slightly angular. Surface marked by faint, distant, concentric, lamellose lines of growth.

This species is more elongate and cylindrical, less arcuate, and more equivalve than C. inflata. The lamellose striae have never been so strong, and are more distant.

Formation and Locality—Occurs in the cherty layers superimposed upon the hydraulic limestone of the Devonian formation in Jefferson county, Ky., and in Clark county, Ind. It is a very rare shell, is always silicified, and there are only very few specimens of this species known.

Cypricardinia inflata, var. subequivalvis. HALL AND WHITFIELD.

Cypricardinia inflata, var. subequivalvis, H. and W. 24th Regent's Report, p. 180—1872.
Cypricardinia inflata, var. subequivalvis, H. and W. 27th Regent's Report, pl. 11—1875.

This species is described by Prof. Hall from a single specimen belonging to the cabinet of the late Dr. James Knapp. At the time my plates were prepared, said specimen was missing, and as thus the species was not represented by any known specimen, I omitted it. Since then I have found, myself, two fair shells of this species, and I therefore give here its description.

Shell small, nearly equivalve, sub-quadrilateral; beaks terminal; cardinal and basal margins sub-parallel; left valve slightly smaller, less convex, and straighter than the opposite; the post-umbonal slope distinctly angular, while on the right valve it is sub-angular or rounded.

Surface marked by about twelve to fourteen or sixteen strong, equal, lamellose, concentric ridges. Prof. Hall based its name of equivalvis upon the fact that in crushed specimens both valves appear equal, while good, not distorted, individuals show the slight inequality of valves characterizing the genus.

This shell resembles C. inflata, Conrad, but the valves are more nearly equal, and the right valve is less inflated.

Formation and Locality.—The chert beds overlying the hydraulic cement rock of the Devonian formation, in Jefferson county, Ky., and in Clark county, Ind.

Genus Cypricardites. Conrad.

Cypricardites, Conrad. Ann. Geol. Rep. N. Y.—1841.
Etymology: resembling the genus Cypricardia.

Shells ventricose, sub-orbicular or broad ovate in outline, with an external flattened ligamental area; cardinal teeth, four or five, short, oblique; lateral teeth, two or more, oblique; muscular impressions prominent, anterior one single; pallial line simple. Silurian.

Synonyms: Cyrtodonta and Vanuxemia of Billings, and Palaearca of Hall.

Cypricardites halli. N. sp.

Plate XXXIV., figures 1 to 6.

Shell of medium size; sub-triangular; from moderately ventricose to gibbous; both valves equally convex. Dorsal line almost straight, rounding at its extremity into the anterior and posterior margins; anterior margin slopes down and backwards in a gentle curve, which is slightly inflected, at its center, to the basal margin. The angle formed by the average direction of the anterior margin with the dorsal or hinge-line, measures about sixty degrees.

The posterior margin slopes down from the hinge-line, either at right-angles, or deflecting backwards, and forms a gentle curve; the basal line is very short, and strongly curved, forming almost a linguiform extension of the shell; its most prominent point is either entirely posterior, or below the center of the posterior portion of the hinge-line.

Both valves have their maximum convexity a little above the middle of the shell, from where they slope in a regular curve, which is more or less strong, according to the greater or smaller gibbosity of the shell, towards the sides and front; the slope on the posterior side of the umbonal region appears to be somewhat steeper than the anterior, causing the flattening of the shell along the upper half of the posterior margin, and especially at the posterior cardinal angle. The umbonal region extends from the beak to the base, and crosses the valves in a somewhat diagonal direction, terminating at the basal extremity. The umbones are markedly deflected towards the anterior end; they are only moderately elevated above the hinge-line; the beaks small and closely incurved; the hinge is nearer to the anterior end, at about two-fifths of the whole length from the front. The size of the species is shown by the two specimens illus-trated on plate 34, of which one is only moderately ventricose, while the other is very gibbous.

The surface is marked by closely set, strong, concentric lines of growth, which are more conspicuous near the margins than on the umbo.

Formation and Locality.—Found by me in the Hudson River shales of Oldham county, Ky. Outside of the two specimens belonging to my own collection, I do not know of any others. To contribute my mite, small as it may be, to the many well deserved honors of America's greatest geologist and palæon-tologist, the venerable Prof. James Hall, of Albany, New York, I have selected his name for this beautiful little shell.

Genus Grammysia. De Verneuil.

Grammysia, De Verneuil. Bull. Soc. Geol. France—1847.
Etymology: gramme, a line of writing; *mys,* a mussel shell; in allusion to the transverse furrows which cross the valves from the umbones to the middle of the ventral margin.

Shells equivalve, inequilateral, not gaping, furnished with two muscular im-pressions of very unequal size; pallial line rounded posteriorly, and united with the large muscular impression in such a manner as to leave about two-thirds of it outside of the line; ligament external, much prolonged in the depression of the escutcheon.

Surface traversed by an oblique fold or rib extending from the beak to mid-dle of the inferior border, and by numerous rounded concentric folds. This is De Verneuil's description, which is improved upon by Prof. Hall's, which is as follows: Shell equivalve, inequilateral, varying from sub quadrate to transversely elliptical. Valves ventricose, sometimes inflated; beaks strong, prominent and incurved; hinge-line shorter than the shell, posterior to the beaks. Dentition obscure, or represented only by irregular folds on the cardinal line; ligament external, prominent, extending from beneath the beaks to nearly one-half the length of the hinge-line. Cardinal margin bordered by a small, deep and strongly defined lunule. Anterior and posterior muscular impressions faintly marked, the latter much the larger; pallial line not sinuate but broken into points or ridges, strongly rounded posteriorly, and uniting with the large muscular scar near its anterior border.

Surface of shell often marked by an oblique mesial rib or fold, extending from the beak to the basal border, and by numerous strong, concentric folds or ridges, which are frequently obsolete on the posterior part of the shell. The shells appear to have been thin and fragile, and are usually much crushed and distorted from compression.

Grammysia gibbosa. HALL AND WHITFIELD.

Plate IV., figures 16 to 20.

Grammysia secunda, var. gibbosa, H. and W. 24th Rep. on N. Y. St. Cabinet, p. 199—1872.
Grammysia secunda, var. gibbosa, H. and W. 27th Rep. on N. Y. St. Cabinet, pl. 12—1875.

Shell of medium size, sub-elliptical. Proportion of length and height variable, but the length always less than twice the height; basal margin gently curved, with a distinct but shallow sinuosity anterior to the middle, this incurvation of the basal border is often very obscure, and in some specimens entirely obsolete. Posterior extremity is strongly rounded.

The cardinal line is straight, and measures about two-thirds of the length of shell. Anterior end is short, and regularly rounded. Valves entirely equal, moderately convex below and at the posterior end; becoming gibbous in the middle and above. Beaks almost anterior; of medium size and strongly incurved and closely appressed. In some specimens the beaks of both valves have different elevations above the hinge-line, one overlapping the other; this feature is not natural, but the result of some distortion. In perfect specimens the beaks are of even height, and opposite to each other. The umbonal slope is strongly rounded and extends to the posterior end of the basal margin. A broad but very shallow depression extends from the beaks, crossing the valves obliquely, and terminates at the basal sinus, forming a lateral sinus and producing the basal one. In some specimens the lateral sinus is very obscure and often entirely obsolete. The basal sinus is dependent upon the lateral one; it is well marked, where the latter is plainly visible, and it becomes obliterated, where the latter is obsolete.

Surface of the shells, which occur only as internal casts, is marked by more or less strong, concentric folds or elevations, which are angular on the anterior part of the shell, and become rounded and lower posteriorly. They increase in size from the beak to the margins. In size this shell varies greatly ; the forms illustrated give the average dimensions of this species.

Professors Hall and Whitfield consider it so closely allied to Gr. secunda, as to make a variety of that species ; but to me, the differences between this shell and the mentioned species appear so pronounced, that I place it in an entirely different species, retaining Hall's name, "gibbosa."

Formation and Locality.—Occurs in the cherty layers topping the hydraulic limestone of the Devonian formation, in Kentucky and Indiana, at and around the Falls of the Ohio.

Genus Paracyclas. Hall.

Paracyclas, Hall. Geol. Surv. of N. Y., Rep. of 4th Dist.—1843.
Etymology : para, allied to; *cyclas*, a genus of shells.
Type : Paracyclas elliptica.

Shell equivalve, sub-equilateral, sub-orbicular or broadly sub-elliptical. Anterior end regularly rounded ; posterior end rounded or sub-truncate, somewhat more produced below than the anterior ; beaks small and low, generally rising little above the hinge-line.

Hinge-line short ; post-cardinal slope more or less defined by an oblique furrow or depression, which sometimes leaves the extremity sub-alate.

Surface concentrically striated ; sometimes with strong concentric ridges marking the exterior.

Structure of hinge not fully observed. Ligament supported on each side, internally, by a narrow plate, and leaving in the cast two diverging grooves directed forward from the beak. Muscular impression on the post-umbonal slope. Pallial line parallel with, and a little within, the margin of the shell.

This fossil possesses many of the external characters of the finely striated forms of modern Lucina ; and the distinguishing characters are not strongly marked.

(Copied from Hall's Lamellibranchiata.)

Paracyclas elliptica. Hall.

Plate II., figures 1, 2 and 3.

Paracyclas elliptica, Hall. Palæont. N. Y., Vol. 5, part 1, page 440, plate 72, figures 23 to 33.
Lucina elliptica, var. occidentalis, H. and W. 24th Ann. Rep. N. Y. St. Mus., page 189.

Shell large, sub-circular or broadly elliptical ; length and height about equal. Pallial margin regularly curving from the extremities of the hinge. Cardinal line short, more than one-third the length of shell, slightly arcuate,

Valves regularly convex, somewhat regularly gibbous in the middle. Beaks a little anterior to the middle, small, appressed, and closely incurved, rising but little above the hinge-line. Umbonal slope defined above by a depression extending from the beaks to about the middle of the posterior extremity, distinctly limiting the post-cardinal slope of the valves.

Test thin; surface marked by fine concentric striae, which are sometimes aggregated into fascicles at irregular distances.

Ligamental groove narrow and elongate. Posterior muscular impression just within the post-cardinal margin and below the ligamental groove. Pallial line parallel with the basal margin, marked in the cast by a row of elongated nodes, which are the terminations of low ridges from above. Interpallial area pustulose on the cast. (Hall.)

This species resembles Lucina proavia of Goldfuss to such an extent that it is impossible to distinguish the German species from the American. I have in my possession a large number of perfectly preserved specimens of our shells, and two equally well preserved specimens of Lucina proavia from the old country, but so far none of my geological friends has been able to pick out the foreign species.

Prof. Hall says the hinge of the German shell is much more declining, and the anterior end is more elevated and sub-auriculate, as shown in Goldfuss' figures. If such a difference is shown in the figures, which I do not doubt, it may be that they were taken from a peculiarly formed specimen which did not represent the average form of the species, or the figure may not be a correct copy of the specimen from which it was taken. Small differences, as those marked out by Prof. Hall, taken from figures, should always be considered doubtful, and never used without other evidences to establish a new species. I have not the least doubt that, in the course of time, the identity of P. elliptica and L. proavia, will be acknowledged by all American geologists, and the fossil will then be known under the name of Paracyclas proavia. The generic name Lucina, has to be dropped for other reasons.

Formation and Locality.—In the Corniferous rocks of Kentucky and Indiana, around and at the Falls of the Ohio, where specimens of exquisite beauty and perfection, with the exterior shell as well as internal casts are found.

Paracyclas elongata. N. SP.

Plate II., figure 8.

This shell resembles very closely P. lirata of Conrad, but it differs from it greatly in form, so much so, that any one must distinguish the two species at the first glance. While P. lirata has almost the shape of a regular circle, this shell has the form of an ellipse, in which the larger axis exceeds the smaller one considerably. In this shell the width is only about three-fourths of the length. It is covered with strong concentric striae, which are sharply marked, almost all parallel to each other and equidistant. The depression of its dorsal margin in front of the beaks is very conspicuous ; the illustration does not show this at all, or very faintly. The beaks are close to the anterior margin ; the anterior slope is steep, while the posterior one has only little fall. The size of this shell varies in different specimens ; it agrees generally with that of P. lirata. Both valves are moderately convex.

It differs from P. lirata by its elongate shape and by the position of its beaks, which is sub-anterior, while the position of the beaks in P. lirata is almost central.

Formation and Locality.—Found in the cherty layers superimposed upon the hydraulic limestone of the Devonian formation, in Jefferson county, Ky., and in Clark county, Ind. It may be possible that some intermediate forms exist which connect this new species with P. lirata ; but it appears to me that both species are sufficiently different to guarantee the existence of the new one.

Paracyclas lirata. Conrad.

Plate II., figures 4, 5, 6 and 7.

Posidonia lirata, Conrad. Geol. Surv. N. Y., Ann. Rep.—1838.
Paracyclas lirata, Hall. Pal. N. Y., Vol. 5, pt. 1, p. 441, pl. 72, figs. 2-19.

Shell of medium size, sub-circular or broadly elliptical; length a little greater than height; margins regularly rounded. Cardinal lines short, less than half the length of the shell. Valves moderately convex below, becoming gibbous on the middle and above.

Beaks anterior to the center; small, appressed, rising but little above the hinge-line. Post-cardinal slope not defined.

Surface marked by fine concentric striae, and by strong, sub-angular, concentric ridges, which are more or less sharply defined, depending upon the condition of the specimen and the nature of the matrix in which the fossil is imbedded.

Ligamental grooves distinctly marked and only moderately divergent from the cardinal margin.

In form this shell is very like the elliptica, but considerably smaller in size, and marked by more or less distinct, angular, concentric ridges. It also resembles Lucina lineata of Goldfuss, from the Devonian formation in Germany, with which it may be found specifically identical. (Hall.)

The size of this species is very variable, as may be seen from the figures on plate 2, which are of natural size. Prof. Meek, in the first volume of the Palæontology of Ohio, has figured and described a Par. ohioensis, which bears a very close resemblance to Par. lirata, and differs only from the latter by a flange attached to the margin of the shell. It is considered by some geologists as identical with Par. lirata.

Formation and Locality.—In the Corniferous limestone of the Devonian formation in Jefferson county, Ky., and in Clark county, Ind., where it is found rather abundantly, and in well preserved specimens, which are always entirely silicified.

Paracyclas octerlonii. n. sp.

Plate XXXI., figure 18.

The shell of this species agrees, in every particular, with that of the preceding species, except in size and form. It is considerably smaller than elliptica, measuring somewhat less in width, and considerably less in length. Its form is peculiar, having its anterior and posterior margins almost straight and parallel. Orlando Hobbs, Esq., of Jeffersonville, Ind., presented me with the first specimen of this species, and drew my attention to its peculiar shape, which could not be the result of distortion, inasmuch as the shell did not show the least sign of any violence. Afterwards I came in possession of a great number of specimens, all of which have exactly the same figure; but I never obtained forms which, as intermediates, could have connected them with the elliptica. These differences are so well marked, and appear to be constant, and I, therefore, considered them sufficient to base upon them a new species. Should hereafter such forms be found, which will connect them with the elliptica, they will, even then, retain at least the character of a variety.

Most all distorted specimens of Par. elliptica, which came under my observation, I found to be compressed in the direction from base to hinge-line; never in the direction from the front to the rear, which is easily explained by the fact that the Lamellibranchiata generally rest upon the base of their shell, placing the hinge on top. Any compression will be caused by the weight of superimposed bodies, and will result in reducing of the width and enlarging of the length.

Formation and Locality.—This species is found associated with the preceding species in the Corniferous limestone of Kentucky and Indiana, at and near the Falls of the Ohio. It is somewhat rare, at least well preserved specimens are seldom found. I have named this species in honor of Dr. John A. Octerlony, of Louisville, Ky., who is not only an excellent physician, but also an ardent student of Natural Sciences, and especially of Geology and Palæontology

Paracyclas ohioensis. Meek.

Plate V., figure 20.

Lucina ohioensis, Meek. Proc. Acad. Nat. Sci. Phil., p. 6—1871.
Compare Posidonia lirata, Conrad. 1838, see fig. 12, pl. 2, 13th Rep. on St. Cab. of N. Y.
Lucina (Paracyclas) *ohioensis*, Meek. Pal. of Ohio, Vol. 1, p. 199—1873.

Shell of less than medium size; compressed or only slightly convex, and more or less nearly circular, though in some specimens greatly deviating from that form, as is shown in the specimen illustrated on plate 5, figure 20; beaks small and appressed, and very little elevated above the dorsal margin; they are situated about in the center of the dorsal border. The anterior margin is rather abruptly compressed above, just in front of the beaks; hinge-margin short and rounding into the posterior dorsal outline; posterior dorsal slopes of each valve marked by a strongly oblique sulcus, extending from the back part of the beaks to the upper portion of the posterior margin, to which it imparts a slightly sinuous outline at its termination.

Surface ornamented with small, more or less regular, concentric undulations, which are most strongly defined on the umbones. The average size of shells belonging to this species is represented in the specimen illustrated on plate 5, figure 20.

This species is closely allied to Par. lirata, with which it is considered identical by some palæontologists; but its peculiar posterior dorsal sulcus is such a prominent feature, that it may be regarded of sufficient importance and value to base upon it a separate species.

Formation and Locality.—It occurs, together with its associates and congeners, the Par. elliptica, lirata, elongata and octerlonii, in the upper strata of the Devonian formation, in Jefferson county, Ky., and in Clark county, Ind. It is, however, very rare in our rocks, where, so far, only a few specimens have been found.

Genus Goniophora. Phillips.

Goniophora, Phillips—1848.
Etymology: gonia, an angle; *phoros*, bearing.

Shell equivalve, very inequilateral, rhomboidal or trapezoidal in outline; obliquely truncate behind and rounded in front. Cardinal line usually straight and not oblique. Beaks small, closely incurved, situated within or about the anterior third of the shell. Umbo prominent. Umbonal slope continued as a strong angular ridge to the post-inferior margin. The valves are crossed obliquely, sometimes vertically, by a broad, undefined sinus, extending from anterior of the beaks to the basal margin, which is usually slightly constricted at this point.

Surface marked by more or less regular concentric striae, which may be either simple throughout or fasciculate on the anterior portion of the shell. Some species are marked by strong, radiating striae upon that portion of the valves between the umbonal ridge and the sinus.

Hinge furnished with a strong oblique fold or tooth in the left valve, situated just beneath the beak, and a corresponding depression in the right valve. No lateral teeth have been observed. Ligament external, strong; its attachment to the shell is marked by one or more defined grooves. Muscular impressions two; the anterior one deep and strongly marked, situated a little anterior to the beak and just within the anterior margin. Pallial line simple, continuing nearly parallel to the basal margin until it crosses the umbonal ridge, and recurving to the posterior muscular impression, which is large and shallow, and situated on the posterior cardinal slope, sometimes near the middle of length of shell.

This genus was proposed by Phillips in 1848, as a generic designation for the original Cypricardia cymbiformis of Sowerby, but without generic definition or illustration of internal characters, and, so far as known, the genus has never been heretofore described.

Goniophora truncata. HALL.

Plate IV., figures 21, 22 and 23.

Goniophora truncata, Hall. Pal. N. Y., Vol. 5, pt. 1, pls.—1883.
Goniophora truncata, Hall. Pal. N. Y., Vol. 5, pt. 1, p. 298—1885.

Shell of medium size, in a side and front view sub-triangular, in a dorsal view sub-elliptical. Length about twice as great as height; anterior end of the basal margin rounded, middle portion slightly sinuate, and the rear portion nearly straight or slightly curved to the post-basal extremity; posterior margin obliquely sub-truncate, slightly curving. Cardinal line short and straight. Anterior end short and rounded. There is a broad, shallow depression extending from the beaks obliquely across the valves to the central point of the basal margin; this last feature is only faintly expressed in some specimens, and in others entirely obsolete. Valves convex below the umbonal ridge, gibbous in umbonal region. The area above the umbonal ridge, which I called in Cypricardinia cataracta the dorsal incline, is usually flattened or very slightly convex; in some shells it is even concave. The beaks are entirely anterior, acute and incurved; in some shells they are closely appressed, while in others they are separated by a small interspace.

The umbonal ridge is strongly defined, forming a very sharp edge, separating the lateral areas of the valves from their dorsal incline. Cardinal line is short and straight, the umbones are more or less prominent and somewhat angular. Test is of moderate thickness, the entire shell marked by stronger and finer radiating and concentric striae, which differ in their character, according to the places they occupy. On the baso-lateral area of each valve there are sub-angular, abruptly elevated, concentric striae in their course from the anterior margin to the umbonal ridge, where they terminate parallel to the anterior and basal margins. These elevated striae have flat interspaces of different width, sometimes three or four times as large as the striae. Some of these interspaces are smooth, while others are occupied by one to three finer striae. Between the umbonal ridge and the sinus, mentioned above as a shallow depression crossing obliquely the valves, these interspacial finer striae become more prominent, and some more are added by intercalation, thus causing them to appear somewhat crowded. In this region, limited by the umbonal ridge and the lateral sinus, the concentric striae are crossed by fine, closely arranged radii, giving that portion of the surface a cancellated, somewhat rugose appearance. This cancellated belt commences at the apical end of the umbonal ridge, increases regularly, but rapidly in width, until it occupies, in the basal margin, the whole posterior half of the shell.

The dorsal incline is covered by subequal, rounded, and closely set radii, which start from the posterior portion of the cardinal line, and extend along the cardino-posterior margins to the umbonal ridge; they increase in number by bifurcation and interpolation.

I do not know any other Goniophora, and can not, therefore, compare this species with any of its congeners. Prof. Hall compares it with G. perangulata of the Schoharie grit, with which he thinks it may be identical. In comparing my specimens with his figures of that species, it appears to me that there is a vast difference between both species.

Formation and Locality.—This shell occurs in the Corniferous limestone of the Devonian formation in Kentucky and Indiana, at and around the Falls of the Ohio. It is a very rare shell; the two specimens in my own collection are, so far, the only individuals found in our rocks.

Genus Modiomorpha. Hall.

Modiomorpha, Hall. Prel. Notice of Lam. Shells—1870.
Etymology : Contracted from *modiola,* a genus of shells; and *morphe,* form or shape like Modiola.

Shell inequivalve, very inequilateral, compressed, sub-ovate in outline, largest posteriorly; beaks small, compressed, usually situated within the anterior third of the length. Surface of shell marked by rugose or undulating concentric striae, which usually coalesce or become fasciculate toward the anterior end. The valves are crossed obliquely by a more or less distinctly defined sinus passing from the beak to the base, and constricting the basal margin; the anterior end is rounded, forming a projecting lobe of greater or less extent beyond the beak. Hinge characterized by a single, strong, wedge-form tooth in the left valve, and a corresponding cavity in the right; no lateral teeth exist. Anterior muscular impression sub-circular, situated within the anterior extension of the shell; posterior impression large and superficial, situated near the cardinal border; pallial line entire. Ligament external, attached to the thickened margin of the shell.

This genus is allied to Modiola, Modiolopsis and Cypricardites, but differs from Modiola in the toothed hinge; from Modiolopsis in not having lateral teeth, and from Cypricardites in general aspect. Modiomorpha concentrica may be considered the type of this genus.

Modiomorpha affinis. HALL.

Modiomorpha alta, in part (Conrad), Hall. Pal. N. Y., Vol. 5, part 1, Plates and Explanations pl. 37, figs 13 and 14—1883.

Modiomorpha affinis, Hall. Pal. N. Y., part 1, page 284—1885.

Shell large, robust, obliquely ovate, arcuate; length about one-third greater than the height; basal margin straight or slightly arcuate, curving rather abruptly both at the anterior and posterior extremities; posterior margin abruptly curving below and more gently forward to cardinal margin; cardinal margin arcuate from the beaks to the post-cardinal extremity. Anterior end short, scarcely defined; narrow, declining from the hinge-line and regularly rounded below.

Valves convex, very gibbous in the middle and umbonal region; depth more than half the height of shell. The umbonal elevation extends from the beaks, curving above the middle to near the post-basal margin, forming an undefined arcuate ridge.

Hinge-line oblique, extending more than one-third the length of the valves. Beaks small, sub-anterior, and closely incurved.

Test comparatively thick, marked by fine concentric striae, which are fasciculate and pass into strong abrupt ridges upon the umbonal and anterior portions of the shell. Interior unknown.

An individual of average size, among the specimens of this species in my collection, measures as follows: length, twenty-one lines; height, sixteen lines, and thickness, eleven lines.

This form resembles Mod. alta, but is more elongate, distinctly arcuate; the anterior end is narrower below the beaks; the posterior end is more produced, and curving more abruptly forward in the upper part, with the post-cardinal angle rounded. The anterior end is less produced than in typical forms of Mod. mytiloides.

Formation and Locality.—Found in the cherty layers superimposing the hydraulic limestone of the Devonian formation, in Jefferson county, Ky., and in Clark county, Ind. Almost all my specimens of this and other species of Modiomorpha were found in the cement quarries at Watson Station, in Clark county, Ind., about six miles distant from the Falls of the Ohio,

Modiomorpha alta. CONRAD.

Plate XXVI., figure 10.

Cypricardites alta, Conrad. Geol. Surv. N. Y., Ann. Rep., p. 52—1841.
Modiomorpha alta (Conrad), Hall. Prelim. Notice Lamellib. 2, p. 75—1870.
Modiomorpha alta (Conrad), Hall. Pal. N. Y., Vol. 5, pt. 1, pl. and exp.—1883.
Modiomorpha alta, Hall. Pal. N. Y., Vol. 5, pt. 1, p. 278—1885.

Shell above medium size, broad, rhomboid-ovate; length about one-third greater than height; the basal margin, for two-thirds of its length from the anterior curve, is nearly straight, varying from slightly concave to nearly straight, abruptly curving at the post-basal extremity, and continuing to the post-cardinal margin in an oblique, gently curved line.   In some examples, the posterior margin is regularly curved, cardinal margin sometimes forming a nearly straight line, usually gently arcuate.   Anterior end produced beyond the beak from one-sixth to one-fourth the length of the shell; obliquely truncated, obtuse, rounded below; its greatest extension is below middle of the shell.

Valves convex, gibbous on the umbonal and medial portion of the shell; the umbonal ridge is gibbous and arched upward; the point of greatest convexity is about the middle of the shell or a little posterior.   The depth of both valves is equal to two-thirds of the height of the shell.

Hinge-line straight, oblique, extending for less than half the length of the shell.   Beaks rounded, somewhat appressed, directed forward.   Umbonal region not strongly defined, depressed anteriorily, becoming gibbous in the middle of the shell, gradually merging into the general contour in the posterior portion.

Test of moderate thickness, marked by irregular concentric striae, which become fasciculate and produce strong concentric ridges at irregular intervals. The surface is marked by fine vascular lines, similar to those on Mod. mytiloides.   The anterior muscular impression is situated close to the anterior margin of 'the shell, with a small retractor scar above it.   Other characters of the interior unknown.

The specimen illustrated on plate 26, figure 10, is rather shorter than the average.   An individual of average size has the following dimensions: length, twenty-three lines; width, fifteen lines, and thickness, ten lines.

This species has a greater proportional height than Mod. mytiloides, a broader and often sub-truncate posterior end, while the anterior end is usually broader and less extended; the umbonal ridge is arcuate; in other features it is very similar.   In some of its conditions this species is not easily distinguished from Mod. mytiloides.

Formation and Locality.—Found associated with Mod. concentrica, mytiloides and affinis, in the cherty strata topping the hydraulic limestone, in Jefferson county, Ky., and Clark county, Ind.

Modiomorpha charlestownensis. N. SP.

Plate V., figures 7, 8 and 9.

The shell illustrated on plate 5, figures 7, 8 and 9, has evidently its valves dislocated. The right valve is more than one-eighth of an inch removed backward.

Shell of about medium size, elongate, sub-elliptical, very ventricose or gibbous; greatest height at about one-third of length from the anterior extremity; valves strongly convex, the greatest convexity being a little anterior to the middle of shell. Hinge-line oblique, almost straight, and of about one-half the length of shell. Beaks anterior or sub-anterior, acute and closely appressed. Umbonal region strongly convex, angular, and inflected on its dorsal slope near the beaks, regularly curved on its ventral and posterior slopes, and also in the posterior half of its dorsal slope; prominently ridged. The course of the umbonia ridge forms an acute angle with the cardinal line, and runs somewhat diagonally to the posterior extremity, where the post-ventral and post-dorsal margins meet in a very abrupt curve.

Ventral or basal line almost straight, only slightly incurved in its central portion; at its posterior end it curves regularly and gently upwards into the abrupt curve at the posterior extremity. The posterior part of the dorsal line forms a gentle regular curve from posterior end to hinge-line

Anterior end short, its margin straight and sloping almost rectangular with the cardinal line down to the basal margin, which it meets in a short curve.

Surface covered by fine concentric lines of growth, which, at irregular intervals, have been raised into imbricating lamellae, leaving strong varices on the cast.

A portion of the shell remaining shows the concentric lines as closely set as on Mod. concentrica, and if the form of my shell did not differ so greatly from that of Mod. concentrica, I would have placed it with that species. Its elongate form, its great gibbosity, its linguiform posterior end, and the marked concentric zones on its surface, distinguish it from its other congener, with which it is associated in our rocks.

Formation and Locality.—The chert beds over the hydraulic limestone of the Devonian formation in Jefferson county, Ky., and in Clark county, Ind.

Modiomorpha concentrica. CONRAD.

Plato II., figures 9, 10, 11, 12 and 14.

Pterinea concentrica. Conrad. Geol. Surv. N. Y., Ann. Rep., p. 116—1838.
Cypricardites concentrica, Conrad. Geol. Surv. N. Y., Ann. Rep, p. 52—1841.
Cypricardites oblonga, Ibidem.
Modiola concentrica, Hall. Geol. Surv. N. Y., Rep. 4th Dist.—1843.
Modiomorpha concentrica, Hall. Pal. N. Y., Vol. 5, pt. 1, p. 275—1885.

Shell of medium size, ovate, extremely variable in its proportions; length less than twice the height; basal margin often nearly straight, usually a little concave on the anterior one-third; posterior margin rounded abruptly below, but gently curving above. Cardinal margin oblique in the prevailing forms, moderately arcuate, often nearly straight; sub-alate in many specimens. Anterior end produced beyond the beaks, many specimens only slightly, abruptly rounded, sometimes nasuate, limited by a broad depression extending from the beak to about the anterior third of the basal margin. In our Kentucky shells the shape differs as regards the anterior end, which is not at all, or at least only slightly produced beyond the bend; the anterior margin is almost straight or little curved, and turns at the beaks abruptly down to the basal margin.

Valves moderately convex, but somewhat gibbous along the umbonal slope; the point of greatest convexity is about one-third of the length from the anterior margin. Hinge-line extends generally to the middle of shell, sometimes even beyond the same.

Beaks sub-anterior (in our western shells anterior), small, sharply angular, appressed, directed forward. Umbonal region a more or less prominent subangular elevation, extending obliquely from beak towards the post-basal margin, but usually dying out about the middle in the length of the shell.

Test comparatively thick, and ornamented by concentric, rounded or subangular striae, which become lamellose and coalescing on the anterior end of the valves, where they are less prominent.

Anterior muscular impression strong, striated, situated just within the anterior margin, with a small retractor scar above it. Posterior impression large and shallow. Pallial line moderately impressed. Hinge furnished with a strong cardinal tooth just posterior to the beak in the left valve, and a corresponding depression in the right valve. No proper lateral teeth have been observed, but the cardinal margin is thickened and grooved from the beak backward about half the length of the cardinal line. It is impossible to give in figures the dimensions of the different individuals, nor the different sizes of the specimens. The proportion of length, width and thickness is as variable as the sizes of the different shells. The illustrations on plate 2 give the sizes of average specimens.

Formation and Locality.—Found associated with Ptychodesma knappiana in the cherty layers of the Devonian limestone, in Jefferson county, Ky., and in Clark county, Ind., at and around the Falls of the Ohio. It occurs rather abundantly in fractional shells, but fair specimens are not often met with. The shell illustrated by figure 14, plate 2, has two beautiful crania attached to its surface.

Modiomorpha mytiloides. Conrad.

Cypricardites mytiloides, Conrad. Geol. Surv. N. Y., Ann. Rep.—1841.
Modiomorpha complanata, Hall. In err. Pal. N. Y., Vol. 5, pt. 1, plates and explanations, pl. 38, figures 1-16—1883.
Modiomorpha planulata, Hall. Prelim. Notice Lamellib. 2, p. 74—1870.
Modiomorpha mytiloides, Hall. Pal. N. Y., Vol. 5, pt. 1, p. 277—1885.

Shell larger than medium size, rhomboid-ovate, oblique; length less than twice the height; basal margin nearly straight, or very slightly concave anterior to the middle, curving to anterior and posterior extremities; posterior margin abruptly curving below, and more gently recurving toward cardinal line; cardinal margin arcuate. Anterior end narrow, extended, abruptly curved on the margin; somewhat defined by the sinus, which extends from anterior of the beak to the middle of the shell.

Valves moderately convex, in old shells gibbous in the umbonal region. Hinge-line oblique, extending to about the middle of length of shell.

Beaks appressed, situated a little more than one-fourth the length of shell from anterior end. Umbonal region not defined; convex in young specimens, becoming more gibbous in older ones.

Test of moderate thickness, concentrically striated with irregular lines of growth, which are sometimes elevated into concentric ridges. The post-cardinal slope in well-preserved specimens shows fine vascular markings. The anterior muscular impression is well marked, and situated just within anterior margin below beak. Other interior characters are not known.

An average sized individual of this species has the following dimensions: length, twenty-six lines; width, seventeen lines, and thickness, ten lines.

This species resembles somewhat in form Mod. concentrica, but its anterior end is more produced, and it does not show the concentric striae of that species. It also resembles some forms of Mod. alta, but is more elongate, and possesses a more regularly rounded posterior extremity, and a narrower anterior end.

Formation and Locality.—Occurs in the chert of the Devonian formation in Jefferson county, Ky., and in Clark county, Ind., in company with its congeners, Mod. concentrica, alta and affinis. Watson's Station, in Clark county, Ind., on the Ohio and Mississippi Railroad, furnishes fair specimens in a silicified condition.

Genus Nucula. Lamarck.

Nucula, Lamarck. Hist. Nat. Des. An. Sans Vert.—1815.
Etymology: nucula, a little nut.

Shell small, equivalve, inequilateral, trigonal or transversely elliptical or sub-circular. Anterior or posterior extremity sometimes produced, usually rounded. Beaks anterior or posterior to the middle of the length, often sub-central. Cardinal line arcuate ; escutcheon marked. Surface marked by concentric striae, which, in some species, are regular and rugose.

Hinge furnished with a triangular, spoon-shaped cartilage-pit beneath the beaks, with a series of small transverse teeth on each side. There are two principal muscular impressions in each valve, with usually a smaller retractor scar adjacent, and also the cavity of the beaks often shows several pits for the attachment of umbonal muscles. Pallial line simple.

Examples: Nucula varicosa and N. randalli. (Copied from Hall's Lamelli-branchiata.)

Genus Nucula. Lamarck.

Etymology: nucula, a little nut.

Nucula herzeri. N. SP.

Shell small, elongate, sub-trigonal ; very gibbous.; length one and one-half the height ; both terminal extremities very narrow, almost pointed ; beaks prominent and closely incurved ; situated about one-fourth of the whole length from the anterior end ; basal margin in its main portion only slightly convex, even at its anterior end, where it joins the anterior margin, which is most prominent close to the basal line ; at the posterior end the basal margin turns in a light regular curve upwards to the very narrow, often pointed, posterior margin. The cardinal margin slopes in a straight line down to the posterior extremity, and with an inflected curve very abruptly to the anterior extremity ; umbones very ventricose, making the thickness of the shell equal to its height.

This species is associated with Nuc. niotica and neda, which it resembles in some points, but is easily distinguished from them by its elongate form, its pointed terminal extremities, and the equality between its depth and height. An average-sized specimen of this species has the following dimensions: length, one-half inch; height and depth, one-third of an inch.

Formation and Locality.—Occurs in the cherty layers overlying the hydraulic cement rock of the Devonian formation around the Falls of the Ohio in Kentucky and Indiana. I dedicate this pretty little shell to Rev. H. Herzer, formerly of Louisville, Ky., who devoted his spare time to the study of Natural Sciences, and especially to that of Palæontology. It was he who rekindled in me the love for Geology, which was almost extinguished by many years of hard work, but which since has afforded to me so many hours and days of genuine enjoyment.

Nucula neda. HALL AND WHITFIELD.

Plate V., figures 5 and 6.

Nucula neda, H. and W. 24th Reg. Rep., p. 191—1872.
Nucula neda, H. and W. 27th Reg. Rep., pl. 11—1875.

Shell cuneiform, sub-trigonal, with the umbones ventricose; the beak a little more than one-third from the anterior end, prominent and incurved. Cardinal margin sloping to the anterior and posterior extremities; basal margin straight.

The cast shows strong anterior and posterior muscular impressions, with three or four umbonal muscular scars; a narrow pedal scar just within the cardinal line, anterior to the posterior muscular area, as usual in the genus Nucula.

The surface has been marked by fine concentric lines of growth. It is associated with Nucula niotica, which it resembles in many features, but it differs from it in several points, which are given in the description of that species.

Formation and Locality.—Occurs in the chert beds superimposed upon the hydraulic limestone of the Devonian formation, around the Falls of the Ohio, in Kentucky and Indiana.

Nucula niotica. HALL AND WHITFIELD.

Plate V., figures 2, 3 and 4.

Nucula niotica, H. and W. 24th Regent's Rep., p. 190—1872.
Nucula niotica, H. and W. 27th Regent's Rep., pl. 11—1875.

Shell small, obtusely cuneiform; the beaks prominent, incurved, with the umbo inflated; height from beak to base equal to three fourths the length of the shell. Surface marked by fine, even, concentric striæ, with sometimes strong varices of growth. The internal casts show the evidence of strong, anterior and posterior muscular impressions, and three distinct umbonal pedal muscles, seven or more posterior and five anterior teeth in a specimen of medium size. Hall's description.

We find three distinct Nucula in our rocks; two of the species have a cuneiform sub-trigonal form, as shown in Prof. Hall's figures of Nucula neda and niotica; they must, therefore, be the two species in question; but which is neda and which is niotica? Prof. Hall's descriptions and figures of both species may answer to either one. There is only one point in the descriptions which may decide the question; this is the character of the respective umbones. According to Hall, the umbo of N. niotica is inflated, and the umbo of the neda is ventricose. Basing my identification of the two species upon this single point of difference, I will try to point out a few more distinguishing features. Nucula niotica differs from Nucula neda in the following characters:

1. In N. niotica the umbo is inflated, in Nucula neda it is very ventricose.

2. In N. niotica the depth is only one-half of the depth of neda, measured in specimens of the same size, at the point of their greatest convexity.

3. In N. niotica both slopes of the beaks are concave, while those in N. neda are almost straight.

4. In N. niotica the basal margin is broadly curved, while that of N. neda˘ is straight or even inflected.

Formation and Locality.—In·the chert beds over the hydraulic limestone of the Devonian formation, in Jefferson county, Ky., and in Clark county, Ind. Found in silicified, fairly preserved specimens; not very rare.

Yoldia ? valvulus. Hall and Whitfield.

Plate IV., figures 4 and 5.

Yoldia ? valvulus, H. and W.   24th Regent's Rep., p. 190—1872.
Yoldia ? valvulus, H. and W.   27th Regent's Rep., pl. 11—1875.

Shell elongate, narrow, sub-elliptical, more than twice as long as high, the depth a little more than half the height; anterior end nearly one-fourth wider than the posterior.   Beaks situated at three-fifths the length from the anterior end; an obsolete post-umbonal ridge extending from near the beak to the post-basal margin; posterior extremity not recurved.

Surface marked by somewhat coarse, wavy, concentric lines to the post-umbonal ridge, above which they are even and much finer.

Formation and Locality.—Occurs above the hydraulic limestone in the cherty layers of the Devonian formation, in Jefferson county, Ky., and in Clark county, Ind., where it is found rather abundantly in silicified specimens.   It is represented by fair individuals in several collections in the Falls Cities.

Genus Aviculopecten. McCoy.

Etymology: resembling the shells of the genus Avicula.

Aviculopecten crassicostatus. Hall and Whitfield.

Aviculopecten crassicostatus, H. and W.   24th and 27th Reg. Reps., p. 188, and pl. 11—1872 and 1875.

Shell below medium size, its body broadly ovate or sub-elliptical.   The left valve is only known to me, and shown in the specimen before me; it is depressed convex; body of the shell oblique; hinge-line straight, equal to three-fourths the length of the shell; anterior wing very small, separated from the body of the shell by an abrupt deep sinus; posterior wing narrow, obtusely pointed, and extending nearly as far as the posterior extremity.

Surface marked by strong, coarse, angular ribs, of which there are about thirteen or fourteen on the body of the shell, with intermediate smaller ones ; about five obscure rays on the posterior wing ; the radiating costae crossed by coarse, distant, lamellose, concentric ridges.

Formation and Locality.—Found in the hydraulic limestone of the Devonian formation at the Falls of the Ohio, in Kentucky and Indiana, where it is a rather rare shell.

Aviculopecten fasciculatus. HALL.

Plate III., figure 4.

Aviculopecten fasciculatus, Hall. Pal. N. Y., Vol. 5, pt. 1, page 11—1883.

Shell small, obliquely and transversely ovate ; height about equal to length, the former measuring more than seven-eighths of the latter. Pallial margins regularly rounded, becoming more convex towards the middle of the posterio lateral margin, and extending in a straight or slightly concave line to the beaks. The left valve is only known to me ; it is slightly convex in its basal half, but more so in the umbonal region ; the umbo is prominent, and the beak pointed and incurved. The hinge-line is straight and shorter than the width or length of the shell ; this is situated anterior to the middle of the cardinal line. The anterior ear is considerably smaller than the posterior wing ; both are triangular in shape, and both are defined by a sulcus, of which the posterior one is more expressed and deeper. The posterior wing is very attenuate at the extremity. Figure 4, plate 3, does not show the correct shape of the rear wing ; it should be more extended in the hinge-line, and should reach downward only half as far as it does in that figure. The terminal margins of both wings should be concave, and should join the lateral margins of the shell in a regular curve, and not, as represented in the figure, by straight lines.

The test of this shell is ornamented with numerous filiform, radiating striae, which are often fasciculate, and by fine concentric lines of growth. In young shells the radii are regular, with a slight fasciculate arrangement. The concentric lines are sharper and more crowded on the wings, while the radii are very much subdued, almost obscure. The interior of this shell is not known, neither have I ever seen its right valve.

The specimen here figured and described measures eight lines in height, nine lines in length, and its hinge-line is five lines long. This species has some resemblance with A. formio, princeps and pecteniformis, but differs from them partly by its form, and partly by its surface-markings ; from A. princeps mainly by the presence of radii on its wings.

Formation and Locality.—Found in the Corniferous limestone of the Devonian formation in Kentucky and Indiana, at and around the Falls of the Ohio.

Aviculopecten pecteniformis. Conrad.

Plate III., figure 1.

Avicula pecteniformis, Conrad. Jour. Acad. Nat. Sci. Phil.—1842.
Aviculopecten pecteniformis, Hall. Pal. of N. Y., Vol, 5, pt. 1, p. 4—1883.

Shell sub-ovate, oblique to the hinge-line; length about equal to height; anterior and basal margins regularly rounded, while the posterior margin of the body forms an almost straight line to beak. Left valve almost flat, only moderately convex in the umbonal region. The hinge-line is straight, and of about two-thirds the length of shell, or even somewhat more. Umbo moder ately elevated, abruptly sloping to the wings, thus forming a demarcation-line between the ears and the body of valve. These umbonal lines form an angle of a little more than ninety degrees. The wings have a triangular form and are of medium size, the anterior one having but little more than half the area of posterior wing. The beak is of moderate size and pointed; it is located anterior to the middle of the cardinal line. The terminal margins of the wings are more or less concave. The interior of this shell and its right valve are not known.

Test is thin and ornamented by about thirty-five sharp and strong radiating striae, with intermediate finer ones, which are crossed by fine, imbricating, concentric lines of growth, some of which are more prominent, and divide the surface in different concentric zones.

On the wings the radiating striae are obsolete, and even the lines of growth are there scarcely visible. This species is variable in its dimensions in differ- ent specimens. The one before me measures twenty-five lines in height, by two inches in length, and with a hinge-line of one inch and one-half.

This species has great resemblance to A. princeps, from which it differs, however, by its smaller ears, and by its coarser or stronger principal radii, while the intermediate finer striae are so fine as being scarcely visible to the naked eye, which makes the interspaces between the principal striae appear to have three times the width of these radii.

Formation and Locality.—Occurs in the Corniferous limestone of the Devonian formation at and around the Falls of the Ohio, in Kentucky and Indiana. It is a rather rare species, especially in fair or well preserved specimens. •

Aviculopecten princeps. Conrad.

Monotis princeps, Conrad. Ann. Rep. N. Y. Geol. Surv.—1838.
Avicula parilis, Conrad. Proc. Acad. Nat. Sci. Phil., Vol. 8—1842.
Aviculopecten princeps, Hall. Pal. N. Y., Vol. 5, pt. 1—1883.
Aviculopecten sanduskyensis, Hall. Pal. N. Y., Vol. 5, pt. 1—1883.

Shell large, obliquely broad-ovate; axis inclined more than sixty degrees to the hinge-line; length and height nearly equal, varying within moderate limits. Anterior margin convex, the convexity increasing to the middle of the postero-lateral side, thence truncated and extending in a straight line to the beak, making an angle of from thirty to forty degrees with the hinge-line.

Valves depressed; left valve regularly convex; right valve nearly flat or only slightly convex. The hinge-line is straight, having a length of from two-thirds to more than three-fourths the length of the shell, and extending anteriorly as far as the anterior margin. The beaks are obtuse, rounded and anterior to the middle of the hinge-line. Umbo of left valve is little convex, somewhat inflated, and the lines of demarcation between it and the anterior and posterior wings form an angle of about one hundred and thirty degrees. The wings comparatively only of medium extent; the anterior considerably smaller than the other; both are triangular in shape. The anterior ear is separated from the body by a distinct sulcus, while the posterior wing is defined by the abrupt slope of the posterior side of the umbo. This slope is formed by an almost rectangular deflection of the posterior margin, and has a height of about one line. The terminal margins of the beaks are more or less concave, becoming convex at the hinge-line. Byssal sinus broad, rounded, well defined, and indicated on the ear by a sulcus extending to the extremity of the beak.

Test is thin, marked by numerous regular alternating rays or radii, which increase in number by interstitial additions, and become broader and stronger towards the margins. These radii are crossed by very fine, sharp lines of growth. On the wings the radiating striae are obsolete, while the lines of growth are there sharper and stronger than on the body of the shell.

The dimensions of the shells in this species are very variable; there are very large and also very small specimens. The one before me, which is one of the largest ever found, measures thirty lines in height, thirty-two lines in length, and has a hinge-line twenty-seven lines long; here the length exceeds the height, and the hinge-line is shorter than height or length; but we find specimens belonging to this species where all three dimensions are nearly equal.

This species resembles A. pecteniformis, but differs from it by its larger wings and by its more numerous and less prominent radii. This is one of the largest shells of the genus Aviculopecten, and is easily identified by its form and surface-markings. All the forms heretofore placed in the two species of A. sanduskyensis and A. parilis, belong to the present one. The apparent specific differences noted in the description of these three forms are neither constant nor well defined, and not even sufficient to base upon them a separation into different varieties.

Formation and Locality.—This species occurs in the Corniferous limestone at and around the Falls of the Ohio, in Kentucky and Indiana, where fair specimens are not very rare, though not abundant either.

Genus Glyptodesma. Hall.

Glyptodesma, Hall. N. Y. Rep., Vol. 5, pt. 1.
Etymology: glyptos, curved; *desma*, a ligament.

Shell aviculoid, erect or moderately oblique ; inequivalve. Ligament external. Ligamental area striated, continuous. Hinge with two strong, lateral teeth, and numerous irregular transverse plications along the cardinal margin. In form the shells of this genus resemble Actinodesma, but they have not the permanent diverging teeth of that genus. Surface marked by concentric striae.

Glyptodesma cancellata. N. SP.

Plate V., figure 1.

Shell large, regularly oviform in its body, almost erect or slightly oblique ; height exceeding length ; anterior and posterior margins broadly rounded ; front or base strongly curved ; posterior wing large ; its posterior margin concave, and its extremity produced to a salient point; anterior wing defective in the specimen before me, but it appears to be short, and of the shape as indicated in figure 1, plate 5. The hinge-line is about equal in size to width of the shell. Only the left valve is known ; it is very convex and gibbous in the umbonal region, from where it slopes in a gentle curve to the margins in the basal half of the valve. The lateral slopes of the umbonal region are abrupt, the anterior somewhat more than the posterior. There is no sharp dividing line between the body and wings. The posterior wing is very convex, sloping rapidly or even abruptly to the cardinal line, which is entirely straight. The interior of this shell and its right wing are unknown. The umbo is prominent, and the beak elevated and incurved over the hinge-line ; it is located anterior to the middle of the shell, and has an anterior direction. The surface is marked by strong, simple, rounded, radiating plications, with wide, flat interspaces, which are about three times as wide as the ribs. There is scarcely an intercalated plication observed on the whole valve ; no bifurcation takes place.

The specimen here described and figured is well preserved, with the exception of the anterior wing, which is either broken or covered with rock; this shell measures thirty-one lines in height, by twenty-nine lines in length. The surface is divided by several strong lines of growth into concentric zones.

Formation and Locality.—Found in the Corniferous limestone of the Devonian formation at and around the Falls of the Ohio, in Kentucky and Indiana. The specimen illustrated on plate 5 is, so far, the only one known.

Glyptodesma occidentale. HALL.

Plate III., figure 5.

Glyptodesma occidentale, Hall. Pal. N. Y., Vol. 5, part 1, page 157—1884.

Shell large, broadly ovate ; body nearly erect; height somewhat greater than the length. The specimen before me measures thirty-eight lines in height by thirty-four lines in length. All the margins are regularly curved, with about the same radius.

Of the two valves of the shell, only the left one is known ; it is somewhat gibbous at the umbo, from where it slopes in a gentle curve down to the base and to the basal half of the anterior and posterior margins ; in the upper half of the valve the lateral slopes of the umbonal region are abrupt, more so on the anterior than on the posterior side. The hinge-line is straight and considerably shorter than the width of the shell ; in our specimen it measures about two-thirds of the greatest width of shell. Prof. Hall's figure, on plate 86, of volume 5, part 1, shows an enormously extended wing, and consequently a very large hinge-line, but it appears to me, that in restoring the wing, which in Prof. Hall's specimen was missing to the extent of an inch and one-quarte on the posterior margin, a considerable mistake was made in regard to its length, although the concentric lines, near the edge of the broken wing, indicated a very mucronate one. My specimen is almost perfect and shows a wing as illustrated in figure 5, plate 3. The beak is anterior to the middle of the shell, with a strong inclination to the anterior end ; it is prominent and acute. The anterior wing is short, defined by a deep sulcus, and marked byssal inflection or sinus just anterior to the beak. Posterior wing is large, depressed, convex, moderately extended, joining the body of the shell at the middle, and defined partly by the recurving of the striae, but more decidedly by a small but plainly visible depression, which extends in a straight line from the cardinal line near the beak along body of the valve to the posterior margin at the middle of the shell. The posterior margin of the wing is slightly concave, and its extremity somewhat produced, but not to such an extent as shown in Prof. Hall's figure.

Test thick, marked by numerous fine striae or lines of growth, which at intervals are crowded into fascicles, producing an undulating surface. These striae are more closely arranged, and become lamellose on the anterior part of shell. On the posterior wing the striae are regular, and at distant intervals a single stria becomes sharply elevated. The interior of this shell and its right valve are unknown.

This species resembles G. erectum, but appears to be a more robust form ; the shell is more orbicular, the umbonal region more gibbous, the surface more rugose from the undulations of the fascicles of striae, and the limitation between the body and the posterior wing is less strongly defined. These are the differences marked out by Prof. Hall. It appears to me that in all these points shells may differ and still belong to the same species, and especially in this case, where the most important distinction, the last mentioned one, disappears, inasmuch as Prof. Hall did not notice in his specimen the dividing sulcus between body and posterior wing, which my shell so plainly shows.

Formation and Locality.—Found in the Corniferous limestone at and around the Falls of the Ohio, in Kentucky and Indiana.

Genus Actinopteria. Hall.

This genus is established by Prof. Hall in his N. Y. Rep., Vol. 5, part 1, Lamellibranchiata. His description is:

Characterized from Pterinea in the absence of a broad striated ligamental area and strong cardinal teeth. Right valve sub-convex. Surface with fine rays.

Actinopteria boydi. Conrad.

Plate III., figure 2.

Avicula boydi, Conrad. Jour. Acad. Nat. Sci. Phil.—1842.
Avicula quadrula, Conrad. Jour. Acad. Nat. Sci. Phil.—1842.
Actinopteria boydi, Hall. Pal. N. Y., Vol. 5, pt, 1, p. 113—1883.

Shell of medium size, rhomboidal; body ovate, varying in the proportion of its dimensions. Its longitudinal axis forms with the hinge-line an angle of from forty-five to sixty degrees. Length and height sometimes nearly equal, but in some specimens the length is one-fourth greater than height. The margins in the basal half of the shell regularly rounded; in the upper half of the valve anterior margin of the body is almost straight or very little curved, while the posterior border of the body is entirely straight or even slightly concave. The post-basal part of the shell is extended. The left valve, which is only preserved in the specimen before me, is moderately convex throughout the whole body. The umbo is somewhat more elevated; its anterior slope is gentle, while the posterior descent is abrupt, meeting surface of the posterior wing almost at right-angles, thus forming a sulcus by which the rear wing is defined.

The hinge-line is straight from the anterior side of beak to the posterior extremity. Beak anterior, acute, prominent, inclined forward, and rising above the cardinal line; the umbonal margins form an acute angle of less than sixty degrees. Front ear short, oblique, limited by a deep, but not sharply defined sulcus. Terminal margin of the rear wing concave, and the cardinal extremity acute.

The test is thick; the left valve, in well preserved specimens, is covered by numerous strong, simple, sharp, radiating striae, which are continuous from the umbo to the margin; intercalated radii are very seldom, but when they exist they are finer than the balance. The radii are crossed by regular, sharp, elevated, concentric lamellae, which, in well preserved specimens, are produced into sub-tubular, spiniform extensions upon the rays. On the wings the radii are less conspicuous, while the concentric lines of growth are there more prominent and crowded. The specimen here described and figured measures in both height and length fifteen lines, and its hinge-line thirteen lines.

Formation and Locality.—Occurs in the Corniferous limestone of the Devonian formation at and around the Falls of the Ohio.

INDEX TO GENERA AND SPECIES DESCRIBED.

PROTISTA.

PLATES.

Brachiospongia
digitata...35, 36

BRYOZOA.
Ptilodictya
hilli 35

BRACHIOPODA.
Ambocoelia
umbonata 17

.·nastrophia
internascens..32

Athyris
vittata 16

Atrypa
aspera 14
calvini 32
ellipsoida ....
reticularis...14, 15
reticularis, var. niagarensis...32

Camarella
congesta ....

Centronella
glans-fagea..31

Chonetes
acutiradiata 18
subquadrata...
yandelliana 17, 31

Crania
bordeni 2

PLATES.

Cyrtia
    exporrecta 27
    exporrecta, var. arrecta 27, 32, 34

Cyrtina
    crassa.. 13
    hamiltoniae 13
    hamiltoniae, var. recta 13

Discina
    doria ....
    grandis 3

Leiorhynchus
    quadricostatus ....

Leptocoelia
    hemispherica 32

Lingula
    triangulata 31

Meristella
    nasuta 15
    unisulcata... 15

Meristina
    maria 20
    nitida... 33

Nucleospira
    concinna 32
    elegans ....
    pisiformis 33

Orthis
    biforata 29
    borealis 34
    elegantula.. 32
    flabellum 34
    goodwini 17
    hybrida 32
    livia 16, 17
    linneyi 34

PLATES.

Orthis—Continued.

nisis 27

propinqua 16

rugaeplicata 27

subnodosa...

vanuxemi 16

Pentamerella

arata 13

papilionensis ....

thusnelda 31

Pentamerus

complanatus 27

globulosus ....

knappi.. 28

knotti 32

knighti 29

littoni 27

nucleus 27, 33

nysius, var. crassicostus... 28

nysius, var. tenuicostus ....

oblongus 33

oblongus, var. cylindricus.. 30

pergibbosus 29

uniplicatus 33

ventricosus 33

Productella

semiglobosa 26

subaculeata, var. cataracta 17

Rhynchonella

acinus 32, 26

bellaforma ....

carolina.. 13

gainesi 31

increbescens.. 34

indianensis... 33

louisvillensis 31

pisa 32

rugaecosta 32

saffordi 27, 33

PLATES.

Rhynchonella—Continued.

    saffordi, var. depressa 33

    stricklandi 29, 27

    tenuistriata 17

    tethys 13, 31

Rhynchotreta

    cuneata, var. americana 32

Spirifera

    acuminata 8

    arctisegmenta 12

    atwaterana 9

    byrnesi 10

    conradana 7

    crispa, var. simplex 17

    davisi 12

    divaricata 11, 12

    dubia 33

    duodenaria 12

    euruteines 6

    euruteines, var. fornacula 6

    foggi 32

    gregaria 8, 10

    grieri 9

    hobbsi 10

    knappiana 7

    macconathii 11

    marionensis

    medialis 26

    mucronata 31

    oweni 7

    radiata 29

    raricosta 17

    rostellum 27, 29

    sculptilis 31

    segmenta 13

    varicosa 10

Streptorhynchus

    arctostriata 31

    subplanus 29

    tenuis

PLATES.

Stricklandinia
    louisvillensis. --- 34

Strophodonta
    demissa --- 33, 18
    hemispherica -- 18
    inequistriata -- 17
    nacrea ---
    perplana -- 18
    plicata --
    profunda -- 17, 29
    striata --

Strophomena
    rhomboidalis (Devonian) ----------------------------------- 18
    rhomboidalis (Silurian) -------------------------------------

Terebratula
    harmonia --- 17
    jucunda ---
    lincklaeni ------------------- ----------------------------- 17
    roemingeri --- 16

Trematospira
    hirsuta --- 16
    helena --- 32

Tropidoleptus
    carinatus --- 17

Zygospira
    kentuckiensis --- 34

PTEROPODA.

Styliola
    fissurella --

Tentaculites
    sialariformis --- 31

GASTEROPODA.

Bellerophon
    leda --- 17

PLATES.

Bucania
devonica 26

Callonema
bellatula 20
clarki 24
imitator 20

Cyclonema
cancellata 20
multilira 22
rugaelineata 33

Euomphalus
deceini 21
sampsoni 21

Loxonema
hamiltoniae 31
hydraulicum 20
laeviusculum 22
rectistriatum ....

Macrocheilus
carinatus 20

Murchisonii
desiderata 26
petila 31

Platyceras
bucculentum 23
compressum 25
conicum 25
dumosum 23
dumosum, var. rarispinum 23
echinatum 31
erectum ....
milleri 25
multispinosum 25
rictum ....
symmetricum 23
thetis ....
unguiforme ....
ventricosum 25

PLATES.

Platyostoma
lineata... 19, 21
lineata, var. callosa 21, 22, 25
niagarense 33
turbinata... 21
turbinata, var. cochleata ....

Pleurotomaria
arabella... 26
casii 26
lucina..
procteri 21
sulcomarginata 21

Polyphemopsis
louisvillae.. 20

Strophostylus
varians 22

Trochonema
fatua ....
rectilatera 20
yandellana.. 20

Turbo
shumardi 19, 22

CEPHALOPODA.

Gomphoceras
oviforme 21
turbiniforme 21

Goniatites
discoideus.. 20

Lituites
marshi 30

Nautilus
maximus.. 24

LAMELLIBRANCHIATA.

PLATES.

Actinopteria
boydi 8

Aviculopecten
crassicostatus ....
fasciculatus 8
pecteniformis 8
princeps ....

Clinopistha
antiqua ....
striata 4
subnasuta 4

Conocardium
cuneus 5

Cypricardinia
cataracta 4
cylindrica... 4
inflata, var. sub-equivalvis ....

Cypricardites
halli 84

Glyptodesma
cancellata 5
occidentale 8

Goniophora
truncata.. 4

Grammysia
gibbosa 4

Limoptera
cancellata 3, 4

Modiomorpha
affinis...
alta.. 26
charlestownensis... 5
concentrica 2
mytiloides ....

PLATES.

Nucula
  herzeri ....
  neda' 5
  niotica 5

Paracyclas
  elliptica.. 2
  elongata 2
  lirata 2
  octerlonii 31
  ohioensis 5

Ptychodesma
  knappianum... 2

Yoldia
  valvulus 4

INDEX TO SPECIES DESCRIBED.

PROTISTA.

PAGE.

Brachiospongia digitata 29

BRYOZOA.

Ptilodictya hilli 30

BRACHIOPODA.

Ambocoelia umbonata 86
Anastrophia internascens 47
Athyris vittata 87
Atrypa aspera 88
    calvini 89
    ellipsoida 90
    reticularis 91
    reticularis, var. niagarensis 92
Camarella congesta 48
Centronella glans-fagea 153
Chonetes acutiradiata 66
    subquadrata 67
    yandelliana 68
Crania bordeni 32
Cyrtia exporrecta 93
    exporrecta, var. arrecta 94
Cyrtina crassa 95
    hamiltoniae 96
    hamiltoniae, var. recta 97
Discina doria 32
    grandis 33
Leiorhynchus quadricostatus 71

PAGE.

Leptocoelia hemispherica 152
Lingula triangulata 34
Meristella nasuta 98
    unisulcata 99
Meristina maria 101
    nitida 102
Nucleospira concinna 103
    elegans 104
    pisiformis 104
Orthis biforata 35
    borealis 36
    elegantula 37
    flabellum 38
    goodwini 39
    hybrida 39
    livia 40
    linneyi 41
    nisis 42
    propinqua 43
    rugaeplicata 44
    subnodosa 44
    vanuxemi 45
Pentamerella arata 49
    papilionensis 50
    thusnelda 51
Pentamerus complanatus 53
    globulosus 54
    knappi 55
    knighti 57
    knotti 56
    littoni 58
    nucleus 59
    nysius, var. crassicostus 60
    nysius, var. tenuicostus 60
    oblongus 60
    oblongus, var. cylindricus 61
    pergibbosus 62
    uniplicatus 63
    ventricosus 64
Productella semiglobosa 70

	Page
Productella subaculeata, var. cataracta	69
Rhynchonella acinus	73
bellaforma	73
carolina	75
guinesi	76
increbescens	83
indianensis	76
louisvillensis	77
pisa	78
rugaecosta	78
saffordi	79
saffordi, var. depressa	80
stricklandi	81
tenuistriata	82
tethys	83
Rhynchotreta cuneata, var. americana	85
Spirifera acuminata	105
arctisegmenta	108
atwaterana	107
byrnesi	109
conradana	110
crispa, var. simplex	111
davisi	112
divaricata	113
dubia	115
duodenaria	114
euruteines	115
euruteines, var. fornacula	117
foggi	117
gregaria	119
grieri	120
hobbsi	121
knappiana	122
macconathii	123
marionensis	124
medialis	125
mucronata	126
oweni	126
radiata	130
raricosta	128

PAGE.

Spirifera rostellum 129
    sculptilis 132
    segmenta 132
    varicosa.. 134
Streptorhynchus arctostriata 140
    subplanus 141
    tenuis 142
Stricklandinia louisvillensis 65
Strophodonta demissa 143
    hemispherica 144
    inequistriata 145
    nacrea 146
    perplana 147
    plicata... 149
    profunda 148
    striata 149
Strophomena rhomboidalis (Devonian) 150
    rhomboidalis (Silurian) 151
Terebratula harmonia 154
    jucunda.. 154
    lincklaeni 155
    roemigeri 155
Trematospira hirsuta 136
    helena 137
Tropidoleptus carinatus 46
Zygospira kentuckiensis 138

PTEROPODA.

Styliola fissurella 157
Tentaculites scaliformis 156

GASTEROPODA.

Bellerophon leda 158
Bucania devonica 160
Callonema bellatula 175
    clarki 175
    imitator 176

PAGE.

Cyclonema cancellata 187
    multilira 188
    rugaelineata 187
Euomphalus decewi 181
    sampsoni 182
Loxonema hamiltoniae.. 177
    hydraulicum 178
    laeviusculum 178
    rectistriatum 179
Macrocheilus carinatus 180
Murchisonia desiderata 169
    petila 170
Platyceras bucculentum 160
    compressum... 162
    conicum 161
    dumosum 162
    dumosum, var. rarispinum 163
    echinatum 164
    erectum 165
    milleri 165
    multispinosum 166
    rictum 166
    symmetricum 167
    thetis 168
    unguiforme 168
    ventricosum 168
Platyostoma lineata 183
    lineata, var. callosa 184
    niagarense 185
    turbinata 184
    turbinata, var cochleata 185
Pleurotomaria arabella.. 171
    casii 171
    lucina.. 172
    procteri.. 173
    sulcomarginata 174
Polyphemopsis louisvillae 180
Strophostylus varians 186
Trochonema fatua 189
    rectilatera.. 189
    yandellana 190
Turbo shumardi 191

CEPHALOPODA.

	Page
Gomphoceras oviforme	103
turbiniforme	194
Goniatites discoideus	194
Lituites marshi	195
Nautilus maximus	196

LAMELLIBRNACHIATA.

Actinopteria boydi	229
Aviculopecten crassicostatus	223
fasciculatus	224
pecteniformis	225
princeps	225
Clinopistha antiqua	200
striata	200
subnasuta	199
Conocardium cuneus	203
Cypricardinia cataracta	204
cylindrica	205
inflata, var. sub-equivalvis	206
Cypricardites halli	206
Glyptodesma cancellata	227
occidentale	228
Goniophora truncata	214
Grammysia gibbosa	208
Limoptera cancellata	198
Modiomorpha affinis	216
alta	217
charlestownensis	218
concentrica	219
mytiloides	220
Nucula herzeri	221
neda	222
niotica	222
Paracyclas elliptica	209
elongata	210
lirata	211
octerlonii	212
ohioensis	213
Ptychodesma knappianum	201
Yoldia valvulus	223

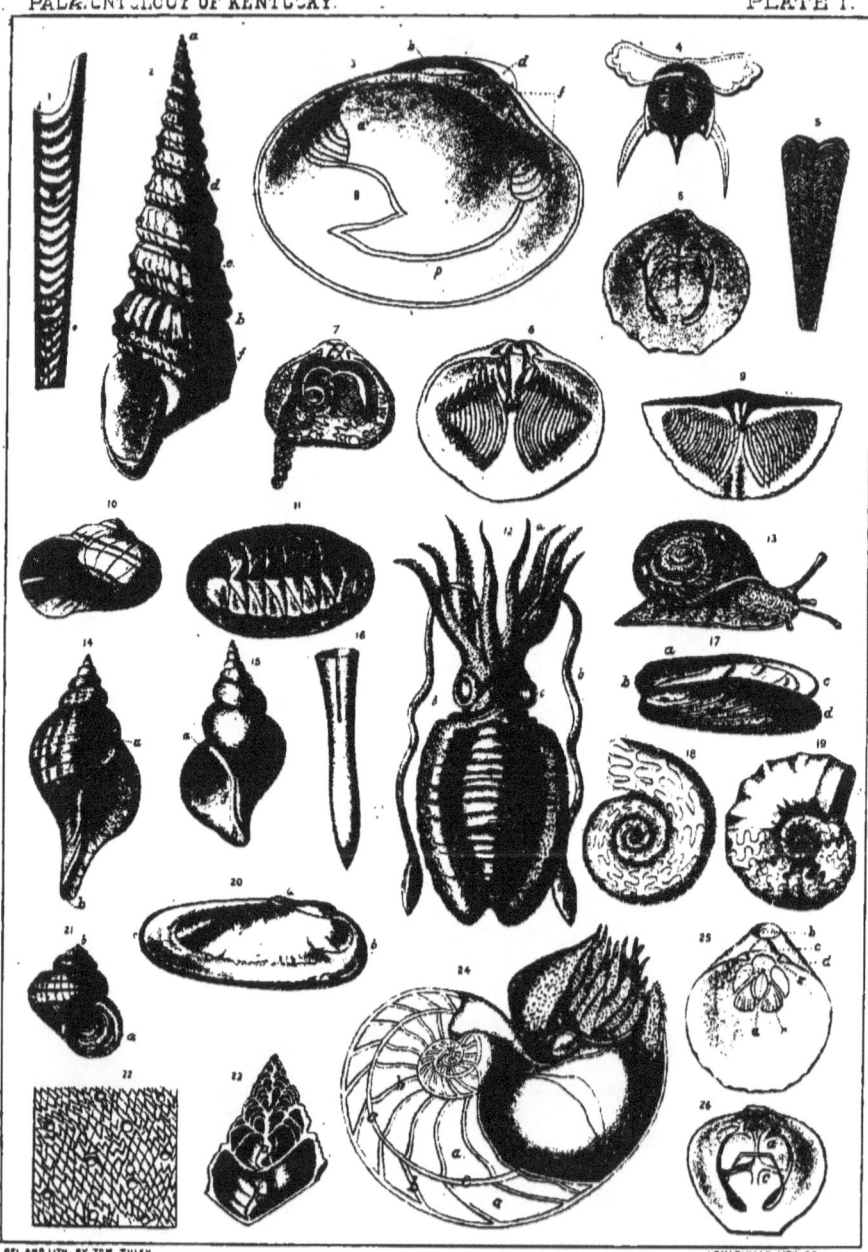

PLATE I.

CEPHALOPODA.

Belemnitella mucronata. SOWERBY.

Fig. 16. View of the internal shell. Page 22

Sepia officinalis. LINNÉ.

Fig. 12. View of a specimen. Page 22
    a. Arms.
    b. Tentacles.
    c. Eyes.

Nautilus pompilius.

Fig. 24. View of the animal and shell, the latter sawed through
    the middle. Page 22
    a a. Air chambers.
    b b. Septa.
    c c. Siphuncle.

Goniatites henslowi. SOWERBY.

Fig. 18. View of a specimen, the outer shell entirely removed. Page 22

Ceratites nodosus. BRUGUIÈRE.

Fig. 19. View of a specimen, outer shell entirely removed. Page 22

Turrilites costatus. Lamark.

Fig. 2. Apertural view of a specimen.   Pages 22 and 23
    a. Apex.
    a f. Spire.
    b.
    c. } Sutures.
    d.
    g. Aperture,

Baculites anceps. Lamark.

Fig. 1. View of the internal shell.   Page 22
    a. Aperture.
    b. Septa.
    c. Sutures.

PLATE I.

GASTEROPODA.

Triton corrugatus. Lamark.

Fig. 23. Longitudinal section of a specimen. The upper part of the
spire has been partitioned off many times successively.   Page 23

Fascioloria tulipa. Linnè.

Fig. 14. Apertural view of a specimen. Dextral.   Page 23
    a. Posterior canal.
    b. Anterior canal.
    d. Labrum.

Fusus antiquus. Mueller.

Fig. 15. Apertural view of a specimen.   Sinistral.   Page 23
   a. Posterior canal.
   b. Anterior canal.
   f. Labrum.

Paludina listeri. Hanley.

Fig. 21. Apertural view of a specimen.   Dextral.   Page 23
   a. Aperture, closed by operculum.
   b. apex.

Ampullaria bolteniana. Chemnitz.

Fig. 10. Apertural view of a specimen.   Sinistral.   Page 2ε

Chiton squamosus. Linné.

Fig. 11. Dorsal view of a specimen.   Page 22

Helix desertorum. Fosskal.

Fig. 13. View showing animal and manner of bearing shell.   Page 22.

PLATE I.

PTEROPODA.

Hyalaea tridentata. Lamark.

Fig. 4. Dorsal view of a specimen.   Page 23

Conularia trentonensis. Hall.

Fig. 5. Front view of a specimen.   Page 23

PLATE I.

BRACHIOPODA.

Terebratula dorsata. Smelin.

Fig. 26. View of a dorsal valve.   Page 24
    a. Crura of the loop.
    b. Loop.
    c. Septum.

Fig. 22. Magnified section of shell of Terebratula.   Page 24

Waldheimia australis. King.

Fig. 6. View of dorsal valve.   Page 24
    b. Loop.
    l. Reflected portion of loop.
    m. Abductor.
    p. Hinge plate.
    s. Septum.

Waldheimia australis. King.

Fig. 25. View of ventral valve.   Pages 23 and 24
    a. Single abductor impression.
    b. Foramen.
    c. Deltidium.
    d. Teeth.
    r. Cardinal muscles.
    v. Portion of the vent.
    z. Attachment of pedicle sheath.

Spirifera striata. Sowerby.

Fig. 7. View of dorsal valve showing spiral cones.   Page 24

Athyris concentrica. Buch.

Fig. 8. View of dorsal valve showing spiral cones.   Page 24

Rhynchonella ptissacea. Chemnitz.

Fig. 9. View of dorsal valve, showing spiral arm unrolled.   Page 24

PLATE I.

LAMELLIBRANCHIATA.

Modiola lithophaga. Linnè.

Fig. 17. View of right and left valve.   Page 25
    a. Dorsal margin.
    b. Anterior margin.
    c. Posterior margin.
    d. Posterior margin.

Cytherea chione. Linnè.

Fig. 3. View of left valve.   Page 25
    à Anterior abductor.
    a. Posterior abductor.
    e. Cardinal tooth.
    d. Umbo.
    h. Hinge linament.
    f. Lunule.
    p. Pallial impression.
    t'. Lateral teeth.
    s. Sinus.

Glycimeris siliqua. Chemnitz.

Fig. 20. View of a left valve.   Page 25
    a. Dorsal margin.
    b. Anterior margin.
    c. Posterior margin.

NOTE.—All figures on Plate I. are copied from "A Manual of the Mollusca. A Treatise on Recent and Fossil Shells. By Dr. S. P. Woodward, A. L. S., F. G. S., Second Edition. Lockwood and Co., London, England, 1871."

PLATE II.

Paracyclas elliptica.

Fig. 1-3. Right, left and cardinal view of specimen.   Page 209

Paracyclas lirata.

Fig. 4. Left view of a specimen.   Page 211
Fig. 5-7. Left, right and cardinal view of specimen.

Paracyclas elongata.

Fig. 8. Left view of a specimen.   Page 210

Modiomorpha concentrica.

Fig. 9, 10, 14. Left view of specimen, showing variations in size and ornamentation.   Page 219
Fig. 11. 12. Right and profile view of specimen.

Crania bordeni.

Fig. 14. View of two specimens adhering to left valve of Modiomorpha concentrica.   Page 32

Ptychodesma knappianum.

Fig. 13. Profile view of a specimen.   Page 201
Fig. 15. Left view of a specimen.
Fig. 16. Left view of a smaller individual.
Fig. 17. Right view of a specimen, showing striated ligamental area.
Fig. 18. View of left valve enlarged, showing striated ligamental area.

PLATE II.

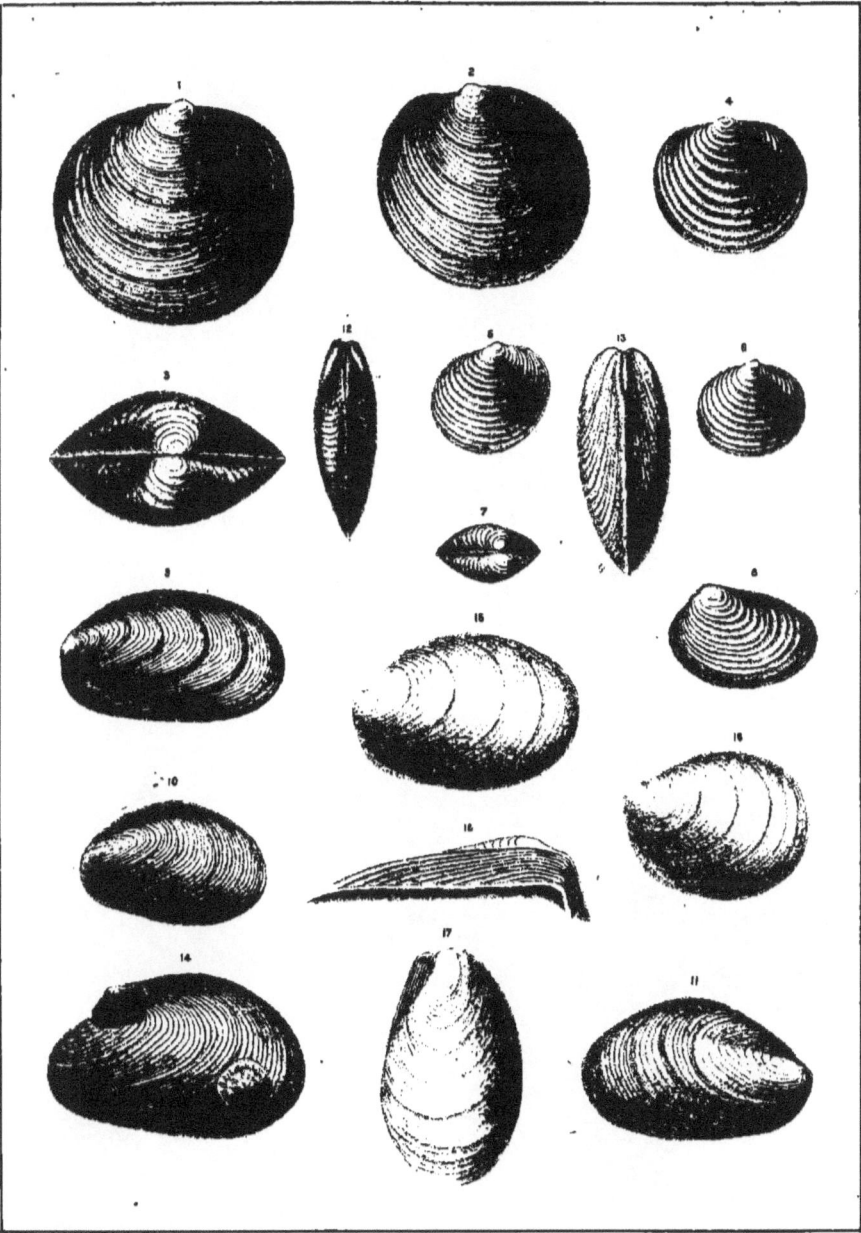

DEL.AND LITH. CHAS. STARCK. LOUISVILLE LITH. CO.

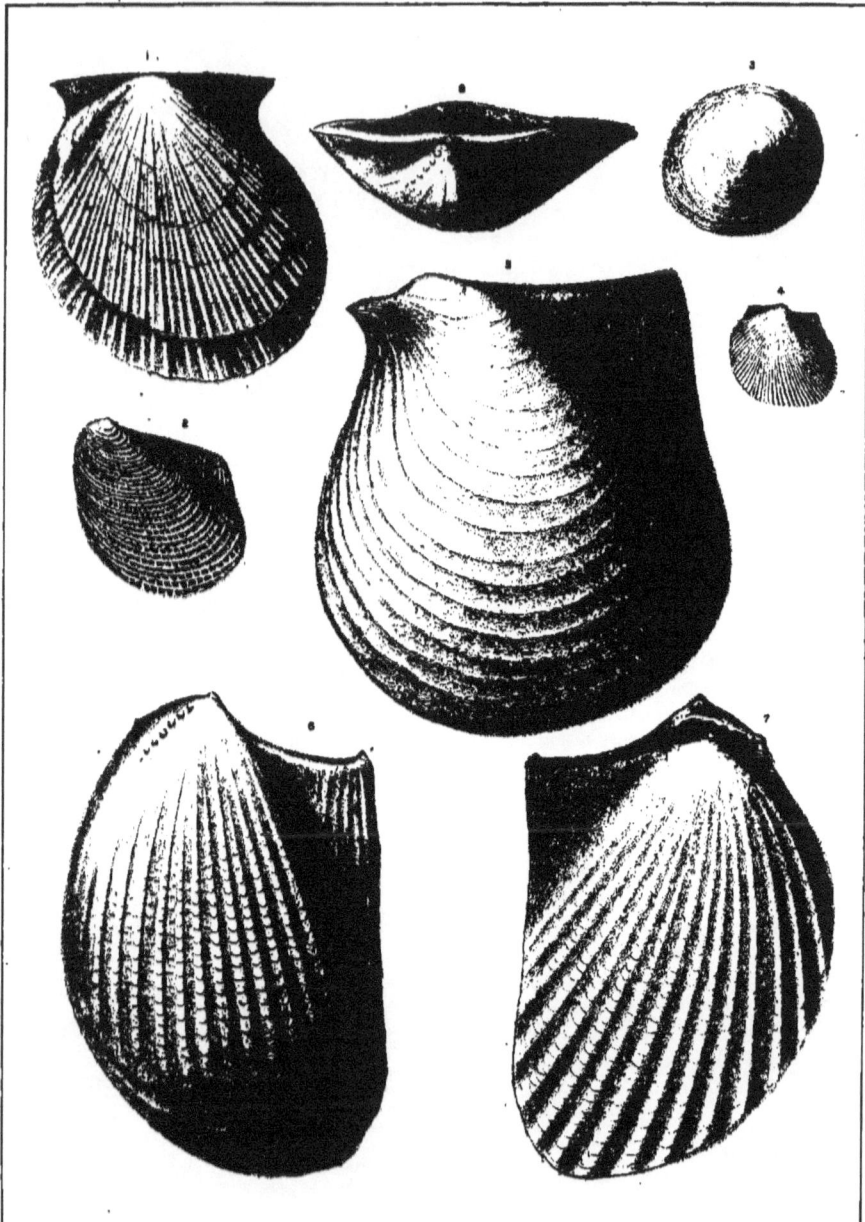

PLATE III.

Aviculopecten pecteniformis.

Fig. 1. View of a left valve.   Page 225

Actinopteria boydi.

Fig. 2. View of a left valve, showing surface ornamentation.   Page 229

Discina grandis.

Fig. 3. Dorsal view of a specimen.   Page 33

Aviculopecten fasciculatus.

Fig. 4. View of a left valve.   Page 224

Glyptodesma occidentale.

Fig. 5. View of a left valve.   Page 228

Limoptera cancellata.

Fig. 6-8. Left, right and cardinal view of specimen.   Page 198

PLATE IV.

Clinopistha striata.

Fig. 1, 2. Right and left view of specimen   Page 200

Cypricardinia cataracta.

Fig. 3. Left view of a specimen.   Page 204

Yoldia ? valvulus.

Fig. 4, 5. Left view of two specimens.   Page 223

Clinopistha subnasuta.

Fig. 6-8, 12. Left, cardinal, right and posterior view of specimen.   Page 199

Clinopistha antiqua.

Fig. 9-11. Right, cardinal and left view of specimen.   Page 200

Cypricardinia cylindrica.

Fig. 13-15. Left, cardinal and right view of specimen.   Page 205

Grammysia gibbosa.

Fig. 16, 19, 20. Cardinal, left and posterior view of specimen.   Page 208
Fig. 17. Right view of a specimen.
Fig. 18. Right view of a smaller specimen.

Goniophora truncata.

Fig. 21-23. Posterior, side and cardinal view of a specimen.   Page 214

Limoptera cancellata.

Fig. 24. View of a young individual.   Page 198

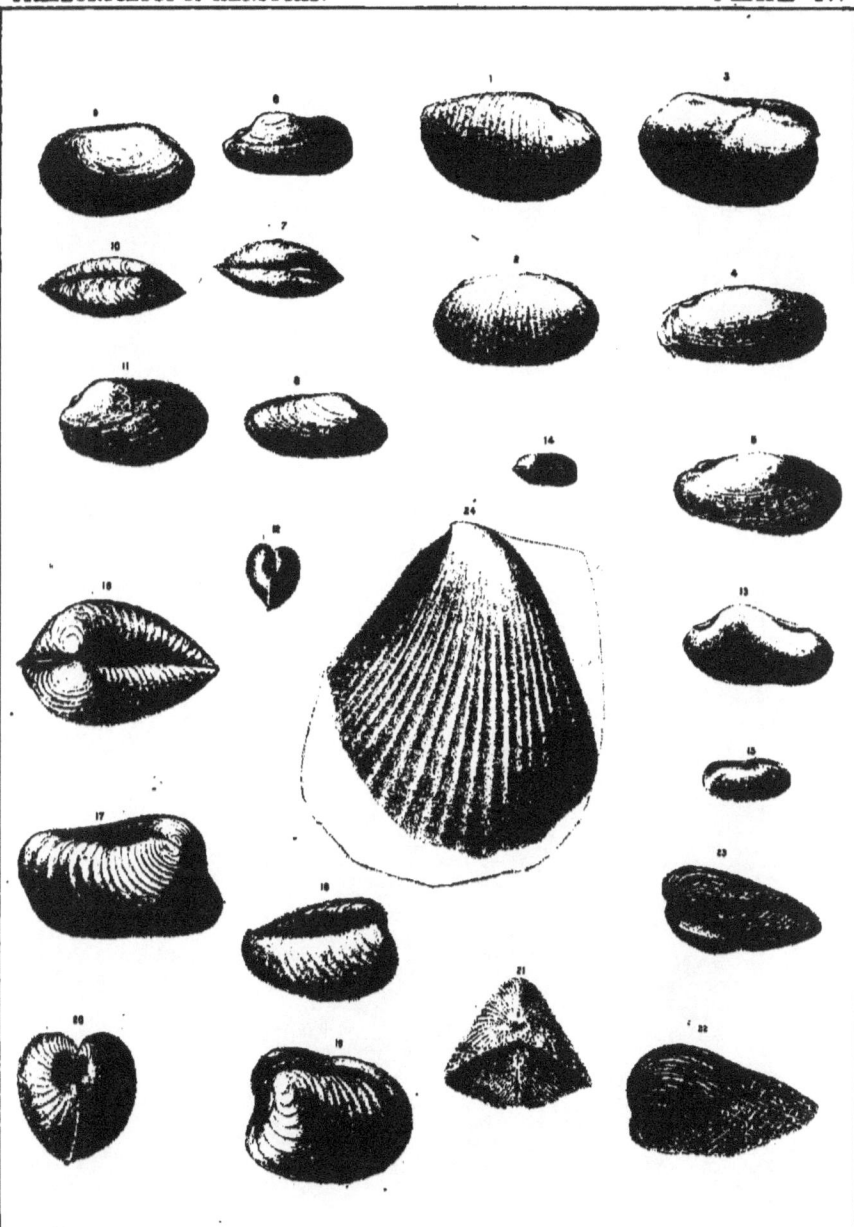

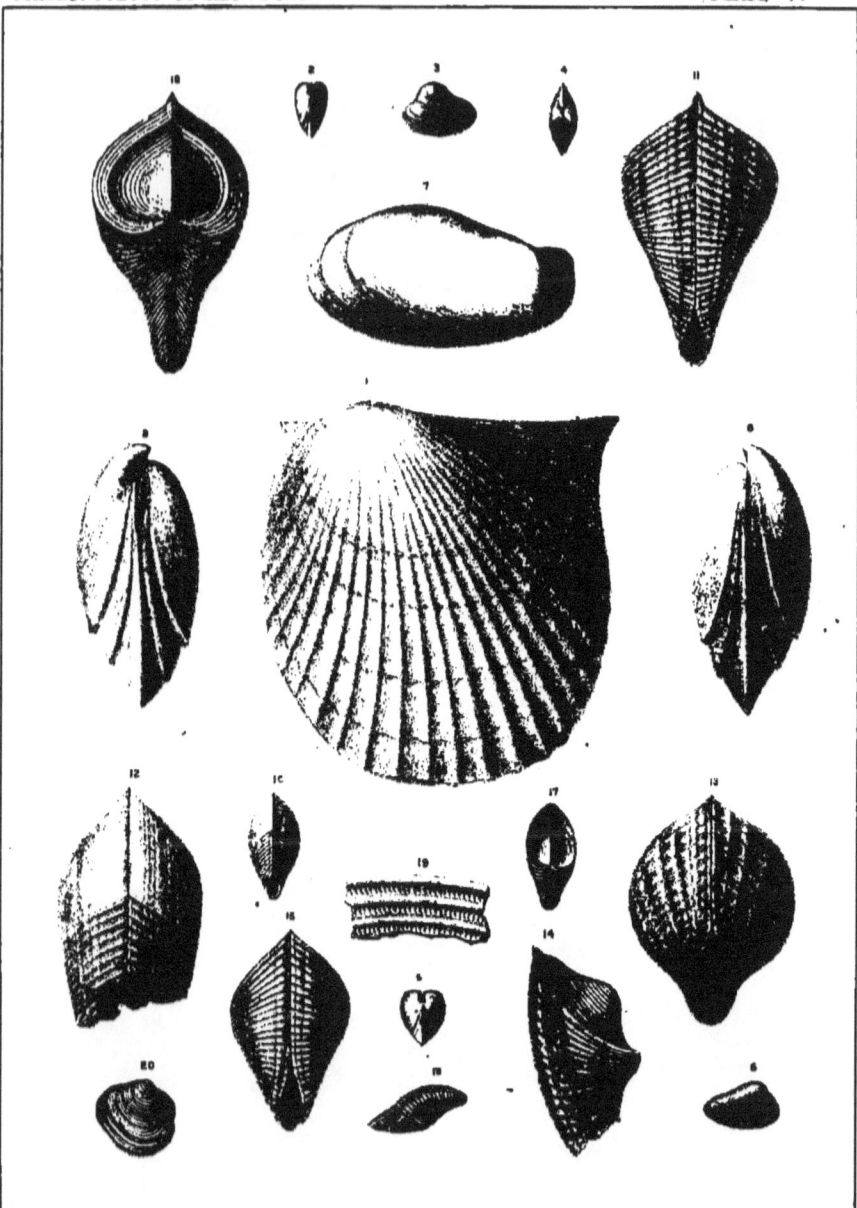

PLATE V.

Glyptodesma cancellata.

Fig. 1. View of a left valve. Page 227

Nucula niotica.

Fig. 2-4. Anterior, left and cardinal view of a specimen. Page 222

Nucula neda.

Fig. 5, 6. Right and anterior view of a specimen. Page 222

Modiomorpha charlestownensis.

Fig. 7. Right view of a specimen. Page 218
Fig. 8, 9. Profile view of two specimens.

Conocardium cuneus.

Fig. 10, 11. Dorsal and ventral view of a specimen. Page 203
Fig. 12, 13, 15. Ventral views of three specimens, showing variations
    in size and ornamentation.
Fig. 14. Lateral view, showing shield.
Fig. 16. Ventral view of a young specimen.
Fig. 17. Dorsal view of a young, very perfect specimen.
Fig. 18. Side view of a young specimen.
Fig. 19. Enlargement of a fragment of test, showing ornamentation.

Paracyclas ohioensis.

Fig. 20. Right view of an average size specimen. Page 213

PLATE VI.

Spirifera euruteines.

Fig. 1-7, 9, 11-17. A series of specimens showing principal varieties of
   form.   Page 115
Fig. 21, 22. View of two specimens broken so as to show the spiral
   cones.

Spirifera euruteines, var. fornacula.

Fig. 8, 10. Cardinal and ventral view of a large specimen.   Page 117
Fig. 18, 19, 20. Dorsal, ventral and profile view of a small specimen.

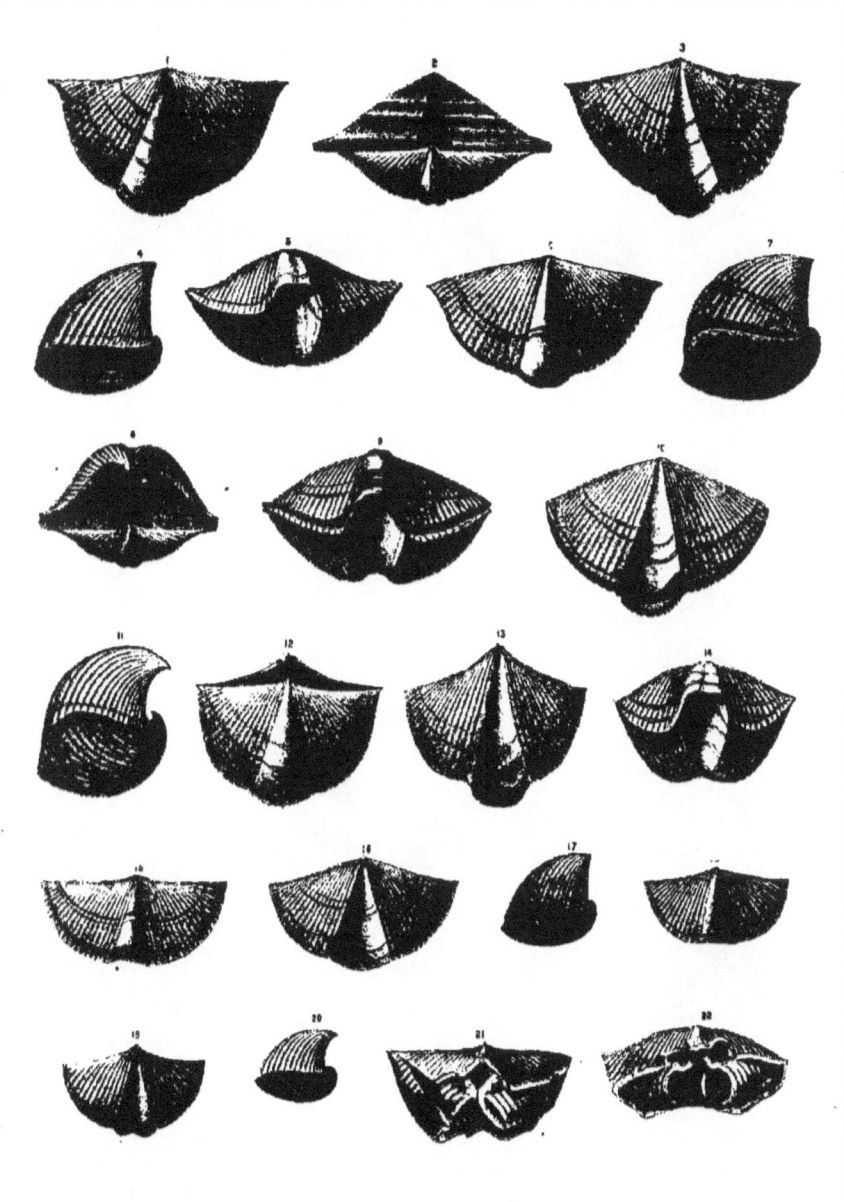

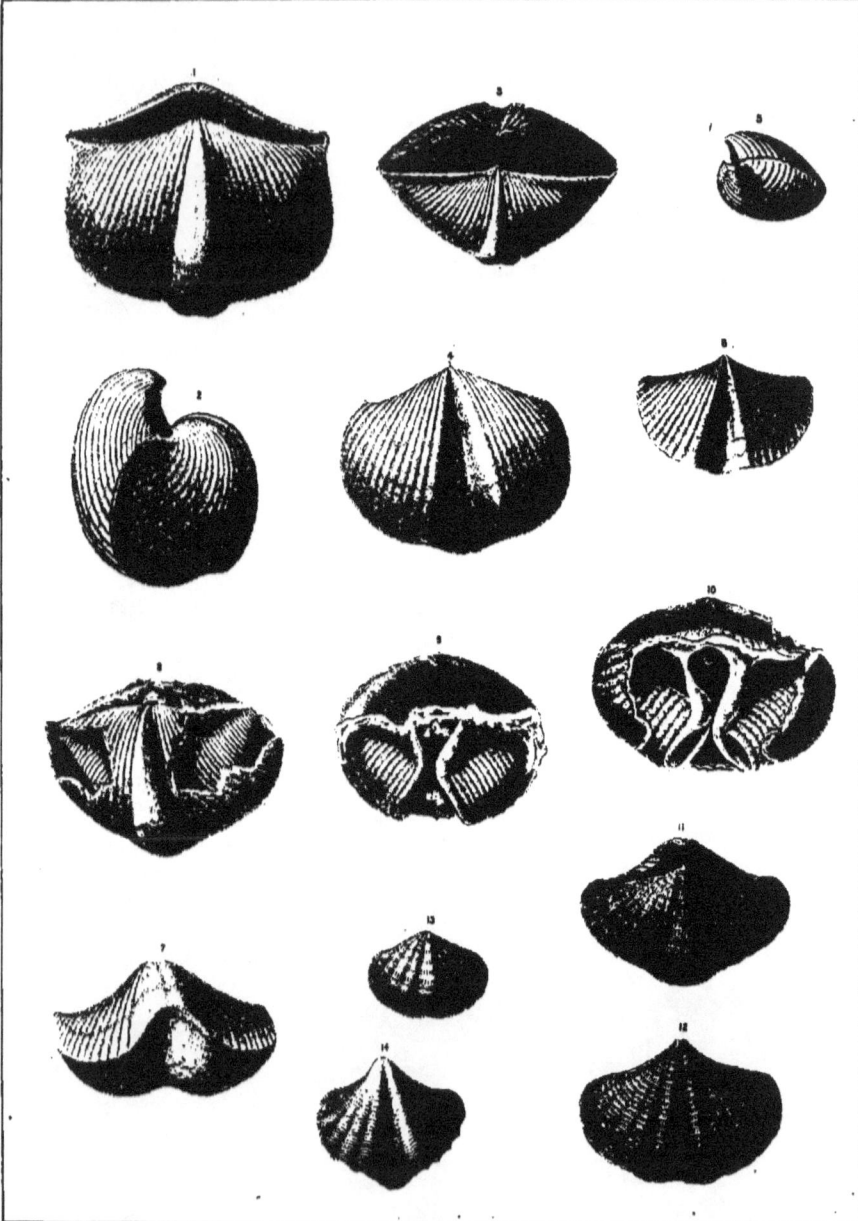

PLATE VII.

Spirifera oweni.

Fig. 1-4, 7. Dorsal, profile, cardinal, ventral and front view of specimen.   Page 126
Fig. 5, 6. Lateral and dorsal view of a young specimen.
Fig. 8, 9, 10. View of three specimens broken so as to show the
spiral cones.

Spirifera conradana.

Fig. 11, 12. Dorsal and ventral view of a specimen.   Page 110
Fig. 13. Dorsal view of a small specimen.

Spirifera knappiana.

Fig. 14. Ventral view of a specimen.   Page 122

PLATE VIII.

Spirifera acuminata.

Fig. 1. Dorsal, ventral, profile, front and cardinal view of a specimen.   Page 105
Fig. 6, 7, 8. Cardinal, ventral and dorsal view of an internal cast.

Spirifera gregaria.

Fig. 9-13. Ventral, dorsal, front, profile and cardinal view of a specimen.   Page 119

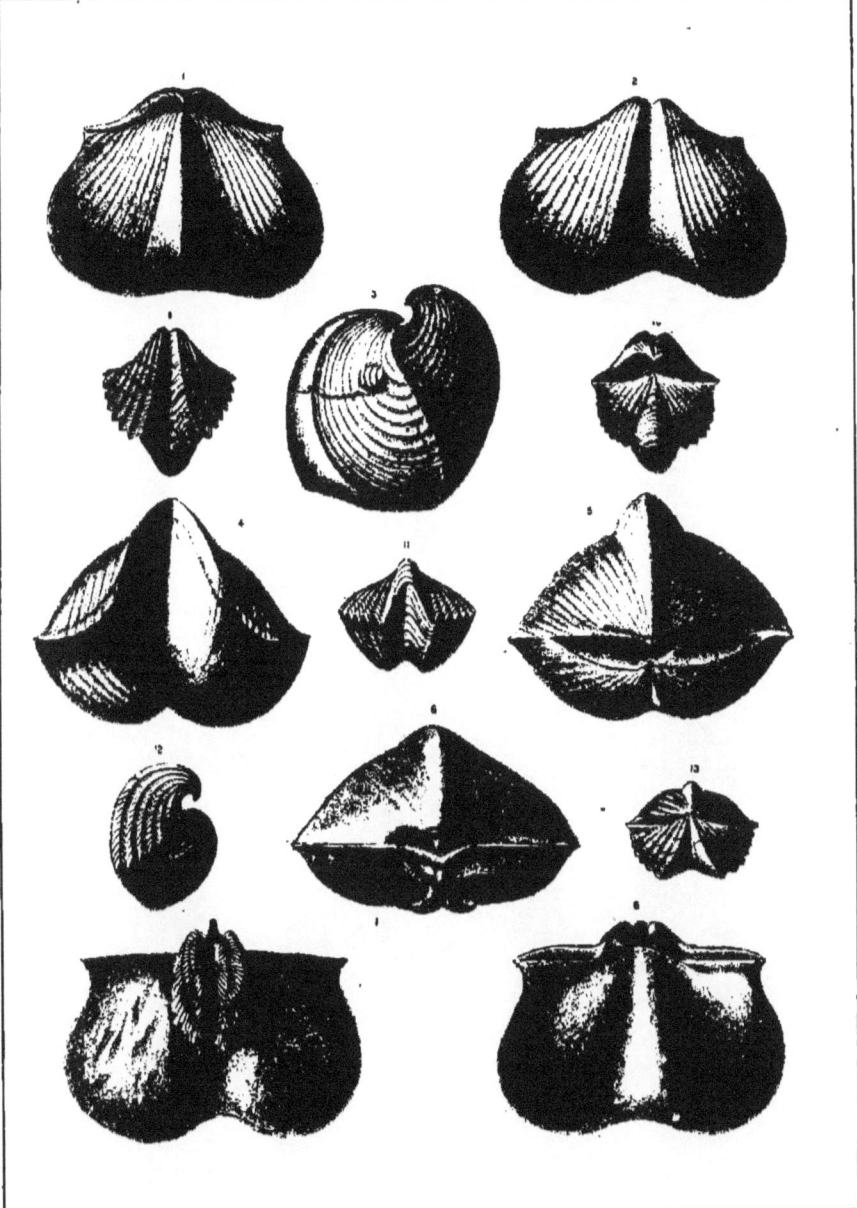

DEL.AND LITH. BY CHAS. STARCK. LOUISVILLE LITH. CO.

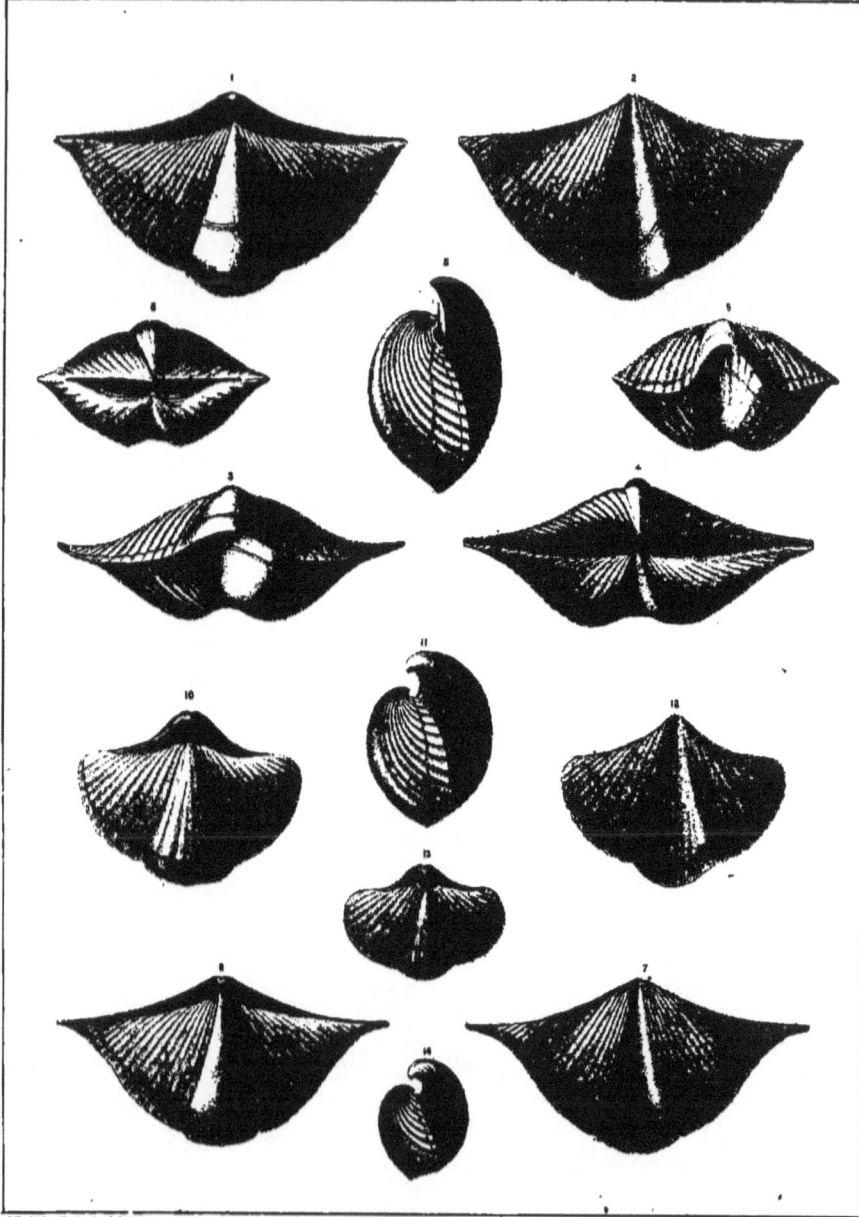

PLATE IX.

Spirifera atwaterana.

Fig. 1-5. Dorsal, ventral, front, cardinal and profile view of a specimen.

Page 107

Fig. 6, 7. Dorsal and ventral view of a smaller specimen.

Spirifera grieri.

Fig. 8-12. Cardinal, front, dorsal, profile and ventral view of a specimen.

Page 120

Fig. 13, 14. Dorsal and profile view of a small specimen.

PLATE X.

Spirifera byrnesi.

Fig. 1-5. Dorsal, ventral, front, cardinal and profile view of a specimen. Page 109

Fig. 31-34, 36-39. A series of specimens, showing variety in form and
ornamentation.

Spirifera gregaria.

Fig. 6-10. Dorsal, ventral, front, cardinal and profile view of a specimen. Page 119

Spirifera varicosa.

Fig. 11-20, 23-25. A series of specimens showing variety in size, form
and ornamentation. Page 134

Spirifera hobbsi.

Fig. 21, 22. Dorsal and ventral view of a specimen. Page 121

Fig. 26-30. Dorsal, ventral, front, cardinal and lateral view of specimen.

Fig. 35, 40. Dorsal and ventral view of a specimen, showing extreme
extension of hinge-line.

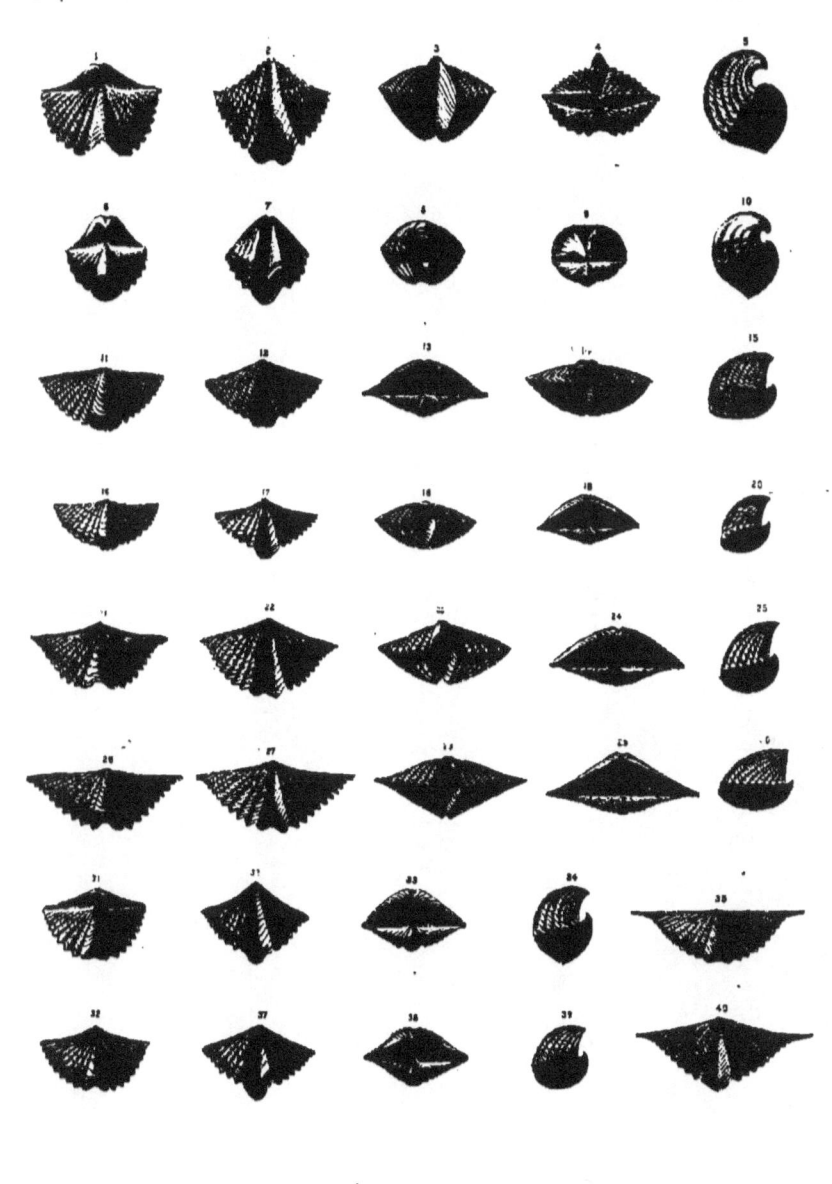

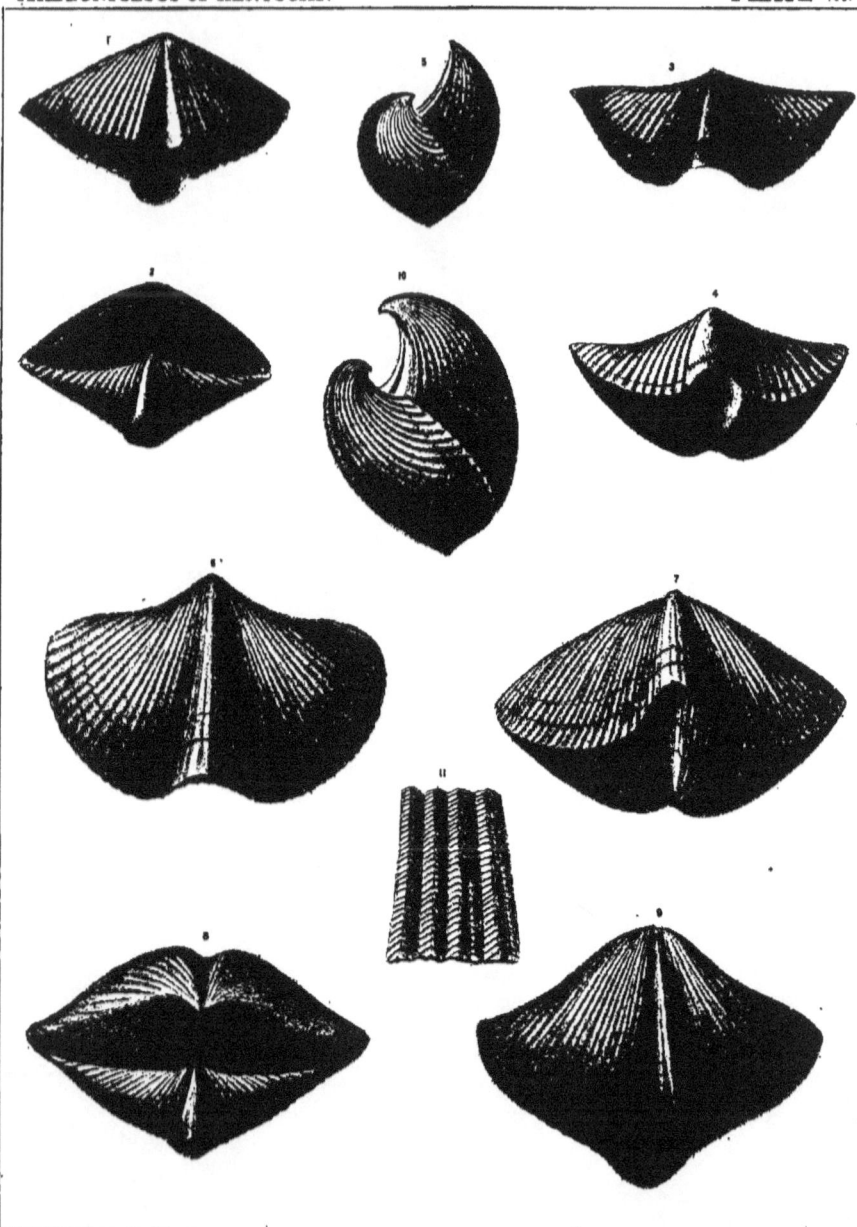

PLATE XI.

Spirifera mcconathii.

Fig. 1-5. Ventral, cardinal, dorsal, front and profile view of a specimen.   Page 123

Spirifera divaricata.

Fig. 6-10. Dorsal, front, cardinal, ventral and profile view of a specimen.   Page 113

Fig. 11. An enlargement of a portion of the test of a specimen.

PLATE XII.

Spirifera davisi.

Fig. 1-4. Dorsal, front, ventral and profile view of a specimen.   Page 112

Spirifera divaricata.

Fig. 5-11. A series of specimens showing variations in form and size. Page 113

Spirifera duodenaria.

Fig. 12, 13, 16. Ventral, dorsal and profile view of a specimen.   Page 114

Spirifera arctisegmenta.

Fig. 14, 15. Ventral and dorsal view of a specimen.   Page 108

PLATE XIII.

Rhynchonella tethys.

Fig. 25-33. A series of specimens showing variations in size and number of plications.   Page 83

Spirifera segmenta.

Fig. 36-38. Dorsal, ventral and profile view of specimen.   Page 132

Rynchonella carolina.

Fig. 1-3, 34, 35. A series of specimens showing variations in size.   Page 75

Cyrtina hamiltoniae.

Fig. 4-12. A series of specimens showing variations in size and ornamentation.   Page 96

Cyrtina hamiltoniae, var. recta.

Fig. 13. View of a small dorsal valve.   Page 97
Fig. 14. Ventral view of a specimen.
Fig. 15. Profile view of a specimen.
Fig. 16. View of a larger dorsal valve.

Pentamerella arata.

Fig. 17-20. Dorsal, ventral, front and profile view of a specimen.   Page 49

Cyrtina crassa.

Fig. 21-24. Ventral, cardinal, profile and dorsal view of a specimen.   Page 95

PLATE XIV.

Atrypa aspera.

Fig. 1-5, 7-11. A series of specimens showing variations in form and
    size.   Page 88
Fig. 6. Interior of a ventral valve.

Atrypa reticularis.

Fig. 12-17, 19. A series of specimens showing variations in form and
    size.   Page 91
Fig. 18. Dorsal view of a specimen, broken so as to show spiral cones.
Fig. 20. Ventral view of a specimen, broken so as to show spiral cones.
Fig. 21. Side view of a specimen, broken so as to show spiral cones.
Fig. 22. View of a single spiral cone.
Fig. 23. View of interior of a ventral valve.

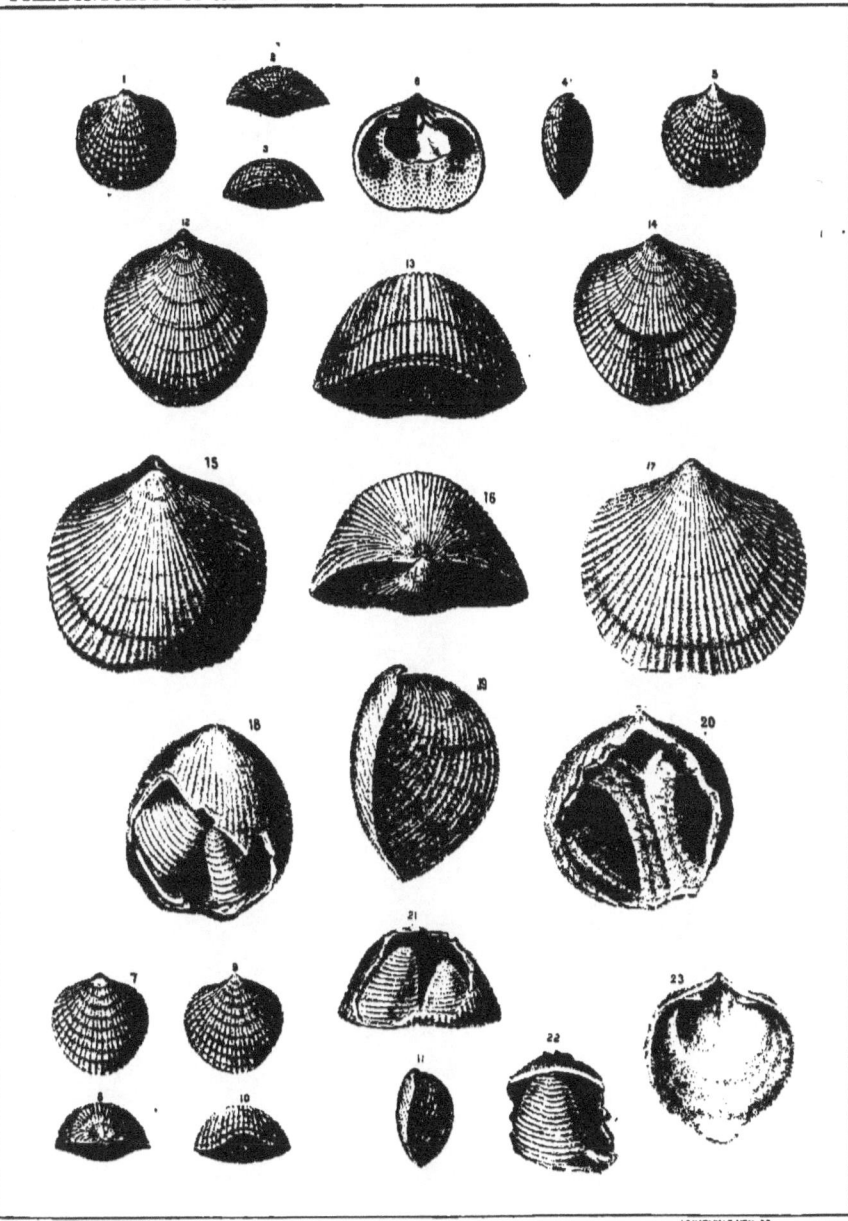

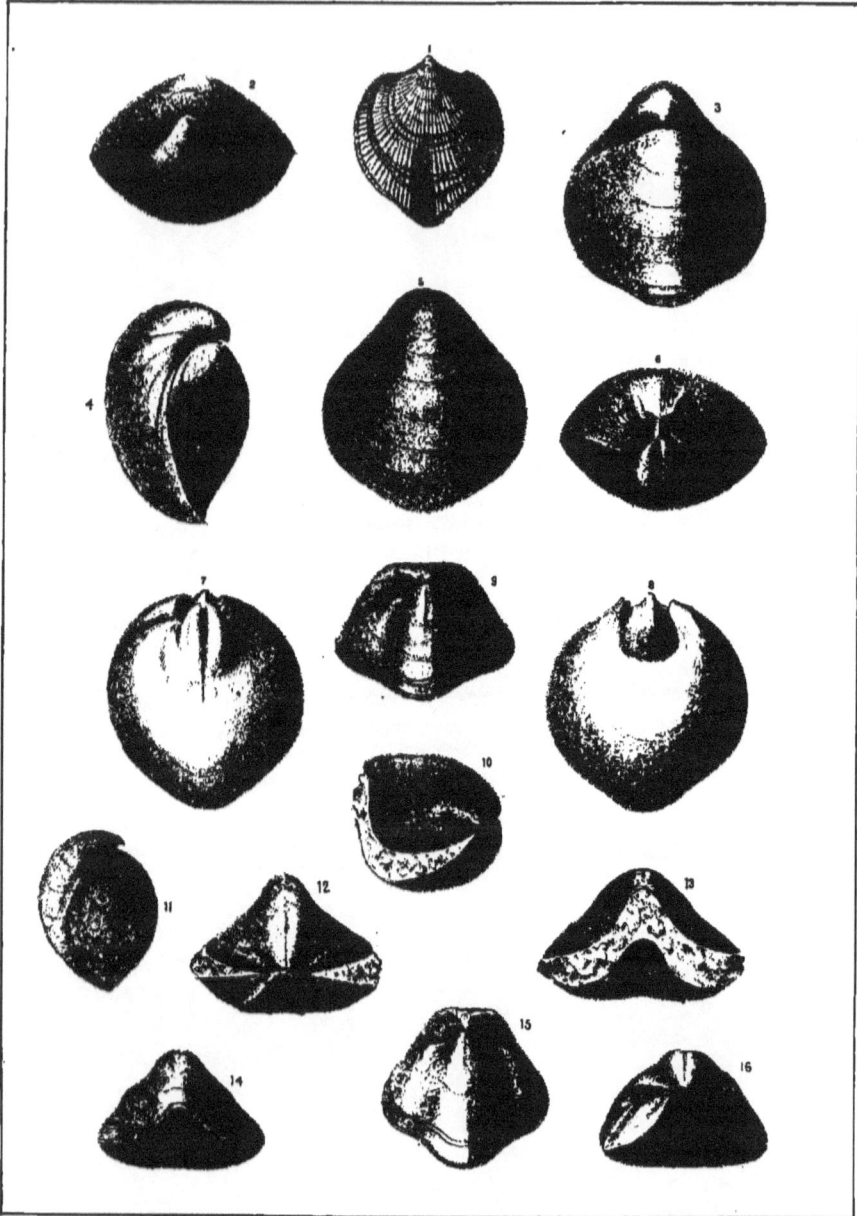

PLATE XV.

Atrypa reticularis.

Fig. 1. Ventral view of a very rugose specimen.   Page 91

Meristella nasuta.

Fig. 2-5. Cardinal, dorsal, profile and ventral view of specimen.   Page 98
Fig. 6-8. Cardinal, ventral and dorsal view of an interior cast.

Meristella unisulcata.

Fig. 9-16. A series of specimens showing variations in size and form.   Page 99

PLATE XVI.

Orthis propinqua.

Fig. 1-3, 7-11. A series of specimens showing variations in size.   Page 43

Orthis vanuxemi.

Fig. 4-6, 12, 12a-14. A series of specimens showing variation in size.   Page 45

Trematospira hirsuta.

Fig. 15-19. Profile, dorsal, ventral, front and cardinal view of specimen.   Page 136

Terebratula roemingeri.

Fig. 20-22. Profile, ventral and dorsal view of a specimen.   Page 155

Orthis livia.

Fig. 23, 24. Dorsal and ventral view of a specimen.   Page 40

Athyris vittata.

Fig. 25-29, 31, 32. A series of specimens showing variations in size
and ornamentation.   Page 87
Fig. 30. Ventral valve broken to show position of spiral cones.

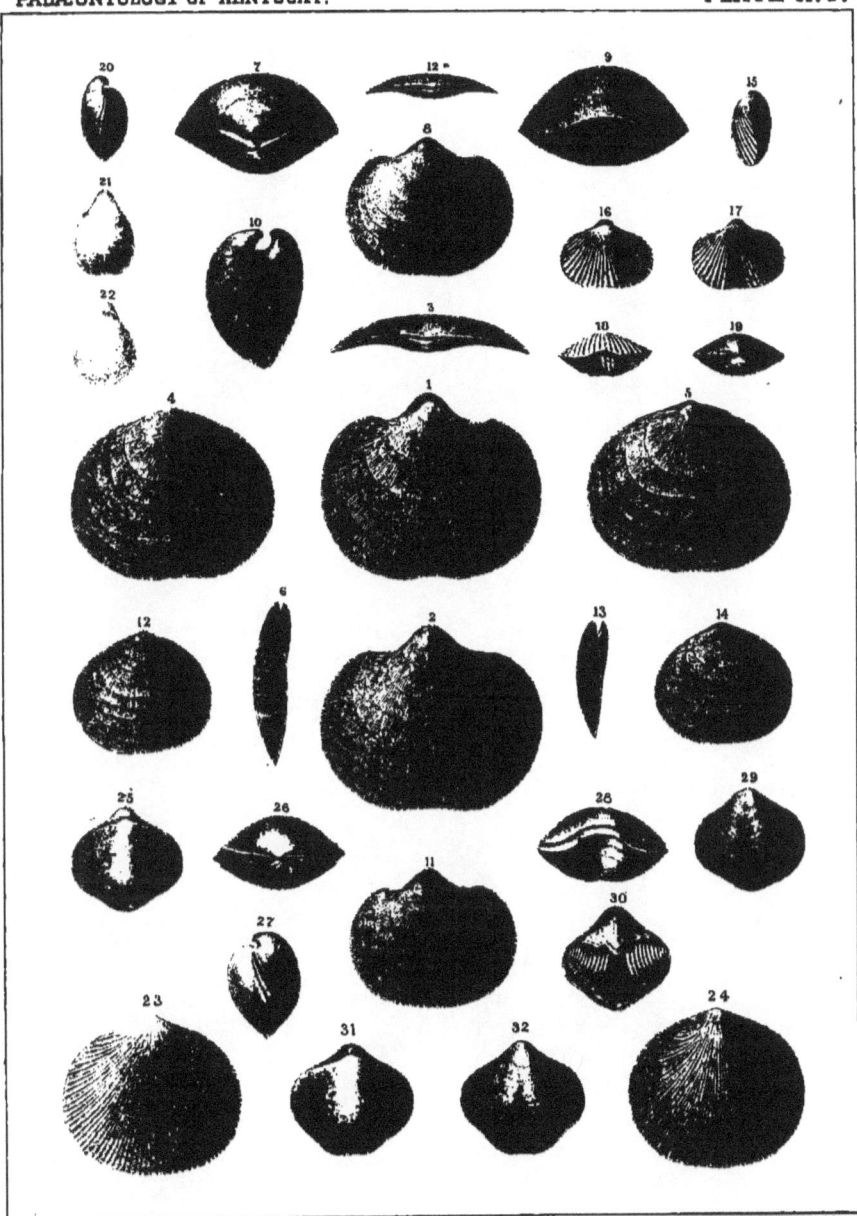

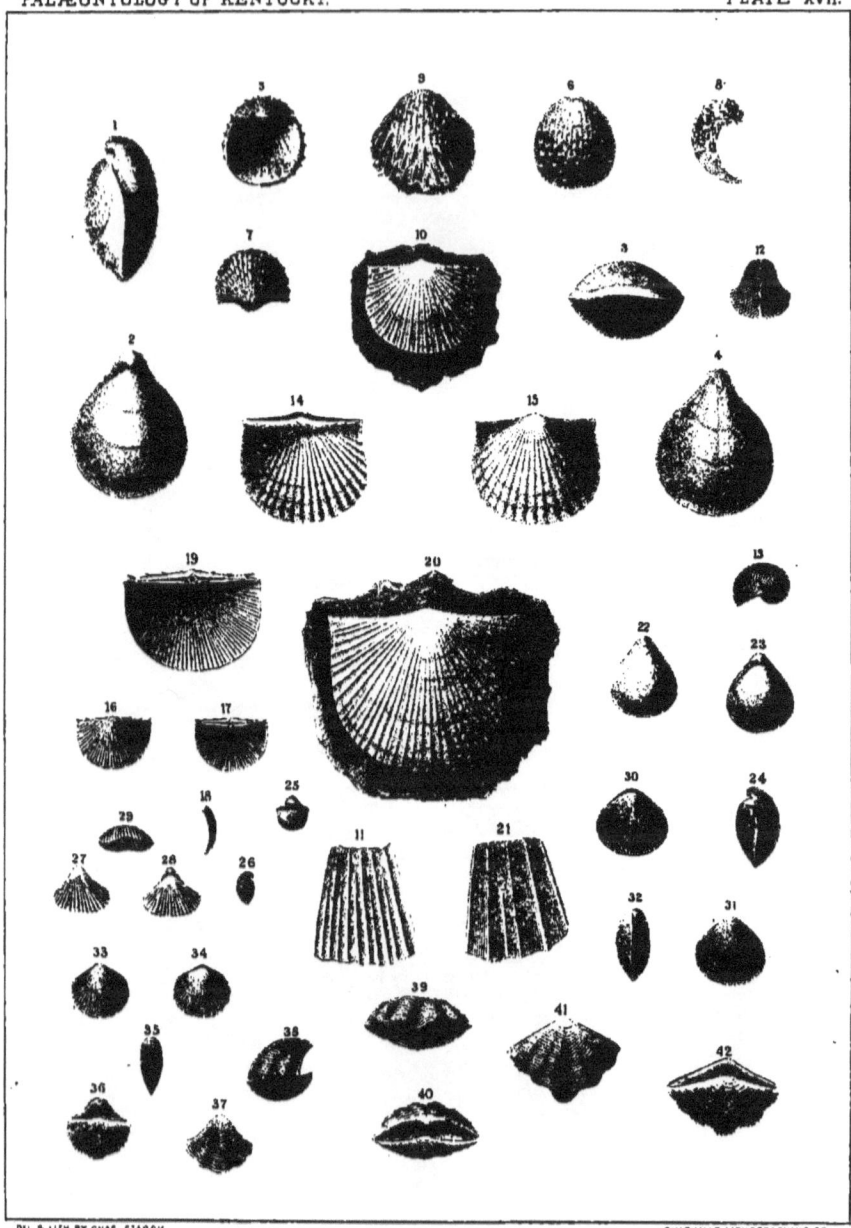

PLATE XVII.

Terebratula harmonia.

Fig. 1-4. Profile, dorsal, front and ventral view of a specimen.　　　　Page 154

Productella subaculeata, var. cataracta.

Fig. 5-8. Dorsal, ventral and front and transverse view of a specimen.　　　　Page 69

Fig. 9. Ventral view of a specimen, showing almost perfect spines.

Strophodonta inequistriata.

Fig. 10. Ventral valve of a specimen.　　　　Page 145

Fig. 11. An enlargement of a portion of the surface, showing intercalated striae.

Bellerophon leda.

Fig. 12. 13. Profile and side view of a specimen.　　　　Page 158

Tropidoleptus carinatus.

Fig. 14, 15. Dorsal and ventral view of a specimen.　　　　Page 46

Chonetes yandelliana.

Fig. 16-18. Ventral and dorsal view and transverse section of specimen.　　　　Page 68

Fig. 19. Dorsal view of a larger specimen.

Strophodonta profunda.

Fig. 20. Ventral valve of a specimen.　　　　Page 148

Fig. 21. An enlargement of a portion of the surface showing radiating striae.

Terebratula lincklaeni.

Fig. 22-24. Ventral, dorsal and profile views of a specimen.   Page 155

Ambocoelia umbonata.

Fig. 25, 26. Dorsal and profile view of a specimen.   Page 86

Rhynchonella tenuistriata.

Fig. 27, 28, 29. Ventral, dorsal and front view of a specimen.   Page 82

Orthis goodwini.

Fig. 30-32. Dorsal, ventral and profile view of a specimen.   Page 39

Orthis livia.

Fig. 33-35. Ventral, dorsal and profile view of a specimen.   Page 40

Spirifera crispa, var. simplex.

Fig. 36, 37. Dorsal and ventral view of a specimen.   Page 111

Spirifera raricosta.

Fig. 38-42. Profile, front, cardinal, ventral and dorsal view of a specimen.   Page 128

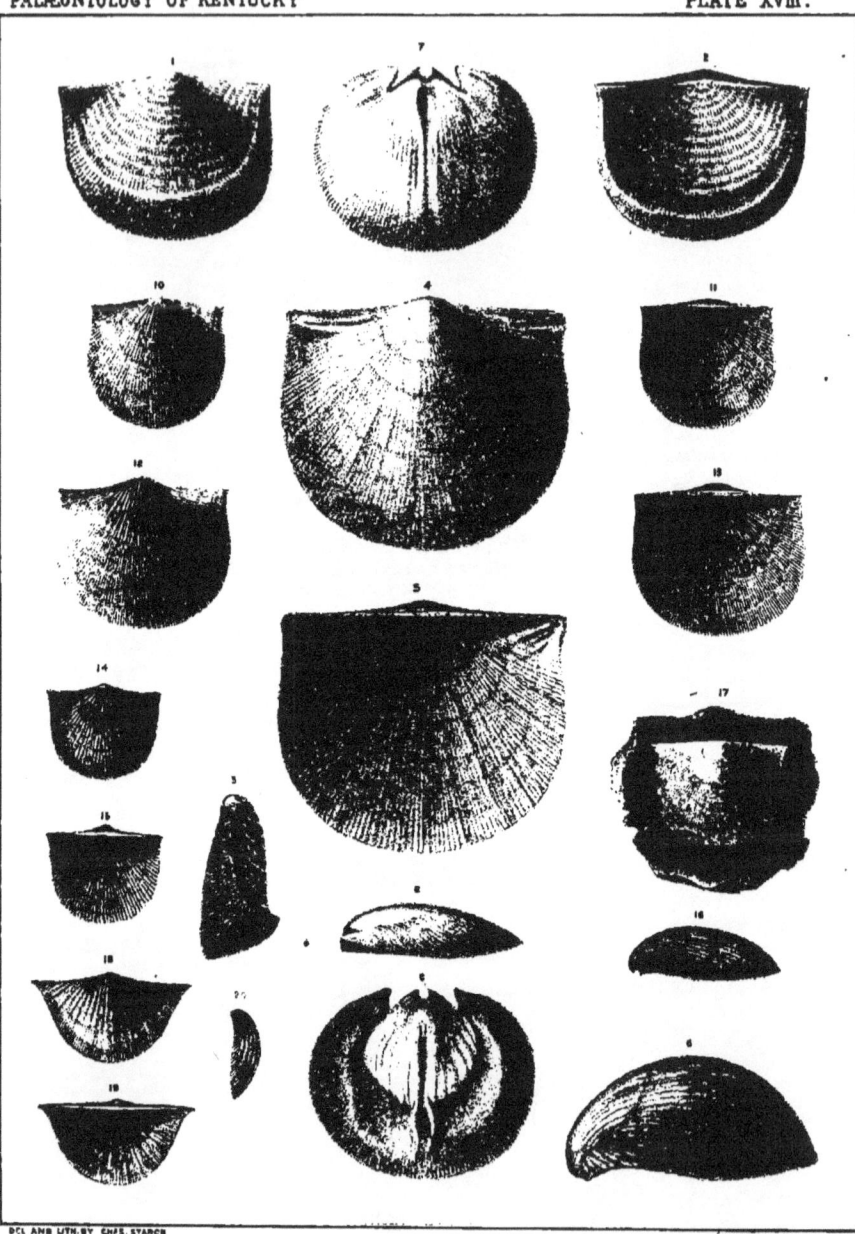

PLATE XVIII.

Strophomena rhomboidalis.

Fig. 1-3. Ventral, dorsal and profile view of a specimen.   Page 150

Strophodonta hemispherica.

Fig. 4-6. Ventral, dorsal and lateral view of specimen.   Page 144
Fig. 7-9. Dorsal, ventral and lateral view of an internal cast.

Strophodonta demissa.

Fig. 10-15. A series of specimen showing variations in size.   Page 143
Fig. 16. Lateral view of a specimen.

Strophodonta perplana.

Fig. 17. Ventral view of a specimen.   Page 147

Chonetes acutiradiata.

Fig. 18-20. Ventral, dorsal and profile view of a specimen.   Page 66

PLATE XIX.

Turbo shumardi.

Fig. 1. Apertural view of a specimen.   Page 191
Fig. 2. Dorsal view of a specimen.
Fig. 3. Vertical view of a specimen.
Fig. 4. Vertical view of a larger specimen.

Platyostoma lineata.

Fig. 5. Vertical view of a specimen.   Page 183
Fig. 6. An enlargement of a portion of the test.
Fig. 7. Apertural view of a specimen.
Fig. 8. Dorsal view of a specimen.

PLATE XX

Polyphemopsis louisvillae.

Fig. 16-19. A series of specimen showing variations in size.   Page 180

Macrocheilus carinatus.

Fig. 20-23. A series of specimen showing variations in size.   Page 180

Trochonema rectilatera.

Fig. 1, 2. Apertural and dorsal view of a specimen.   Page 189

Trochonema yandellana.

Fig. 3. Apertural view of a specimen.   Page 190

Callonema bellatula.

Fig. 4-7. A series of specimen showing variations in size and ornamentation.   Page 175

Loxonema hydraulicum.

Fig. 8, 9. View of three specimen enclosed in matrix.   Page 178

Cyclonema cancellata.

Fig. 10, 11. Dorsal and apertural view of a specimen.   Page 187

Callonema imitator.

Fig. 12, 13. Vertical and apertural view of a specimen.   Page 176

Goniatites discoideus.

Fig. 14, 15. Basal and profile view of a specimen.   Page 194

PLATE XXI.

Euomphalus decewi.

Fig. 1, 2. Profile and upper surface view of a specimen.　　　Page 181

Euomphalus sampsoni.

Fig. 3, 4. Profile and lateral view of a specimen. ·　　　Page 182

Platyostoma turbinata.

Fig. 5, 6. Dorsal and vertical view of a specimen.　　　Page 184

Platyostoma lineata.

Fig. 7, 8. Vertical and dorsal view of a specimen.　　　Page 183

Pleurotomaria procteri.

Fig. 9, 10. Dorsal and vertical view of a specimen.　　　Page 173
Fig. 13. Dorsal view of a small specimen.

Pleurotomaria sulcomarginata. ·

Fig. 11, 12. Vertical and dorsal view of a specimen.　　　Page 174

Platyostoma lineata, var. callosa.

Fig. 14. Lateral view of a specimen.   Page 184

Gomphoceras turbiniforme.

Fig. 15, 16. View of two specimens showing variation in size.   Page 194

Gomphoceras oviforme.

Fig. 17. Side view of a specimen.   Page 193
Fig. 18. View of the aperture of a specimen.

PLATE XXII.

Turbo shumardi.

Fig. 1. Dorsal view of an internal cast of a specimen.   Page 191
Fig. 2. Dorsal view of a perfect specimen, very large.

Bucania devonica.

Fig. 3, 4. Vertical and front view of a specimen.   Page 160

Cyclonema multilira.

Fig. 5. View of a gutta percha cast.   Page 188

Strophostylus varians.

Fig. 6, 7. Dorsal and vertical view of a specimen.   Page 186

Loxonema laeviusculum.

Fig. 8. View of a somewhat distorted specimen.   Page 178
Fig. 9. View of a more perfect specimen.

Platyostoma lineata var. callosa.

Fig. 10, 11. Side and summit view of a specimen.   Page 184

DEL. & LITH. BY CHAS. STARCK.

LOUISVILLE LITHOGRAPHING CO.

PLATE XXIII.

Platyceras dumosum.

Fig. 1-4. A series of specimen showing variations in size, distribu-
tion and condition of spines.   Page 162
Fig. 5, 6. View of two specimen exfoliated, and showing spine bases.
Fig. 12. Vertical view of a young specimen.

Platyceras dumosum, var. rarispinum.

Fig. 7, 8. Dorsal and lateral view of a specimen.   Page 163

Platyceras bucculentum.

Fig. 9, 11. Lateral view of two specimen, showing variation in size.   Page 160

Platyceras symmetricum.

Fig. 10. Lateral view of a specimen.   Page 167

PLATE XXIV.

Nautilus maximus.

Fig. 1. Side view of a specimen.   Page 196

Callonema clarki.

Fig. 2. Summit view of a specimen.   Page 175
Fig. 3. Side view of a specimen.
Fig. 4. Apertural view of a specimen.
Fig. 5. Side view of a smaller specimen.

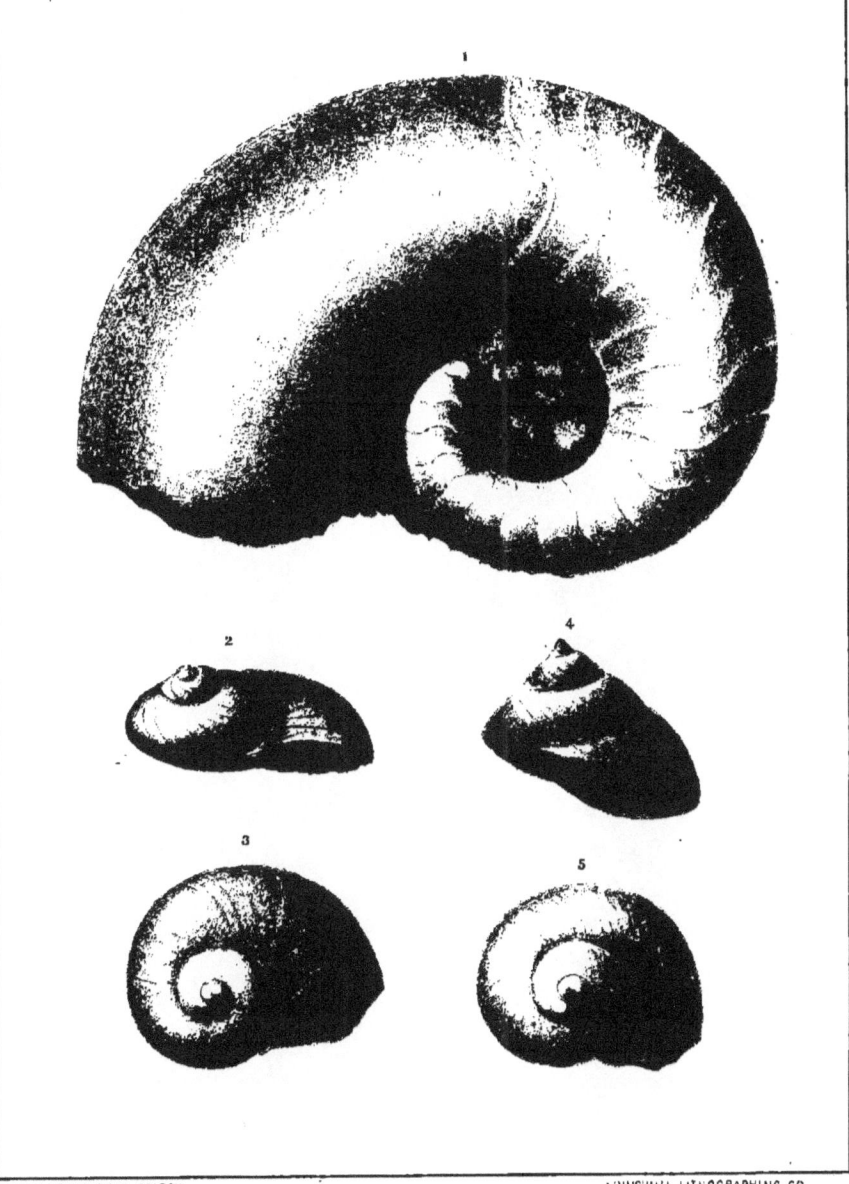

PLATE XXV.

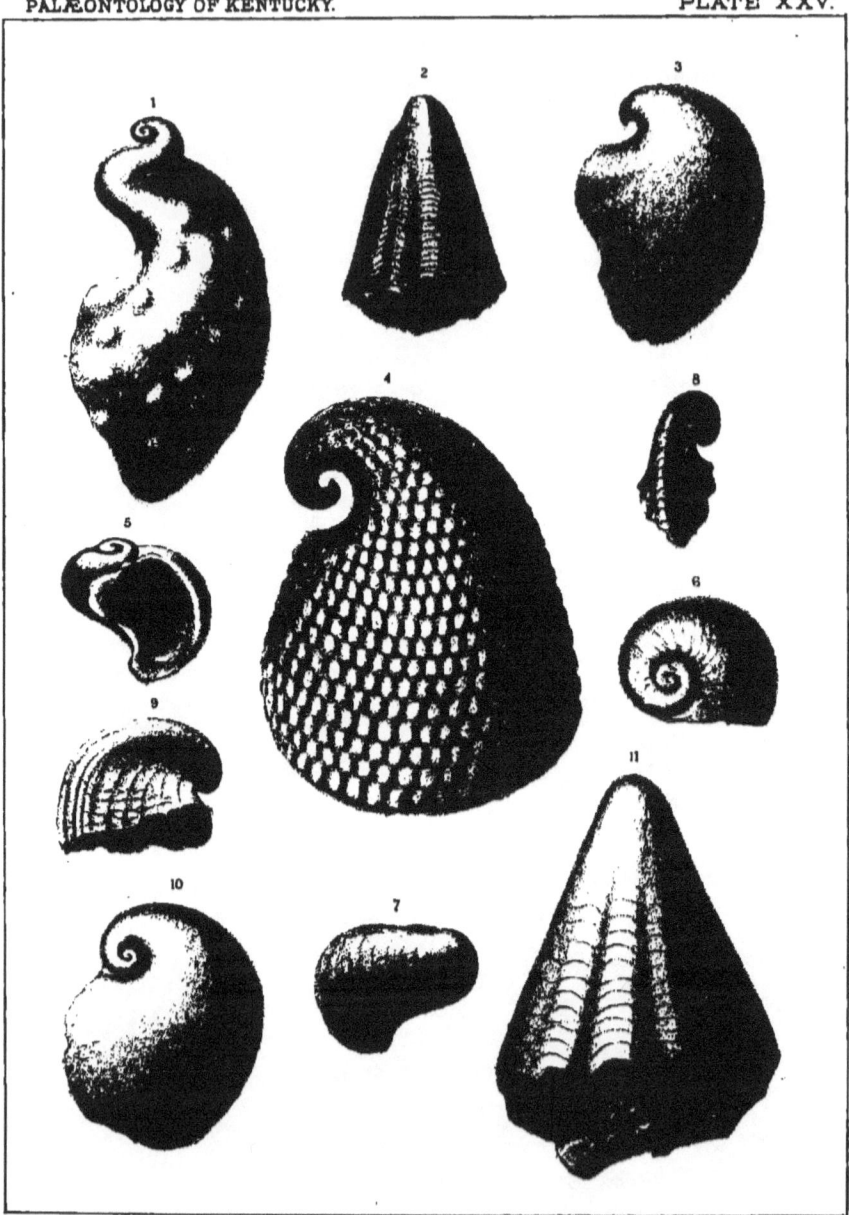

PLATE XXV.

Platyceras milleri.

Fig. 1. Anterior view of a specimen.   Page 165

Platyceras conicum.

Fig. 2, 11. Dorsal view of two specimen, showing variation in size. Page 161

Platyceras bucculentum.

Fig. 3. Anterior view of a specimen.   Page 160

Platyceras multispinosum.

Fig. 4. View of a cast of a very large specimen.   Page 166

Platyostoma lineata, var. callosa.

Fig. 5-7. Apertural, side and dorsal view of a specimen.   Page 184

Platyceras compressum.

Fig. 8, 9. Dorsal and posterior view of a specimen.   Page 162

Platyceras ventricosum.

Fig. 6. Anterior view of a specimen.   Page 168

PLATE XXVI.

Lingula triangulata.

Fig. 1. Ventral view of a specimen.   Page 34

Spirifera medialis.

Fig. 2-5. Cardinal, ventral, dorsal and profile view of a specimen.   Page 125

Rhynchonella acinus.

Fig. 6, 13, 14. Dorsal, profile and front view of a specimen.   Page 73

Productella semiglobosa.

Fig. 7. Ventral view of a specimen.   Page 70

Murchisonia desiderata.

Fig. 8. View of an internal cast of a specimen, which is entirely covered by an incrusting coral, studded with somewhat irregularly distributed tubercles.   Page 169

Bucania devonica.

Fig. 9. View of an internal cast.   Page 160

Modiomorpha alta.

Fig. 10. Left view of a specimen.   Page 217

Pleurotomaria casii.

Fig. 11. Dorsal view of a specimen.   Page 171

Pleurotomaria arabella.

Fig. 12. Apertural view of an internal cast retaining a small portion of the test.   Page 171

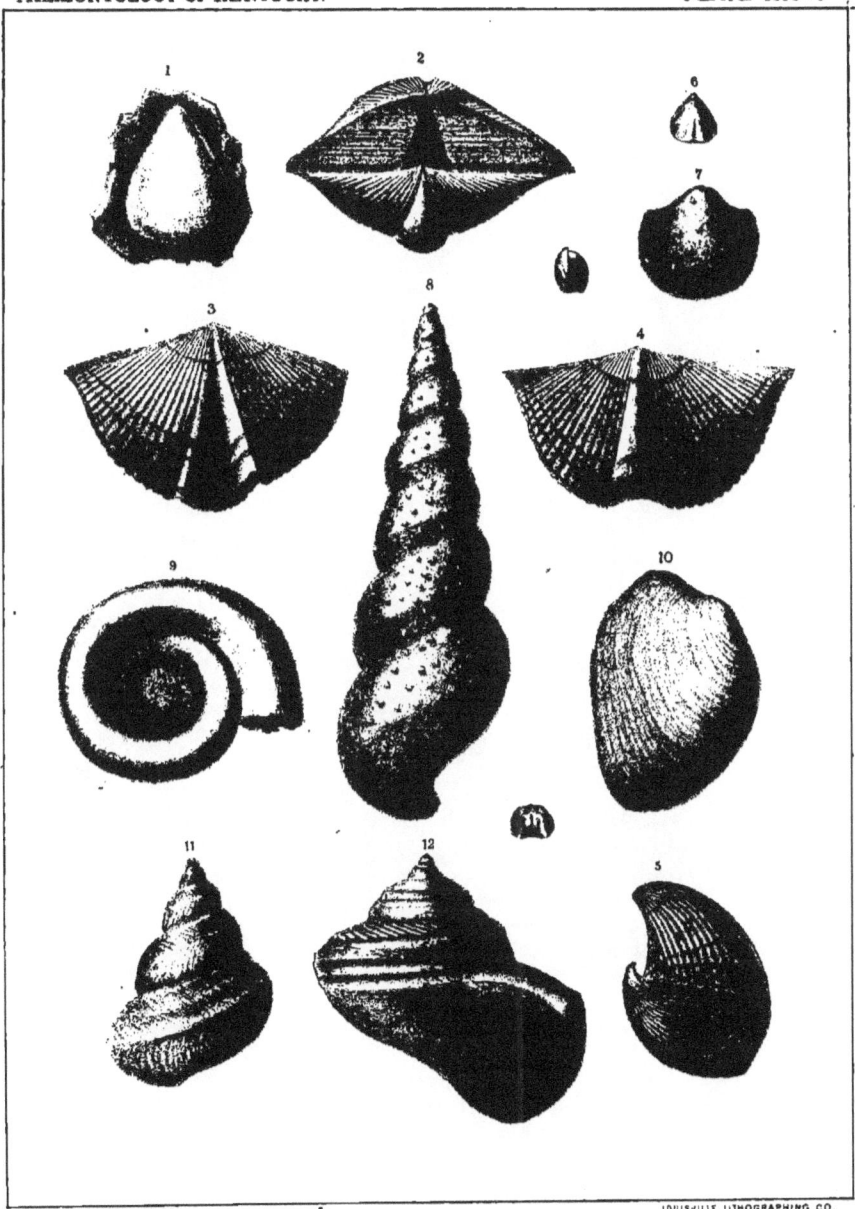

DEL & LITH. BY CHAS. STARCK.　LOUISVILLE LITHOGRAPHING CO.

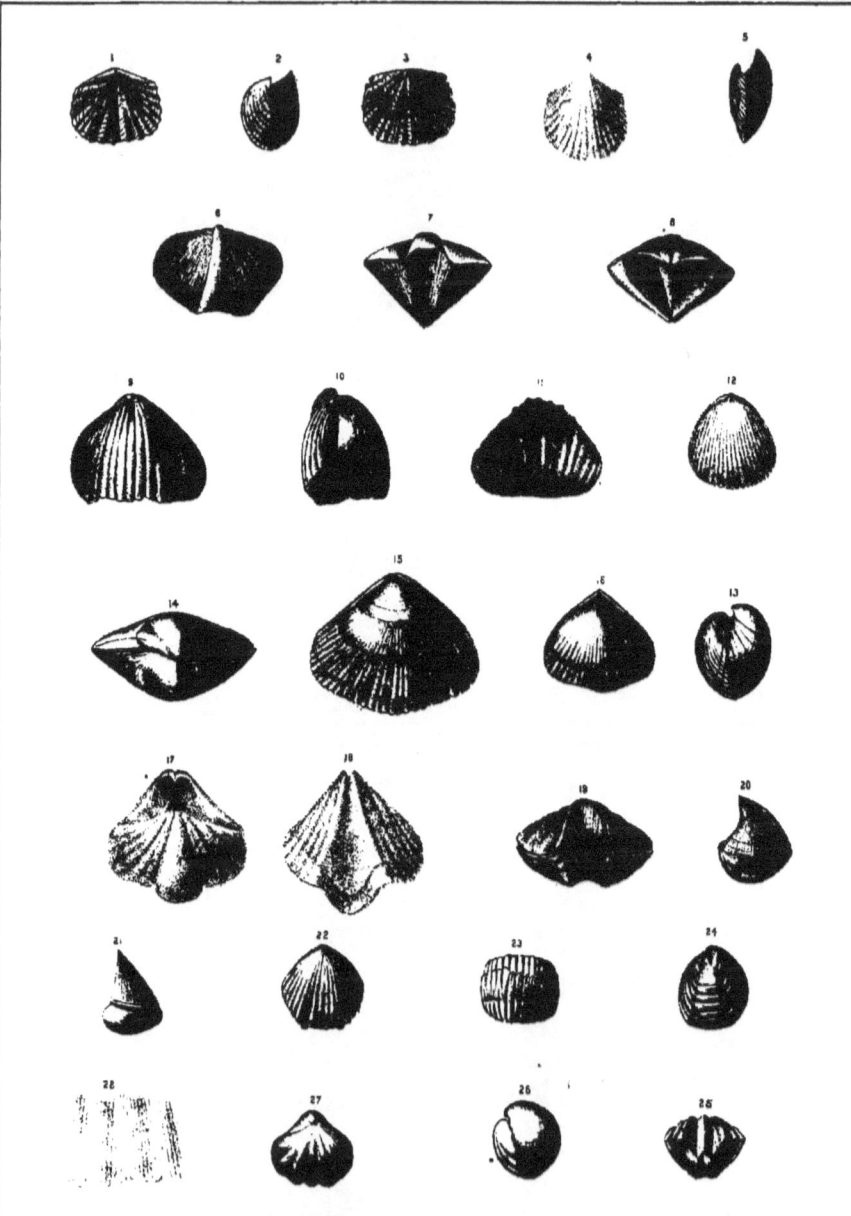

PLATE XXVII.

Orthis rugaeplicata.

Fig. 1-3. Dorsai, profile and ventral view of a specimen.   Page 44

Orthis nisis.

Fig. 4, 5. Ventral and profile view of a specimen.   Page 42

Cyrtia exporrecta.

Fig. 6, 7, 8, 20. Dorsal, front, cardinal and profile view of specimen. Page 93

Rhynchonella stricklandi.

Fig. 9-11. Dorsal, profile and ventral view of a specimen.   Page 81

Pentamerus littoni.

Fig. 12, 13. Dorsal and profile view of a specimen.   Page 58

Pentamerus complanatus.

Fig. 14. Cardinal view of a specimen.   Page 53
Fig. 15, 16. Dorsal view of two specimen, showing variations in size.

Spirifera rostellum.

Fig. 17-19. Dorsal, ventral and front view of a specimen.   Page 129

Cyrtia exporrecta, var. arrecta.

Fig. 21. Profile view of a specimen.   Page 94

Rhynchonella saffordi.

Fig. 22-24. Dorsal, front and profile view of a specimen.   Page 79

Pentamerus nucleus.

Fig. 25-27. Front, profile and dorsal view of a specimen.   Page 59
Fig. 28. An enlargement of a portion of surface of test.

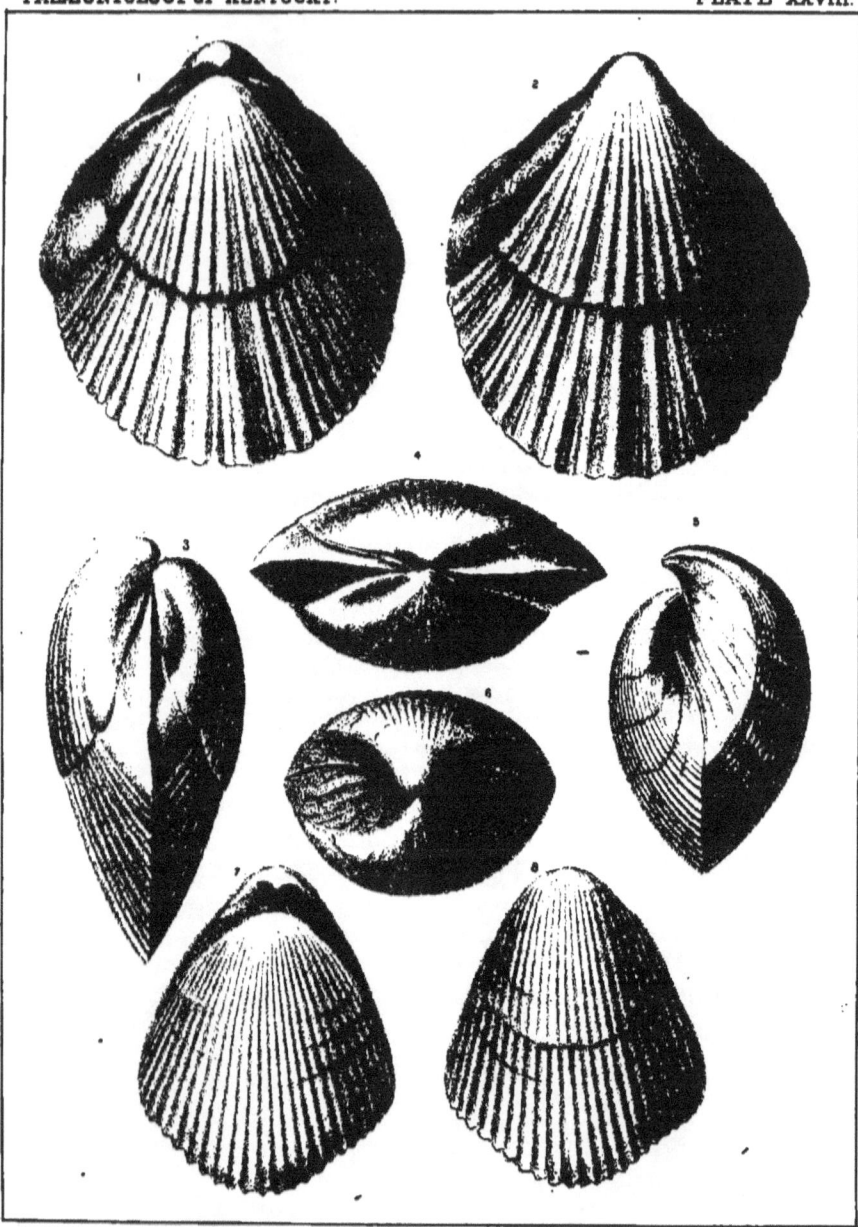

PLATE XXVIII.

Pentamerus knappi.

Fig. 1–4. Dorsal, ventral, profile and cardinal view of a specimen.   Page 55

Pentamerus nysius, var. crassicostus.

Fig. 5–8. Profile, cardinal, dorsal and ventral view of a specimen.   Page 60

PLATE XXIX.

Pentamerus knighti.

Fig. 1, 2. Dorsal and profile view of a specimen.   Page 57
Fig. 17. Profile view of an unusually large specimen.

Rhynchonella stricklandi.

Fig. 3-6. Dorsal, cardinal, profile and front view of a specimen.   Page 81

Meristina maria.

Fig. 7-10. Dorsal, ventral, profile and front view of a specimen.   Page 101

Streptorhynchus subplanus.

Fig. 11, 12. Profile and ventral view of a specimen.   Page 141

Spirifera radiata.

Fig. 13-16. Dorsal, ventral, profile and cardinal view of a specimen. Page 130

Orthis biforata.

Fig. 18-22. Ventral, profile, dorsal, front and cardinal view of a
  specimen   Page 35

Pentamerus pergibbosus.

Fig. 23, 24. Profile and dorsal view of a specimen.   Page 62

Spirifera rostellum.

Fig. 25. Dorsal view of a specimen.   Page 129

Strophodonta profunda.

Fig. 26. Ventral view of a specimen.   Page 148

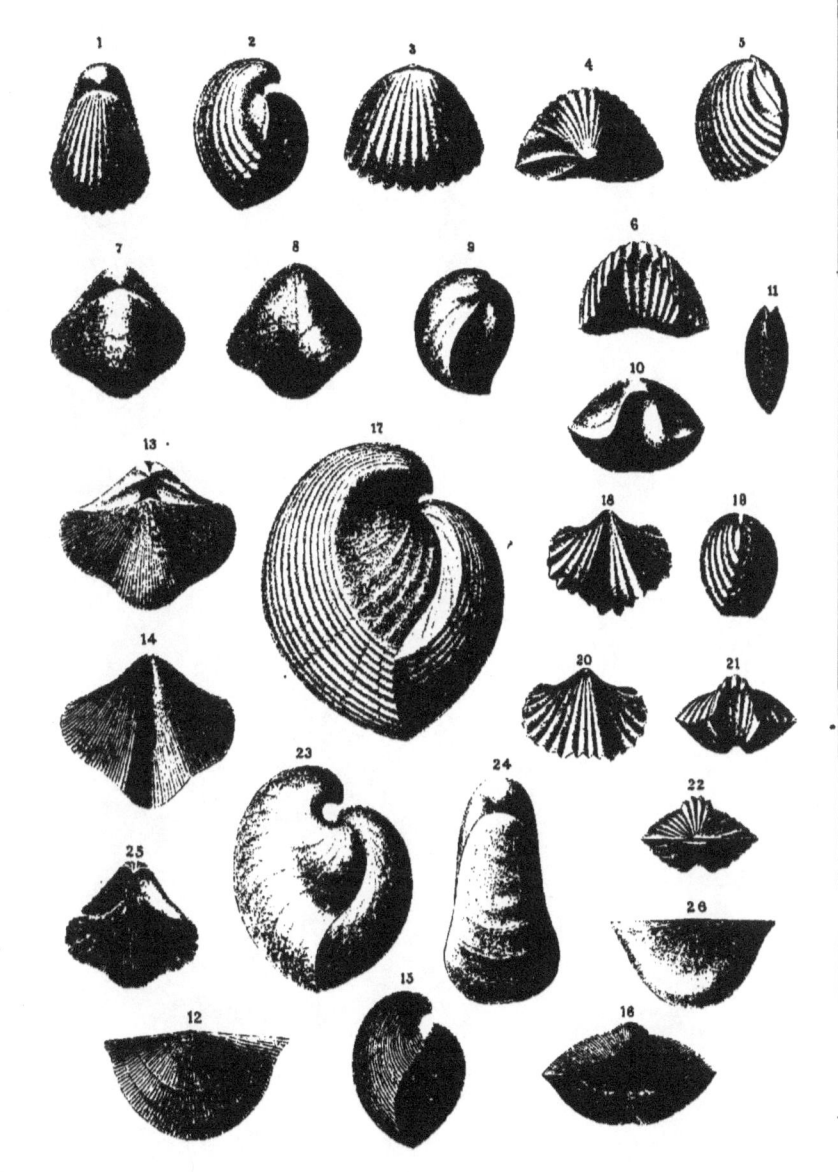

DEL.& LITH. BY CHAS. STARCK.　　　　　　　　　　　LOUISVILLE LITHOGRAPHING CO.

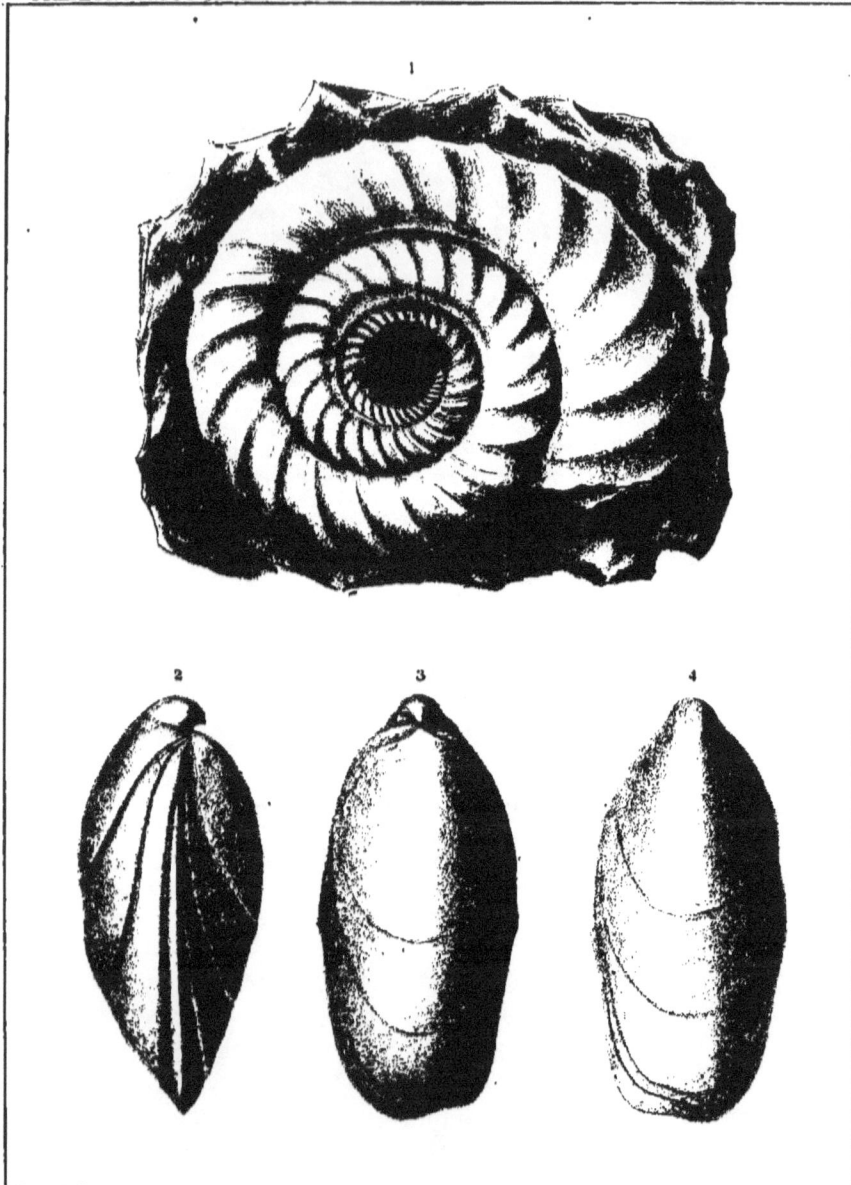

PLATE XXX.

Lituites marshi.

Fig. 1. Anterior view of a specimen.　　　　　　　　　　Page 195

Pentamerus oblongus, var. cylindricus

Fig. 2-4. Profile, dorsal and ventral view of a specimen.　　　Page 61

PLATE XXXI.

Rhynchonella louisvillensis.

Fig. 1–4. Dorsal, ventral, front and profile view of a specimen.   Page 77

Murchisonia petilla.

Fig. 5. View of an internal cast.   Page 170

Rhynchonella gainesi.

Fig. 6, 7. Dorsal view of two specimens.   Page 76
Fig. 8, 9. Front and ventral view of a specimen.

Spirifera mucronata.

Fig. 10, 11. Ventral and dorsal view of a specimen.   Page 126

Tentaculites scalariformis.

Fig. 12. View of a specimen, enlarged xi.   Page 156

Spirifera sculptilis.

Fig. 13. Ventral view of a valve.   Page 132

Centronella glans-fagea.

Fig. 14–17. Front, profile, dorsal and ventral view of a specimen.   153

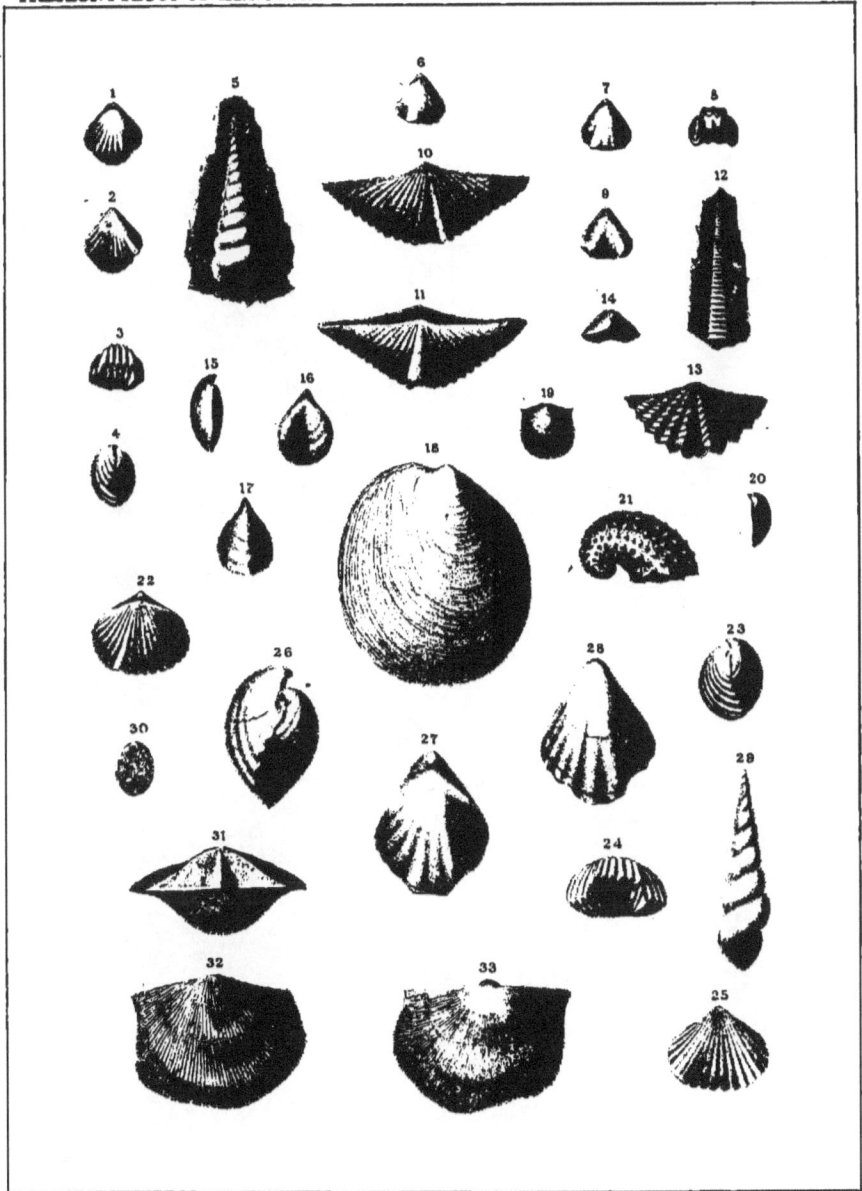

Paracyclas octerlonii.

Fig. 18. Left view of a specimen.   Page 212

Chonetes yandelliana.

Fig. 19, 20. Ventral and profile view of a specimen.   Page 68
Fig. 30. Transverse section of a specimen.

Platyceras echinatum.

Fig. 21. Side view of a specimen.   Page 164

Rhynchonella tethys.

Fig. 22–25. Dorsal, profile, front and ventral view of a specimen.   Page 83

Pentamerella thusnelda.

Fig. 26–28. Profile, dorsal and ventral view of a specimen.   Page 51

Loxonema hamiltoniae.

Fig. 29. View of a rather perfect specimen.   Page 177

Streptorhynchus arctostriata.

Fig. 31–33. Cardinal, ventral and dorsal view of a specimen.   Page 140

PLATE XXXII.

Nucleospira concinna.

Fig. 1–4. Dorsal, ventral, front and profile view of a specimen.　　　Page 103

Atrypa reticularis, var. niagarensis.

Fig. 5–8. Profile, dorsal, front and ventral view of a specimen.　　　Page 92
Fig. 44–47. Dorsal, ventral, profile and front view of a specimen, show-
　　ing variation in size.

Pentamerus knotti.

Fig. 9–12. Dorsal, profile, ventral and front view of specimen.　　　Page 5

Rhynchonella acinus.

Fig. 13–16. Dorsal, ventral, profile and front view of a specimen.　　　Page 73

Anastrophia internascens.

Fig. 17–20. Dorsal, ventral, front and profile view of a specimen.　　　Page 47

Leptocoelia hemispherica.

Fig. 21–23. Dorsal, ventral and profile view of a specimen.　　　Page 152
Fig. 36–39. Profile, front, ventral and dorsal view of a larger speci-
　　men.

Rhynchonella pisa.

Fig. 24–27. Profile, dorsal, ventral and front view of a specimen.　　　Page 78

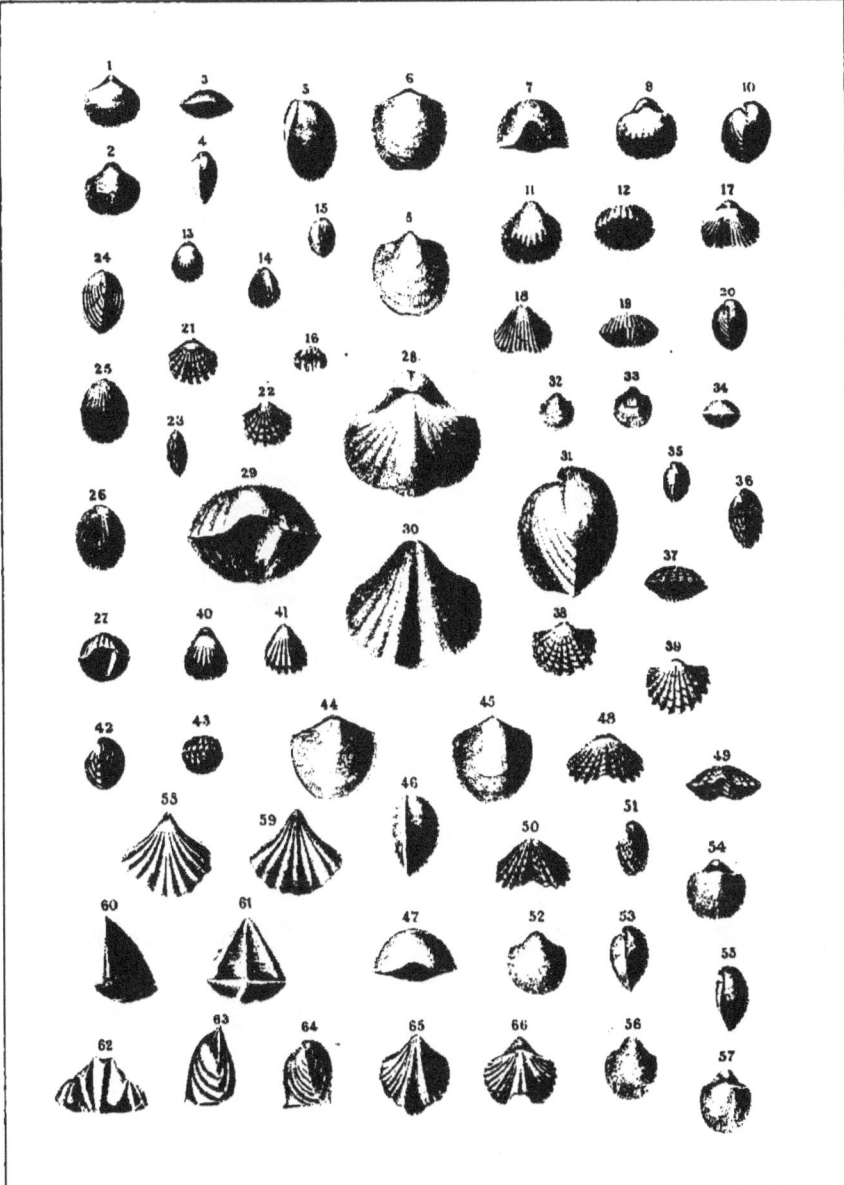

Spirifera foggi.

Fig. 28–31. Dorsal, front, ventral and profile view of a specimen.   Page 117

Orthis hybrida.

Fig. 32–35. Dorsal, ventral, front and profile view of a specimen.   Page 30

Trematospira helena.

Fig. 40–43. Dorsal, ventral, profile and front view of a specimen.   Page 137

Rhynchonella rugaecosta.

Fig. 48–51. Dorsal, front, ventral and profile view of a specimen; all
    enlarged xi.   Page 78

Orthis elegantula.

Fig. 52–57. A series of specimens showing variations in size.   Page 37

Rhynchonella cuneata, var. americana.

Fig. 58, 59. Dorsal and ventral view of a specimen.   Page 85
Fig. 62, 63. Front and profile view of a specimen.

Cyrtia exporrecta, var. arrecta.

Fig. 60, 61. Profile and cardinal view of a specimen.   Page 94

Atrypa calvini.

Fig. 64–66. Profile, ventral and dorsal view of a specimen.   Page 89

PLATE XXXIII.

Rhynchonella saffordi, var. depressa.

Fig. 1–3. Dorsal, ventral and profile view of a specimen.　　Page 80

Rhynchonella saffordi.

Fig. 4–6. Profile, dorsal and ventral view of a specimen.　　Page 79

Nucleospira pisiformis.

Fig. 7–9. Profile, dorsal and ventral view of a specimen.　　Page 104

Meristina nitida.

Fig. 10, 11. Dorsal and profile view of a specimen.　　Page 102

Pentamerus ventricosus.

Fig. 12–14. Dorsal, profile and ventral view of a specimen.　　Page 64

Pentamerus oblongus.

Fig. 15–17. Dorsal, profile and ventral view of a specimen.　　Page 60

Rhynchonella indianensis.

Fig. 18–20. Dorsal, ventral and profile view of a specimen.　　Page 76

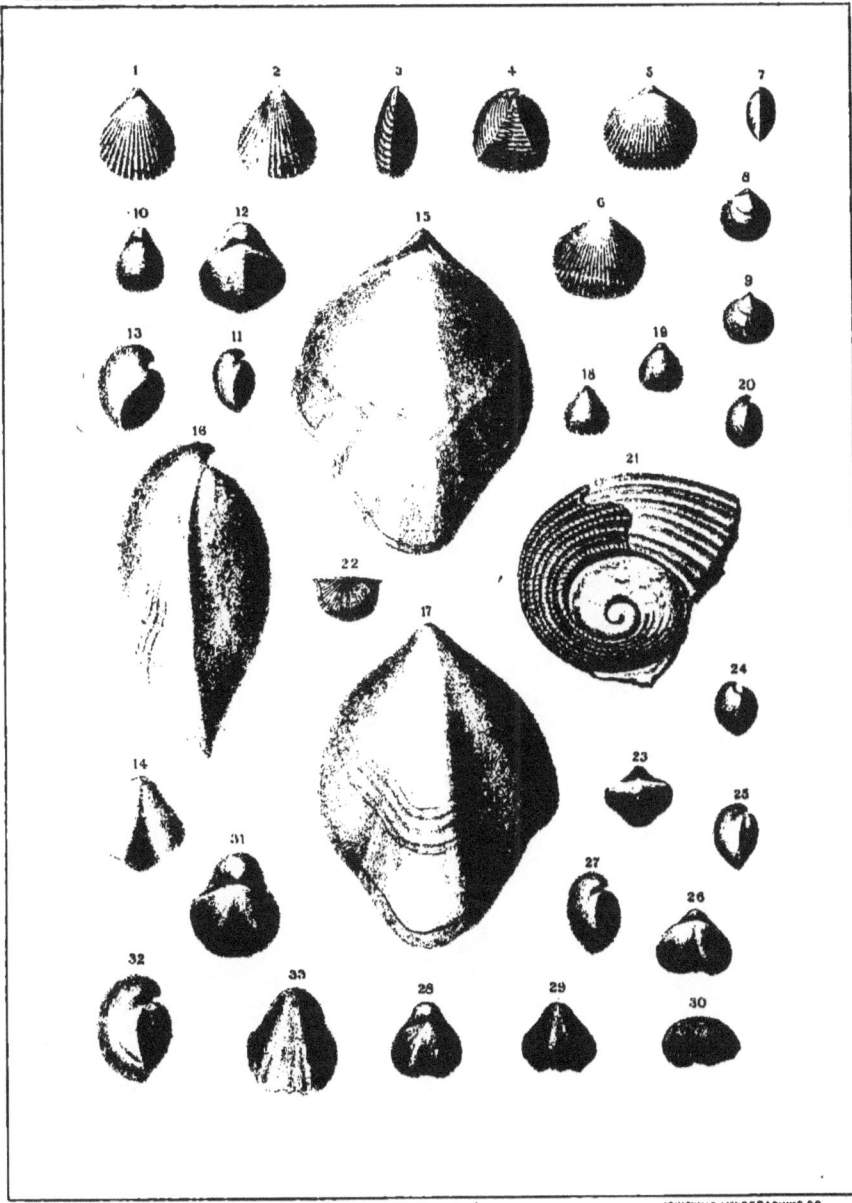

Cyclonema rugaelineata.

Fig. 21. Anterior view of a partly exfoliated specimen.   Page 187

Strophodonta demissa.

Fig. 22. Ventral view of a specimen.   Page 145

Spirifera dubia.

Fig. 23, 24. Dorsal and profile view of a specimen.   Page 115

Pentamerus uniplicatus.

Fig. 25, 26. Dorsal view of a specimen   Page 63

Pentamerus nucleus.

Fig. 27-29, 31-33. A series of specimens showing variation in size.   Page 59

Platyostoma niagarense.

Fig. 30. Vertical view of a young specimen.   Page 185

PLATE XXXIV.

Cypricardites halli.

Fig. 1–6. A series of specimens showing variation in size and form.   Page 206

Orthis linneyi.

Fig. 7–13. A series of specimens showing variation in size and form.   Page 41

Orthis borealis.

Fig. 14–20. A series of specimens showing variation in size and form.   Page 36

Zygospira kentuckiensis.

Fig. 21–25. A series of specimens showing variation in size and form.   Page 138

Rhynchonella increbescens.

Fig. 26–29. Dorsal, ventral, front and profile view of a specimen.   Page 83

Orthis flabellum.

Fig. 30. Dorsal view of a specimen.   Page 38

Stricklandinia louisvillensis.

Fig. 31–34. Ventral, dorsal, profile and cardinal view of a specimen.   Page 65

Cyrtia exporrecta, var. arrecta.

Fig. 35. Cardinal view of a specimen.   Page 94

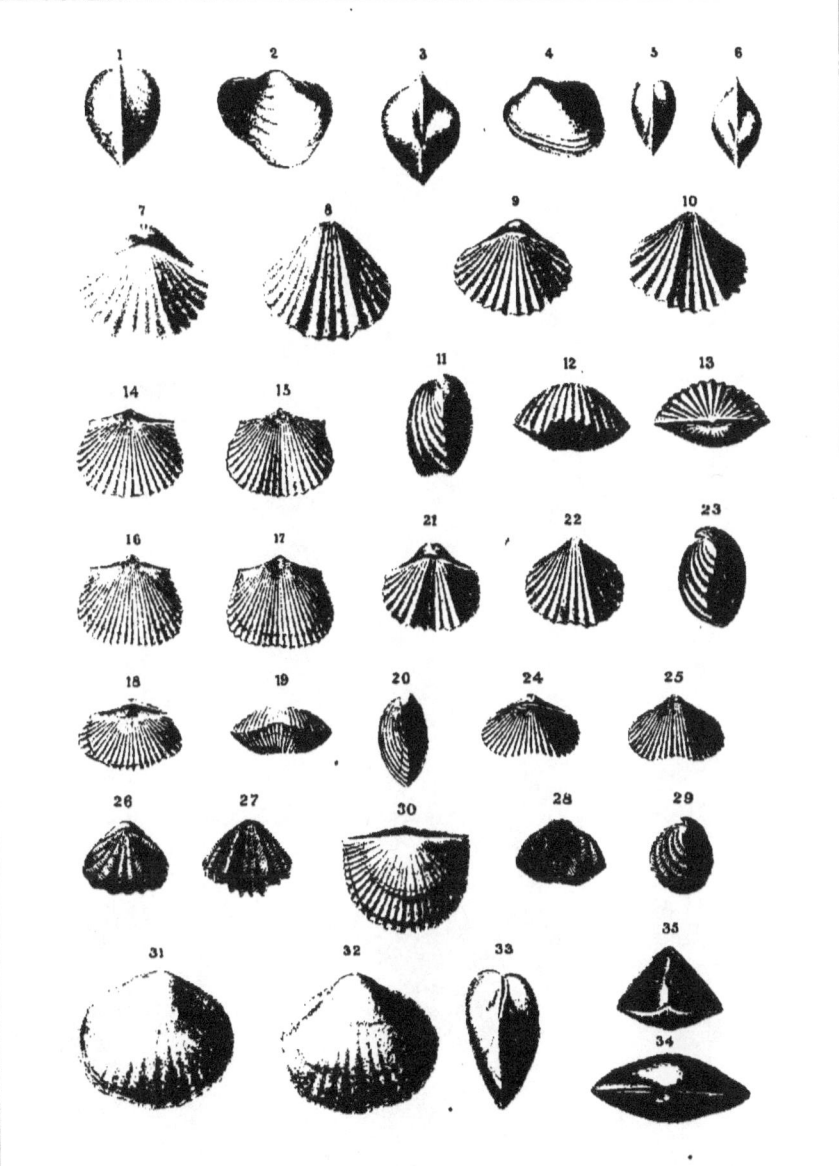

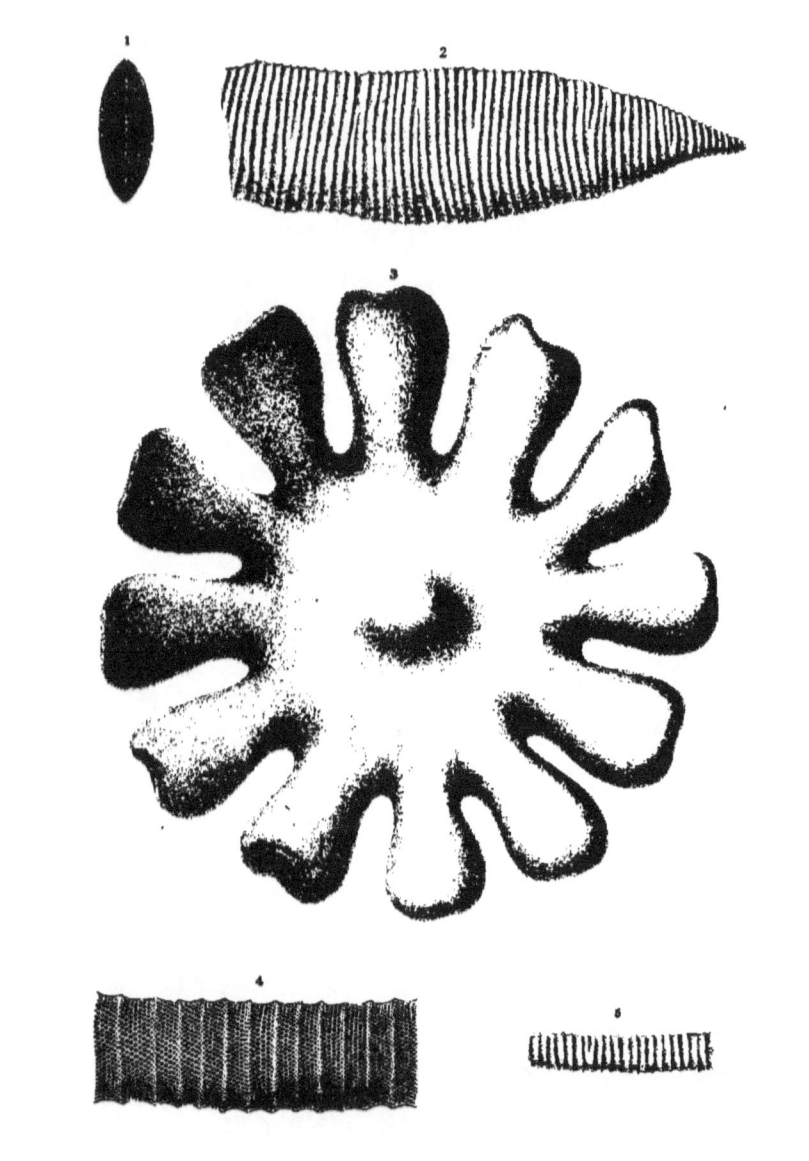

DEL.& LITH BY CHAS. STARCK.   LOUISVILLE LITHOGRAPHING CO.

PLATE XXXV.

Ptilodictya hilli.

Fig. 1. Transverse section of a specimen.   Page 30
Fig. 2. View of an unusually large front.
Fig. 4. A portion of a frond enlarged.
Fig. 5. View of a small, imperfect frond.

Brachiospongia digitata.

Fig. 3. Basal view of an unusually perfect specimen.   Page 29

PLATE XXXVI.

Brachiospongia digitata.

Fig. 1. Front view of the specimen figured on Plate XXXV.　　　Page 29

Fig. 2. Summit view of the same.

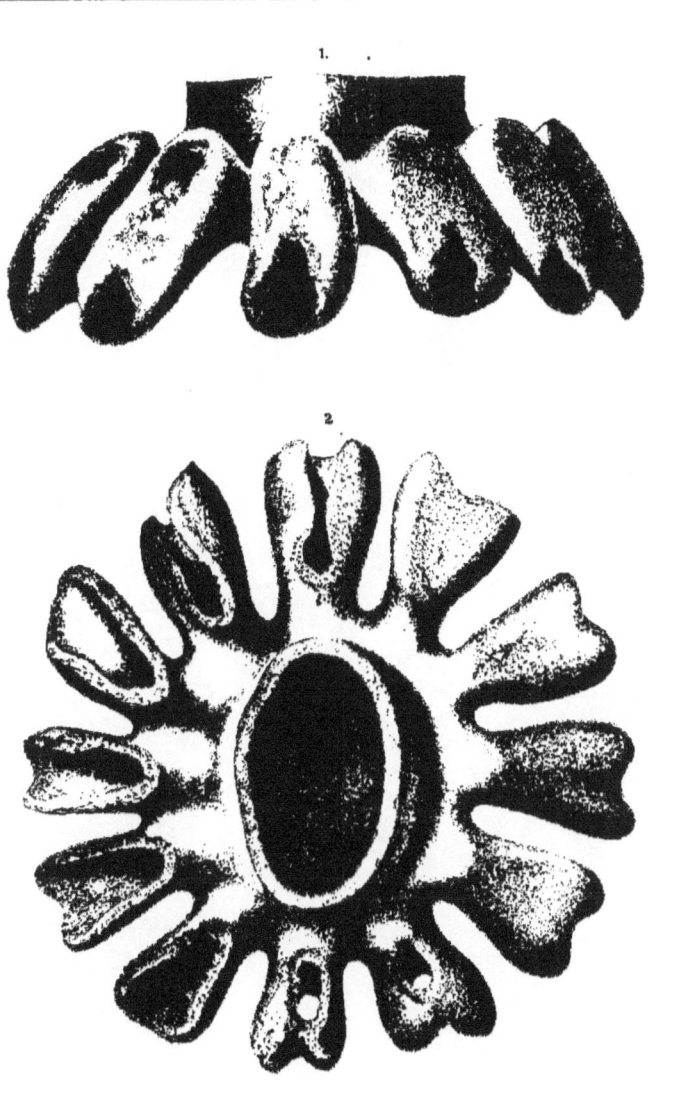

ERRATA.

PAGE.	LINE.	
17	10	Read Eozoön.
17	26 and 27	Read R. I. Murchison.
30	10	Read Polyzoa.
30		Under PTILODICTYA HILLI add ; *Ptilodictya hilli*, James. The Palæontologist, page 4, 1878. The original description of this species makes it unbranched and not digitate. None of the figured specimens show any indication of branching.
31	25	Read H. H. Hill.
32		Under reference to 27th Regents Report add : The two different references and dates given here arise from the fact that the plates illustrating the descriptions published in 1872, were not published until 1875 when the 27th Report was issued. These plates are numbered "24th Report," and should always be included with it, though not published until three years later.
33	19	Read p. 17.
37	17	Read vol. II.
38	7, 8, 9	Read FLABELLULUM.
39	3	From bottom, read vol. II.
41		After ORTHIS LINNEYI, add James. *not* n. sp. ; also add *Orthis (?) linneyi*, James. The Palæontologist, page 41, 1881.
42	8	From bottom, read Hall & Whitfield.
42	5	From bottom, read figs. 4–8.
43	17	Read 1867.
44	6	Read Hall & Whitfield.
45	14	Read pp. 135, 136.
46		Add to TROPIDOLEPTUS, 10th Rept. State Cab. Nat. Hist., p. 151, 1857.
47		After line 6 from bottom, add, *Anastrophia internascens*, Hall, 28th Rept. State Cab. Nat. Hist., p. 168, 1879.

PAGE.	LINE.	
49	7	From bottom, read 1841.
50	7	From bottom, read 1858.
53	12	Read tenuicosta.
55	15	Read Hall & Whitfield.
58	18	Add 1859.
59	1	Read Hall & Whitfield.
60	1	Read Hall & Whitfield.
60	3	Read p. 185, 1872.
60	4	Read 4–7.
60	25	Read Hall & Whitfield.
60	4	From bottom, read Ibid. Idem.
60	2	From bottom, add 1852.
68		Make line 13, 14 instead.
71	21	Read p. 168.
71	22	Read *Atrypa (Orthis) quadricostata.*
75	3	Read pl. 54.
83	3	From bottom, read 1847.
83	5	From bottom, read *Rynchonella capax,* Conrad., and add below; *Atrypa capax,* Conrad. Jour. Phil. Acad. Sci., vol. 8, p. 264, 1842. *Rhynchonella increbescens,* Hall. 12th Report State Cab. Nat. Hist., p. 66, 1859. 13th Report State Cab. Nat. Hist., p. 66, 1861. *Rhynchonella capax,* Billings. Pal. Foss. Can., vol. 1, p. 142, 1862. *Rhynchonella capax,* Meek. Pal. Ohio, vol. 1, p. 123, 1873.
84	25	Read 1876.
85	3	Read 1876.
85		Under Ambocoelia add; *Ambocoelia,* Hall. 13th Rep. N. Y. State Cab. Nat. Hist., p. 71, 1860.
88		Add between line 8 and 9 from bottom, *Atrypa spinosa vel aspera.*
93	11	From bottom, read trapezoidalis.
93	10	From bottom, read trapezoidalis.
103	10	From bottom, read pp. 25, 26.
104	7	From bottom, add p. 221.
104	4	From bottom, read pp. 301, 302.
105	13	From bottom, add 1867.
108	10	(Note.—This reference is evidently to the extra or author's edition of the paper published in the 10th Annual Report, with new pagination.)

PAGE.	LINE.	
110	5	Add 1867.
112	3	From bottom, read W. J. Davis.
113	4	Read *venustus.*
113	5	Add 1867.
120	23	Read 27 and 28.
124	23	Add vol. I, part 2.
126		Add to references of S. oweni; *Spirifer oweni.* Hall. 10th Rep. State Cab. Nat. Hist., p. 129, 1859.
128	5	Read p. 132.
129	11	Read Hall & Whitfield.
	13	Read 1872.
	14	Read 1875.
132	4	Read 1867.
	7	From bottom, add p. **131.**
135	25	Add 1867.
136	3	Read p. 168.
	4	Read 14th Report, 1861.
138		Under *Zygospira kentuckiensis* add; *Zygospira modesta,* var, *kentuckiensis,* James. The Palæontologist, p. 7, 1878.
143	15	Read 1857.
	16	Add vol. 1, part 2, and read 1858.
145	6	From bottom, read 1867.
147	15	Read 1857. Add to references *Strophodonta perplana,* Hall. Pal. New York, vol. 4, pp. 92, 98-101, 1867.
151	5	From bottom, after *Leptocoelia* add *Leptocoelia concava,* Hall. 10th Report, Reg. State Cab. Nat. Hist., p. 107, 1857. *Leptocoelia,* Hall, 12th Rept. State Cab. Nat. Hist., p. 32, 1859.
156	4	From bottom, read *Tentaculites,* 1879.
157	5	From bottom, read 1879.
158	6	From bottom, read 24th.
159		Under *Bucania,* add Pal. of New York, vol. 1, p. 32.
161	21	Read 1879.
163	7	From bottom, read 1879.
165	4	Read p. 32.
	6	Read 1879.
166	7	From bottom, read 1879.
167	16	Read 1879.
168	5	Read 1879.

PAGE.	LINE.	
168	5	Between line 4 and 3 from bottom add; *Platyceras ven-tricosum*, Hall. 12th Rept. State Cab. Nat. Hist., p. 17. 1859.
170		For *petilla* read *petila*.
174	8	From bottom, add p. 50, 1879.
179	9	Read p. 130.
183	23	Read 1879.
184	12	Add part 2, p. 23.
188	9	From bottom for pl. 12, read p. 36.
194	12	From bottom, add pl. 13, as var. *Ohioensis*.
196	13	Read 1879.
198	12	Read 1884.
199		After Clinopistha add; Proc. Phila. Acad. Nat. Sci., p. 43, 1870.
	12	From bottom, read pl. 11.
203	4	Read pp. 171, 172.
	6	Read 1885.
205		Place (?) after *Cypricardinia* in references.
209	5	From bottom add; & p. 95, fig. 18, 1885.
	4	From bottom, add 1872.
211	19	Add 1885.
224	8	Read 1884.
225	4	Read 1884.
	4	From bottom, add pp. 1–4, and read 1884.
229	19	Read 1884.
Plate I.		Description, transpose figs. 7 and 9.
Plate VIII.		Description, for fig. 1 read fig. 1-5.
Plate X.		For 32 in lower left hand corner read 36.
Plate XIII.		Change 23 on second line of figures from lower left hand corner to 32.
Plate XXV.		In description for fig. 6, last line, read fig. 10.
Plate XXVI.		Add 13 to upper, and 14 to lower one of the two unnumbered figures.
Plate XXXI.		Read Murchisonia petila for M. petilla.
		Fig. 12, read enlarged twice.
Plate XXXII.		After Rhyn. knotti, read p. 56.
		Under Rhyn. rugaecosta, read enlarged twice.
		For Rhynchonella cuneata, etc., read Rhynchotreta.
Plate XXXIV.		For Rhyn. increbescens, read R. capax.
		For Orthis flabellum, read O. flabellulum.